STONE 588

BY GERALD A. BROWNE

STONE 588
19 PURCHASE STREET
GREEN ICE
SLIDE
HAZARD
11 HARROWHOUSE
IT'S ALL ZOO

GERALD A. BROWNE

STONE 588

ARBOR HOUSE / NEW YORK

Copyright © 1986 by Pulse Productions, Inc.

Designed by Richard Oriolo

Manufactured in the United States of America

10 9 8 7 6 5 4 3 2 1

Library of Congress Cataloging in Publication Data

Browne, Gerald A.
  Stone 588.

  I. Title. II. Title: Stone five hundred eighty-eight.
PS3552.R746S7 1986   813'.54   85–20130
ISBN: 0-87795-539-5

For Merle Lynn Browne,
Maggie Browne Miller,
Cindy Montana Browne,
Peggy and Whip Alley

ACKNOWLEDGMENTS

The author is grateful to all those who helped him in the bringing about of this book.

Especially Jonathan W. Stewart, M.D., Assistant Professor of Clinical Psychiatry at the Columbia University College of Physicians and Surgeons and Research Psychiatrist, New York State Psychiatric Institute; Marvin S. Belsky, M.D.; Dr. Ruth Ochroch; Roger D. Powell, M.D., orthopaedic surgeon; Joyce N. Cox, R.N.; Thomas Gouge, M.D., New York University Medical Center.

And Ben Jacobson, Detective (ret.), New York City Police Department; Jerome Allan Landau, attorney, former Special Agent, U.S. Treasury Department, Internal Revenue Service, Intelligence Division, and U.S. Strike Force Against Organized Crime; Scott Towner, gemologist, G.I.A.; Simon Abraham, president, Amasian Gems, Inc., New York, Bangkok, Geneva.

And Adnan Khashoggi; Robert Shaheen; Robert J. and Patricia Lovejoy; Richard and Anastasia Capalbo; Bernard and Patricia Nunez; Lucienne Dodge; Pia Kazan, Paris editor, *Harper's Bazaar;* Michael and Susan Torlen; Jack Tirman.

And Sterling Lord and Ann Harris.

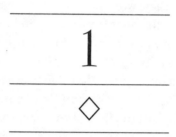

1

◇

Brushing her hair again.

Janet Springer sat in her fat armchair and gave little mind to what she was doing. Only when she pulled the bristles of the Mason Pearson brush too painfully across her scalp did she let up, relax her grasp of the handle, and go back to normal brushing.

She'd been at it for over an hour. Three hours was not unusual. Cadently, stroke after stroke, through the strands on the right side of her dark, straight, shoulder-length hair. It caused tiny electrical crackles that Janet considered encouraging. At the end of each stroke she gave the brush a sharp snap, as though to cast a substance from it. She often told herself it was silly, that she didn't really believe an inch of the idea that brushing, no matter how strenuously, might help the inside of her head. Nevertheless she was drawn to the brush, especially when she felt her between days slipping away.

Janet's right arm, doing the brushing, seemed independent of the rest of her. The rest of her was still as rock. Her feet were precisely together on the floor, the knobs of her ankle bones touching. Her knees were aligned and her thighs served as a vise for her free hand. She sat exaggeratedly erect, the upper part of her stiffened, her hips locked, breasts, throat, and chin thrust forward by the bow of her spine. She appeared to be in a contrived posture, perhaps begging for audience. However Janet had not, on an impulse of solitary dramatics, struck the pose. It had come over her while she was sitting there, a change degree by degree that tightened her lips, clenched and covered her eyes so they were now seeing inward more than out.

Thoughts were darting about in Janet's mind so rapidly that even the most unrelated ones overlapped. She felt her brain was deliberately trying to confuse itself, mazing among the convolutions in her skull. She knew the symptoms. What they were leading her to. From all the times before she knew it was futile to battle them. She hadn't expected, just hoped with the merest of hope, that she might remain indefinitely in the phase of between. Even a few more days of it would have been a blessing.

Signs of shift.

Had begun in her a week ago. Only an edginess at first, but before long that had grown into explosions of irritability. Set off by inconsequential things such as not being able to find at once her place in a book she'd been reading, or having a postage stamp slip and stick awry on the corner of an envelope. She also dropped things more, and when she did, dropped her eyeglass case or whatever, her immediate reaction was to blame it, kick at it. She talked louder, faster. She was stuffed with energy, expelled some by lying on the floor to hook her feet in under the couch and do a hundred sit-ups. She used a white wool sock like a mitten to wipe dust from the floor beneath the bed and the dresser. Pecked lint from her dark wool sweaters at two in the morning. Her sleep was brief, black intermissions. She came wide awake the instant her eyelids parted.

Last night she hadn't slept at all. For hours she lay nude with the covers thrown off. Shivering was a diversion. At intervals a face had peeked in at her through the clear plastic square in the door. Each time she'd sat up and glared, a disturbed look. Once she'd gotten up and paced the room for a long while, with her eyes closed because that helped her pretend she was walking straight, going places. When she returned to the bed and was lying face up, closing her eyes made everything worse. Thoughts dropped to the back of her head in a deranged heap from which they were fired back up at her in no sensible order.

Chanceless wishes.

Addictive memories.

Numerous sexual impossibilities.

At dawn she considered packing. She mentally sorted through her many pretty things and put aside some that would be right for this month, April, in Rome.

Twenty-six-year-old Janet Springer.

She had been at High Meadow for three years. It was the longest time she'd spent at any clinic. During the ten years before High Meadow there had been five other private clinics. They were always huge Connecticut houses, the former country retreats of wealthy city families back when there'd been no concern about heat or help. Protected by acres, situated as though hidden, such houses were perfect for their present purpose. (Who knows over the years how many in the line of the original owners had returned and were, even now, tucked away in familiar rooms?)

Janet called the clinics "keeping places." They were where she was kept. Within driving distance of home.

She had been moved from one keeping place to another because she was more of a problem than she was worth. Those clinics that admitted her sooner or later regretted having done so. They made up thin excuses for insisting she be removed. Some were honest about it to a point, let it be known they couldn't cope with her. She was too complicated a case, could not be properly treated. Their preference was a patient like a tame bird into whose mouth they could drop on schedule doses of compliance and predictability. Thus the staffs of the clinics, from ordinary attendants to head doctors, were, in their own way, as hooked on antipsychotic drugs as the patients. So many milligrams of this or that prevented bedlam.

Janet was an exception. It wasn't that she refused to take the drugs; she would have willingly done so and been grateful for the relief.

Thorazine was the first antipsychotic medication tried on her. Her system could not tolerate it, or any of the chlorpromazines. When given haloperidol she also had an adverse reaction. The drug that promised the most for Janet was lithium carbonate. She asked for information on it and read every word they brought her, over and over, until she was convinced that lithium was intended for her and all the problems she'd had with drugs up to then had been necessary —leading her to lithium. Lithium was a wonder. It could alleviate her emotional extremes, the agitations and the funks. It could keep her balanced. No longer would she be swung by her sick head on that terrible pendulum. Lithium had helped other manic-depressives.

She wanted it.

She prayed to whatever force that controlled her body to allow her body to accept it.

The chief of the clinic reviewed Janet's medical history, more thoroughly this time. Her past intolerances to drug therapy made him reluctant. He noticed that, for some reason, lithium had never been tried on her. Perhaps it had been too new, radical, considered dangerous. Up to now, he himself had had only positive results prescribing it. If it worked on this difficult patient it would be a feather in his medical cap. It might even call for a paper for the *American Journal of Psychiatry*.

The doctor ordered that Janet be given three hundred milligrams of lithium three times a day, a cautious initial dose. His double-underlined instructions were that a blood sample be drawn from her each morning prior to medication to determine her serum level. If her serum level went above 1.6 or if any adverse symptoms were observed, he was to be notified, personally, at once.

When Janet's lithium therapy began she was optimistic. She didn't have any apparent adverse reactions to it, and with each passing day her hope increased.

Out of psychological habit she was, of course, sensitively aware of her moods, and when she felt herself mentally lifted in a lighter, unfamiliar direction she was sure it wasn't her imagination. She was in the outer limits of happiness, she believed. She actually felt giddy, as though her throat was crowded with tiny lighter-than-air bubbles she couldn't possibly hold in.

The most ordinary things amused her: the snug adjacency of her own toes, a bird outside cocking its head, the naive blankness of a piece of letter paper. She giggled while alone at a water stain in a corner of the ceiling—her private Rorschach that she purposely supposed into the craziest creatures and situations she could think up. It was fun for a change to be genuinely elated. The lithium was indeed working.

She noticed other changes.

She was dizzy at times, which seemed to go along with her giddiness. Her mouth was dry and had an unpleasant metallic taste, which persisted no matter how often she rinsed. Her hands twitched, jumped often as though startled. Nothing important, she told herself. Her hope wouldn't let her complain.

The eighth day of lithium began with:

"Good morning, Janet."

"Good morning."

"How are you today?" the nurse asked.

"Better, thank you." Janet's words seemed to come out swollen and stuck together. She remained in bed, extended her arm. The nurse drew the daily blood. Janet sat on the edge of the bed. She looked in the direction of the bathroom and was about to rise and go to it when she felt a glowing hollowness inside, just below where her ribs came together in front. Suddenly, her head turned aside on its own and her right arm flew upward like a puppet's and her eyes rolled in their sockets.

She fell to the floor, just dropped.

She cried out, one short sound that seemed squeezed from her. Her legs knifed up, knees to chest. Her elbows dug hard into her. She gasped for breath, apparently unable to get air past her throat. Her skin took on a blue pallor. There was no stopping it.

Her body went completely limp, as though drained of all its substance.

But the next moment she was invaded by more tension than she could possibly contain, tightening her tissues to the tearing point.

Foam came from her mouth.

The convulsions lasted for several minutes, then ceased abruptly. Her eyes were open, but she was unconscious when they lifted her onto the bed. Her pupils were fixed, dilated. The nurse removed the ballpoint pen she had in emergency forced between Janet's teeth to protect her tongue. Deep teeth marks were visible on the shaft of the hard pen.

When Janet came to she was confused, couldn't recall the seizure, none of it. She felt tired, sleepier than ever. Her last thought before giving in to sleep was how disappointed she was.

The blood that had been drawn that morning showed Janet's lithium serum level at 2.2, more than high enough to cause toxicity in her central nervous system. What puzzled her doctor was how subtly and quickly the lithium had built up in her system. He had escaped having her death or coma on his reputation by perhaps only a day or two. When he entered the episode on Janet's medical record, his bottom-line notation, printed in capital letters not to be overlooked, was: CAUTION: LITHIUM CARBONATE SHOULD NEVER BE ADMINISTERED.

At other clinics other approaches were tried on Janet. Dosages were halved and halved again for her, until they were practically unmeasurable. Whenever a new psychotropic drug was brought out, Janet managed to have it given to her. Nothing worked. She suffered reactions, not just severe side-effects but often life-threatening direct effects.

The doctors were challenged and stumped. Three of the country's leading psychopharmacologists were consulted. They studied and speculated but were unable to recommend a beneficial course. They chalked it up to having something to do with Janet's natural psychochemistry, which was obviously complicated and messed up enough to be unique.

Janet Springer.

Given up on.

Now, there she sat in her room on the third floor at High Meadow. Her fat armchair faced a large double window of numerous individual panes, small panes of safety glass. The frames of the window appeared to be made of wood but were really formed steel that had been painted. Less disheartening than bars or mesh.

As much as possible had been done to make Janet's room unclinical and yet safe for her. It would never be as nice as home, of course, but those who loved her had seen to it that she was surrounded by familiar and cherished things. Against one wall was her own bed, and along the opposite wall a soft sofa from home. Other furnishings that had been brought were her father's six-drawer upright dresser and a small Queen Anne–style writing desk her mother had always treasured. On the floor was a 9-by-12 Chinese rug, a nice thick one that had been carried in on the shoulders of her two brothers.

Other normal touches had accumulated: a particularly friendly pillow, a colorful handmade throw, certain books they knew she liked to reread. Audrey, the woman her brother Phillip loved, had given her, among other things, a subscription to the weekly newspaper called *W,* somehow knowing she would at times be entertained by that snobby nonsense.

Photographs of those she could not be with were hung and placed around. A few were serious portraits but most were candid snapshots of special good times that helped her feel included. A photograph of her father was in his last passport, which she kept standing open on the dresser top: him looking out with an impatient expression, the officially embossed State Department seal marring his plain, small, knotted tie and dark, correct suit. Nearly all the stamped entries on the pages of the passport were London and New York. The last foreign one, on a page by itself and stamped so hard its magenta ink had smeared, was Belgian. It was dated ten days before he'd died. Janet often imagined him alone and not feeling well in Antwerp.

The passport was something of his that she had asked to have. As was the oval-shaped, shallow silver dish which, on his dresser top, had always held his ordinary incidentals: collar stays, shirt studs, cuff links, foreign coins, and his reminder stone. She kept the dish and its contents exactly as she believed she remembered. The only thing that had been on the dish that she wasn't allowed to have were several straight pins with round blue heads, removed by him from a new shirt, no doubt.

Janet thought of her room as territorial, divided and claimed by her psychological phases.

The sofa. It was where depression always drove her, where her face burrowed into the crevices of the cushions and she cringed to a shape that deserved being overlooked. The sofa was where her arms and legs and spine turned to iron and where she often stayed in one position so long she was close to paralysis. It was during sofa time that she'd put those crisscross scars on the insides of her wrists: death kisses, she secretly called them. She was no longer inventive or conniving about suicide. She'd take it if it was offered, of course, but there'd be no more scaffolding of furniture to get within reach of the wire-covered ceiling bulb so she could poke something in, jab, and shatter the bulb for a tiny shard of glass, for example.

The bed. It was where her mania always eventually carried her, where she was forced to lie like a Gulliver, her strength trussed, futility spewing from her in obscenities.

Situated appropriately between the sofa and the bed was the armchair. Good old stuffed friend. Its slick chintz-covered lap was as far as she ever got from her extremes, as close as she would ever come to being well, she believed. In the fat armchair was her between time.

It was running out on her again.

She brushed faster, spiked her scalp with the bristles, and then, in the middle of a stroke, stopped abruptly. Her hand was on its way to placing the hairbrush on the side table when her mind flung it anywhere. She heard the brush skitter across the floor and ricochet sharply off the baseboard beneath the bed, but she had no sympathy for it.

The rigidity left her body as she gave in.

She freed her other hand from between her thighs. She slid down in the chair, slouched way down so she was nearly horizontal, her head at a right angle to the rest of her, chin to collarbone. She extended her feet to the windowsill. There were no laces in her white sneakers. Their long tongues stuck out insubordinately. She dealt with them with snapping kicks left and right. The sneakers flew off.

She brought her bare feet back into position on the sill, and that put New England springtime beyond her toes, half-developed leaves in the upper reaches of the maples outside. She focused on those momentarily and could easily make out their paler green underveins. Her eyesight was now keener than anyone who had eyes, she was a fucking human telescope, she told herself.

Cars were moving swiftly along the highway a half mile away. Through the small spaces in the branches of the maples Janet caught the speed of their colors. The briefest of flashes. Her thought was she didn't give a shit where they were going. Possibly they were headed for a crash, one crammed carload hitting another carload head-on. The image amused her, especially the prospect of explosion and fire, and it occurred to her that if she were able to concentrate intensely long enough she could probably will it. Supernatural her. Nothing she couldn't do. It was for her amusement and everyone's well-being that she pretended her limitations.

Her bare feet were jiggling, keeping time with some internal composition she didn't hear.

She stood quickly.

Her narrow figure had a hint of leftover lankiness to it, in keeping with the filling-out experiences she'd missed. She was also pretty, though that had to be appreciated through layers of agony. Tension had caused a discernible pull from the corners of her mouth to the corners of her eyes.

She moved about the room, darting as though she had purpose, hesitating as though she had destination. To the desk to the dresser to the chair and around again. The thought that she'd browse the latest issue of *Vanity Fair* was lost to the thought that she'd try on some of the evening dresses Audrey had brought her last week was lost to the sound of the only door to the room being opened.

It was Mawson, the male attendant Janet disliked most. A tall, knobby-boned man with a pronounced Adam's apple and a neglected brush mustache.

"Pudding time," Mawson announced, singsongy. He was carrying a small laminated plastic tray. He placed it on the table next to the armchair.

Janet ignored him.

"Butterscotch today."

"Stick your prick in it," Janet suggested flatly.

Mawson wasn't fazed. He liked his job, the opportunities it gave him to be as condescending as he wanted, seeing usually privileged people at their worst.

Janet crossed the room. As though alone, she brought her bare foot up onto the arm of the chair and scratched her instep. The sound of fingernails to skin seemed loud. She scratched slowly, all the while looking off, apparently oblivious to her skirt hiked up, her thigh and crotch exposed.

Mawson knew better. He never refused a benefit and this was more than a mere flash. She wasn't wearing underpants.

Still not looking at him, not acknowledging his presence, Janet stopped scratching, but she kept her leg up. She moved her leg slowly from side to side, parting and closing, denying and offering.

Mawson told himself to be satisfied just knowing he could fuck her. Whatever she did would be all her own doing, none of his. No way they could fire him for seeing. He ran his tongue up into his mustache, shoved the fingers of both his hands into the tight rear pockets of his white jeans.

Janet continued her taunting. She glanced peripherally at Mawson.

He was coming at her!

She would scream when he got beyond stopping with his grabs. She had the scream ready, an alarm in her throat.

However, Mawson's movement was only a shift of his stance.

Janet was disappointed. Impatience poked at her. Damn him! Impatience broke through the delusive membrane of the situation and caused a measure of her own arousal. She would not have screamed. There were craving reaches in her pelvis. She brought her leg down. She disliked Mawson all the more now.

Across the chair she said, "Hand me my pudding."

Mawson was trained to think twice before responding to a patient's request, but this seemed harmless. The pudding was in a cardboard bowl on a cardboard saucer with a cardboard spoon and two Nabisco sugar wafers. He picked it up, extended it to her. She reached across for it, and the moment it was transferred from his hand to hers she flung the bowl and all at him.

Mawson got most of the butterscotch pudding in the face. It looked like excrement on his brows and lashes and mustache. Glops of it stuck to his white shirt. "Fucking bitch!" he shouted.

Janet laughed as though she'd just been told a mildly humorous story.

Mawson was using the sleeve of his shirt to wipe pudding from his eyes when Janet crouched and got hold of the underframe of the large chair. She didn't look strong enough to do it, but in a sudden, single motion, she heaved the chair up and over at him. He jumped away quickly or would have gotten more than painfully bruised shins.

Mawson's anger now broke one of the clinic's primary rules: Never attempt to control a violent patient alone. He grabbed for Janet.

She was too quick for him.

He stalked.

She was more amused than fearful.

He lunged at her.

She evaded, threw magazines at him and newspapers. The sheets of the newspapers separated, opened up midair to be her protective obstacles, and when they were underfoot on the carpet, Mawson slipped on them and went sprawling.

He was furious. The television camera up in the corner of the ceiling didn't matter. He was on duty at the monitor. No one was watching. He'd catch her. He'd get her in a hammerlock and pressure just short of breaking her arm, and while he was at it, during the tussle, he'd shove his thumb up her cunt.

Across the room Janet took up something from the floor: the laminated plastic tray. She held it by its edge and let it go with a sidearm motion, like throwing a Frisbee. The tray scaled the air, came at Mawson so fast it was all he could do to hunch and protect his face with his arms.

The edge of the tray struck about six inches below his armpit. As

11

it gashed in, Mawson let out a painful grunt. No doubt ribs were fractured. He pressed the panic button on the remote signaler attached to his belt. And retreated from the room.

Janet wasn't done.

Mawson had only been included in her enthusiasm. Now she gave her energy to the couch, flung cushions. She rampaged around the room, intent on shambling it, feeling her exhilaration soar as anything that came into sight was victimized. Neatness was most vulnerable. With merciless backhands she swept everything from every surface. She easily overturned her father's dresser.

Four attendants came.

They forced her down among the mess she'd made of things. It took all four to do it. They underestimated her strength at first and she managed to free one leg to kick a face and cause a nosebleed. They finally got good enough holds to lift her to the bed.

Mawson came bringing the Posey restraints. His shirt was bloodied and he was stiffly favoring his left side. He had wanted to use leather restraints, knowing they would be less comfortable and with them Janet would be more apt to hurt herself. Usually at least two sets of leathers were kept in the clinic's medical storage closet, but although no other patients had gone berserk, those restraints were not there today. Mawson thought it likely that someone on staff had taken the leathers home for a bit of kink. He had to settle for using soft restraints, made of a woven cotton material similar to a lightweight, supple canvas. Anyone seeing them for the first time would hardly guess their function. Each restraint was six inches wide and five feet long and had a reinforced slit into which one end was inserted and pulled through to form a loop.

As now, with Janet. While she was held down on the bed, front up, the loop of a restraint was drawn snug around her wrist, then wrapped once around and tied with a clove hitch, the prescribed knot for these circumstances because a patient's pulling at it only made it more binding. The two free ends of the restraint were led down and tied to the metal frame of the bed. When Janet's other wrist and both ankles were restrained in the same manner she was spread-eagled and no longer a threat.

Mawson volunteered to remain with her, on the pretense of overseeing that the restraints were properly taut and she didn't hurt herself. The senior attendant made him go have his injury cared for. One of the other attendants stayed on.

Janet screeched her repertoire of profanities, rapid and nonstop, as though they were on a string being pulled from her mouth. Her incessant adjective, of course, was *fucking,* but some of the other obscenities she combined were so impossible the attendant couldn't help but be amused.

From the struggle her skirt was twisted up around her waist. The attendant pulled it down and neatened it. He checked the restraints all around, adjusted the slack of the one that held her right ankle, and made sure she had adequate circulation. He plumped a pillow. Placing it beneath her head brought his face in range. Sure as a snake, she aimed spit at his eyes. He recoiled, wasted no further attention on her, left the room.

Janet alone.

Demonstrated that her ferocity was not performance. Rage came discharging from her with more intensity. All the stored storms within her churned and gathered and riled, to come—a boiling flood —from her body. Beasts hunched in her most reptilian recesses flicked their tongues and lashed their scaly tails. She writhed furiously, bucked up, arched to the limit of her spine. Time after time she snapped her pelvis upward and twisted her buttocks, trying to shake herself loose. The restraints were lined with flannel to cushion them, but with all her pulling and straining, her wrists and ankles were raw. If she kept on they would bleed, but paroxysms are anesthetic and hardly self-preserving. An undriven body would have surrendered to exhaustion but she refused to let up, fought the restraints with vigorous heaves and wrenches, all the while shrieking the vitriol of mad whores.

For almost two hours.

It was then that Janet first felt within her the demand to hush. The space around her became a soft die that enclosed the precise shape of her with quiescence. Her will flared up, proposing that her struggle continue. This was swiftly damped—not *by* her, somehow, but *for* her.

There she lay, splayed, absolutely stilled. She was now able to admit to the ceiling and its familiar imperfections, and the well-known near wall, and the circumstances of her position. Also, now, she sensed a more equitable communion with her body and was told, it seemed, that something was happening to it. She thought perhaps she was dying. Perhaps all there was to dying was such an inner call to concede. Good. She would give in to it, would, for as long as it lasted, enjoy all its phases and nuances. She closed her eyes, the better to see inside where, naturally, death would occur.

The Righting of Janet had begun.

Her suprarenal glands, those two that sit cocked like floppy Robin Hood hats atop the kidneys left and right, had already been influenced to stop overproducing adrenaline. The hormone those glands had already sent into her bloodstream was offset, brought down from an incited level. Normally, the excess adrenaline would have been expelled over a dozen or more hours with no experienceable change such as the calming hush Janet had felt come over her. It was understandable, of course, that she thought it her choice when she surrendered to the hushing. Although, in fact, by then she was well infected with compliance.

Vibrations.

Vibrations of a magnitude more subtle than might be thrown from the glint of a prism from the angle of a crystal goblet were entering her. Gentle and too slight for our ways of measuring, yet they entered her with purpose. They seemed to know her well, traveled the courses of her inner systems as though having been over them countless times, going by a perfect master pattern. Around and around with her blood, throughout the circuits of her nerves, to the finest farthest ends.

Each of her organs was explored and assessed. As were the integrants of each organ. All the way down to the microcosmic landscape of her cells.

The cause of Janet's mental disorder was determined.

A concentration of nerve cells in two areas of the hypothalamus of her brain were abnormal, malformed. They had axons too short. That made the gaps across to other cells twice as wide as they should have been.

At times that were almost a schedule, the chemical neurotransmitter called norepinephrine accumulated at the ends of each of those short axons, like traffic jams at bridges that are out. The more the secretions of this substance ganged up, the more hell they raised.

As a result Janet experienced mania, phases of belligerance, and, ultimately, violence.

At other times the chemical neurotransmitter acetylcholine brought its inhibiting qualities to the brinks of those abnormally wide gaps and collected there in unmanageable batches. Overdoses of its squelching influence got to the mental system. Janet was then overwhelmed by a phase of depression, her every thought and action stifled with dark ingoingness.

A bipolar disorder of a major affective disorder.

That was the diagnostic label the doctors put on what Janet had. Manic and depressive to extremes. The doctors had no way of knowing that malformed axons in the hypothalamus were behind it all. And even if they had known, there was nothing they could do about it. Brain cells don't change or repair. How ironic that the great suffering of Janet was the penalty of such an infinitesimal mistake, a matter of a few millionths of an inch. Born with it, she was stuck with it.

Now, restrained on her bed in her room at High Meadow, she lay absolutely still, compelled to stillness for some reason. She was unaware of the energy oscillating within her. It traveled now as though in response to a call, gathered in her brain and then, more specifically, in the domain of her hypothalamus. Concentrated, it focused upon the malformed axons.

The changes that took place within Janet's brain during the next two hours would have been impossible for the unaided eye to notice. Perhaps even the most powerful scanning electron microscope might not have picked them up.

Changes on the molecular level.

The defective axons, all the millions of them, were ever so gradually perfected—increased in length, five millionths of an inch. Just enough to perfect the width of the gap from cell to cell. Within a short while the neurotransmitters, acetylcholine and norepinephrine, were gotten into line. Secreted in tiny quantas, they began firing across the gaps at a nice, normal rate.

Altogether, the Righting of Janet took four hours.

Which would be about average.

For Janet it was a lifting of miasmas. Layer after layer of all the old interposing mists and overcasts were dissipated. Diffusion gave way degree by degree to a mental clarity as pure as washed air.

Janet did not trust it. The feeling was too strange for her to trust. With her eyes yet closed she lay there, not believing in it, suspecting it was a cruel tease, that she was merely being given a taste of sanity. She thought perhaps this was the moment before death when utmost wants were granted—although it felt more like life, she had to admit.

Ten minutes passed.

She hung on to it, believed it tenuous, breathed gently not to disturb.

A half hour.

Her outlook improved.

Warily, she opened her eyes.

The afternoon light was mostly gone, the room in dusk. It was later than suppertime. No one had come to look in on her, at least not that she knew of. Where had the time gone?

The window was in direct view. She saw outside, blessed outside, where the new green of the maples was black against a sky with some indigo and mauve in it. She loved the leaves, the sky, the lenient colors it was presenting in this hyphenation of day and night. Her chest and eyes were crying.

The incongruity of her hands took her attention to them. They were still fisted. There was something hard in her right fist. From the feel of it she believed she knew what it was. She unfurled her fingers. Her hand was still held by a restraint so she had to raise her head to look at it.

It was from tip to tip a smidgen longer than an inch. Three quarters of an inch at its widest point. Octahedral in shape, like a pair of pyramids fused base to base, forming eight triangular sides. It wasn't a geometrically perfect octahedron. All its sides were not precisely the same measure, but nearly. One tip of it was incomplete, apparently chipped off. Except for that tip its surface was whitish-opaque, as though hazed with frost.

A rough crystal.

A stone.

Her father's reminder stone.

It had been among the belongings of his she'd had on his old dresser. During her rampage she must have unintentionally grabbed it up.

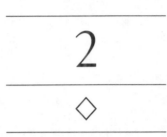

2

◇

Forty-seventh Street between Fifth and Sixth Avenues is not really
a good place to walk a dog. Nor, for that matter, is it the best of
places to walk a mistress.

Diamonds are why.

Rubies, sapphires, emeralds, and pearls too, but mainly diamonds.
There are well over a thousand jewelry shops and concessions, counting from corner to corner along both sides of the street. Every
window is arranged like an altar to avarice. On tier above tier in tray
after tray precious stones are set, perfectly angled to wink and keep
winking. They take such advantage, naked as they are against black
velour. They are teasers, motionless Salomes. They flick their selves
iniquitously on the stages of motives behind the eyes of in-lookers,
suggesting the wantonness that might be given the giver in return.
Or, for the wanter, bringing up new resolves to accommodate old
erotic persistencies, after which nothing could possibly be denied. Of

course, the same is true of such offerings at Cartier, Bulgari, Van Cleef's and other Fifth Avenue establishments, however, there the lust is rather oblique, more decently disguised and not so thoroughly atmospheric.

A fifteen-carat marquise diamond appears self-conscious of its relationship to the word REDUCED. In the same window is a tray that contains twenty-seven apparently identical diamond rings, each set with three quarters of a carat, pear shape. A platoon of rings, their shanks sunk in separate slots in the black velour, five slots down, six across. Three slots are purposely unoccupied, stuck with red plastic buttons that have the word SOLD imprinted on them, three of thousands of lies.

The street.

People in the trade now even leave off the number when they speak or think of it. Pelikaanstraat in Antwerp is a diamond place, as is Hatton Garden in London. But 47th in New York is "the street." It handles, one way or another, over half the finished diamonds in the world.

Such industry is unbelievable—at nine o'clock at night. Come night the street looks depressed. Shop next to shop next to shop appears vacated, the windows stripped, empty, exposing fades and dust boundaries on the velour surfaces. And beyond in the unlighted interiors the shelves of glass display cases are barren. The impression is that everyone packed up every carat in a hurry and fled. Truth is, of course, the precious stuff has been given over to the deep dark of vaults and safes. But it never sleeps. Darkness is an imposition to facets, perhaps even a suffering.

Come the day, the street awakens, more instantaneously vigorous than any other commercial street in Manhattan. It flashes open. Store windows and display counters are swiftly kindled with cold blaze, and the pitch seems already under way before it starts.

Especially outside along the sidewalks. They are sidewalks as ample as those of most east-west New York blocks, but here they are too narrow. Here the sidewalk is a place for negotiation, where men pause and stand together to conduct business in a manner that really isn't as much happenchance as it appears. For many the sidewalk is office, pockets are vaults. Many of that many are Hasidim, the most pious of orthodox Jews, unmistakable in their long black coats and beards. No neckties, white home-laundered shirts buttoned at the collar. Beneath the crowns of their black wide-brimmed hats, long hair hides, except in front on both sides, where gathers of strands to the chin are braided or curled into tubelike locks with a curling iron. The Hasidim—or beards, as they are called—seem less arduous somehow and therefore more confident. Their black outfits probably enhance that; surely their legion does. Whatever, the scurry goes past and around them, such as the carrying of stones from place to place. Every moment lots of the precious hard things are being taken to be seen, being returned. Those who bear them cut and thread through the street traffic swiftly, avoiding jostle, never allowing contact, stepping off the curb so as not to be brushed. Incidents of pocket-picking have taught overcaution.

The milieu of the street: Add the furtive hustlers wanting to look like thieves in their cheap shoes and team-type jackets, because it will help them pass off twenty-dollar-a-carat cubic zirconium as hot diamonds at two fifty a carat, take a quick two hundred. Then there are the authentic thieves, the swifts, small-time independents trying *not* to be taken for what they are in their cheap shoes and team-type jackets. They shift along in pairs or threes, unable to be casual, their score of the night before concealed on them as remotely as possible. They go in at places, come out, confer. They're angry that no interest has been shown in a gold-filled cameo brooch, or they're disappointed and pissed because the most they've been offered for a clean two-carat square-cut still in its Tiffany mounting is not even half of half what their minds have already been spending.

Add in too: the flavor of Colombians. Usually gaunt and tight-suited young men but sometimes older, with a paunch that a jacket can just barely be buttoned over. They are in from a barrio of Bogotá or Cartagena, cocaine mules who have gotten through and unloaded. They have also brought their bonus, have it in the safest pocket: one or two hundred carats of cut emerald to peddle. They look only slightly more out of place than the middle-aged ex-wives in from Huntington or Paterson or New Haven wanting to sell away some of their recent alienation. Rings, pins, minor bracelets, things that actually never were favorites serve the vengeance.

All this at street level.

Above is where the heavier action is, in the buildings that with only one or two exceptions are prewar. The tallest is thirteen floors, the average is seven. The reason there are no new high-rises on the street is that no one, neither landlords nor tenants, wants to lose what can be made during the months needed to tear a building down and put another up. Thus, the old buildings have been divided and subdivided to the bulging point.

Precious stones are small. Even the largest dealers can make do with little room. It also helps that it is against the grain of the trade itself to try to impress. Still, even with cramp, there is not enough of the street. Like a garden taking over, it has spread north to 48th and south to 46th and, as well, grown around all the corners it shares with its adjacent avenues.

The diamond firm of Springer & Springer was part of that spillover.

But by choice.

It preferred being just around the way at 580 Fifth. That building was somewhat newer and taller, and Springer & Springer considered itself satisfactorily in place on the twenty-fourth floor with north exposure. Its space there was ample but certainly not excessive. Seven hundred and eighty-some square feet partitioned into a reception area, three windowed offices, and a small catchall room that had a coffee-making machine and a refrigerator in it. Wall-to-wall wool carpeting in a gray shade was unifying to some extent, though it would have been too much of a stretch to say the place was decorated. Furnished was closer to fact. The reception area was a grade better than the rest. The desk of polished chrome and thick clear glass matched the low table in front of a chesterfield sofa of black leather. Next to that a ficus was getting along fairly well in a blue glazed porcelain planter that was sort of Chinese. Otherwise there wasn't any evident try for coordination or color. The walls, ceilings, and doors were all painted as white as possible for no reason other than to keep the diamonds honest.

On the third Friday of May, Phillip Springer was at his desk. Seated across from him was a dealer named Arthur Drumgold.

Springer had never done business with Drumgold before. He could only vaguely remember having heard mention of him, which was strange considering the man claimed acquaintance with Springer's late father.

"Our ways converged occasionally," was how Drumgold put it. "We shared a few amusements and consolations."

He was British, thickly accented. His hair was yellowish white, sparse, combed straight back and held stiffly in place by whatever he used on it. One could see the tracks made by his comb's teeth. "Honorable man, your father . . ."

Springer was used to hearing it.

". . . but likable as well," Drumgold said, implying the two qualities together were rare in the business. He asked Springer's permission to smoke and brought out an antique silver and enamel case too small for today's cigarettes. He had snipped an inch off his Rothmans so they fit.

Springer hadn't thought Drumgold would be so old. Late seventies was his guess. It was not unheard of but unusual for a man Drumgold's age to still be out peddling stones from country to country. Springer didn't put too much stock in his observations that Drumgold's shirt cuffs were a bit too frayed for starch to conceal, that his business card was inexpensively ink embossed rather than engraved, and that there were several lighter spots on his tie where he'd dabbed it with cleaner. The ethic that only the totally heartless would bargain to the bone with a man in need was too often used to advantage. Besides, Springer was overwary by habit when it came to business. Only moments after receiving Drumgold's call requesting an appointment and using Fred Holtzer as reference, Springer had placed a verifying call to Holtzer in Geneva. Holtzer's admission to the referral was somewhat apologetic, but Springer recognized that as typical self-exoneration before the fact—in case anything went sour.

"Let's see what you have," Springer told Drumgold to begin.

The words corrected the course of Drumgold's thoughts. He'd

been momentarily coveting the youth of this Springer fellow, the energies in store, all the chances not yet taken. He crushed out his cigarette in the ashtray, thoroughly, and brought his good but far from new Moroccan leather briefcase to his lap. He had a little trouble with one of its snaps but got it unstuck. He didn't fumble inside the case, evidently had come well organized. He brought out a "briefke," a sheet of paper folded five times a certain way down to 3½ by 2½ inches. He placed it on the desk.

Springer hardly lifted it from the surface as he opened it, deftly, although mainly with his thumbs. It was something he'd done countless times. The folds of a briefke form a pocket to hold stones. This one contained melee, ten-pointers in this case, or, in other words, at the standard 100 points per carat, stones that were one tenth of a carat. Fifty of them. Springer examined them only for a moment before setting the briefke aside.

Drumgold presented another.

More melee. Twenty pointers of a better quality. A hundred carats in the lot.

Springer also set these aside without revealing interest. He turned partly away from Drumgold, not actually giving attention to what was outside his window. His usual view: tarred rooftops and standpipes, the dun-shaded symmetry of Rockefeller Center, the spires of St. Patrick's cathedral contrasting with the ominous black of Olympic Tower, and, a few blocks farther up the avenue, Trump Tower, also black and attractively sinister. To Springer they were like the elements of a painting or a photograph he'd looked at so often there were no more discoveries.

After another lot of melee of nearly the same size and quality, Springer asked, "Did Holtzer say these are the sort of goods I might want?"

"No."

"All you have is melee?"

"At the moment," Drumgold said, his eyes dropping.

The point had been reached where Springer could kiss Drumgold off, do something else with his time, perhaps sort through and match up some of the two-carat stones now in inventory. However, Drumgold's last three words moved Springer to consider all the fine precious stones that had probably passed through this man's hands. All the glowing times when he'd bought well or sold well. Beautiful deals made and celebrated. Now the years, like a sieve, had him down to melee.

"These your best?" Springer indicated the three briefkes he'd opened.

Drumgold had several briefkes in hand. He thumbed through them and extracted one.

Springer unfolded it. After a glance he tilted it, and the diamonds flowed down the groove of a crease and out onto the white paper sorting pad on his desk.

He ran the edge of his tweezers over them, gently disturbing them, provoking scintillations. When bunched as they were, they borrowed brilliance from one another. He wanted to see how they did on their own. There were eighty stones in the lot. Round-cuts of a quarter of a carat each. Twenty carats total. Springer separated about a third of the diamonds from the rest. Using the tweezers he turned those over one at a time, so they were all table down, their pointed bottoms up. He did it with professional swiftness, arranged the stones into a single row, spaced about an eighth of an inch apart.

This enabled him to observe their color through their pavillion facets. He went over them bare-eyed and then with the help of a tripod table loupe that magnified them ten times. Bent over with his eye close down to the loupe he inspected the color of each stone, compared it with its companions, while also searching for inclusions, specks of carbon, clouds, or any other imperfections.

"Aikhal goods," Drumgold said.

Springer had already figured they were Russian, from their colorless quality. They were so white they looked frozen, an appropriate characteristic inasmuch as they had been mined in a region of Siberia called Yakut, where the earth never thawed. Aikhal diamonds were the finest out of Yakut, and, as nature's frequent perversity would have it, they were also the most difficult to get at.

Springer took up a single stone with his tweezers, used an eye loupe to look at it. Its cut appeared perfectly proportioned, the underpart of the stone in proper ratio with that above its girdle. Its facets were clean, sharp-edged, and precisely angled so the spread of its face was right. Everything about the cut contributed to getting the greatest possible brilliance from the stone.

"Nice make," Springer said, to the stone as much as to Drumgold. He inspected the cut of several others. They were identical. It was known the Soviets were now using electronic devices that could be set to cut to such perfection.

"How much?" Springer asked.

"Finest water, those," Drumgold said. The old epitome of British praise for diamonds.

A maybe shrug from Springer. He sat back, pushed back from his desk a way. "You regularly handle Russian goods?"

Drumgold told him no, regretfully. "I happened onto these in Hong Kong. They were part of a larger lot. The far better part, I must say."

Nothing unusual about that. Sellers nearly always fattened their better lots with stones of lesser quality.

"I went a bit overboard on them," Drumgold admitted.

Springer took that as part of Drumgold's sell.

Drumgold did a little scoffing grunt and diverted his eyes. "By now I should be beyond such foolishness, not heeding my common sense, allowing diamonds to have the final say." He paused briefly to consider his words. Again the stones prevailed. "But they are lovely goods, aren't they?"

"Yes."

"Be something, wouldn't it, if they were each twenty carats?"

Springer didn't go along with that dream, but the times of his own similar losses occurred to him, when the owning of a certain lot or stone had mattered more to him than his better judgment. It hadn't happened much, however. Perhaps, he thought, the tally had been no greater for Drumgold when *he* was thirty-four. "What price have you put on them?" Springer asked.

Drumgold didn't reply quickly and firmly as he should have. "Sixteen," he said, meaning sixteen dollars a point, sixteen hundred a carat.

Springer looked to Drumgold's eyes, saw the off-color of their whites, the shade of old yellowish pearls, outlined by the pink of his inflamed lids. What business battle was left in the gray of the irises was not enough. "Will you take a check?" Springer asked him.

"Of course," Drumgold managed to say. He was stunned that there'd be no haggling.

"I can give you cash."

"Whichever accommodates you. A check will be fine."

Springer gathered up the Russian melee with a small flat scoop. On the counter within reach of his chair was an electronic scale about the size of a toaster oven stood on end. He transferred the stones from the scoop to the shallow pan housed within the scale. The hitting of the little diamonds on metal sounded disproportionately loud. The readout in green numbers on the face of the scale settled on 20.60 carats.

"Make it an even twenty," Drumgold said.

That sixty points just conceded was worth $960. Springer held back from refusing it. Better he should allow some reciprocity. He poured the stones back into their briefke and closed its folds. Drumgold put away his other goods while Springer wrote out a check for $32,000.

"How long will you be in town?" Springer asked.

"Perhaps a week. It's been a while since I was last here. I find everything even taller and faster than I remember. London is my home field, naturally."

"So then you're probably a sight holder." After a deal, Springer usually eased things down with conversation: a tactic his father had instilled.

"Used to be. For many years I was one of the chosen. Got struck off."

Only Springer's eyes inquired.

Drumgold told him. "Business was tight for . . . various reasons. I had difficulty raising payment for a couple of packets. Presold them seal unbroken to an Indian dealer. The System got wind of that, of course. Didn't approve. Didn't approve of an Indian getting such goods nor of my financial bind. My very next packet was half again larger—only half, mind you—but the price The System put on it was three times as much. Three million. They had me. I couldn't presell the packet. I couldn't buy it. I was out."

Springer's nod was genuinely sympathetic. He was well acquainted with The System and its ways, as hard and insensitive as the diamonds it controlled.

Drumgold continued. "That was in 'seventy-seven, just before the *bren.*" Meaning, like a fire out of control, the run-up of diamond prices from $8,000 to $63,000 per D-flawless carat. It lasted from 1978 to 1980. "Unfortunate timing for me. Could have recouped, possibly even made a bundle." Drumgold's good-loser smile was incongruous with his recollections. His teeth were tea-stained.

Springer got up and went to the safe, situated within a recess of the near wall. When he swung open its heavy door he realized why he hadn't waited for Drumgold to leave before putting away the Russian melee. He took his time, enough to deal with the ambivalence he felt, and then removed from the safe one of several small zippered leather cases. He returned with it to his desk.

Inside the case were at least fifty briefkes. They were neatly filed with contents coded in pencil in their upper left corners. Springer fingered through them. Withdrew one, considered, and decided against two others. "I take it you'll be calling on other people while you're here."

"Yes, I'd thought I would."

"Then perhaps, as a favor, you wouldn't mind showing some of our goods around."

"Happy to oblige."

Springer opened four briefkes. Each contained a diamond: a 2.30 carat, a 3.05 carat, a 2.26 carat, and a 2.01 carat. They were brilliant cuts, E to F in color and of VVS1 quality: that is, only very very slightly imperfect. These diamonds were part of a parcel that had recently arrived at Springer & Springer from one of its contract cutters in Antwerp, had just been placed in inventory. Springer took a pad of memos from his desk drawer, listed the stones on it along with their weight and price per carat. In the diamond trade a memo serves as combination record, receipt, and promissory note that is made out whenever a stone but not money changes hands. Drumgold's signature acknowledged his having received the goods and assumed responsibility for them up to the amount indicated. Springer kept the memo original; Drumgold got the carbon copy. He shook Springer's hand across the desk and again at the door as Springer showed him out.

Back at his desk Springer was in the wake of what he'd just done. He felt his father's presence admonishing but also commending. He could have bought the Russian melee from Drumgold for less, surely for twelve, maybe ten. Was it a weakness that he hadn't been able to put his knee on that old neck? Actually, nothing was lost other than the profit not taken. He was sure that a client, a jewelry manufacturer in Chicago, would pay sixteen for that melee.

The four stones from inventory were, however, something else. The price per carat he had stipulated on the memo would just about cover cost. Drumgold would be able to sell them easily, make a nice profit for himself, twenty-five thousand minimum. Well, hell, that had been the idea of it, hadn't it? That and to supply the old casualty with something to go in with to make him a bit more significant than melee.

Springer zipped up the leather case, returned it to the safe. There was no sin in being soft in such a hard business once in a while, he told himself. At least he thought that was himself he heard.

At that moment Linda looked in to see if Springer was alone. She was the all-around assistant, a graduate gemologist who appreciated that she was in a good spot with Springer & Springer. She'd been with the firm for four years. She was twenty-five, and not merely attractive, a natural blonde who helped herself to some strawberry. Linda was extremely capable. She knew diamonds, could even grade rough when necessary. Her real love, however, at least when it came to stones, was color, especially sapphires. Springer shared that with her.

"Mal called," she said. She came all the way in.

"Where is he?"

"I'm sure I heard the rustle of satin sheets."

"No clinking of glasses?"

"Just rustle. He said he was on his way in, whatever that might mean."

"I have to leave in a half hour. If Mal doesn't get here, can you cover?"

"No problem. I was supposed to meet a hunk at Lutece but I'll order lunch in."

"Go to Lutece."

"I would," she flung at him on her way out, "if it was the truth."

Springer could only damn Mal's behavior.

Malcolm was his uncle, his father's younger brother. Malcolm was sixty-one. A bachelor by nature and preference, he believed he knew and had the wherewithal to provide what most thirty-year-old women needed. That confidence was probably the moving force behind his numerous carnal successes, although the fact that he was a diamond dealer must have often counted considerably.

Uncle Malcolm's libidinal irrepressibility was a principal reason for the early assumption that Springer would follow in the business. His father, Edwin Springer, had long ago given up any hope that brother Malcolm would change his ways. Edwin had believed that left solely to Malcolm the firm would be taken over by the banks or be in chapter eleven within a few years—perhaps even sooner—reduced to nothing by paternity suits.

Springer & Springer was founded in 1908 by brothers Willard and Bernard Springer. Bernard was the elder by eight years. They were the sons of an unenterprising merchant whose farm supply store, located in New Milford, Connecticut, did not expand an inch or show an increase in profit for twenty-five years. Not taking after his father, Bernard set out to do better when he was twenty-five. Willard, who was seventeen, tagged along. They went places, shipped out of Boston as deckhands. However, they had no ultimate destination until the possibility of precious stones took over their optimism.

In 1901 their ship had them in Salvador, Brazil. They signed off there and went inland four hundred miles to the province of Minas Gerais. Diamonds had been discovered there in 1725.

What Bernard and Willard first learned was that diamonds were not to be plucked right off the ground and, as for Brazil, they were late, had even missed the tail end of the pickings. They shipped out of Salvador and, via the circuitous routes endured by hired seamen, finally made it to Johannesburg, South Africa.

They made their way north to the diamond fields and became caught up in the frenzy of greed and grit. The claims they worked yielded barely enough to keep their bodies and hopes alive, but they kept at it. Until one day they were unable to encourage one another. They left everything they couldn't carry and began wandering.

Naturally, they kept their eyes to the ground.

Observed doing that around Dutoitspan and Bultfontein, they were chased off by De Beers officials. They ran into the same trouble at Jagersfontein and Koffiefontein. Thus they were more or less forced into taking a direction that put them up the Orange River and then farther up along its main tributary, the Vaal.

There, in a dry bed that was merely one of thousands of runoffs, Bernard and Willard found that the first lesson they had learned in Brazil was not necessarily true. Because there, right there, *were* diamonds to be plucked right off the ground.

No shout of joy or kicking up of a jig. The finding was anticlimactic. Bernard and Willard squatted and began methodically picking diamonds from among the gravel. Alluvial diamonds with a misty-like skin on them. Fine river whites.

Each found about five hundred stones: some no larger than a ladybug, quite a few three times the size of a bumblebee. Willard took off his socks and, because of holes, knotted them at the toes.

Two sockfuls of diamonds. That's what they carried home.

Springer & Springer was in business.

In 1908 it opened to deal in diamonds at 84 Nassau Street. Then and for the next twenty-five years that area of lower Manhattan—Nassau Street, John Street, Canal Street and Maiden Lane—was New York City's diamond district. In the early thirties, about the time when Rockefeller Center was built, many of the downtown jewelers and dealers moved up to 47th Street to be closer to the spenders.

Springer & Springer remained on Nassau Street. Willard and Bernard Springer were against making such a move. However, when

Bernard died in 1945 and Willard passed away four years later, Willard's two sons assumed responsibility for running the firm. Springer & Springer it would still be. Edwin was then thirty-two, Malcolm twenty-five.

Within a year after Willard's death Edwin and Malcolm agreed to move the firm uptown. They were both of the conviction that Springer & Springer would have done better had it made the move earlier, and indeed, within the first year of operation out of its new location at 580 Fifth Avenue, business improved. Springer & Springer was never one of the supereminent diamond dealers. It did not do an enormous volume or have high-level clout with The System. Nevertheless its niche was worthy as one of the few truly solid upper-middle-ground firms, well known by the trade because of its equity and the consistency of its reputation. A diamond, rough or finished, from Springer & Springer could be counted on to be what Springer & Springer claimed it was. If, for example, the cut of a stone was slightly off, Springer & Springer, instead of trying to squeeze it through, would inform its client of the discrepancy and accordingly call attention to the price adjustment it had made. That is not to say Springer & Springer wasn't tough when it had to be. It hondled and hacked and bluffed with the best of them. But no firm was fairer.

For thirty-one years, Edwin Springer was the axis for such standards. He constantly tended and nourished Springer & Springer's reputation, kept it impeccably structured for the years ahead.

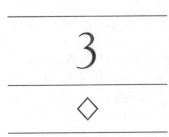

3

It was an extreme disappointment to Edwin when his first-born son, Norman, showed no interest in the business. Edwin was patient in his attempts to motivate Norman, but it was evident that Norman's heart would never be in it. To him a diamond was valuable but not fascinating. Eventually Edwin gave up trying to influence him. Norman would be whatever he would be.

Edwin could hardly wait for his second son, Phillip, to be old enough. When Phillip was still toddling, Edwin brought diamonds home that he and Phillip would play with on the rug in the family apartment at 28 East 72nd. Of course, Edwin had to keep careful watch or the child would have them in his mouth. The way the stones seemed to dazzle Phillip, the way his tiny fingers found and enclosed them, Edwin was encouraged.

For his eighth birthday Phillip received *A Child's Dictionary of the Supernatural* from his mother, Mattie, and from his father a volleyball and a set of master stones. He liked the volleyball. He went around bouncing it off every possible surface, including, to his mother's horror, his baby sister Janet's bassinette. But it was the set of master stones that surprised and pleased Phillip most: six round-cut diamonds, one-quarter carat each, in their own special black leather case. They were inset exactly in place and labeled according to their grade of color: D, E, F, G, H, and I. Many diamond dealers used this same type of master set to compare and verify their stones. It was expensive, by no means a toy. Phillip treasured it, handled it with care. He kept it safely locked away in a metal strongbox in a locked drawer and wore both keys on a chain around his neck.

After that Edwin would frequently bring a few diamonds home and challenge Phillip to grade them. Phillip was glad to put his master set and opinion to work.

"This one's an F and this one might be a D to some people, but I think it's closer to an E."

"You have exceptional eyes," Edwin told him. And soon Phillip was classifying stones without relying on the master set, using it only to check himself.

Edwin continued to teach him diamonds in much the same manner as he had been taught by his own father, with challenges and praise and tactical consternation.

"I'm considering buying this stone. It's supposed to be flawless but . . . well, what do you think?"

The stone in question, a three-carat round, was handed over to Phillip for his examination under the ten-power of his father's loupe.

"It looks clean."

"Really? I'd certainly hate to pay the price that's being asked, if it isn't."

"I don't see anything in it."

"Not even a speck of carbon . . ."

"Pretty stone."

" . . . or a hairline fracture?"

"Nope."

"Good. I feel better now that—"

"Hey, wait a second! I think I just caught on something. Yeah, there it is, a flake of black right under the crown facets and the edge of the table. Like it was hiding under the table."

"Or hidden?"

"Or hidden."

"Well, what do you know."

That was when Phillip was twelve, with a protégé's understanding of such diamond complexities as high shoulders, lumpy girdles, included crystals, and cleavage cracks. Sometimes he was a bit cocky about his special knowledge, and Edwin would have to let him see how much he still didn't know.

"What would you say is the weight of this stone?"

"Four carats."

"You're sure?"

"Give or take a few points."

"You're off, way off. It's less than three carats."

Phillip remained dubious until the stone was on the scale and registering 2.92 carats. Edwin said it was a "swindle."

"A gyp?"

"Not if someone knows better," Edwin told him pointedly and explained that a swindle was what those in the trade called a stone that was cut with so much spread to its table that the stone appeared larger than it actually was.

To Phillip it was personal trickery. He took his volleyball and headed for the park. He could usually find a game in progress or get one up. Where he played mostly was in the vast open area called The Sheep Meadow. Sometimes the games there were serious, the players older guys, and Phillip could only stand around and watch. More often, however, it didn't matter how many were on a side or how old or tall one was. It was a free-for-all, on a surface that was grass run to dust, with hardly any team play, and as many as four or five guys converging on the ball. The larger, taller guys dominated, but Phillip was gutsy, went for it, and was often crushed. He vowed that when he was older he would be an absolute ball hog. Whenever he was in a game only with fellows near his own age he never gave up, made sacrificial dives for balls that seemed impossible to reach, and for that he'd already made some saves remarkable enough to remember. He broke his collarbone twice.

When he wasn't in the park playing volleyball he was most likely somewhere on 47th Street. He'd go looking along, interested in every shop window. There was always something new to see because of the street's constant turnover of goods. A ten-carat square-cut making its debut or refreshed comeback could hold his attention for a half hour that seemed to him no more than a couple of minutes. His approach was to first give a stone its due and then try to realize its flaws.

He was the same with people. He got to know just about every jeweler on the street and every stall owner in the arcades. In the course of their adult business seldom was a youngster such as Phillip around so regularly, and for a while he was regarded as an outsider, a possible nuisance. However, eventually, when he'd never gotten in the way or cost anyone a sale, they accepted him. Not only the street jewelers with their flourishing stores but as well the stall keepers with lesser offerings, the bead stringers, the sellers of findings—all those little gold snaps and rings and catches and bezels—the watchmakers, the repairers, even those who sold only the special boxes jewelry requires. If they weren't busy sometimes they would schmooze with him. His inquisitiveness was often flattering, an opportunity for, say, a man who knew opals to share a bit of his expertise, or a pearl dealer to show him how much better were the beauties that came from the Asian oceans before the oyster beds were contaminated.

"You don't see pearls like this anymore."

Actually, Phillip on his meanderings saw numerous pearls of such quality or better, but he kept that to himself. He was psychologically precocious in that respect, knowing when *not* to say anything. It gave him a chameleonlike advantage.

He got to know early the bright conspicuous side of 47th and also its criminal underbelly. He could pick out the shylocks, some connected well enough to come up with a half million or more within an hour to get some dealer deeper in the hole. He recognized their collectors, potential bullies, making rounds. He saw the same faces of the same fences come with diamonds, rubies, sapphires, emeralds popped from mountings and therefore unidentifiable, surely unincriminating. A stone is a stone is a stone to be set anew and sold again and, chances were, stolen again. So went the cycle. Just from overhearing and observing he was able to make out which were the pushy corruptors, the larcenous and the slippery, the mob guys.

Phillip would never forget a particular mob guy who operated out of a booth in one of the busier exchanges, a small booth with a smattering of ordinary gold chains in its finger-smeared glass case. The man's name was John. No one seemed to know him by more than that, so they called him Just John. And apparently he didn't mind. He was a short, thick man with a large face, who always wore a white shirt with its sleeves rolled not quite to the elbow. No tie. Expensive black shoes. Just John's booth was situated far in the back so he had a total view of the place and could see anyone coming in his direction well in advance. He was brought things he might want to buy. Not anyone could approach him, only certain guys, the same guys every day. If someone else offered to sell him something, he wasn't interested, no matter how fine and cheap the goods. Just John had the next to the last word. Only rarely did he have to ask whomever it was whether or not he should make a buy. When he asked he always went outside on the street to a pay phone.

Once Phillip watched as Just John dealt with a guy. Just John was smiling amiably one second and the next his face was cold stone. Phillip would always remember it, how all the while it must have been there just beneath the smiling surface—that sudden death.

One day.

On the street outside the exchange of Just John.

"Hey, kid."

Phillip glanced around and thought perhaps he'd heard his imagination because no one was there except a boy about his own age, a dark-haired, dark-eyed boy with the beginnings of a first mustache like a charcoal smudge above his lips. He had on light tan gabardine slacks, a pale green tight-fitting shirt, well-shined hardly worn brown shoes. He was leaning against the facade of the place. "Come here," he said.

Phillip was used to having to decide whether or not to ignore someone. He was already stopped. He took three steps forward, which was about halfway to the boy.

The boy took his three.

Five minutes later they were together at a table in the cafeteria down the way, having milkshakes. The boy paid for them with a fifty, although, Phillip noticed, he had smaller. He introduced himself as Danny Raggio, said people who really knew him called him Danny Rags. By comparison Phillip thought his own name sounded stiff and unsuitable so he told Danny to call him Springer.

Danny was new on the street. He'd had a fight in school, literally in it. All the way down the school corridor, throwing punches and anything else he could get hold of.

"Who won?" Phillip asked.

"The fuckheads broke it up."

Phillip liked the honesty.

"They expelled me so my father got me this job."

"Doing what?"

"I'm a runner for Just John. You know Just John?"

Phillip nodded.

"He's my uncle." Not mere fact the way Danny said it. Some boast in it. And the next time Danny smiled Phillip tried to read through it, but there was no lurking icy lethalness that he could see.

"You ever been up around Arthur Avenue?" Danny asked.

"I don't think so."

"In the Bronx."

"I've been to the zoo."

"It's not far from there."

"Is that where you live?"

"Yeah, the zoo."

"It's all zoo," Phillip said.

Laugh for laugh.

"I'll take you up with me sometime," Danny promised. "Show you around. We'll have some parmigiana or something. One of my other uncles owns a couple of restaurants." There was a hollowness to his words because he was speaking into the wax container, had it inverted, trying to get the last foamy part of his shake to slide into his mouth.

"Use your straw," Phillip suggested, which was advice his older brother Norman used to give him. But for Danny, to rely on a straw would evidently be violation of a personal code.

"How many uncles do you have?"

"Six," Danny told him. "Two in the joint."

"What did they do?"

"Don't ask. You're not supposed to ask. Want another shake?"

"No, thanks."

"You work here on the street?" Danny asked.

"Yeah."

"Figured that when I saw you around so much. What are you into?"

"Diamonds," Phillip replied and, being cautious, let it go at that.

From then on he and Danny spent some of nearly every day together. Phillip knew the street and was glad to teach it to his new friend. He pointed out things that weren't what they seemed and showed him some of the nice and many of the seamy aspects of 47th. It was a trade-off. For Phillip, just being around Danny further magnified his outsight. For one thing he had greatly underestimated the weight of the traffic in swag.

When Phillip graduated from high school with a B average that would have easily been an A if he hadn't been so distracted, his father rewarded him with a trip to London. Edwin was scheduled to attend a sight at The System.

They stayed at the Savoy.

Edwin was well known there, had been a guest ten times a year for many years. In his opinion the Savoy was more conscientious than similar hotels in the West End. As well, it was more convenient to number eleven, the headquarters of the Consolidated Selling System. Eleven Harrowhouse Street.

Ten times each year The System sent cables to a select list of diamond dealers throughout the world, notifying them that a sight was to be held and they should attend. Altogether five hundred dealers received such word, which really was more a summons than a notification. Those on the list of five hundred were called sight holders, and although they were the buyers, the clients of The System, it was The System that extended the favor, The System that was always right.

At rock bottom of that paradox was the fact that The System had the corner on diamonds. Ninety percent of the world's output of gem quality rough, accumulated from its own high-yielding mines in Africa and through tight arrangements with Russia and other diamond-producing countries. Thus to be in the business of diamonds to any substantial extent, a dealer had to be in the good graces of The System and take care not to offend.

Furthermore, the dealers, even the most significant, had to accept whatever quality rough The System chose to dole out. With nothing to say about what they bought, it would seem the dealers certainly would not put up with having no say about how much they paid for it. Nevertheless, that was how it was.

A dealer showed up precisely at his appointed time at number eleven. He was accompanied to the sight room and his parcel was brought to him. He might as well have left at that point for what difference it made. However, as a matter of courtesy and perhaps curiosity, he opened his parcel then and there: broke its ornate wax seals to get to its contents, the rough diamonds he had bought. Probably there would be some of the fine quality that he'd requested —but, no doubt, more of the lesser quality The System wanted to get out of their inventory or felt that dealer deserved. The dealer swallowed his resentment and ended the transaction expressing his gratitude with a tone he hoped sounded genuine.

Dealers tolerated this demeaning one-sidedness simply because it was more profitable over the long run. The rough diamonds in The System's parcels were usually, eventually, worth more than the pride or dollars paid for them. Anyway, that was the way the cartel known as The System did business, the way it kept control of the world's supply of diamonds and, often, of the lives of certain men.

Edwin Springer was such a sight holder, as his father had been before him and as Edwin hoped someday Phillip would be. He would not, however, on this trip take Phillip to number eleven and introduce him. He'd considered doing that and decided Phillip would see enough of those people in his lifetime, spare him now.

Phillip was impressed with London, and, although nothing direct had been said, he had the feeling that the city was impressed with him. Especially for the trip he had bought a new dark gray vested suit and three ties more conservative than he'd ever owned. Up to then he'd avoided wearing a tie whenever he could, believed a tie was a hang-up, a noose around his neck, but when he dressed in front of the mirror in his room at the Savoy he was quite conscientious about the knot he made.

He also felt taller for some reason, as though he'd shot up a few inches in just a couple of days. He was already five-ten, only an inch shorter than his father, but he hadn't taken special notice of that or thought it important until London.

While his father did business, Phillip had time to himself. He appreciated that his father hadn't told him not to get lost or warned him about the city, merely said they'd meet back at the hotel at such and such a time. Phillip had ample pocket money for taxis and he took them when necessary; however, he preferred to walk. There he went, down the Strand, careful not to gawk, his right thumb in the watch pocket of his vest. Young girls passing appreciated him with their eyes and he was aware but not entirely sure of them and they became opportunities lost.

He went to the Tate for confrontations with Van Dyke, Gainsborough, Reynolds, and Blake. He was particularly taken with the Whistlers, those paintings titled like musical compositions, nocturnes and symphonies. He bought a cashmere sweater at Harrods for Danny, a camel shade, although he almost chose black. Walked Hyde Park from Kensington Palace all the way to Park Lane, watched perfectly groomed horses ridden by perfectly outfitted people along Rotten Row. Decided he wouldn't go to see the changing of the guard at Buckingham Palace and then unwittingly walked right into it. It seemed to him that every piece of brass in London was polished every day, that Christopher Wren built nearly everything, that the royal family had always been great customers, according to the numerous shops that displayed crowns and rampant lions and plaques bragging they were or had been royally appointed at one time or another. He didn't want to be so obviously a tourist but it seemed unavoidable. He even had to suffer the close-call cringe from having been just missed by a fast truck because he stepped off the curb of Kensington High Street after looking the wrong way.

On his third London afternoon he bought four greengage plums at Fortnum & Mason and returned to the Savoy. In his box at reception was a message from his father. For business reasons his father would not be back until very late. He was to have dinner on his own. It was, Phillip thought, a good grown-up message.

He didn't go straight up to his room. Instead, he went to the lounge off the lobby, where he was shown to a small round table situated along a velour banquette. He ordered tea and was pleased when along with it came several little frosted rolls that he hadn't asked for. He was sipping and nibbling and envisioning the world as a sphere, and where he was on it, when—"They're tastier when you butter them," he was told by a woman's voice.

She was seated alone at the next little table: a woman in a navy blue felt cloche hat with wisps of brunette hair showing at her temples. Her dress was also navy, of a lightweight material, high at the neck and contrasted by a narrow white collar. She wasn't beautiful, none of her features, not her nose or mouth or eyes, was predominant; however, they went together in an equitable, pretty way. Her eyes were exaggerated by makeup, darkly outlined and shaded.

"Here, let me," she said, and before Phillip had a chance to decline she reached over, broke open one of his rolls, and smeared it with butter.

She was an older woman in Phillip's eyes. At least thirty. Her teacup was half empty, her rolls partially eaten. Evidently she'd been there but he hadn't noticed. He thanked her for her attention. She was very pleasant.

"How do you find London?" she asked.

"I like it."

"I see you've gotten to Fortnum & Mason."

His greengage plums were wrapped in that store's paper and tied with its identifiable ribbon. He subdued the impulse to open the package and offer her one.

"What have you been doing for amusement?" she inquired.

He told her he'd gone to a play the night before. She didn't, as he expected, ask him which play or whether or not he'd enjoyed it, so he continued on, told her all about it, a Noel Coward play.

She didn't interrupt but listened intently, although, when he was through, she told him she adored the play, had seen it twice. "I get fidgety at plays," she confided.

"So do I." He laughed.

"Thank goodness for intermissions. Shall I pour for you?" She assumed control of his teapot and, while she was at it, signaled for a fresh one and had the waiter move her table closer to Phillip's.

"That's better," she said, settling. "Much better." Her voice had a throaty quality to it that, along with her British stretching and broadening of vowels, captivated Phillip. Especially so when she said who she was: Lady Irith Ward-Lambdon. She taught him how to correctly pronounce her given name. "Like the flower, iris, only with a lisp."

When he told his name she said it aloud twice as though she were tasting it. It sounded different, better said by her, Phillip thought.

They talked for another two hours. Phillip commented lightly on Lord Nelson's column in Trafalgar Square, wondered if Nelson had been such a hero why he'd been put way up there where no one could really see him.

Lady Irith thought that a very good point.

Phillip told her how close he'd come to being smacked dead by a truck on Kensington High Street.

Lady Irith cautioned him to be careful, very careful, as though his safety truly meant something to her.

Her nail enamel and lipstick matched, Phillip noticed.

Enough tea, enough of the lounge.

Offhand, she suggested, "Why don't you show me to my rooms?"

Her rooms were on one of the highest floors, a large suite. She invited him in. First thing, she removed her hat, fussed her hair neat in the mirror. They sat opposite one another, and although Phillip tried to make conversation she apparently was all talked out. Except for her eyes. He almost believed he could hear her eyes but he wasn't sure enough. She kept them right on him. He wasn't made to feel uncomfortable; however, he couldn't give it right back at her, eyes to eyes, had to glance away. He thought, if anything, he would have to go over to her.

At that moment she thought how attractive this young man was. Hair dark as her own, slate-blue eyes. Not a pretty boy, fortunately —his were strong good looks, virile. She purposely hadn't asked his age, not to draw attention to that. She'd decided on seventeen, possibly only sixteen. No matter, he wouldn't bolt.

Lady Irith got up, smiled at him, and left for the bedroom. Her dress was wrinkled in the back from so much sitting, Phillip noticed.

He remained where he was for two extremely long minutes and then went in.

She wasn't undressed or anything, just standing there waiting for him. She put out her arms and he went into them, and they held pressed for a while and he breathed the fragrance of her expensive powder on the fine skin of her neck. She was careful with her mouth, skimmed it slowly across his cheek to come upon his with gentle and reassuring hunger. Her hands, both of them, moved down and she withdrew herself from against him enough to find him down there. She was pleased that he was already so hard. It confirmed her.

Phillip was not the first much younger man for Lady Irith. He was her second. The first had occurred under somewhat similar circumstances at the Hotel Hermitage in Monte Carlo. That time the idea of the perversity of what she had dared do was more exciting than what she'd actually done. That, she felt, would not be so with Phillip. There was no fumbling or clumsiness to him; his hands, his fingers, were confident while they traveled her. He stroked and respected her skin as though it were delicate fabric and helped himself with tender assertion to whatever part of her he wanted. She had anticipated his lovemaking would be vigorous. The quality of it, however, so astonished her that it was a while before she stopped externalizing and gave entirely into it.

Lady Irith's body was a ripened woman's body. The first for Phillip. Unlike those intermediate merely promising shapes he had experienced. There was an insistence rather than defensiveness to her wanting. When he was above her and in her she drew her legs up so the backs of her calves were against his shoulders to have as much of him as possible. She rolled over and haunched up to have even more from behind. She made little animal whines that sounded somewhat painful, and when she had adequate breath she described aloud what he was doing to her.

After the first comings she went into the bathroom for only a short while and returned looking as fresh as though nothing had happened. Brought a warm wet washcloth and towel and tended to him. She plumped and piled the pillows cateringly. He lay back on them. She lay front down across the foot of the bed, the upper part of her supported by her elbows, her forearms and hands flat on the sheet.

"What a marvelous lover you are," she declared.

"So are you," he told her, as though he'd had many comparisons.

"Who taught you to love like that?"

"No one." Certainly he hadn't learned much those two times Danny had led him to the Upper East Side apartments of girls who were paid for it.

"You're just blessed, is that it?" Lady Irith grinned.

"Could be."

Positioned sphinxlike as she was and with her eyes darkly made up, she reminded Phillip of a painting by Dante Gabriel Rossetti he had seen at the Tate. A *femme fatale,* irresistible and evil, who would take pleasure from depletion.

For the rest of the trip Phillip saw very little of London. Whenever his father inquired about how he'd spent the day he was prepared with places and descriptions borrowed off the pages of a tourist guidebook. He disliked having to fib.

Phillip gained some useful insights from his brief, fiery entanglement with Lady Irith. He learned that women were not really so physically mysterious, and that, with them, he should always have the confidence to rely on tenderness. They were so easy to please when they wanted to be. He also learned from a phone call Lady Irith made—while bare in bed with him—to her husband in Sussex, sweetly informing him that she'd decided to do a few more days' shopping in town. "Might as well get what I need while I'm at it," were her exact words Phillip would remember.

* * *

That fall Phillip began at New York University. Every weekday morning he subwayed downtown to his first class, and often he felt he got more from that ride and those making it than from the droning lectures he had to endure. He had difficulty deciding on a major study. He thought he'd head into law until he had a dull talk with a couple of bored lawyers. He finally settled on business and that turned out badly. He found the courses uninspiring. Time Management, Effective Supervision, and Marketing Plans were unrealistic and overcomplicated. He'd already been exposed, too influenced by the simpler honor-of-word no-cash-register 47th Street way of doing business. Nevertheless, he persevered, received his B.B.A. degree, and that was that. He went right to work full-time at Springer & Springer.

Edwin was relieved. His shaping had paid off. Careful not to spoil, he started Phillip out with more responsibility than salary.

Meanwhile, Phillip's older brother Norman was practicing medicine in Washington, D.C. Norman had determined his direction early and never swerved from it. He had taken his premed at Cornell and graduated at a precocious eighteen; he also got his M.D. there with highest honors. He interned spectacularly at Mass General, became a favored assistant to the Head of Cardiology. To add extra icing to his already impressive credentials he spent two years at the Center for Cardiac Care in Lyons, France, reputed to be the most advanced clinic of its kind in the world.

Dr. Norman B. Springer.

Washington was quick to take him to its most important hearts. Their anginas and hypertensions and infarcts became his charge. All the better that he was young: He was up-to-the-minute in knowledge. Good that his fees were high: It expressed self-confidence and kept him exclusive. A medium-high-up in the State Department was first to find him, and from then on he was a badly kept top secret.

"The Ambassador just got back from two bad weeks in Cairo. He's feeling shaky and his eyes look like pissholes. We're worried. Can you fit him in this afternoon? Doesn't matter how late."

Norman rarely got up to New York except for the big holidays, and he even had to miss some of those. He phoned often, talked to his parents and brother, asked about Janet, became more of a voice than a person. "If you need me for any reason I'm here," he would say long distance and Phillip would hold back from saying, "Exactly."

One Christmas visit he and Phillip went out together for a drink. Phillip wanted to go to a casual neighborhood place where they could talk easily and recoup some of their relationship. Norman chose the Oak Bar at the Plaza.

The Oak Bar was jammed with serious drinking well-offs. Cigar smoke and babble. Phillip suggested they go someplace else. Norman parried with the excuse that they'd already checked their coats. He seemed in his element, the way he apologized as he forged roughly through the crowd, aggressively wedged into and widened a space at the bar, demanded a pair of Dewar's on the rocks as though he'd been long slighted.

They touched glasses.

Norman said a perfunctory "cheers" and took a gulp.

They had thought they'd have a lot to talk about, but now they didn't know where to start. Actually they didn't have much in common, not even in their looks. Norman was shorter, about five-eight. His upper body was too chunky for his legs. The gray in his hair and the natural slackness of his mouth added years to him. On the starting line of going to jowls, was the impression he gave. The one obvious resemblance between these brothers was their eyes, of an identical shape and slate-blue shade.

"You look tired," Phillip said.

"Thanks."

"Been going with anyone?"

"Not seriously. No time for it. You?"

Phillip nodded. "You don't know her." He waved away a puff of cigar smoke that had floated into his face. "You know, you ought to at least be living with someone, have her take care of you."

"I've got a housekeeper," Norman said with a tinge of insinuation in case Phillip let it go at that.

"I hope she's blond, Swedish, and grateful."

"Gray, Irish, and dependable," Norman admitted.

Phillip imagined what Norman's routine was like, thought he probably ate and fucked on the run, looked after everyone's heart but his own. Numerous times over the years he'd envied Norman's independence, Norman's having a profession that, no doubt, evoked more response than was possible from his own mute stones.

But not any more.

The way he now saw it Norman was the less fortunate, leading a sacrificial existence. Phillip wished there was some way he could come right out and express his empathy without the chance of its being taken as belittling.

"I've got a shot at the White House," Norman said.

"You're going to make an attempt on the President's life?"

"You might put it that way—but don't!" He glanced around. "Not in a place like this. Full of spooks."

"Sorry."

"What I meant was I might have the President as a patient. Nothing definite yet, but there have been overtures."

"How do you know?"

"His people have been checking, stirring up my background, authenticating it. Making sure I'm really who I am. Besides, the Secretary of State tipped me off on it and he's not the mind-fucking sort."

"I hope it works out."

"It could mean a lot."

Norman was obviously delighted with the prospect and Phillip was proud of him, but they kept it light.

"I thought you didn't make house calls," Phillip quipped.

"Only White House calls."

"Anyway, congratulations. I hope it works out." Phillip extended his hand.

"It's too early yet. Don't want to jinx it." Norman declined the handshake and ordered another round of Dewar's. "Sorry I didn't get up to see Janet this time," he said. "For sure next time."

"Next time," Phillip repeated as he envisioned Norman stethescoping the chest of the most powerful man in the world and telling him to hold his breath.

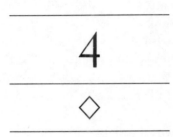

4

◇

In 1980, in the very early hours of August eighteenth, Edwin Springer died. He died the kindest way, of a sudden stroke while he slept. To spare his mother, Phillip took care of arrangements. Services would be held at the Frank E. Campbell Funeral Chapel at 81st and Madison.

Norman came up from Washington as soon as he got word. Phillip met him at LaGuardia. In the corridor of the off-ramp they embraced and drew solace from one another, patted backs.

Norman asked how their mother was taking it.

Her beliefs would see her through, Phillip said.

During the service at Campbell's both Phillip and Norman gave extemporaneous eulogies. They took their time about it because for this purpose there would be no other time. Said what they felt as it came to them and were not self-conscious when grief choked their words. They just paused and cried.

All one hundred of the foldaway seats in the chapel were occupied and there were people standing. Many of the diamond trade, from important dealers to journeyman cutters, had come to pay respects. Six high-ranking members of the Diamond Dealers Club acted as pallbearers. They bore the bronze coffin out onto Madison Avenue and into the waiting black Cadillac hearse. A black stretched limousine was for family. Phillip and Norman rode with their mother, Matilda Springer. It was a two-hour journey to New Milford.

The open grave that awaited was on the hilliest part of Center Cemetery; in a plot with an old but still mostly intact fancy cast-iron border. The long-ago farm-supply storekeeper Ephraim Springer, his sons, Bernard and Willard, and their wives, already lay there. Grassy thick, sunken uneven in places, the ground had grown used to having them. The mound of dirt that had been shoveled out for Edwin was off to one side, partially covered by a green canvas tarpaulin.

The family stood around the poised coffin. Cemetery attendants bided their time nearby.

No minister.

Matilda hadn't wanted one. There would be no worn religious mutterings. There was no need to impress anyone, she said; the fact was that Edwin had merely passed from this life to another just as he had passed into it from another. No reason to say farewell forever to Edwin. They were all related recurrences; they would all, sooner or later, be with him again, she promised.

Matilda Springer's sadness was like that felt for someone greatly loved who would be away for quite a while. Her eyes cried as they smiled.

The coffin was lowered.

The Springers, silent prayers said, turned and walked away. Except Phillip. He was aware that the cemetery attendants wanted to be done. He gestured them to come forward and begin. Dirt was shoveled down onto the coffin. Phillip heard the pebbles in it striking the bronze surface. He saw, protruding from the dirt along the sides of the grave, various-size common Connecticut rocks. His father deserved better.

Phillip took up a fistful of dirt. He made sure of the shovelers' eyes before he flung it down upon the coffin, where it was immediately covered over. Along with it had gone twenty-five carats of diamonds, ten of the finest-quality stones from the Springer & Springer inventory.

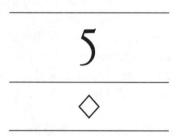

5

◇

Now in his office in the diamond district, Springer tidied his desk. He tore off and discarded the top sheet of his large white sorting pad so, come Monday, he'd be starting fresh. The small black-faced quartz clock that was almost hidden behind the phone told him eleven forty-three. He knew it was lying, that it was always exactly sixteen minutes ahead of the truth.

He had told Audrey he'd be out at eleven thirty sharp. He'd make it this time. He called for Linda. She came in. He asked, "Will you be needing anything from the safe?"

"I doubt it. Schiff said he was coming by but he's bringing back, not taking. I've got a few things out." She had a small raised-border sorting tray in her hand. "You want to close the safe now?"

"I suppose Mal can close it when he gets here."

"Close it," Linda advised.

Offhand, Springer couldn't remember what the dealer Schiff had, and he didn't want to take the time now to go looking through the memo book.

"Only a few carats," Linda told him, then said archly, "I'll hide them somewhere on my body."

"Where they will surely be found."

"I wish." She put her tray and its contents into the safe, careful with it, so as not to disturb the sorting she'd done.

Springer's intercom buzzed. One of the phone lines was blinking on hold.

"Who is it?" Springer shouted out to the receptionist, who was actually only ten feet and a partition away.

"It's Gayle," the receptionist shouted back.

"Tell her . . ." His intentions seemed to hit a wall. "Oh, shit," he muttered and picked up the receiver, said a mannerly hello.

"Where the hell are you?" Gayle asked.

"You dialed."

"You said you'd be here midmorning. Jamie's been waiting over an hour."

He knew what she was pulling. "You bitch," he said.

She wasn't fazed. "Jamie is extremely upset with you. He asked me to call."

"Gayle, last Tuesday I told you I'd have to be out of town this weekend."

"Nothing of the sort. You told me you'd be here Friday midmorning."

"No."

"I'm a liar then, is that it? You're calling me a liar again."

"If the pot fits, sit on it."

That got to her. Her biggest battle with her body was her butt. "You don't deserve visitation," she said.

"Where's Jake?"

"He's right here, but don't call him Jake."

"He's hearing all this?"

"What do you expect?"

"Put him on." The phone was handed.

"Hi, Dad."

Springer detected an undertone of disappointment in the eight-year-old's voice.

"What do you say, Jake?"

"Not much."

"How's the elbow?" A grass-burned elbow from some volleyball they'd played last weekend.

"Almost gone."

"I can't be with you this weekend, Jake."

"Where you going?"

"Out of town," Springer said evasively.

After a pause Jake told him, "That's okay."

"You sure?"

"Next time can we go up to see Mr. Malo and Mr. Bueno and those guys?"

"Maybe. You weren't supposed to mention that."

"She didn't hear me. She went to the bathroom for a minute."

"Everything's Jake, right?"

"Sure."

The disappointment was gone from his voice.

"You're not miffed?"

Jake laughed. "Not at you."

"That's my boy."

"Here she is."

Gayle came back on. "Well"—she sighed, a martyr—"now I'll have to cancel my plans. But that doesn't matter. Jamie comes first." Her voice brightened purposely. "We'll treat ourselves to a good show and have some Japanese afterward."

For perhaps the five thousandth time he wanted to strangle her. Gayle.

Springer had made, he figured, nine or ten major mistakes in his life. She was the worst. Up until the moment they were married she was sweetness and light and willing passion to the bone. It was as though the vows that were said in that ceremony were an incantation that transformed her. Shrewed her face, voice, body, and disposition. Springer chalked it up to newlywed nerves for as long as he could. Then he began questioning his judgment. It seemed impossible to

53

him that he hadn't perceived the way Gayle really was. Had he been that blindly smitten? Of course, she wasn't shrewish all the time. To treat someone badly with maximum effect, he has to be granted a portion of good treatment every so often.

"Incidentally," Gayle was saying, "a cousin of one of my friends will be calling to see you. She wants . . ."

"Gayle, I'm running late. I have to go."

". . . She wants a two-carat square-cut. I told her you'd let her have it at your cost."

"I don't have any two-carat squares in stock," Springer said, wanting to avoid wasting some future hour with another of her remote acquaintances, who would poke around in the best and end up going cheaper for size and unobvious inclusions.

"You'll show her something," Gayle predicted.

Springer said goodbye with the receiver already halfway to its cradle. He locked the safe and, as was his habit, gave the rug around his desk a swift onceover for a possibly dropped stone. He reminded Linda to set the alarms.

On Fifth Avenue the black BMW 745i was waiting in a bus stop zone in front of the 580 Building. Springer cut across the pedestrian flow and got into the passenger seat. Audrey started the car but got bullied by two buses before she could pull out into traffic. She went left on 46th and had to stop momentarily behind a Wells Fargo armored truck making a pickup. Neither she nor Springer had said hello. They never did. Just as they never said goodbye. It was their way of not acknowledging the time they spent apart.

She leaned to Springer, presented her face. "Give us one, love," she said brightly.

He kissed her. Not his best. She had expected one of his best. "I went around the block eleven times," she said, mixing fact and complaint.

Springer wouldn't tell her about the call from Gayle. He never spoiled their time together with Gayle.

"Want to drive?" Audrey asked.

"Not really."

"You drive and I'll crawl into the back and sleep." Audrey loved sleep. She could close her eyes and drop off in a moment, practically anywhere. She had enjoyable dreams.

Springer vetoed sleep.

"Okay," she told him, "I'll drive, you fondle."

That drew his nice laugh from him. "You're oversexed."

"Underloved," she contended.

"Not by me."

"Maybe you feel you overlove me?"

Impossible, he thought, but, then, he'd been wrong before.

Traffic on Madison was thick and competitive. She enjoyed it, defying fenders, dilating the most meager openings. They went straight uptown through Harlem and got onto the Major Deegan Expressway, where, to the delight of Audrey's right foot, the going was faster. She shoved a cassette into the stereo slot, a Crystal Gayle that started in the middle.

Come back
When you can stay forever,
Love's not really love
Unless it lasts that long.

Audrey sang along, word for word, inflection for inflection.

Springer wished she'd just leave it up to Crystal. Audrey's singing voice was dreadful: sharp one note, flat the next. However, as far as Springer was concerned, that was about the only thing wrong with her.

He'd first set eyes on her a little over a year ago. At La Goulue on East 70th. It was a special night for him because his divorce from Gayle had come final that afternoon. His dinner companion was a nearly passé Ford model named Elise whom he'd been seeing now and then. They'd had two Scotch and Perriers and Elise was saying she was considering going to work in Milan again, where she was more appreciated, when Springer just happened to shift his head five inches to the right and look past Elise's synthetically studded left ear to see, reflected but partially obscured by some peeling and flaking of the mirror's silver back, a woman's face that stunned him.

He thought the mirror was playing tricks, that it and the amber lights of the restaurant were being too kind to the woman. He was tempted but could not without being obvious turn for a direct appraisal of her. He had to be satisfied with the view he had—and kept —throughout another drink and Elise asking about the entrees and his ordering of roast lamb for two and the waiter reprovingly repeating the way the menu had it: *médaillons de selle d'agneau.*

Springer's view also included the back of the head of the man the woman was with. He saw her amused by the man, laughing enough to show her teeth. A white, perfect flash. He saw her use her fingers to unmindfully comb through her jaw-length dark hair. Her hair seemed to parenthesize her face, particularly her eyes, wide-set and large. Springer felt a thief the way he was stealing from her, but no matter, she was oblivious to it, he thought. Besides, whatever was stolen from such riches wouldn't be missed.

Finally, he could take no more. He excused himself to Elise, got up, turned, and, for as little time as it took for him to move his chair in place, looked right at that woman.

She looked back but without a hint of acknowledgment.

He continued on to the men's room.

In there alone, looking into another mirror, he told himself he was acting strange. She was not that beautiful, actually. She hadn't really affected him all that much. Chalk it up to divorce day.

Thus fortified with self-possession he opened the men's-room door.

There she was.

In the access way barely wide enough for two. She was standing at the pay telephone on the wall with its receiver up to her ear. At that intimate distance there could be no doubt whom her attention was on. She was purposely holding the telephone receiver with her left hand to show herself unmarried, Springer thought. He seized the moment.

"Where can I get in touch with you?" he asked.

Her eyes intensified, narrowed slightly, trying to take in more of him than was possible. She said nothing during the long moment she needed to decide. She stopped pretending with the phone, placed the receiver on its hook. She extended her hand.

Just for a touch, a brief holding, Springer believed, but the next thing he knew, her hand had his grasped firmly and he was on his way, being led past occupied tables and waiters and out onto 70th Street.

It was extremely cold. Some snow had fallen, just enough to coat everything, including the Rolls-Royce Camargue waiting at the curb with a chauffeur in it.

She hesitated.

Springer sensed from that she was somehow related to the car. She hooked her arm in his and tugged and they hurried, coatless conspirators, to the corner of Madison. She was tall, Springer now realized; her head was almost level with his. He glanced back in the direction of the restaurant, saw only their footprints in the new snow; it occurred to him how easily they might be tracked.

He waved at a fleet cab that appeared available but there was a passenger in it, the driver high-sticking, not turning on the meter, so he could pocket the entire fare. Other cabs with their off-duty lights on ignored Springer. She clutched against him. He felt her shivering. She had on only a white, amply cut long-sleeved silk blouse, a full skirt of gray Ultrasuede, and the merest black evening pumps.

Springer's place was the old family apartment on 72nd, just two blocks away. He chose not to suggest it.

They went down Madison in a hug against the cold that made their walking awkward and caused them to slip more. Her teeth chattered and she tried to laugh. Their breaths combined in the air. They were rescued by a Greek coffee shop, a long narrow place with twenty red plastic-covered rotating stools at a Formica counter. Only two other customers. A counterman immediately placed two heavy mugs of coffee before them as though he'd read their minds.

After they'd taken some of the scalding stuff, Springer told her his name, and, when she didn't respond with hers, he asked, "Who are you?"

She smiled soft commas into her cheeks and said, "Maybe I'm a thousand-dollar hooker."

"If so, you're undercharging," he said, and that got to her. He wanted to say all the right things. It was crucial. Clever was okay but take care not to come off smart-ass, he told himself.

She blew at her coffee. "That was rude of us, wasn't it." Referring to the companions they'd deserted at La Goulue.

"But unavoidable," Springer assured.

"They'll get together."

"Probably."

"Might be the match of the century."

"I only hope he pays her check."

She got off that topic by telling her name. Audrey Hull.

It suited her, Springer thought. Audrey. He'd never personally known an Audrey, never realized how well those two syllables went together.

Close by on the counter, displayed on a stainless steel pedestal, was an enormous cake: frosted white and textured with abundant coconut.

"I want a piece of that," Audrey said.

Springer ordered it.

Audrey watched closely as the counterman measured a slice. Before he could cut it, Audrey told him, "Larger." The counterman obliged.

Springer didn't believe she could possibly eat that much cake. A five-inch slice, no less. Between bites she put the first vital question to him.

"Divorced," he replied.

"When?"

"This afternoon."

She wasn't surprised, just momentarily thoughtful. "Mine was final the day before yesterday," she said matter-of-factly.

With modest bites that determined the tempo of the conversation, Audrey ate every morsel of the cake and then used the side of her fork to scrape up all the frosting from the plate. Springer considered it an achievement. He informed her that she had a crumb clinging near the corner of her mouth. Her tongue tried for it, didn't get it. He stopped her hand as it went for her napkin. She remained permissively still, not even a blink when he closed in on her and tenderly kissed away the tiny golden morsel.

That was the start of them.

Love at first sight, or more aptly, as the French express it, *des coups de foudre*. Thunderbolts.

Springer and Audrey.

For them there was none of the usual lie-for-a-lie. No doubt-sowing insinuations or intentional punishments or deliberate with-holdings. They made a pact early on to not waste time on all that tricky stuff. Others might need it to maintain the high temperatures of their relationships but not they. They would help each to be sure of the other, allow their love and all its consequences to happen honestly.

Springer wanted Audrey to understand how his marriage had been, hoped to get it out of the way once and for all. He spared her the sordid details and managed to conceal whatever permanent bit-terness it had caused. As for his disillusionment, that, with the entrance of Audrey, felt gone for good.

"Tell me just one thing she did that was particularly disgusting," Audrey said, wanting it to put Gayle into that kind of mental niche.

There were so many bad things that Springer had trouble deciding on which he should divulge.

"Can't come up with even one?" Audrey pressed.

Springer considered telling her of the psychological tug-of-war games she'd played with their son, the shabby use she made of the child to get her own way. Instead, he told Audrey, "She'd ball up her used sweat socks and jam them into the toes of her sneakers, then chuck the sneakers into the back of my closet. Stunk up all my suits."

"Is that the worst thing she ever did?"

"No."

"That's good." Audrey claimed she wasn't jealous of Gayle, but she made Springer promise he'd never speak the name in her pres-ence. When mentioning Gayle was absolutely unavoidable he would use *she* or *her*. Audrey would know to whom he was referring.

Springer believed that fair enough.

It was especially important to Audrey that Springer see her marriage in its true light. The person she'd been married to (she didn't say *man*) was Tyler Briggs. She'd known him most of her life. They had, as they say, gone to different schools together. Tyler was her age, twenty-eight, born the same month, in fact. She'd felt all along that a marriage to him wouldn't work, but it had always been not a matter of Are you going to marry Tyler Briggs? but When? Her Aunt Libby had been the most insistent promoter. Aunt Libby was always quick to point out anything Tyler did that might be entered on the positive side of his ledger, and for him, going to his tailor was an accomplishment. On the good side, Tyler had a quick mind, an attractively cynical sense of humor, and was capable of sorties of thoughtfulness if they weren't expected of him. He was a victim rather than a survivor of extremely wealthy parents. An only child because his mother was dead set on never having to go through *that* again. It was impossible for Tyler to commit to anything that asked for effort, be it a career or a dutiful sit-down dinner, Audrey said. She hadn't, of course, realized how terribly hopelessly lopsided he was until after they were married. Not to bitch, just to relate, Tyler was the world's worst loser *and* winner. Whenever he lost, at backgammon or tennis, for example, he would brood and snap and go into a pout. Whenever he won he rubbed it in and gloated as though that was his real reward. Honestly, Audrey told Springer, as rationalizing as it might sound, the main reason she married Tyler was to get it over with. Was that weak of her?

"No," Springer assured her too quickly.

"Besides," she added, "at the time there were just too many damn Tylers around by one name or another."

(One afternoon the next September, Springer and Audrey were bound for a couple of hours with Monet and his friends at the Met. They happened onto Tyler. He was standing there on the sidewalk in front of the museum looking at girls in skirts, who, by being seated on the steps above, were unknowingly exposing their panty-covered crotches. Tyler made no pretensions about what he was doing. He resented being interrupted. Audrey introduced Springer and there was some neutral small talk. Tyler, as visualized by Springer, was a slim-to-bony, under-height, vainly dressed, superior-nosed, privileged-looking sort. The real Tyler was six-foot-five and two hundred forty. A lot of pudge in a dark-blue hard-finished business suit and a plain dark tie, knotted too tight up into the straining top button of his white shirt collar. His prematurely receding hairline provided more forehead to perspire. He appeared closer to forty-eight than twenty-eight.

"See you," Tyler said dismissively and continued with his diversions.)

Springer was relieved to learn the extent of Audrey's marriage. He told her she could mention Tyler any time.

What did disturb Springer, however, was Aunt Libby. He knew her—at least knew of her: Elizabeth Hopkins-Hull. Those with her measure of social and financial power, no matter how they went on with their liberal rantings and posturings, did not want any middle-bracket diamond dealer seriously turning the head of one of their darlings. The prudent way to cope with Aunt Libby, Springer decided, was to keep away from her.

The Aunt Libby problem was not on Springer's mind now, as Audrey, at the wheel of the BMW, turned off at exit 3 of the Major Deegan to take the Cross County Parkway. Springer was lost in one of his favorite pastimes: stealing from Audrey. This day she was wearing the palest of blues. Her oversize linen blouse was deep at the neck and gave a side view of the beginning of a breast. Her wrap skirt parted high in front, offering the inside of a thigh.

Audrey glanced and caught him at it.

"You're spiffy." He smiled and concentrated some on her hair. There was a lot of red in her hair, especially in certain lights, as though she'd sprinkled shining cinnamon all through it. That went beautifully with her skin, creamy and fine-textured, which was advantageous for her eyes, their irises as green-bright as underwater moss contained within hoops of black. There was an elegant quality to her face. Her nose was so straight and nicely narrow it was suspect, her chin well-defined but not aggressive. Her upper lip was fuller, giving her mouth constant expression, innocence on the verge of seduction.

A painstaking woman, was the impression of her most frequently assumed. Especially by other women. Surely she was given to vanities, centered a major portion of each day on herself. How otherwise could the complexion of her neck and face be so flawless, she remain so slender, appear so well-dressed?

Actually, Audrey was one of those rare fortunates who could look superb without much effort. A beauty ritual such as a facial masque was for female play, not something to be taken seriously. Usually she wore only minimal makeup, an outline here, an exact smudge of shading there, a few strategic powdery fluffs with a fat brush. Her slenderness was natural and, at least for the time being, perpetual. If she gained a little it didn't show. She never bothered to get on a scale. Because she was slim and tall, clothes looked well on her, and, although she kept one eye on the latest fashions, she didn't kowtow to their extremes. She took hints but there was no need to tell her what to wear, not when she could throw on almost any old thing and be smashing to some degree. Her sense of style seldom failed her. It amazed Springer, whenever on the spur of the moment he suggested going out, how quickly she got ready. Often she had to wait for him.

Her hand moved with the steering wheel. The ring on her second finger caught sun. It was a cabochon sapphire of ten carats set in plain yellow gold. Not the finest quality sapphire, but a Ceylon chosen by her for the very reason that it was worth less: its washy blue color. The flare it threw diverted Springer from the knob of her ankle. He looked out and realized they were now on the Hutchinson River Parkway with all its swoops and swerves. He leaned across and kissed Audrey on the neck and simultaneously got a look at the speedometer. It indicated twenty over the posted limit. Not to worry, he told himself, Audrey was intuitive when it came to lurking police cars. She also had Aunt Libby for a fix.

Audrey turned down the volume on a Bruce Springsteen and asked, "Do you ever get existential anxiety?"

"Such as?" he stalled, trying to decipher it.

"When you're bored."

"I don't get bored."

"Never?"

"Not any more."

She didn't accept that. "Practically everyone at one time or another feels he's not enjoying life and it's not life's fault."

She could be testing, he thought. He'd be vague. "I suppose."

"Then you've had the feeling?"

"Have you?"

"No fair answering a question with a question. Know what Nietzsche said?"

"Which Nietzsche?"

"He said, Even the gods get bored and can't do anything about it."

"Nietzsche and God were talking over a couple of beers and God complained that he didn't know what to do with himself."

"I'm serious and you're being a smart-ass."

Springer looked out and saw they were passing by the Maple Moor Country Club, a section of it that was occupied annually by a large flock of wild geese. Four stylish golfers were pulling their bag carts along the fairway, stepping with care among the goose droppings.

"Well?" Audrey prompted.

What was she getting at? Why was boredom on her mind? Maybe she was coming in obliquely. "Are you trying to say we're getting predictable?" For his comfort she took too long to reply.

"I think I've enough curiosity about you to last a lifetime."

That was how he liked to hear her talk.

"Besides," she went on, "you've got boredom all wrong. Boredom's not bad. It's a healthy nudge in the direction of a move . . . a more highly charged life."

"So let's have a little boredom, is that it?"

"I think maybe the only thing we lack is some danger."

"Living is dangerous."

"I mean danger in the ordinary sense."

"Give me a for-instance."

She considered a few things such as sky diving and cliff climbing but they were too commonplace. "It just seems living would be appreciated more if some risk of survival were *de rigueur.*"

Springer decided it was only driving talk. Going along with it, he went tough. "Have you ever put it all on the line?"

"No," she was sorry to admit.

"Want to?"

"Yeah."

"Okay. How about botulism? This weekend we'll have some peaches my mother canned three years ago."

Up went Audrey's chin. Her lips tightened. "I just stopped loving you," she announced.

Springer didn't react.

After a few miles she turned to him with a smile and told him, "I'm loving you again." It was her contention that love was full of such stops and starts, might as well admit it.

"I'm hungry," Springer said.

"Eats are in the back."

"All I had for breakfast was a bagel." Springer reached to the rear seat for a brown-paper shopping bag. He placed the bag on his lap and from it brought out a couple of devil's-food Twinkies. He tossed those back in and rummaged around in the bag among some Goldenberg Peanut Chews, a cylinder of Pringle's potato chips, Goobers, Good & Plentys, a box of Sweet 'n Swinging donuts, a tangle of strawberry red laces, a Bloomingdale's bag containing a dozen Mrs. Fields macadamia and butter-sweet chocolate chip cookies, and so on. He should have known. For her a feast of quick food was no less enjoyable than eight courses at Lutece. After a junk-food binge she would sometimes expiate by putting herself through what she called a cleanse, which meant eating nothing but watermelon, for example, for two or three days.

"Christ, Audrey, I need something solid . . ."

"Give me a Devil Dog, will you?"

"There aren't any Devil Dogs." Springer was rankled. His blood sugar was low and his stomach was crabbing.

"I know for certain I bought some Devil Dogs."

Springer dug roughly in the bag and found what she wanted. He used his teeth to tear the corner of its cellophane wrapper, peeled the wrapper away, and handed to her the piece of chemically loaded devil's-food-like cake. She went right at it.

"*I* need something I can get my teeth into," he grumbled.

"Have a Big Jerk," she suggested.

He refused silently. Tossed the shopping bag of stuff into the back. However, five miles later he was tugging with his teeth at a tough pepperoni stick and wishing he could assuage himself with the promise of a marvelous home-cooked meal at their destination. His mother, however, was a dreadful and unimaginative cook. About her best effort was instant cocoa.

The BMW went ten miles farther up major highway 684. There it turned off at exit 6 and got onto lesser Route 35 for a little more of New York before it crossed over into Connecticut and the town of Ridgefield. In a hilly estate area, set back on a winding road between Ridgefield and Wilton, was High Meadow Clinic. Audrey got a small squeal from the tires as she turned in at the entranceway and proceeded up the crunching drive.

Janet Springer was seated on the front steps of the once-private mansion. She'd been waiting, watching for the car, and she stood quickly when it came into view. She'd taken care with her appearance for the occasion, had on a neat tailored suit of beige wool and appropriate high-heeled pumps. Gathers of a small French-blue silk square peeked from the breast pocket. Her hair was clean and held back from her face by a perfectly placed barrette. She was also wearing an excited smile.

She kissed and held first Springer, then Audrey. Springer went into the clinic and signed her out. He loaded her three pieces of luggage into the trunk of the car. "Are these all?" he asked.

"For now," Janet said. "We'll be sending for the rest."

She sounded so positive about that, Springer thought. She'd said in her letters and telephone calls to him that she'd undergone a change for the better but she hadn't elaborated, and he took that to mean she herself didn't altogether trust it. Apparently she was more sanguine about it now. As the car went down the drive she didn't even look back at High Meadow, and during the forty-five-minute trip to Sherman she was excited only to a normal extent over the prospect of going home. She gazed out appreciatively at the passing countryside and made easy contributions to the conversation. She wasn't asked and she didn't volunteer what had brought about her transformation.

Springer could not recall ever having seen his sister when she wasn't either too far up or down or in the erratic shift between. It was one of his old hopes that she would somehow come out of it, and, of course, he loved seeing her this way. But he wasn't convinced. During the ride home he put his arm over the back of the seat and she put her hand in his hand, clasped it instead of squeezing it desperately.

Home was on a bend of Connecticut's Route 37 where the countryside opened above the Housatonic Valley. The dirt drive from the road to the house was potholed from the winter and spring storms. Maples mingled their branches to form arbors over it. The place had been a working farm before Willard Springer had bought it in 1930. There were still remnants of those farming days around, but now all that was grown was in a twenty-row vegetable garden out near the principal barn.

The heart of the house was two hundred and fifty years old. It was originally a modest saltbox with small low-ceilinged rooms arranged around a center chimney. Over the generations and various owners, it had been added on to in almost every direction so it was now large and somewhat of a hodgepodge. The land of the place was fifty acres, some of it woods but most of it inclined fields and meadows that a dairy farmer neighbor mowed twice a year for hay so they always looked either lush or tended.

Matilda Springer came around from the side of the house to greet them. Janet stood beside the car and presented herself to her mother. Mattie, which was what she preferred being called, gave Janet a welcoming hug, then held her at arm's length. She looked steadily into Janet's eyes for a long moment, one eye at a time, apparently examining them. She seemed relieved by what she saw. She hugged Janet again, acceptingly this time, and told her, "So many people have been sending you their healing light."

Janet nodded compliantly.

Mattie welcomed Springer and Audrey with an exchange of kisses and led the way into the house. "You'll have to overlook the mess," she said, offering no excuse for it. That was something Mattie always said, although the house was always clean, just somewhat scattered and patined from being thoroughly lived in. Mattie had the taste but not the time or inclination for any homes-and-gardens projects. Abandoned bird's nests that she'd found blown from trees were placed inside on many of the windowsills. Some contained stream pebbles smooth as eggs. A huge carved and gilded Buddha sat presidingly on the piano.

Springer carried Janet's luggage upstairs to her room. Then he and Audrey got settled in. Their space was as remote as possible from the house proper, a rectangular-shaped shed with a cement floor that had a shallow gutter along one side of its length. Except for the gutter and a couple of galvanized steel pipes that extended just above head height from beam to beam, there was no evidence that it had at one time been a slaughtering shed. A full bath had been built on. There were stretched and gathered curtains on the windows, a woven grass rug on the floor, and a white matelasse spread on the bed. The walls wore watercolors and racks and shelves for fishing rods and tackle. A pair of French doors opened to the shoulder of a wide sloping field.

After changing into jeans and a shirt, Audrey went to be with Mattie. It always seemed to Springer that Audrey wasn't quite his Audrey when she and Mattie got together. He sensed a league of sorts between them that he would never be asked to join. No doubt gender had something to do with it, but also there was the tie of the way they regarded the meanings of life and the impermanence of death. To their way of thinking nothing was impossible, the laws of physics were often easily mutable, preexistence and reincarnation were fundamental, and anything could be unequivocally decided with the use of a pendulum. Numerous times Springer had sat and withheld comment while in complete accord they discussed something such as bilocation, the appearance of a person in more than one place at the same time. Springer reasoned that if he tried to make one logical point he would be held in at least temporary contempt. So he just left them at it. No harm to him. Besides, when it came to spiritual concepts he had no strong personal beliefs. Who knew what the hell was really what?

For a couple of hours he wandered around the farm, finding memories. Then he drove the five miles down to New Milford and had a steak and fries at a cafe on Bank Street. It was dark when he returned home. He expected Audrey and Mattie would be well into a metaphysical tête-à-tête, but he found Audrey in the *boucherie,* as they called it. She was fresh out of a bath and had on a silk-charmeuse floor-length kimona. She gave him a brief but communicating kiss. He headed for the shower.

She leaned against the bathroom doorway and said, "At the clinic they gave Janet every kind of test."

"How do you know?"

"Janet told us. She had Minnesota Multiphasic Personality Inventories, thematic apperceptions, Szondies, Rorschachs, EEGs by the dozens. The works."

"And?"

"She came out well within normal."

"Doesn't seem possible, getting better all at once like that."

"Mattie thinks she's probably a walk-in."

"A what?"

"Janet wanted to give up on life, so some spirit on the other side agreed to take over her body and everything."

"Like assuming a lease," Springer quipped.

"You might say. Did you know some guy in Sweden is Einstein's walk-in?"

"What about you?"

"Huh?"

"You're just the original you, aren't you?"

"Must be. I've never given up. Where did you go tonight?"

He told her.

"Thought you might be having a go with some local piece."

He got out of the shower. She tossed him a towel and used another to dry his back. She ran her lips over the knob at the base of his neck. When he was entirely dried off he yanked on the tie of the sash of her kimona. Slickly, willingly, it came undone, fell, and allowed the kimona to hang open in front. She merely relaxed her shoulders, and with a single shrug it dropped from her.

She had on pale peach tap panties of lightweight silk. A lingerie seamstress in Paris made them especially for her by the dozens. They were bias-cut, purposely full in the leg and crotch, and instead of elastic at the waist they were held up by a mere loop around one tiny pearly button. Her matching mules had narrow four-inch heels.

Springer rarely misread her at such times, her preference. He believed he recognized this one. He didn't touch her.

She turned, left the bathroom. Her walk was for him to steal from the trimness of her legs, the natural tightening motions of her buttocks. She opened the French doors, slipped off her mules, and stepped out into the night.

Springer clicked off the light and waited the required short while before going outside. It was a pure country night, the air a consistency that made it consciously a substance. The sky seemed not so high with more of it visible, cloudless except for a few wisps. The moon was only slightly elliptic. Audrey would be cold, Springer thought. It was something they had done twice before during the previous summer but it had been warmer then.

He looked to the field. The grass was nearly three feet tall, thick with the fuzzy heads of rye. The disturbance Audrey had caused was a line that could be easily traced. He waded it at a deliberate and quiet stalk.

Came upon her, captured her with his presence. Her bareness seemed luminous. She was lying on her side, arms wrapped, legs doubled up, possibly cowering. Springer loomed above her for a long moment. He reached down and found the waistband of her panties, yanked at it.

The button flew.

The silk tore down the side. The sound of tearing was a hiss. He tore the panties elsewhere and they were off.

He lay down beside her. She unwound her arms and straightened her legs, allowing him to be full-length close. His mouth, as though drawn by some invisible attachment, went directly to her mouth, a light, brief placement. His hand flat on the small of her back pressed her to him. They held like that for a while before his hand began traveling.

Her skin he found was wet, especially her lower legs and thighs, from having waded the dewy grass. His hand accumulated water as it skimmed her, and he felt the texture caused by the night's coolness that his touch could smooth away. His hand was both trespasser and owner as it circumspectly and yet surely moved over her surfaces, her rises and dips, slopes and turns.

Without interrupting she rolled to be front up.

He fingertipped across her abdomen and down along the fringes of her pubic hair. He burrowed a finger into the left and right creases created by the tangency of her mound and thighs, creases that disappeared, became sinewy sockets when she spread her legs and arched them up.

It was ritual, not tease.

He knelt up between her. He listened for her breath. She was holding her breath. She was already swollen and unfolded when he parted her more with his tongue. She was the fragrance of daffodils. Her hands held the back of his head as though it were a bowl feeding her.

She came twice that way.

Then, with her avidity primed, she wanted him in her.

There was no need to guide him. However, she wanted to take hold of his hardness. She appropriated it, stroked herself with it, ran its head up and down in her wetness, and he withheld entering her. When she could no longer bear having him out she heaved up suddenly and slipped herself around him. She wanted him all in, all at once. He pushed his pelvis hard against her, grasped her by her hipbones to prevent her from moving. She understood and remained still. A mere clench might spoil it.

Soon he stirred in her and his initial short thrusts became full length, which told her she could rely upon his control and it was liberating for her to be able to make contributions.

"I love you," he said into her.

She felt the breath of his words on the back of her throat.

"I love you," she said into him.

She had never been brought to feel what he made her feel. She shuddered whenever she thought how far short of her potential passion she would have spent her life without him. What tissue of inhibition there had been, he and his love and her loving response had easily broken through. They were, together, not subject to shame and therefore infinite.

That night in their nest in the high grass, down among all the tinier creatures who run brave and wild after dark, they loved one way or another and another for as long as it took the moon to move halfway across the sky.

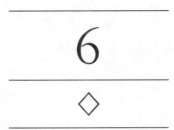

6

◇

The following morning Springer came up out of the kind of dream that needed the verification of touch. He reached with his legs for Audrey. She wasn't there. He opened his eyes, called out to her, and got no reply.

Her Cartier travel clock on the nightstand told him ten thirty. He noticed his knees were extremely grass-stained. Some of the stains had rubbed off on to the sheet. There were fragments of straw and dry grass on her pillow. He got up for the bathroom, decided he wouldn't shave. He had to scrub vigorously with a washcloth to remove the green from his knees and, as well, from his chin.

He went into the main area of the house, through to the kitchen, where he poured merely warm water into a mug and spooned in a couple of heaps of Folger's Instant. He heard voices from the side porch and decided he would go out to them.

Mattie, Audrey, and Janet were seated on faded yellow canvas chairs around a glass-topped table. Springer lifted the back of Audrey's hair and delivered a good-morning kiss to the nape of her neck.

"Tell your brother," Mattie said to Janet.

Janet looked Springer's way, smiled, and said, "Good morning."

"Something wrong?" Springer asked.

"No," Audrey said.

"Tell him," Mattie urged.

"He'll think I belong back in the nut bin," Janet said.

Audrey's Sweet'n Swinging donuts were on a plate on the table. Springer helped himself to a couple. No matter how much he stirred his coffee the crystals wouldn't completely dissolve. He noticed a bordering bed of fatheaded zinnias enjoying the sun. He could have brought Jake along, he thought. He observed Janet. She was the same as she'd been yesterday, bright, relaxed, well in touch with herself. He recalled what Audrey had said about how thoroughly she'd been tested. Time would tell, Springer believed.

Janet met his gaze. She smiled, aware that she was being evaluated.

"What is it you're reluctant to tell me?" Springer asked her.

"No comment until I'm done?"

"Deal."

She related the circumstances and what had occurred during that afternoon and evening a month ago at High Meadow when she had gone off the manic end. She'd been over it time after time in her mind, hadn't verbalized it until that morning. Now, in telling it again to Springer, she was able to remember more details. She did not spare herself, was graphic in her description of her provokings and violence and how she had to be placed in restraints. She had almost total recall of the sensations that had passed through her as she lay bound and alone, her inability to resist during the process her body underwent, the degree-by-degree repair that resulted in blessed mental clarity. She told how she'd discovered the stone was in her hand and her impression that it was instrumental in her recovery.

Springer saw it now, resting on a paper napkin on the table. His father's reminder stone. He didn't quite know what to say. Perhaps he had misinterpreted Janet's words. Neutrally, he asked her, "Are you implying that you believe that diamond helped you in some way?"

"She's not implying, she's saying," Mattie said.

"It didn't help, it healed," Audrey put in.

Janet nodded.

Before joining them on the porch, Springer had thought perhaps their topic of conversation would be something only as incredible as, say, levitation. He asked Janet, "Have you spoken about this to Norman?"

"Not yet."

Springer picked up the diamond, held it up to the daylight as though seriously contemplating it. Actually he was using the time to decide how best to handle the situation. He knew the stone well, probably better than anyone. He knew it outside and in, because as a boy for practice he had examined it with a loupe countless times, gone over its surface and looked into it through its natural window, where one tip of its octahedral formation was chipped away. He had also used it to practice weighing, so, although over the years thousands of diamonds had passed through his mind and hands, it was still easy for him to remember this one weighed 56.41 carats. He put the stone down on the napkin and asked Audrey, "Have you tried your pendulum on it?"

That surprised her. Perhaps, finally, Springer was admitting that her use of a pendulum had merit. She pulled her chair close to the table. From her shirt pocket she brought out a drawstring pouch of chamois which contained her pendulum: a ten-inch length of linen string with a small rectangular piece of polished ivory attached to one end and an emerald bead that resembled a child's marble held by a knot on the other end. The emerald was hazed with numerous internal fractures. Audrey had made the pendulum from scratch. The piece of ivory had been pried from the inlays of an Asprey letter opener left behind by Tyler. The emerald had been found in one of Aunt Libby's boxes of bits and pieces. Audrey was not aware, nor did Libby remember, that the emerald had once come loose from a third-century Hindu dancing girl's ankle bracelet, a tangling arrangement of rounded emeralds and rubies that Libby had donated years ago to the Smithsonian through her personal foundation.

Audrey propped her elbow on the table and, holding the pendulum by its ivory end, suspended the emerald directly above the stone. She concentrated, seemed suddenly removed from her surroundings, as though she and the pendulum had become locked on some mutual frequency.

Springer, as usual, had mixed feelings about the woman he loved doing such a ridiculous thing. Not because she was doing it but because she took it so seriously. Audrey believed the pendulum could determine just about anything. It worked like an all-knowing divining device, a bob of sorts that she could rely upon for guidance whenever she came up against indecision. She claimed that the Egyptians had used pendulums to find out whether or not their wine was spoiled or their food fit to eat. Hundreds of years ago in England children had more easily found pennies and other valuables in the gutters using pendulums made of a thread spool, common string, and any small weighted object. During the First World War a French brigadier used a pendulum to locate German sea mines. There were countless substantiated instances, Audrey claimed. She had read and reread her copy of T. C. Lethbridge's *The Power of the Pendulum,* annotated and underlined it so much it looked like a scribbled coloring book. She insisted that Springer read it. Inasmuch as it was only 138 pages he obliged, skimmed through it.

From what he gathered, an ultimate pendulum was precisely 40 inches long and worked on the principle of cardinal points and coordinates, like a compass. Every thought and substance had its particular coordinate, and, by playing out or winding up the length of string a fraction, the possibilities of determining things were endless. For example: The idea of love, according to Lethbridge, had the coordinates 20/20, which meant with love in mind and the string 20 inches long the pendulum always swung in the direction of 20 degrees. (That 20/20 also signified perfect vision occurred to Springer.) Sex was a 16/19 combination. The coordinates 29/29 were shared by femininity and danger, for some reason. Lethbridge contended that it all had to do with allowing a certain higher energy to flow and communicate through the superconscious. So-called sensitives were supposed to be best at it. Springer knew for sure that Audrey was a sensitive, though perhaps not the sort Mr. Lethbridge had in mind. According to the book's jacket, the man had been Keeper of Anglo-Saxon Antiquities at the Museum of Archaeology and Ethnology at Cambridge University.

Audrey's use of the pendulum was not nearly so complicated. She asked only a yes or no from it. (Should they go to see *that* play? Had the housekeeper nipped and then diluted the cognac? Was the crab-meat salad fresh?) Audrey was by no means too dependent on the pendulum but she always kept it handy, a backup.

Springer put no stock in any of it. Nevertheless he had to consider her pendulum his ally. No doubt Audrey had at various times asked it questions regarding him, and apparently so far it had responded in his favor. He hoped it never turned on him.

Now, holding the pendulum above the diamond, she swung it a bit to get it started. The emerald bead rotated slowly. It seemed to be indicating a *no*. But then its motion gradually became elliptical and even more so until it was swinging straight back and forth. A definite yes.

Audrey, satisfied, put the pendulum back into its pouch.

Springer wanted to know what she'd asked.

"I asked, Does this stone have the power to heal?"

"The power to make right would have been more precise," Mattie said. "To the old mystics a healing was a righting, a correcting of physical faults."

"Anyway," Audrey said, "you saw the answer."

"It's by no means new that a stone should have such influence. The Incas strapped chunks of jade to their backs to dissolve kidney stones."

"Topaz prevents epilepsy."

Springer watched a pair of barn swallows playing jet fighter around the barn.

"Some garnets can stop hemorrhaging. During the Crusades the Saracens rubbed them on their wounds."

"Rubies are also good for that."

"And spinels."

Springer watched a dragonfly come in for a landing on the porch railing. Along the flagstone bordering the steps, a single file of ants was bound for some task or treat.

"They say a sapphire held under the tongue will act like a tonic when someone's run down."

"In India the Ayurvedic doctors use gems to cure everything from hiccups to leprosy. They burn the stones and mix the ashes into ointments and powders."

"This very moment in India one could walk into any Ayurvedic pharmacy and buy ashes of pearls or rubies or whatever."

"They call the ashes *bhasmas*. I remember because when Edwin and I were in New Delhi, he came down with terrible runs. An Ayurvedic doctor prescribed a tincture made from the *bhasma* of a five-caret emerald, and a pretty stone it was, I must add. After just two doses Edwin felt fit enough to go out for a huge curry dinner. From then on he swore by it. Never traveled anywhere without it. We used to send to New Delhi for it."

Springer headed for the barn, a familiar red-peeling sanctuary. He thought he'd give the old tractor a try, not do any work with it, just take a ride on it to the lower meadow, see if the stream that ran through the property was right for fishing. He couldn't imagine his father gulping down a five-carat emerald no matter how bad he had the shits. Springer inserted a stick into the gas tank of the tractor. It came out dry. He wasn't about to go back to the porch for more of Mattie and Audrey's ridiculous volleying.

Those swallows came swooping through the barn.

Springer was hugged from behind. A long tight hug.

It was Janet. She pressed her cheek against his back. Finally she loosened the hug and he turned to her. Her eyes asked to be looked into, wanting him to realize her equilibrium. She smiled to lighten the moment.

"I know it must have sounded crazy to you, what I said about the stone."

"Sometimes just believing enough in something can work wonders."

"I was going to keep it to myself."

"Why didn't you?"

"It kept pushing at me to be told."

"Well, whatever happened, Jan, I'm grateful to it and happy for you."

"So am I," she said cheerfully, emphatically. "But I don't think it was merely a matter of believing. Maybe it was and I don't want to accept that because it's too tenuous. Anyway, do something for me?"

"Sure. Anything."

"Take a closer look?"

She tucked their father's reminder stone into the pocket of Springer's jeans.

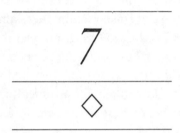

7

◇

A diamond can have a pedigree.

Like some horses and dogs.

In fact, getting a pedigree is much easier for a diamond. No concern, of course, with lineage and breeding. The only requirements are that the diamond be cut and polished, unmounted, and weigh at least one carat.

Since 1952 the Gemological Institute of America has done a tidy business testing and grading diamonds for the trade and issuing pedigrees in the form of its own official-like certificates. Each certificate states what the GIA found—bad, good, or better—about a particular stone. Any diamond, especially one of importance, unaccompanied by such a GIA certificate is viewed with qualms. "Where are its papers?" a cautious buyer wants to know, suspicious that the stone may not be as fine as his personal appreciation says it is—or that the certificate is being held back because the rating the GIA put on the stone does not justify the price being asked for it. The GIA didn't invent the standards, but it defined them and took over as *the* authority. Its gemologists have more than good eyes and opinions. The most advanced testing and evaluating devices are used to put a diamond through its paces.

At nine-thirty Monday morning it was only an elevator stop out of the way for Springer to go to the GIA. Its gem-testing laboratory was located on the second floor at 580 Fifth Avenue, in the same building where Springer & Springer had its offices. Springer was a longtime regular customer and therefore known by the receptionist on the other side of the eleven-sixteenths-inch laminated polycarbon-glass bulletproof window. A .357 magnum pistol fired point-blank at her might make her flinch but not bleed. As a concession to Springer, the receptionist relaxed her eyebrows. He asked to see Joel Zimmer.

Zimmer came out. He had small, chronically strained eyes, large ears, and the sort of beard that made him look in need of a shave an hour after he'd shaved.

Springer told him, "I need a favor."

"You're already two behind."

"Payday's coming."

"My wife needs studs."

"Most guys wouldn't admit it. Anyway, studs are five favors."

"So now I'll be on the second ear. What is it you want?"

"A rundown on this." Springer handed his father's reminder stone to Zimmer, who hardly gave it a glance.

"We don't do rough," Zimmer said.

"You can do anything." It wasn't flattery. Zimmer was the GIA's best. Not only a thoroughly experienced gemologist but a serious crystallographer as well. Springer thought of him as his resident expert. Whenever Springer wasn't sure about a diamond he relied on Zimmer's judgment. Zimmer could bare-eye a stone and be more right about it than most guys could with a loupe.

"Want to wait?" Zimmer asked.

"No hurry. Give me a call."

Springer went up to his office on 24. Linda got him some coffee, made in a pour-through filter beaker no more than ten minutes ago.

And a fresh prune Danish. Springer opened the safe. Linda brought the memorandum ledger and the stones Schiff had returned Friday afternoon. For her own ease she showed those stones to Springer before canceling the memo that pertained to them and putting them back into inventory. Linda dressed drably and wasn't talkative on Mondays.

"Seggerman at the Parker Meridien at eleven," she said.

"I know."

"Want me to select for it?"

"I'll do it."

Linda took her sorting tray and work in progress from the safe and went into her own office.

Springer sat at his desk, feeling that he could have used another hour or two of sleep. After driving back from Connecticut to her place, he and Audrey had watched a cassette of *The Sailor Who Fell from Grace with the Sea* for the sixth or seventh time, and it was close to two when they'd turned off the lights and she'd snuggled into the cave of his shoulder and it seemed they would fall to sleep like that. However, again their hands were like independent roaming animals.

The strong coffee was helping. Springer tore the Danish apart and dunked it. A hunk of it fell off into the coffee, and he burned his mouth gulping to get it. He picked up the phone and dialed Jake. Gayle answered. He hung up without saying anything.

Mal came in.

It was early for Mal, way early for him on a Monday. Springer checked the impulse to offer a congratulatory handshake. Mal had on a fresh white shirt and a new Sulka tie. He looked relaxed, well-rested. Better than I feel, Springer thought. He told Mal that.

"Got up this morning at six. Went for some steam, a rub, and a half hour under the lamp," Mal said.

"Big weekend?"

"Spent some of Saturday and all of Sunday alone. Pulled the phones out and didn't answer my buzzer." An achievement for Mal. "How are things going?" he asked.

"You mean with the business?"

"The business, you, whatever."

"No problems." Springer thought perhaps Mal wanted an increase in his draw.

"Would I be missed for a couple of weeks?" Mal asked.

"Hell, yes." Rather than an unkind *no.*

"I was told about a place down in Pennsylvania. Once you're in you can't get out, and while you're there nobody talks or anything."

"A retreat."

"I don't want to call it that."

"When do you want to go?"

"I made arrangements for being there starting Wednesday." Springer purposely clouded.

"Does that conflict with something?"

"No, that's all right."

"Tell me."

"Well, I was counting on you going over for the next sight."

"When is it?"

"We got notice from The System." Springer consulted his appointment calendar. "It's next Thursday. We're scheduled for three in the afternoon. I know it's my turn but—"

"I'll handle it, forget it."

"Are you sure?"

Mal held his palm up to put an end to it.

Springer had never seen his sixty-one-year-old uncle so relieved. No retreat.

For the next half hour Springer centered his attention on choosing and organizing the various diamonds he would show to Seggerman. He inserted the coded briefkes that contained them into a leather zip-around case, made sure the briefkes were in a certain order. He put the smaller case into his attaché case.

From his bottom desk drawer he selected the less conservative of two ties, a small figured blue on brown. He was wearing a pale blue shirt, gold collar clip, and a double-breasted English wool worsted brown suit. Seggerman, he knew, was definitely a brown suit.

Springer removed his suit jacket. From the same bottom desk drawer he brought out a Smith & Wesson 9mm automatic and a shoulder holster. He checked to see the gun was loaded and on safety.

The sure way he handled it said how familiar to him it was. He inserted the gun into the holster and secured the Velcro flap around the heel of its grip. He put it on, flexed his shoulders to get it situated right. The holster's elastic straps were snug across his back but wouldn't inhibit his movements. The gun was close against his left side nearly up in under his armpit. He had a license to carry it. He put his jacket back on, tugged his shirt cuffs down, stretched his neck because of the tie, and left the office.

Seggerman was in 3904A, a suite on the 39th floor. Springer used the house phone, and after a dozen rings Seggerman answered and told Springer to give him ten minutes.

Springer gave him fifteen, sat at a tiny table off the pleasant lobby, and had a tomato juice and lime. He was feeling better now that he was more into the day. By late afternoon he'd probably be ready for whatever.

Up at the suite Seggerman answered the door in yesterday's shirt and beltless suit trousers wrinkled across the crotch. The room smelled of Shalimar, cigar smoke, and spilled wine. Seggerman had cleared a low square table situated by the main window, which allowed north light. Springer wanted that northern exposure. With it Seggerman would be able to truly see what he was buying and have no excuses later. (A few years ago Springer had made a sale at the Sherry Netherland under inadequate light conditions. The customer had stopped payment and returned three fair-sized stones, claiming they were not as represented. Truth was the stones he returned were of inferior color, not the ones Springer had sold him.)

Seggerman offered to order up anything. Springer declined. They sat at the table to get to business. Springer noticed that Seggerman wasn't wearing socks. His black conservative shoes made his bare ankle skin appear sickly. Seggerman was tall, with a paunch and a tired, prosperous face. Had a lot of obvious dental work. He was one of the leading jewelry manufacturers in the Northwest, came to New York to buy three or four times a year.

Springer pretended not to hear the door to the adjoining bedroom being closed. He placed a tripod ten-power loupe on the table and unzipped the case that contained the briefkes that contained the stones. He started Seggerman off with some five-caraters of F/G color, VVS1's and 2's. With a couple of exceptions they were the largest and best goods Springer had brought. There was a slim possibility that Seggerman might buy one, but more likely he would merely look. It never hurt to inflate a buyer with such overshow, Springer believed. He knew his man, knew Seggerman was there to buy seventy-five-pointers and one-caraters for rings and single-stone pendants. If larger-sized stones had been Seggerman's interest, Springer's approach would have been just the opposite—from the bottom up.

To Springer's surprise Seggerman reacted strongly to several two-carat stones of very fine quality. He examined those for a long while with the loupe and when Springer asked should he put them away Seggerman told him no and set them off to one side, exposed in their unfolded briefkes. Implying that he would return to them later.

Springer was right about Seggerman. When they got to the smaller stones Seggerman started doing business. He had settled on twenty-some medium-quality one-carat stones and was getting into the seventy-five-pointers when the girl came from the bedroom.

Seggerman didn't get up for her. He introduced her as Darlene. She could have been any age from eighteen to thirty. She'd done the best she could with her hair, had it held back from her face with a rolled and tied scarf. But that emphasized her hairline and the fact that she was at least one blond coloring appointment behind. She was brittle, her eyes and brows overdone, her lips too slick. She had on last night's dress: black fitted crepe from the waist down, loose, plunging black lamé above. What also told Springer she was surely a working girl was her death grip on her little black evening purse.

Darlene stood behind Seggerman's chair. She kissed the top of his head while she surveyed the diamonds on the table. "Look at all the goodies," she said, mainly to herself.

She went around and leaned over the table. The lamé swagged. It was unbelievable the way her breasts were large enough to hang but didn't. She poked at the two-carat diamonds with the tip of an enameled fingernail. Without asking permission, she picked one up and placed it in the crease created by the junction of her second and third fingers. She held her hand out and cocked her head slightly as she considered the stone.

The diamond caught some sun and flared as though angry.

Darlene smiled at Springer. She had lipstick on her teeth. "You shouldn't have," Darlene affected broadly.

"I haven't," Springer said to nip it early.

"What do you think?" Darlene asked Seggerman.

Springer expected Seggerman to tell her to stop interfering with business, but Seggerman told her, "You deserve it, baby, you deserve it."

"You don't just taste sweet," Darlene said to him and went closer to the window with the diamond.

"She should have it, shouldn't she?" Seggerman put to Springer.

"You're the customer."

"You'll throw it in, huh?"

Springer didn't say anything.

"As goodwill."

Springer still didn't say anything.

"For me and Darlene."

"No."

"What do you mean no?"

"If you want to buy her the stone I'll do the best I can for you, but that's all."

"I'm the customer," Seggerman reminded coolly.

"And I'm not the Goodwill."

"Tell you what, Springer, take all your fucking goods and get out."

Darlene made an ugly mouth at Springer. She turned her hand over and the diamond fell to the glass surface of the table. It bounced off onto the carpet.

Springer gathered up the briefkes and put them into the leather case. He had trouble finding the diamond in the deep pile of the carpet, but finally it winked at him. He snapped his attaché case shut.

"There are thousands of diamond dealers in this town," Seggerman said. "You just lost me."

"Up your ass with your diamonds," Darlene threw at Springer as he went out the door.

Springer walked east on 57th Street. The office workers were out. He could smell the pot. The scene he'd just been through kept repeating in his mind. If he had donated the diamond to Seggerman's hooker it would have taken the top off the transaction, at least twenty thousand of it. But what bothered him more was the way Seggerman had him measured, thinking he'd go for it, be that much of a bend-over. Springer told himself he'd done right, put it out of his mind.

He went over to Madison and down to 50th Street to the Helmsley Palace. In the luxurious apricot and silver sanctuary of the Trianon dining room he was led to a table deep in a corner where Dante Sebastian Raggio was waiting.

Danny Rags.

Eighteen years had changed him, of course. Maturity, as it does with many men, had improved his looks. The little lines of years, especially those that webbed from the outer corners of his eyes, gave him the attractiveness of experience. He was undoubtedly a man who would be difficult, if not impossible, to fool. And from his apparent physical strength, one not to fool with.

Those impressions were required. Ten years ago he had been moved into Just John's spot, operating out of the concession in the rear of the Empire Diamond Arcade. He did what his uncle had done, only more. The shylocking part alone now amounted to fifty million, and as a clearing house for swag twice that much came through him. The entire 47th Street area was his territory, and the only answering he had to do went into the ear of the top.

Danny and Springer, despite their different circles, had kept in touch. They had preserved with care the comradery of their younger years. Not once had Danny, though often tempted, offered Springer the in on a really good thing. (Such as the breakdown of a stolen necklace of a hundred and twenty-five unidentifiable, absolutely D-flawless carats that he could let Springer have for half the going price.) Also, as mutually agreed, they never met on the street, always at places where anyone who might know them both was less likely to be. Such as there at the Helmsley Palace.

No sooner was Springer seated at the table than a waiter placed a Dewar's and water in front of him, according to Danny's instructions.

Springer inquired after Danny's wife and kids. "The kids are fine. Nothing new with Camilla," Danny told him. His kids were seven and eight, both boys. They were enrolled in a private school in Rhode Island. Camilla was a handsome and quiet Italian woman who had known beforehand what she was marrying into. She shopped a lot at the Westchester branches of the leading department stores, made her own tomato sauce, and refused to hire a housekeeper to help keep up their ten-room New Rochelle home.

"How's Jake?" Danny asked.

"He's fine."

"And Audrey?" Danny put the tips of his fingers to his lips and threw Audrey a kiss wherever she might be. He had told Springer lightly that she was the only thing that could ever come between them.

"Audrey's okay," Springer said, understating.

"Marry her," Danny advised for at least the twentieth time. He raised his glass to drink to that and Springer noticed his meticulously manicured fingernails.

Danny Rags was living up to his name. A far cry from the raw youngster trying to be well dressed, he was now tastefully attired by Paul Stuart and F. R. Tripler & Co. That wasn't what he wore when on the job at the concession. There he was always in inexpensive black gabardine slacks that were a bit shiny and a white shirt with rolled-up sleeves. After this lunch he would go to the apartment he had on East 50th Street and change.

They ordered.

Springer should have been hungrier than the seafood salad he decided on. He hadn't had a substantial meal since Friday, the steak in New Milford.

"How about starting with some pâté?"

"You go ahead."

"What's the matter?" Danny asked.

"Nothing." Springer didn't feel like recounting the Seggerman episode.

"Somebody giving you some shit?"

"No."

"Anybody gives you any shit let me know."

Springer nodded. For years he'd been hearing that from Danny.

Their table was isolated enough so they could talk easily without being overheard.

"What do you say we go down to AC," Danny said, "maybe some day next week. Play some dice. We'll take the chopper down. Bring Audrey."

"I'd like that."

Danny thought perhaps some inside street talk might bring Springer up out of it. He confided to Springer that the recent five million robbery of a dealer in colored stones had been a give-up: that is, the goods had been stolen with the dealer's knowledge and cooperation so he could collect insurance. The five million figure was inflated. What had been taken was closer to three. Some nice rubies, Danny said, evidently having seen.

He also told Springer in a conversational way that swifts—thieves —were now using the Social Register for their leads. It listed not only the names of the wealthy but their addresses and telephone numbers as well. A swift merely phoned in advance to determine if anyone was at home.

It seemed the time of random break-ins was over. Fences were now providing their teams of swifts with positive leads.

For instance, a doorman at a restaurant or hotel spots a woman loaded with "heavy flash." She's feeling secure, considering the circumstances, the public place, maybe her husband and others with her, a driver. The doorman, satisfied that the situation is right, jots down the license plate number of the car the woman departs in. He gives it to a fence. The fence gives it to a cop. The cop runs it through the Motor Vehicle Bureau and comes up with the name and address. For every such address the fence pays the cop a hundred dollars. The fence gives the address to one of his teams. They keep watch on it until the time is right—like the next time the wealthy couple goes out and again she's wearing all that flash. When they come home they're met in the driveway or in the garage by the swifts. With guns. Sometimes, if she's wearing enough goods, the swifts just take that. Other times everyone goes into the house and the couple is offered a choice: Reveal where the goods are stashed, and nothing more will happen. The swifts will just take the goods and leave. Or, if the couple insists there are no goods and the swifts shake down the house and find there is, the couple will be killed for the lie. Naturally, the swifts impress the couple with how thoroughly they can turn a house inside out. Ninety-nine times out of a hundred the couple, begrudgingly and gratefully, lead the way to the safe, the freezer compartment of the refrigerator, a Kotex box, or wherever.

Danny's talkativeness, lurid as it was, worked.

By the time dessert was presented, Springer had forgotten about Seggerman and was undecided on whether to go for the hot lemon mousse or the eight-layer bittersweet chocolate cake.

"He'll have both," Danny told the waiter.

At three o'clock Springer arrived back at his office. Five messages were on his desk. The top one was from Audrey. The receptionist had put quotes around it: *My place at four.*"

From where Springer was sitting he could see Audrey's place, nine blocks up Fifth Avenue. The thirty-fifth and thirty-sixth floors of Trump Tower, corner apartment. Usually when he gazed up there he tried to picture what Audrey might be doing at that moment. Was she dressed, alone, reading, bathing, penduluming, popping Campfire marshmallows into her mouth, or perhaps at one of her windows looking his way and wondering about him? He had often thought of getting a telescope so he could phone and tell her to wave. He would have phoned her that moment but he knew she wouldn't be home.

Today was one of her work days.

She was in charge of dressing the windows at Bergdorf's, had been for nearly four years. She was almost certain she'd gotten the job on her own with her credentials of art classes taken at Wellesley supplemented by more practical courses at the Fashion Institute of Technology. But even if Libby's pull had gotten her hired, that no longer

GERALD A. BROWNE

mattered. By now the store kept her on wholly for her ability, her
sense of style.

Audrey took her Bergdorf windows seriously, the challenge of
coming up with newer and newer ways to present Bergdorf merchandise to the sidewalkers. The windows of Bloomingdale's, Saks, and
Bendel's were getting more outrageous by the month, but Audrey
kept up. It was, for her, a perfect job. It didn't require full time and
was enough of an accomplishment to satisfy those needs in her. After
all, like Gloria Vanderbilt and Dina Merrill, she didn't *have* to do
anything.

Springer's other four messages were from Joel Zimmer of the GIA
laboratory. Springer phoned him. Zimmer wanted him to come
down. Within the quarter hour Springer was with Zimmer in his
cubicle-like work space, an inner sanctum where only the authorized
were usually allowed. The stone Springer had left with Zimmer that
morning was alone on the surface of the white, impervious-coated
work counter.

"Where did you get that?" Zimmer asked.

"It came along with some other rough we bought," Springer told
him, which was the truth, though omissive.

"You bought it as a diamond?"

"Yeah." Springer grinned. "I'm about to have it cut for Cartier's."

"Never."

Springer was self-conscious about how flawed the stone was. If he
hadn't promised Janet, he would never in his life have put it before
Zimmer's eyes.

"First thing I noticed," Zimmer said, "were all the flaws. They
were enough to make me want to stop right there, but they also
made me want to take a closer look." While he spoke Zimmer took
up the stone and placed it on the viewing field of his Raman laser
microprobe, a type of microscope especially suited for identifying
the flaws in gemstones. It took a few moments to get the stone
exactly situated and in focus. "How much do you know about
flaws?" Zimmer asked.

"They cost me," Springer replied lightly.

"The flaws in this stone are, like most others, included crystals.

Crystals that were formed inside the stone while the stone itself was being formed."

"That's why they're called inclusions. They're included. Right?"

"Forgive me for being too basic. Here, take a look."

Springer pressed his upper face to the ample, fitted eyepiece of the microprobe. Immediately it seemed to him that instead of looking into the stone he was viewing it from a distance of several feet.

Zimmer explained. "Notice that each of those included crystals, flaws, or whatever you care to call them are identical formations of the stone itself. Identical."

Springer saw what Zimmer meant. There were hundreds of included crystals within the stone. Some were extremely tiny, nearly indiscernible. All were in every detail exactly like the stone that contained them, even to the extent of having one tip missing. It was, Springer thought, as though he were looking into a solar system. He felt huge. It occurred to him that if he had magnification enough to view the interiors of those included crystals he would find the same duplication. Again and again.

It was fascinating.

Zimmer was saying, "Normally, included crystals have tension fissures around them, caused by their getting in the way during atomic growth. However, not in this stone. The inclusions in this stone are in there snug and neat, as though it's where they belong."

"So, it's an exception." Springer moved away from the microprobe. "A freak diamond."

"It's not a diamond."

"It's always been a diamond," Springer thought aloud.

"The specific gravity of diamond is three point fifty-two with very slight variance. Your stone is four point thirty-one. I measured three times."

"What other minerals fall in that range?"

"Adamite, witherite, a few others, but they don't come octahedral like this, not eight-sided." Zimmer rubbed his eyes with the knuckles of his first fingers, like a sleepy child. Then he blinked several times rapidly, as though that might dispel the strain. "Diamond," he went on, "is a poor conductor of electricity but an excellent conductor of heat. Actually, diamond conducts heat four times better than copper. Did you know that?"

"No."

"Your stone, when I applied fifteen hundred degrees of acetylene to it, didn't even warm up. However, when I touched it end to end with electrical terminals, the current flowed right through it. Just the opposite of diamond. What's more—" Zimmer removed the stone from the microprobe. From a drawer he brought out a device that resembled a ballpoint pen with a sharp diamond affixed to its tip. He scribbled the diamond harshly across one of the surfaces of Springer's stone. That should have caused deep scratch lines but the stone wasn't affected. "If diamond rates a ten on the Mohs' hardness scale, your stone is an eleven."

"Nothing's harder than diamond."

"Then it's a nothing."

"Okay," Springer said. "If it isn't a diamond, what is it?"

Zimmer dropped the stone into a small, self-sealing, clear plastic envelope, handed it to Springer. "My friend, I could bullshit you. If I needed to protect my reputation I could tell you this stone is some rare but useless mineral such as . . . roméite or whatever . . . and you'd probably never learn otherwise." Zimmer paused, sighed. "You ask me what it is. Well, partly because someday soon my wife will be getting those studs, I'll tell you straight." To be so baffled by a stone was painful for Zimmer. It showed as he admitted to Springer, "I don't know."

From the GIA laboratory Springer walked up Fifth Avenue to Trump Tower. Although along the way he stopped to watch an out-of-towner get taken for fifty dollars on the bottom of an upended cardboard Campbell Soup carton in a very smooth three-card monte game, and he also paused at Cartier's, Townsend's and Winston's to see what diamonds they were showing off, he arrived at Audrey's apartment at one minute to four.

Her apartment was a seven-room duplex done throughout in a muted, complimentary gray and decorated with a tasteful mix of authentic pieces ranging from Louis Quinze to Régence to Art Deco. The apartment had cost three million five. That was merely for the bare undivided space. What Audrey had done with it cost another million, not counting the paintings. Every square inch and every stick had been paid for by the Hull Foundation and, ostensibly, it was the owner. What Springer liked most about the apartment was how beautiful Audrey looked in it. She knew well how to dress her own windows best, so to speak.

Audrey greeted him with a peck of a kiss. "I forgot to tell you to bring that stone," she said.

"Which stone?"

"The one Janet had."

"Why?"

"We've got to hurry." She turned and rushed up the stairs. Springer noticed the never-worn soles of her navy and white suede man-heeled spectators as he followed up after her.

"You're nifty," he said.

She was dressed to go, in a navy flannel, double-breasted, man-tailored suit that fit although it appeared too large for her. A creamy shirt buttoned low at the neck. Her broad-brimmed panama hat had just a hint of a gangsterish cock to it.

"I'll give you five minutes to change," she said.

On the bed laid out for him was a dark blue suit, fresh shirt, tie, and everything.

"Where we going?"

"Don't bother to shower. Just run your razor over your face and splash a bit."

Springer removed his suit jacket, despised his tie the way he slid its knot down and yanked it off.

"Damn," Audrey said, "I wish I'd thought to tell you to bring that stone."

He told her it was in his jacket pocket.

She got it out, examined it, checked to see it was the right one.

Springer undressed. He didn't feel up to much. More than anything he wanted to draw the curtains and take a nap.

"We're expected at five," Audrey told him.

"Where?"

"Aunt Libby's."

"I can't go."

"Why not other than you don't want to?"

Springer thought fast. "I have to go back to the office."

"Like hell."

"I have to close the safe."

"Anyone can close a safe," she said. "Opening a safe is the hard part. You should know that."

"Yeah, anyone can close a safe, but not just anyone will make sure what's supposed to be in it is in it."

"You're just grasping."

"I'm not. I can't neglect my business."

"Why, then, are you standing there bare-ass?"

"Unfair question."

"Is Mal at the office?"

"Probably."

"He can close the safe. I'll call him."

"I don't want to go to Aunt Libby's." Unequivocally.

"You have to, sooner or later."

"I'll take later."

Audrey shoved a hand into one of her trouser pockets, stated her terms: "I gave you five minutes to freshen up and change. I'll give you five more. If you're not ready by then I'll go alone . . . to Aunt Libby's and who knows where else." With that she slung a white kidskin carryall over her shoulder and went downstairs.

Springer glanced at his watch. He went into the bath. His razor, brush, and things were right there on the marble counter. Might as well shave, he thought, he always felt better after a shave. He lathered and gave himself a quick once-over. He ran hot as possible water onto a facecloth. It burned his hands when he wrung it out. He pressed the steaming cloth to his face and rubbed it around the back of his neck. He dried on his way to the bedroom. No hurry, he told himself.

From downstairs he heard the front door slam, a loud pissed-off slam.

Springer legged into the trousers of the blue suit Audrey had laid out for him with such haste he hobbled himself and nearly fell. He slipped on socks and shoes, armed into the shirt, and, without taking time to button or tuck it, grabbed up jacket and tie and rushed down the stairs.

Audrey was in the foyer, leaning against the edge of a console, one leg crossed over the other. She smiled, more lovingly than victorious.

"That predictable, huh?"

"I should hope," she said, helping him button.

"Did you reach Mal?"

"Rest easy, Diamond Jim, the safe is closed."

"Who's driving?"

"Aunt Libby sent a car."

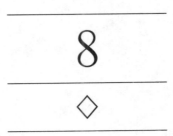

8

◇

The car that Libby sent was a custom-built Daimler limousine. Dark brown. Only someone beyond ordinary wealth would have such a car not be black. The chauffeur, whom Audrey addressed as Groat, was liveried in brown twill with bone buttons. Groat respectfully held his beaked cap in one hand while the other held open the door of the Daimler. He was like an automaton, built for efficiency and protection. His driving did nothing to contradict that impression: gradual, anticipative stops and a steady sixty.

All the way to Round Hill Road in Greenwich, north of the Merritt Parkway.

The Daimler was consistent with the high double gate it turned in at, a seventeenth-century Tijon-style gate with intricate scrollwork in solid repoussé and an H monogram incorporated in its overthrow. The large brick piers that flanked the gate seemed obedient, as, from them, the gate automatically swung open left and right to admit the Daimler.

The house was three hundred yards from the gate, but it was immediately visible because the inner drive was straight. It struck Springer that the relationship of the house to its drive made it look like something with a long white textured tongue sticking out. At him. There were ten-foot-high boxwood hedges perfectly clipped along each side. At regular intervals, recesses accommodated huge pedestaled urns overflowing with Persian blue petunias.

The Daimler came to a stop at the main entrance.

Springer opened the car door before Groat could get to it. He stepped out and paused to take in the house. "No place like home," he quipped.

Audrey pinched his ass, sharply.

The architectural style of the house was uncompromisingly Georgian, a pleasing composition of brick and limestone and numerous double-hung eighteen-paned sash windows. It was two stories, sixty rooms, showing thirty chimneys above the blue-gray slates of its hipped roof.

The entrance door opened. A white-gloved servant emerged as though his sole assignment had been to await their arrival. He was by no means the typical fine-drawn butler but, like the chauffeur, a formidable man well over six feet, more of a bouncer with polish, Springer thought. A dutiful "Good afternoon, Miss," was said to Audrey. Springer got a sort of bowing nod.

Audrey entered the house with the relaxed bearing of one who belonged. Springer felt like a tagalong. He tried not to appear impressed. The crystal chandelier that hung above the wide reception hall was immense and yet so delicate that he would have preferred not to be under it. All the more so because it seemed to be suspended by a mere strip of blue velour, which, of course, was actually a sleeve that covered a length of chain. The feature on one wall of the reception was a full-length portrait by Sargent. On the wall opposite was a French *trumeau* mirror above an important giltwood console holding an extravagant arrangement of rubrium lilies.

Audrey tossed her hat to the butler, whom she called by his last name: Hinch.

Hinch had excellent reflexes. "Everyone is on the lower terrace," he informed her.

Audrey stood tiptoe to peek at herself in the mirror through the mass of lilies. She primped her hair briefly, then extended her hand to Springer to lead the way. They went across the width of the house, passing through several rooms so quickly that Springer got only a vague impression of their spaciousness and elegance.

Tall pairs of French doors opened onto a wide terrace that overlooked the grounds. A broad, gentle slope of flourishing lawn. Mature trees—elm, beech, chestnut—given room, had grown to plump, presiding shapes. Many dogwoods were lesser punctuations. Every edge and angle had been softened by evergreens and flowering shrubs.

From the higher vantage of the terrace, Springer's eyes caught upon a glint of glass in the distance that was the peak of a large greenhouse. Off to the right, obscured by vine, so it might be either ignored or more privately enjoyed, was a tennis court. Also in that vicinity, Springer assumed, would be a swimming pool. He sighted far out, could see no end to the grounds or any neighboring house. No doubt somewhere out there, probably fifty acres away, was a perimeter wall. This in an area where a two-acre building plot went for as much as a half million.

Audrey hurried him down twenty-five wide stone steps and across some lawn to where an expansive brick terrace was contained by the droops of willows.

There, facing the long aureate rays of the late sun, was Libby. She was seated in a deep *duchesse brisée* with her feet up. All but her head was covered by an elaborately embroidered blue silk Fu Manchu dynasty kimona of museum quality. None of the furniture there was meant for outdoors. It was down-filled Louis Quinze upholstered in a pale green silk. Several bergères, tabourets, and a small settee, accommodated by marble-topped side tables. Evidently, the furniture was covered each night or taken inside whenever the weather turned suddenly bad.

On the terrace with Libby were Thomas Wintersgill and Gilbert Townsend. The two men stood as though pulled up, smiling automatically around their greetings. Libby merely tilted her head up to receive left and right cheek kisses from Audrey. Springer was introduced. Handshakes were performed.

"I believe we've met," Townsend said.

"Once," Springer told him.

"Nice to see you again." Townsend was one of the foremost jewelers in the world. His main place of business was on Fifth Avenue only three doors down from Winston's. He and the Winston people were arch competitors, vying for the patronage of the wealthy. Over the years nearly every important or famous stone that came on the market passed profitably through either the Townsend or Winston vaults, some stones three or four times, depending on the whims or the bequests of their clients. Townsend boasted, as did Winston, that he was an exclusive jeweler, while Tiffany and Cartier were department stores.

A short lean sixty-year-old, Townsend was meticulous about his appearance, gave any possible overstatement a wide path. Springer, during an appointment with Townsend a few years ago, had shown some of his better, larger goods. Townsend had treated the stones with disrespect, tossed them carelessly about on his desk, and not even asked their price.

It did not surprise Springer to find Townsend there. Libby was known as one of his choice customers.

Drinks were offered.

A white-jacketed servant appeared.

"We're having Potted Parrots," Libby said.

Springer noticed a frothy orange concoction in the stemmed glasses. "What's in it?" he asked.

"You've never had a Potted Parrot?" Libby said it like *You've never had a pair of shoes?*

"No." Springer expected Libby to urge him to give one a try but she looked abruptly away. "I'll have some stout," he told the servant, just for the contrariness of it, believing stout was probably not to be had.

"A Montrachet spritz for me," Audrey said. She was already seated on the settee with her carryall between her feet, keeping in contact with it as though it contained something especially valuable. She patted the cushion of the settee for Springer to come sit beside her.

A bird somewhere up in the willow's branches let go. Its excrement dropped onto the highly polished toe of Townsend's left shoe. Everyone noticed and stared. Libby condemned the culprit with an upward glance. Townsend apologized, reached down, and self-consciously wiped away the whitish glob with his linen cocktail napkin. Springer hoped Townsend would forgetfully use the same napkin later to wipe his mouth.

The drinks were brought. Springer's stout was Guinness Extra in a heavy crystal mug. He raised the mug to the situation and took a gulp. He disliked the dark, nearly black stuff. To his taste the bitterness of it was a self-infliction. "Not cold enough," he stated and placed the mug on the table by his elbow.

Nose up, Wintersgill informed him, "Stout is best a bit on the warm side."

They'd have to tie him down and shove a funnel in his mouth to get another drop of that bile in him, Springer vowed.

"Before you arrived," Libby said, "we were discussing the Fasig-Tipton sales coming up. From what I've gathered, this year's crop of yearlings isn't much. Except for a couple of Slew and Affirmed colts, there's nothing worth paying two or three million for." She asked Springer, "What's your opinion?"

"I don't know horses," Springer told her.

"I would have thought not." Libby smiled.

It wasn't easy to verbally slice at someone like that and at the same time sweet-smile the way Libby could, Springer thought. Like an executioner beaming amiably as he dropped the blade. Well, this long-avoided head-on with Libby was turning out exactly as he'd always feared it would. He could only hope to get out of it with as little damage done as possible. He had the notion to pretend sudden food poisoning.

Wintersgill cleared his throat and asked Libby, "When do you intend to go down to the farm?"

"Before the Virginia weather gets muggy," she replied.

"You'll skip Keeneland?"

"Christ, yes. Whatever our animals bring they'll bring without my being there. And I can certainly do without all those obligatory dinners, all those idiot hags wilting in chiffon. We used to say July is for the shore, August for the mountains. I still abide."

The conversation went from that to the regretful opinion that Penobscot Bay was deteriorating socially. Townsend contributed little, agreed a lot. Wintersgill grunted and cleared his throat often. Audrey reached over and caressed the back of Springer's neck, a small reward for his forbearance. Springer discreetly appraised his adversary.

Libby.

She was the most victorious time-fighter he'd ever met. Well into her sixties and trying for twenty years less. She was naturally slender, had the fine bone structure of the well bred, which helped considerably in making her various physical renovations more successful. The foremost cosmetic surgeons from Rio to Geneva had done their paring, peeling, tucking, and lifting, so there were no pouches beneath her eyes, no droop to her lids, no furrows across her forehead or striations above her upper lip. They had achieved a perfect concavity for her cheeks, a tight, well-defined chin, and almost done away entirely with the crepiness of her neck. Her body had been taken up or in, like some ill-fitting garment, by its hems and seams. She had healthy, abundant hair, cared for, not the least bit crimpy. Once dark, it had gone gray and was now kept a subtle blond. Her capped teeth were up-to-date.

Springer decided she must have been devastating in her younger years, for now she was certainly an old beauty—sitting there like an empress with her hands concealed in the ample sleeves of her Chinese kimona. Springer didn't like her. Nevertheless he appreciated her.

"Where do you golf?" she asked him.

"I don't," he said.

Again that executioner's smile from her. "You're not much of a sport, are you?"

Springer thought how much he'd enjoy spiking a volleyball right at her. He maintained his composure, what he hoped came off as a pleasant facial expression. He reminded himself that she was the Libby Hopkins-Hull who, not long ago, had purchased and razed a nearly landmark New York hotel merely because it had failed to hold a suite reservation she had taken the time to personally make for one of her friends. The Libby Hopkins-Hull who for the female spunk of it (and a gain of nine hundred million) had tangled what would have otherwise been an expedient merger between two major oil companies. The Libby Hopkins-Hull who, during an afternoon sail on Hobe Sound, had told President Carter that the way to stir the nation's sluggish economy was to simply change the color of the money. Print it with blue ink rather than green and then declare all green money worthless unless officially exchanged within three months. Who would dare declare their unreported cash? Out of the safety deposit boxes, shoe boxes, and coffee cans it would come for one bitch of a spending spree. If Carter had taken her suggestion he would have won a second term, claimed Libby Hopkins-Hull.

"What is it you do?" she asked Springer.

"I told you," Audrey interjected.

"Oh, yes. Now I remember. Diamonds. I suppose you're with Harry Oppenheimer and that bunch."

A smirky scoff from Townsend.

Libby leaned to the table next to her, sipped some of her Potted Parrot up through crystal straws.

At that moment, without even a warning yelp, a pair of Cavalier King Charles spaniels bounded onto the terrace. A chestnut-and-white and a black-and-white. In their eagerness they misbehaved, leaped up onto Libby, trying to get to her with kisses. A wag of tail overturned her Potted Parrot. Her hands came from the sleeves of the kimona to fend off the onslaught of devotion. "Who let these damn dogs out?" she shouted.

A servant rushed to the rescue, carried the spaniels away.

However, by then Springer had seen Libby's hands.

She looked hard at him, daring comment.

Her hands were gnarled with degenerative arthritis, the fingers crooked, their joints enlarged, knotted hard, unable to flex properly. Her hands were a deformity that contradicted her, betrayed her. Ugly old-woman's hands that the cosmetic and ortheopedic surgeons could do little about. She'd had them operated on twice and both times the arthritis returned, determined, it seemed, to be even more monstrous. She loathed the sight of her hands, could easily imagine what others thought. That, of course, was why she'd kept them hidden in the sleeves of her kimona. Well, no need for that now. To hell with it. She threw off the kimona. She had on a white tennis skirt and blouse, tennis shoes, and brief socks with a single fuzzy blue tassel at each heel.

Merely costume, Springer thought, doubting that with the condition of her hands she'd be able to grasp a racquet.

Libby, with some difficulty, took up a cigarette from the table. Townsend jumped to light it for her with his solid gold DuPont. She took a couple of drags, inhaled, and let them out like perturbed sighs. Her fingers couldn't manage. The cigarette fell on her. She slapped at it, causing sparks to fly. She got up, brushed disdainfully at the black smudge that it had made on her skirt, and without another word or look headed for the house.

Audrey told Springer, "Whatever you want just ask for it. I'll be a while." She snatched up her carryall and hurried off to catch up with Libby.

After some awkward silence Townsend asked Springer, "How's business?"

"Things could always be better."

Townsend agreed passively.

Springer caught the attention of a servant who was standing on duty behind the lace of a drooping willow branch. He requested any old Scotch and soda, light on the soda. It was brought. The practically straight Scotch caused him to make a face.

Townsend moved his chair closer to Wintersgill, turned his back on Springer. They spoke in low tones but Springer, without trying, overheard a word now and then. It seemed to him they were discussing a certain stock, that Townsend was imparting some insider information he didn't want Springer to know, but then Springer realized their topic was a person, someone named Ernie or something like that.

Townsend was doing most of the talking. Wintersgill was interested. Wintersgill was in his mid-forties. He had a high-level public relations appearance, a confident show backed up by an abundance of inner fuel, the sort who could, quietly, come on ten different ways in pursuit of his ambition. He was two or three inches over six feet, had a lean, undoubtedly active body. A squash player, Springer thought.

Wintersgill turned, pretended to be looking up to the house while he checked Springer's proximity with his wide-set but narrow eyes, squinty, as though distantly focused. He had a rectangular face exaggerated by pronounced jawbones. A straight strong nose, brown hair side-parted so definitely the part looked like the scar of a knife slash. The suit he was wearing was dark gray, a business suit, but it seemed casual on him. His black-grounded, small-figured tie could not possibly offend. Wintersgill turned away from Springer again, resumed with Townsend.

Springer had no idea who Wintersgill was. He'd heard Audrey mention the name during telephone conversations a few times. Impossible not to remember that name. From what Springer gathered, Wintersgill was in some business way affiliated with Libby.

Springer pulled one of the tabourets over with his foot, put his legs up on it. Couldn't relax. He got up and, with drink in hand, left the terrace. He gazed up the slope at the imposing house, tried to imagine Audrey as a child here, how it had been for her. The picture of her environment that he'd mentally drawn paled by comparison to the real thing. Not because he was naive or lacking sophistication. He had purposely diminished its scope, actually its threat. Perhaps, it occurred to him now, he didn't know Audrey as well as he'd thought. Why, for instance, had she been so quiet, or was it subdued, in Libby's presence? She'd hardly said a word. How much, Springer wondered, would this day cost him?

He meandered down and around the grassy slope. Discovered a reflecting pool, its oblong shape set with patches of water lilies, pale pink ones on their way to closing. The sides and bottom of the pool were black polished granite, so the water, absolutely clear, had a quicksilver quality. About fifty feet away at the opposite end of the pool was a young woman. Seated on the edge with her skirt hiked up and her bare feet in the water.

Springer decided it was better to be curious than pensive. He went to her.

She didn't react to his approach, and even when he was standing beside and above her she didn't move. She seemed entranced.

Springer told her who he was.

"I am here with Mr. Townsend," she said as though her credentials had been requested. Her accent was thick, German. She turned her face up to Springer. She was quite beautiful. Her blond hair was various lengths, purposely styled to appear unkempt. She had green-blue eyes and an expressive, swollen-lipped mouth. The dimensions and attitude of a fashion model. "I am Ernestine," she said, sounding weary about it.

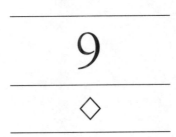

9

Libby allowed her tennis skirt to drop. She stepped out of the circle of it and kicked it anywhere. She'd already sent her blouse and shoes flying. "Fucking dogs," she muttered.

Audrey didn't try to pacify her, knew from past experience that whatever she might say would only sustain the ill temper. Like all such gusts this too would soon blow by.

They were alone in Libby's personal rooms in the south wing of the second floor, a spacious arrangement that consisted of a sitting room, study, bedroom, dressing room, and bath. It was hers within all the rest that was hers, and, in keeping with her wishes, it was accessible only by way of a single door off the upper hallway. When that door was bolted from inside Libby could be sure of her privacy. No one, not even any of the servants, was admitted unless summoned or in Libby's company.

She sat in her dressing room at the Régence ormulu-mounted

bureau plat, a fifty-thousand-dollar Criard piece that she used as a vanity. A giltwood winged mirror was mounted just above it. She glanced into the mirror as though that somehow determined she was really there. She undid her brassiere in front and shrugged herself entirely free of it. Sitting more erect, her eyes returned to the mirror, observed her breasts. She had, she believed, the breasts of a twenty-year-old. Not large; they had never been and she had never wanted them large. Hers were a proud size and firm enough to not need the bra. Her nipples were also convincing. They were like the very tips of baby fingers, encircled by fine-textured, perfectly diametered aureoles. Many women in her opinion had horrid nipples, like spoiled mushrooms, and aureoles like dried peaches. Libby only wished hers were pinker. (She colored them with a semi-indelible dye on special occasions.) As often as she admired her breasts, she never gave credit to the surgeons who had accomplished them. She had succeeded in shoving that back into the mental murk among other things best forgotten.

"How about these for sixty?" She asked Audrey in the mirror.

Sixty-five, Audrey silently corrected and told her, "Incredible." That was not the superlative she'd used for reply last time under these same circumstances. As she recalled she'd used "astonishing," and the time before "remarkable."

Libby leaned to the mirror, turned her face slowly to the left and to the right, studying it critically. The glass of the mirror was true, although the lighting of it was deliberately kind.

"Think I should have another peel?" Libby asked.

"No." The proper answer.

"Your Mr. Springer is extremely attractive."

"You treated him horribly."

"I was merely testing."

"Like hell, you were embarrassingly rude. You owe an apology."

Libby *hmmphed* at the absurdity. She'd never owed anything or ever apologized to anyone. "He doesn't fit," she said.

"He fits," Audrey contended pointedly.

"Exceptional in bed, I suppose."

"Exceptional."

"Well, as long as that's all there is to it. . . ."

"That's not all."

"Oh?"

"I love him."

"Even that's all right if you don't carry it too far. You haven't been thinking of marriage?"

"Thinking," Audrey admitted.

"Spare me."

"I already did a Tyler for you."

"At least Tyler didn't have a money nose like this nothing fellow. I'll bet he's wearing out his knees begging you to marry him."

"He hasn't asked."

"If he does?"

"Then you'll both get an answer."

Libby yanked out a drawer of the *bureau plat,* slammed it shut, yanked out another. "Where the hell are my sleeping gloves?" she grouched.

Audrey found them deeper in one of the drawers Libby had searched: new white cotton gloves, several pairs. While she was at it, Audrey helped by unscrewing the lid from a frosted glass jar that Libby dipped her fingers into and scooped out a glob of a substance that resembled axle grease and smelled like lilacs. A doctor in Montecatini, Italy, had talked Libby into it at five hundred dollars a jar. No doubt the exorbitant price influenced her faith in it.

"My dear," she told Audrey, "there's a lot to be said for class." She slathered the thick, viscous stuff on her hands, worked it in vigorously as she spoke. "Horses, dumb as they are, have more respect for it than people. For instance, a horse with questionable breeding might run an extremely fast mile and win with his own kind. However, put him in a race with horses of a better class and, even if they run slower than he's capable of, he'll hang back, reluctant to win. He knows his place. I've seen it happen any number of times. Horses have a sense about it. People ought to. And that goes for your small-time diamond dealer."

No comment from Audrey. She knew no matter what she said, Libby would have the last word.

Libby inserted her slick-coated, misshapen hands into a pair of the white cotton sleeping gloves. She was psychologically addicted to both the emollient and the gloves, had used up dozens of jars and hundreds of pairs.

She got up, went into the bedroom, and climbed into bed. "A short nap for a long evening," she recited, her customary litany. She situated her extra-plump down-filled pillows exactly as she wanted them, covered her eyes with a silk satin mask, and pulled the hand-embroidered edge of the linen top sheet up around her.

Audrey went across the room and dropped into a puffy fauteuil. She dug into her carryall and brought out the black, white, and pink of a carton of Good & Plentys. Opened one end of the carton and slid several of the capsule-shaped candies into the palm of her hand. For ten minutes she sat there, sometimes melting the candies down patiently in her mouth to their softer licorice centers, at other times crunching right into them. By then Libby appeared to be settled. She was, Audrey knew, capable of dropping off quickly. For a test Audrey shook the half-consumed box of Good & Plentys. The candies rattled loudly. Libby wasn't disturbed.

Audrey went over to the bedside. Libby was sleeping on her side with an arm extended, one of her white-gloved hands lying above the sheet. Again Audrey went into her carryall. She brought out the clear plastic envelope that contained Springer's stone, removed the stone.

Carefully, Audrey stretched open the hem of the glove and tucked the stone down in snug against Libby's palm.

Libby stirred. Thickly, she asked, "What the hell you doing?"

"Trying to improve your disposition for one thing."

Libby, half asleep, flapped her hand. "What is it?"

"Is it uncomfortable?"

"No."

"Don't worry, just nap."

"Nap," Libby slurred.

"Do you mind if I just snooze here on the couch?"

Libby was already oblivious.

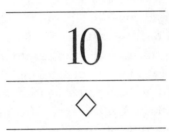

10

◇

The stone.

It was thrown, among others of its kind, like a fistful of sand through the circumferential white light that lay beyond what is now known as the universe.

There was no time then. Time had not yet begun. Nor was there space, there being no matter for space to be between.

The stone and others of its kind were given to the void, sent scattering at speeds that covered distances never measured. They were forethoughts and were well on their way when the idea of the universe detonated.

Although comparatively less than motes, they were not affected by the violent energy caused by the bursting of that idea, were not deterred by the blast or heat of it or the gaseous clouds that were soon all about. They passed easily through those yet individual atoms of hydrogen and helium, which were, after all, a mere one hundred millionth of an inch in size.

At numerous points along the course of the stone those gases swirled into knots, gathered and tightened and formed. Colonies of such formations were everywhere. More than a hundred billion of them occupied the vastness.

Galaxies.

Each with a hundred billion stars.

They incandesced. Some were like the strewing of brilliant jewels, others resembled the fiery yawns of furnaces. Pretty sights. They pinwheeled, and in their spiraling appeared to be throwing off, while actually they were accumulating, attracting more and more star matter into their galactic arms.

There was space now.

And time and distance.

The stone was 96,000,000,000,000,000,000,000,000 (ninety-six billion trillion) miles from its origin, had been under way for fifteen billion years. It had passed by countless newly hatched stars that were glowing baby blue with white centers, like blue ova. Giant orange and red stars, spendthrifts, rapidly depleting their energy. Faint wispy tendrils of tiny stars playing follow-the-leader, swarms of them huddling as though to gossip. The stone shot close by fresh stars that had just shed their dusty coats and revealed their shining nudity. Unstable ones that could only bob and blink. Some that had halos, solitary wanderers, drifters. Others like blazing bullies a hundred million miles in diameter, ready to take on anything.

Keeping to its course, the stone, among others, passed through an enormous cloud of black dust and emerged above the spiraling arm of a particular galaxy. It centered its intent upon the trailing fringe of that arm and continued on, to where a certain star was in its nascency, pulling knots of gas and dust into a core, an organization other nearby gases and dust could not resist. They helped to form a glowing hot sphere.

It was the second time this star had been born. Previously it had burned itself out and collapsed under its own weight and exploded, fragmenting itself in all directions.

Now, once again, it had gathered the proximate bits and pieces.

Not all of them, however.

Some matter, like rebellious factions, refused to be included. It bunched on its own, formed fifty-two separate bodies.

Forty-three moons.

Nine planets.

They didn't go anywhere; couldn't, actually. Bound by the invisible tether of the star, they circled it, as though taunting, out of futility.

For the stone, among others of its kind, one of those planets was destination—the planet that was 8,000 miles in diameter. The outer layers of the planet were still in their molten state; nevertheless the stone plunged right in, penetrated the upper mantle to the depth of a hundred and ten miles.

The stone was not in any way altered as a result of its journey, nor was it affected by the heat and pressure of its environment within the planet. It was not alone there. All around, numerous elements were joining one another.

Calcium, chromium, silicon, and oxygen combined into cubic crystals to become garnets.

Potassium, aluminum, magnesium, iron, lithium, silicon, and oxygen made mica.

Titanium, potassium, and some others in certain amounts joined together to create monoclinic crystals of phlogopite.

Carbon, shunning any association, as though entirely self-satisfied, replicated its cubic atoms into diamonds.

These and other crystals, with the stone among them, remained within the upper mantle of the planet for a billion years, until the crust of the planet cracked apart like a piece of fired pottery too quickly cooled. In many places the crust was so weakened or chinked it could no longer keep capped the pressures of the highly heated substances that lay below. They came spouting out.

One such volcanic gush heaved the stone to the surface. There it was immediately overrun and covered by a layer of molten magma. The eruptions ceased. Rains cooled everything. The magma hardened into an igneous rock, dark gray with bluish reflections.

Then it was a matter of erosion. Two billion years of it.

The rock that contained the stone was worn away. The stone peeked out. For the first time it was exposed to a gentler atmosphere.

With a little more erosion it came entirely free. A rainstorm washed it and carried it a short way to where it became wedged between the spiny outcroppings of two converging rocks.

The stone was held there.

For Amadu Kamara.

Amadu was originally from the village of Banya in the Niawa Chiefdom of Sierra Leone. When he was twelve he was caught at an illicit diamond dig and taken to Kenema Town for a year in prison.

When he was released from prison Amadu was given the traditional penny for a fresh start. He did not go home to Banya. He had heard other prisoners speak of Koidu, sixty miles to the north, where diamonds were lying all around as though they'd been magically sprinkled.

That turned out to be somewhat true.

Nearly everyone in and around Koidu looked for diamonds in the gravel. And often found them. Koidu people even walked differently, bent at the waist, their heads lower than their haunches, constantly scanning the ground. The Koidu stoop, it was called.

Over the years Amadu found numerous diamonds in and around Koidu. Some small, some a bit larger, some good, some not so. As a rule he sold his finds, as did nearly everyone, to the Sierra Leone Selection Trust Ltd., a British firm that had been granted rights to the diamond yield of the area. When in 1956 another British company, called the Diamond Mining System Ltd., opened a buying office in Koidu, all it meant to Amadu was that he could take the few diamonds he found to a different man in a different buying office and receive the same unfair price.

Several times when Amadu happened to hit upon some better stones, he sewed them inside a wad of goatskin that he stuck between his cheek and teeth and trekked thirty miles east through the bush to the Guinea border. They were a dangerous thirty miles even without having to contend with the special diamond police who patrolled the area. Anyone caught in the bush heading the wrong way with diamonds was shot.

Also, finally, there was the Meli River that determined the border between Sierra Leone and Guinea. The diamond police were numerous and especially alert along the river, so it had to be swum at night: a wide river with deceptively strong currents. A swimmer did not know what he was up against until he was out in it.

Across the river in Guinea were the tents of the Lebanese buyers. They did not do business according to any schedule. There were no prearranged rendezvous. They just sat outside their tents at night and flashed their lanterns to attract whoever might be coming across. Sometimes the Lebanese paid twice as much for diamonds as the official buying office. Not out of fairness or generosity, but to feed the rumor that it was better to deal with them. Usually the Lebanese were tighter with their money, argued down the price to below what could have been gotten back in Koidu without the trouble.

When Amadu reached the age of fifty he believed he was too old to ever attempt another trip to Guinea. Besides, a younger man he knew had recently been caught by the police on the outskirts of Kainkordu, a village five miles from the border. The man had swallowed his diamonds rather than have them found in his mouth. The police suspected as much. They cut him open to get them.

Amadu was surely too old for that.

So he limited himself to the Koidu area, seldom venturing beyond the point where he could return home at night to sleep with his second and more cooperative wife.

On an August day in 1957, Amadu was in the vicinity of Dangbaidu, a bush village six miles north of Koidu Town. It was a bright, sweltering day and Amadu had no hat. He said someone had stolen his hat. Actually the Meya River had stolen it when Amadu had bent over to examine a possible that turned out to be only a worthless pebble. Amadu shouted several Niawa curses never forgotten from his childhood as he watched the river carry his hat downstream.

That was the reason he was near Dangbaidu that day. It was miles from the river. Along the river had always been the best place to find diamonds but he blamed the river for taking his hat. Perhaps, Amadu thought, he should not be stubborn about forgiving. He had not found a good diamond in nearly a month, and where he was now did not appear promising. There were not many patches of gravel. The terrain was too flat, baked hard.

Amadu straightened up and, as he'd done so many thousands of times in his life, arched his back to stretch the cramp from it. He swigged some of the water he'd brought along in a cork-stoppered beer bottle, wiped his forehead with his arm, and resumed his Koidu stoop.

Within a few minutes he found a diamond, a tiny one trying to hide among some yellowish rubblestones. It was about twice the size of a pinhead, the sort of diamond that was commonly traded at the taverns for two beers.

Well, Amadu thought, at least he had that much coming.

He went back into his Koidu stoop, kept his eyes to the ground. He was like a sure-eyed bird of prey, scanning the earth, and like that sort of bird the moment he spotted it wedged between two rocks he pounced upon it, clutched it up.

The stone.

Amadu rolled it in his palm, jiggled it, changing its position so he could examine it all around. He was never more certain that he'd found a diamond. A large one. What was it? Forty carats? Perhaps sixty. It was the kind of large diamond the buying office called a special stone.

By the time Amadu walked back to Koidu it was night and only the taverns were open. It was difficult for Amadu not to tell of his find, but he spent the tiny diamond on two beers and did not make his usual contributions to the griping about what an unrewarding day it had been.

The following morning Amadu was first in line at the Diamond System's buying office. Amadu presented the stone. The buyer on duty was not as impressed as Amadu had imagined he would be. The buyer examined the stone with his eye loupe and then placed it on the scale.

Fifty-six carats forty-one points was its weight.

The buyer offered Amadu ten pounds.

Amadu pointed out that it was a special stone.

But very dirty inside, the buyer told him.

Amadu did not want to believe it.

Very dirty, the buyer repeated.

Amadu nodded, and as he folded and put to pocket the ten one-pound notes he told himself he had not been entirely unlucky. He could have found nothing.

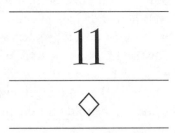

11

◇

Dinner was served.

In what Libby called the *salle à manger intime,* a circular high-ceilinged room in eighteenth-century Adams style that might have been intimate by comparison but was by no means cozy. The predominant color of the room was blue, mainly powdery and French with embellishes and borders of gold leaf. Vertical paneling all around was painted with intricate arabesques, garlands, and bouquets, and considerable plaster work was incorporated throughout, not heavy and obvious but delicate, low-relief, difficult to execute. Giltwood side consoles were topped by *marbre bleu ancien* and the same was laid into a pattern underfoot. Altogether, the atmosphere pleasantly exemplified the gothic and rococo taste of the mid-Georgian period.

Springer hadn't planned to stay for dinner, but he realized now that was what Audrey must have had in mind when she dark-suited and necktied him. Anyway, there he was at table sipping the apéritif, a Kir Royale. He tried to take a positive view of the situation. At least he was going to have a splendid meal for a change, and there was no guessing about that. What he could expect to be served was printed calligraphically course by course on a white card he found lying on the face of his Coalport plate. From the look of it, dining with Libby would be a good deal more than breaking bread.

The seating arrangement puzzled Springer. He was seated on Libby's right, customarily the place of honor. It was, he thought, an error, or else Libby wanted him close so it would be easier for her to take more of her well-honed swipes at him.

The girl Ernestine was seated on Libby's left and then, around the circular table, were Townsend, Audrey, and Wintersgill.

Springer hoped the food was so good mouths would be too busy to talk. He'd say as little as he could get away with, volunteer nothing, and before he knew it, he told himself, he and Audrey would be well fed and driven home.

"Did you know," Libby was saying, "in the days of Louis Treize meals were served wherever the royal family happened to be at the time?"

"Rarely in the bath," Townsend quipped.

"Their food was brought to them on trestle tables," Libby went on, "which was not such a bad idea when you consider all the boring dinner guests they avoided. Do you spend much time in France, Mr. Springer?"

"Not much." Springer anticipated a follow-up slash from her.

But she said, "Nor do I any more. The people have soured me. Better to keep one's distance and steal from their taste."

Springer agreed with a nod.

Libby's smile was soft. "Where do you stay when you're in Paris?"

Here it comes, Springer thought. "The Crillon," he fibbed.

"Excellent choice," Libby said.

"He goes to London more often," Audrey put in.

"And where do you stay in London?"

Springer nearly said the Savoy, which was the truth. Instead he told her, "The Connaught."

"But of course," Libby said, "a marvelous hotel, and superb food."
She took a sip of her Kir, pursed her lips, blotted them gently with
her napkin. "However, Mr. Springer, from now on when you're in
London you mustn't endure even the Connaught." She looked to
Wintersgill. "We still have that place on Chester Terrace, I pre-
sume."

"We do," Wintersgill confirmed.

"Haven't been there in ages," Libby explained. "Not since the
Wimbledon before last." She told Springer, "I do hope you'll use the
place. It has a lovely large garden. Just give Wintersgill an hour or
two notice so the servants aren't caught in their *vêtements de dessous*
or whatever."

"Thank you."

"I do work many times in London," Ernestine said, perhaps
fishing for a similar open invitation.

"I'm sure you do," Libby said and gave Ernestine's hand two pats
that advised patience.

What was Libby up to? Springer wondered. As caustic as she'd
been earlier, she was all charm now. Something told him not to trust
it, that Libby was digging him a pitfall with her niceness. However,
he had to admit she seemed genuinely changed, high-spirited. It was
probably impossible for her to look more radiant. She had assumed
the hostess's perogative and overdressed slightly—in an ivory silk
crepe that was dramatic in its simplicity: cut straight across the base
of the throat, attached tenuously at one shoulder in such a manner
that only the round of that shoulder was exposed above a full,
draping upper sleeve, which gradually tapered to a snugness at the
wrist. The fabric, although opaque, accentuated the absence of a bra.
On the ring finger of each hand was a diamond of twenty carats,
rectangular cuts. The diamonds appeared identical. They transmit-
ted equally intense scintillations whenever Libby moved her hands.

And move them she did.

Her hands were like a pair of birds with huge flashing eyes flutter-
ing around her.

Springer believed the diamonds but not the hands. Those, he was
sure, were not the hands he'd seen only a couple of hours earlier on

the terrace, the hands Libby had taken such care to conceal. There was no gnarl or awryness, no clawlike rigor, none of that. The fingers of these hands were perfectly straight, ideally tapered, and how lithe they were, despite their age. The yet-lovely pampered hands of an older woman.

Springer was bewildered. The first explanation that occurred to him was that Libby had hoaxed him on the terrace. Perhaps she was a perverse practical joker and the deformed, arthritic hands he'd seen had been only a pair of ugly gloves made of the same fleshlike material as Halloween monster faces.

It didn't wash. Not only wasn't Libby the type, Springer was certain of what he'd seen, including her self-conscious pique.

He watched her now take up her glass, hold it between her thumb and second finger, and spin its delicate stem. How could those be the hands that hadn't been able to manage a cigarette?

The only other explanation was one that increased Springer's bewilderment. It would also explain why Audrey had been so insistent on coming here—with the stone—and why, ever since she'd come down to dinner, she'd been grinning like a cat with mice under both front paws. He hadn't had a chance to talk to her. She'd come skipping down the main staircase, given him what he had interpreted as a peck of encouragement, and taken him by the arm into dinner. During those two hours she'd been away somewhere with Libby, it was assumed by Springer that she was working wonders only to the extent of making points in his favor. It now seemed apparent that much more had ensued.

The stone.

No.

Although the evidence was right there being flaunted by Libby's transformed hands, Springer could not easily accept anything so incredible. It went against his rational grain, was asking even more of him than the damn pendulum stuff. But then, Springer thought, what about Joel Zimmer, the way he, the expert of all the GIA experts, had been baffled by the stone? That also couldn't be ignored. No matter, even if everything he was supposed to believe about the stone was true, it was going to take a lot of sinking in.

The Righting of Libby's hands.

It had begun the instant Audrey had put the stone inside her sleeping glove. At once, an energy extraordinary and unobservable had emanated from the stone and flowed throughout Libby's body, just as it had with Janet. According to the divine schema that was its influence, it sought out whatever discrepancies there were in Libby's system and found the osteoarthritis in her hands.

The metacarpals, the five shaftlike bones within the flat of each of her hands, were severely affected. Especially at her knuckles where those bones worked in conjunction with the phalanges, the bones of her fingers. There was boney build-up at nearly every joint. Some joints were worse than others in that regard, the joint cavities necessary for movement spurred or bound with the rigid substance. As a result, cartilage was worn away and her ligaments were no longer supple. Also, the synovial membranes, the thin, saclike layer of tissues that encased the joints from bone to bone, were ruptured in some places or thickened, and the fluid normally secreted by those membranes to keep the joints lubricated was inadequate.

During the Righting of Libby's hands the circulation of blood through the arteries and veins of her arms was markedly increased. At the same time the large multinuclear cells known as osteoclasts proliferated in the areas of her hands. They were being asked to work thousands of times more swiftly than they normally did in disintegrating and absorbing the bony buildup.

The osteoclasts got busy. The interfering bone tissue in and around each joint was broken down into minute particles. Like conveying vessels, the osteoclasts carried the particles off into Libby's bloodstream to be processed as waste material.

Within an hour the spacings between the joints were clear.

Next came a supply of chondrogen, the substance that is the basis for cartilage. It was needed for the making of fresh cartilage cells.

The cells were made.

They accumulated rapidly, formed into ranks like eager soldiers, and created the fibrous tissue that was only one twenty-four-thousandth of an inch thick. The tissue attached itself properly from bone to bone across the joint.

Libby's ligaments, in turn, were similarly repaired, their fibers rearranged so they were parallel or interlaced as they should have been. Pliancy and flexibility returned, and her ligaments were once again a healthy, shiny, silverish color.

It was time then for white tissue cells composed of the protein collagen to bundle together. They arranged their four-sided shapes into single-file rows. Each cell was connected to the next by a cementing substance. Thus bonded, they became the delicate synovial membrane that wrapped each joint like a well-sealed package.

As soon as the joints were perfectly sealed, the membranes began their secreting of the synovial fluid that diminished friction, served as a permanent lubricant, and reestablished normal articulation within Libby's joints.

Throughout the Righting, Libby experienced no sensations. There might have been some, but sleep was her anesthesia. She slept an hour longer than she'd intended.

Now at the dinner table Libby was saying, "Jacqueline de Ribes . . . there's a noble nose for you. And how noble of her to go around profiling it as she does. Wouldn't you agree?" She put the question to Springer.

"Everything you say is true," he told her.

Libby placed her hand lightly on his shoulder. "Am I being too much of a bore?"

He got a whiff of her perfume, decided if she could charm he could charm. He smiled his best smile. "That's a very effective perfume you're wearing."

"I'm pleased that you like it." She offered him the inside of her wrist for a sniff. "Most people don't appreciate subtle qualities. Jean Paul Guerlain personally supplies me with this fragrance."

"It has an oriental topnote."

"My, you do have a keen nose." Libby's insinuation was slight but unmissable. "In fact," she explained to everyone, "this particular perfume was the runner-up when Aimé Guerlain was creating Jicky in 1889. Can you imagine?"

"What's it called?" Townsend asked.

"It's mine," Libby replied. "Literally. Comes with a plain, tastefully understated label with M-I-N-E handprinted on it."

"Guerlain created a perfume especially for Sarah Bernhardt," Springer said. It was something he'd read and happened to recall now for ammunition.

Libby put on a pout. "I know that's true, but how could you steal my thunder like that?"

A contrite shrug from Springer.

"Pas grave." Libby smiled. Her hands were palms down on the table's edge, flanking her plate. Springer watched her fingers extend and retract, her perfectly shaped and buffed nails lightly scratching the linen cloth. He'd seen cats do that and had always thought they were reaffirming their ability to claw.

The second course was served.

A *mousse aux deux poissons.*

And then the third, to freshen the palate.

Sorbet de citron vert à l'Armagnac.

During these courses Libby remained at the helm of the conversation, steering it in various directions and always making sure Springer was on deck.

"I suppose in your business there's a great deal of thievery."

"It happens," Springer told her.

Townsend concurred.

"Nothing I detest more than a thief," Libby said, hardening her eyes. She ignored Audrey, who evidently did not entirely trust the fish mousse and was holding her pendulum above it. "I hope Dante is right about thieves, don't you?" Libby asked Springer.

"Right," he said.

"In Dante's hell thieves have no sense of self, so they're constantly changing from humans to beasts."

Springer thought that sounded like everyday life.

"People who steal try to make up for their lack of identity with things that belong to others." Libby paused for a nibble of mousse. Her tongue flicked at the underside of her fork. "A thief has nothing of his own. No matter how much he manages to steal he remains impoverished."

Wintersgill cleared his throat and contributed. "That, of course, is predicated on the belief that what we own helps us realize what we are."

"I believe," Townsend said, "only someone with a superior sense of self can own precious things without those things owning the person." He raised his chin in Libby's direction as though she exemplified this.

Springer thought how well suited the moment was for a holdup. The main course.

Noisettes de veau aux concombres et morilles. Much was made over the wine that came with it. And justifiably so. It was a Chateau d'Yquem, vintage 1858. "A favorite of Czar Alexander the Second and all the Romanovs," Libby informed them. She had, she said, come onto it in the 1950s when a White Russian emigré in Paris had reluctantly agreed to sell her two dozen cases that had been miraculously saved from the ravages of the revolution. While other White Russians fled with their gold pieces and jewels, this foresightful fellow had made off with the best of the Czar's wine cellar. "It's now worth four thousand a bottle," Libby said, lifting her glass in tribute to its contents.

Springer was dubious about the White Russian's sales pitch. He couldn't imagine anyone running for his life encumbered by such a burden. Most likely he'd only saved the labels. Springer took a sip. It was by far the finest wine that had ever passed over his tongue. It tasted like four thousand a bottle. This was the life. A hundred dollars a swallow. He glanced at Ernestine. She was making the best of it, had already emptied her glass and was being served a refill. He winked at her. She nearly smiled.

Soon enough the excellent food and, even more, the wine reached Springer. By the time he'd finished off two portions of the *Soufflée au Calvados* that was dessert he was feeling thoroughly convivial, viewing Libby in a more favorable light and not resenting Townsend so much.

Libby announced they'd take coffee in the small library.

That room with all its agreeable boiserie and leather bindings awaited them. The down-filled cushions on the three sofas were plumped high and smooth. The lighting was to everyone's advantage.

As soon as they were all seated espresso was served, accompanied by a very fine decanted cognac. A silver tray layered with a linen doily held precise lines of chocolate truffles.

Audrey practically attacked those.

"Do try one, Springer," Libby urged. She'd dispensed with the *Mr.* many words ago.

Springer popped one in his mouth. At once the chocolate began melting and his tongue involuntarily curled greedily around it.

Libby remarked that the truffles were made for her by a chocolatière in Vienna whose identity she kept as confidential as her sins.

"Did you know," Audrey said, "that one of the things in chocolate is . . ."—she paused to get the syllables in order—"phen-yl-thy-la-mine . . . which in the brain is connected with the emotion of loving?"

"Love*making?*" Libby asked.

"Can there be one without the other?" Audrey said archly.

"That being the case . . ." Libby took up three truffles. She ate one and with a flourish extended one to Ernestine, whose mouth opened as though remotely controlled. Before Ernestine could swallow Libby fed her the third truffle and gave her right cheek a couple of *good girl* pats.

Townsend and Wintersgill were restrainedly amused.

There was a lapse in the conversation.

Into it Libby put: "Springer has a most unusual stone. Perhaps with a little persuasion he'll show it to us."

"What kind of stone?"

"You'll see," Libby promised.

As far as Springer was concerned, there was no reason to be secretive about the stone. His only concern was what ridiculing comments Townsend might make. The man's fingers had held so many of the world's finest famous diamonds.

Fuck Townsend. Springer gestured to Audrey and she took the stone from her carry-all. She placed it next to Libby's espresso cup on the large glass table. Libby picked it up and handed it to Wintersgill. He looked at it briefly, grunted, and deferred to Townsend, who held the stone up to the light, squinted, and said what he saw: "Dirty diamond."

"What's so unusual about it?" Wintersgill inquired.

The lump of melting truffle in Audrey's cheek was made more pronounced by her smug smile.

Springer sighed and sipped cognac. This was all old ground to him.

Libby allowed some silence for emphasis before she replied, "It heals."

"What do you mean, heals?"

"Exactly that," said Libby.

Townsend scoffed. He glanced at the stone again. "What are you trying to pull off, another crazy thing like those copper bracelets? Remember, back a way how everyone believed wearing a copper bracelet would ward off rheumatism and all sorts of problems? Is that what you're trying to get going?" Townsend's tone shaded Springer as a small-time promoter.

Libby silenced Townsend by holding up her hand. She held up her other hand and displayed them both, gracefully. "It heals," she contended. She backed up her statement by relating in detail what had happened: her two-hour nap with the stone inside her sleeping glove, her delight when she awakened to find her hands rectified.

Wintersgill had become so used to making it a point not to notice Libby's hands that now he found it difficult to remember them as they'd been. They certainly weren't unsightly now, so some sort of transformation must have occurred.

Townsend had been more observant. He'd noticed the change in her hands right off, at the start of dinner. Those two large diamond rings had drawn his attention to them, of course. He had sold numerous expensive rings to Libby in the past before her hands became ugly. None since. In certain ways, Townsend believed, he knew Libby better than anyone else. He had developed a special sense about her, a sort of barometer that measured her receptivity, told him when her wants outweighed her resistance. It made no difference what had caused the change in her hands. Perhaps next week or next month they would be uglier than ever. What did matter was that this dirty diamond had his premier client completely convinced. He doubted that Springer had the good business sense to realize the advantage. "Interesting," Townsend commented. He placed the stone on the table, told Springer, "Why don't you drop around tomorrow and we'll talk about it."

Audrey picked up the stone, sealed it in its plastic envelope, and shoved it into Springer's jacket pocket. "It's not for sale," she said.

"Would you care for a cigar?" Libby asked Springer, signaling a servant before he'd had a chance to reply. Offered in a sterling replica of a cigar box were Monte Cristo Habanas, the finest from Cuba by way of London. They smelled better unlighted, was Springer's opinion, as he, Wintersgill, and Townsend puffed up individual clouds.

The conversation hopped along from a recent auction of old masters at Sotheby's to what *we* had to do to recapture the America's Cup to the truth behind a recent Palm Beach Murder. Ernestine in her Prussian way was telling a joke that to be funny required the word *cunt* to be said. Libby came to her rescue.

"It's been ages since I've bought a piece of jewelry."

"Last week," Audrey quipped.

"I mean an important piece." Libby frowned. "I've never owned an original piece that was truly important."

Springer would have bet against that.

"Always it's some necklace that once belonged to Empress Marie-Louise or a bracelet that was made for Catherine the Great," Libby complained.

Townsend studied her for a moment, sat back confidently.

"What I want is a piece that *I'll* be remembered for, one that someday a few hundred years from now someone will buy knowing it was once mine." Libby looked to Audrey for concurrence. "That's a reasonable desire, isn't it?"

A why-not? shrug from Audrey.

"That's what I want and that's what I shall have," Libby decided.

"Describe the piece you have in mind," Townsend suggested, assuming he would be the source.

After a thought Libby said, "A necklace. Contemporary, simple. The sort of thing Bulgari might do except with diamonds only. I can't bear what so many jewelers are doing with semiprecious stones these days—with topaz and tourmaline and the like, setting them large as goose eggs as though that somehow compensates for their commonness." She turned to Springer. "Don't you agree?"

He agreed.

Libby asked him, "Could you find for me perhaps ten or a dozen diamonds that are perfectly matched?"

"What size?"

"Say, twenty-five carats each."

Springer hid the expression he thought must surely be on his face with his brandy glass. A large sip put his stomach back where it belonged. His eyes avoided Townsend.

"D color," Libby stipulated, "and flawless inside and out."

"It'll take some looking to come up with perfectly matched stones of that quality and size," Springer said.

"He'll find them," Audrey quickly assured her.

"How much would you be willing to spend for this necklace?" Springer asked.

"Ten to fifteen million. How does that sound?"

"About right," Springer said nonchalantly.

"You, Springer, will supply the diamonds, and you, Townsend, will make the piece." Libby looked to Townsend for agreement.

He managed a believable smile and said, "No problem."

Springer knew Libby was throwing Townsend a bone. Most of the profit would be in the diamonds, the headaches would be in the design and the mounting.

"No objections from the Foundation, I take it," Libby said to Wintersgill, who bulldogged his lips to convey it was a minor matter and shook his head no.

Springer was already wondering how he was going to finance such an order. He didn't have that kind of capital or credit. He was no Townsend.

As though reading his concern Libby told him, "Although this is more or less in the family and trust is not a question, to help smooth the way Wintersgill will arrange with one of our banks for a letter of credit for up to fifteen million. You may draw from it as you need."

Wintersgill said he would take care of that tomorrow. He jotted it down on a little pad that he took from his inside jacket pocket, as though fifteen-million-dollar expenditures were so commonplace they required such reminding.

Springer thanked Libby.

"No," she said, holding up her hands, admiring them and smiling softly. "Thank *you.*"

Springer and Audrey said their good nights and departed for the city at eleven thirty.

Townsend left shortly thereafter. He left alone.

As soon as Townsend was gone, Libby and Wintersgill went upstairs.

The young woman, Ernestine, did exactly as she'd been instructed. She remained in the ground floor reception for fifteen minutes before going up, to that extent hyphenating the evening and making this part of it seem more voluntary.

Ernestine's shoes made subtle gritty sounds on the stairs. She'd been told not to try to be quiet; in fact, to exaggerate each step. So, when she reached the upper landing and proceeded along it, the clicking of her high heels was cadent, the stride of a woman not to be denied her destination. All the way down the landing to the wide hallway of a wing: she counted off four doors on the left.

She entered.

The room was large, with a high ceiling, done romantically in pale brocades and gilt. It was strategically lighted so there would be no hard edges or obvious realities: a flattering magenta tint. The bed had no spread or top sheet on it. Its pale linen covering was fitted, stretched so tight it appeared a surface incapable of being disturbed.

Wintersgill was on the far side of the bed. He was nude, standing stock still. Ernestine did not acknowledge him. Her eyes gave him no more than they gave the furnishings. She moved apparently aimlessly about the room, though actually it was a bit choreographed. Pausing to study a Degas, running her hand over the flower heads carved on the crest of the backrest of a Louis Quinze fauteuil, touching, as though mildly interested in, the hard intricate ormulu mount on the corner of a commode.

She had been told not to hurry. To allow the setting to accept her. She lighted a cigarette and sat at a mirrored dressing table. Studied her reflection, was successful as she could be in conveying the impression that she truly appreciated herself. The minuscule gold flecks on her eyelids shimmered.

A nearly imperceptible ringing sound was heard. It faded.

Ernestine undressed. As though she were alone and impatient to be free of her clothes, she took off everything except her shoes. She had a long body, thin but not unsubstantial. Only the studs of her hipbones were a bit too pronounced. Her navel looked like a vertical knife puncture. Her breasts were circular rises not full enough for even slight pendancy. Aroused-looking nipples.

She stood with most of her weight on one leg, making her buttocks asymmetrical, a widened space between her thighs. As though mindless of what her hands were doing she reached down and tugged at her pubic hair, left and right of herself. It seemed a secondary consideration that she went over to Wintersgill.

She stood off from him a way and looked him up and down, walked around him, examined him. He remained unmoved. It was up to her how she would arouse him. She would not, she told herself, get caught up in it. No matter what. She cared nothing for this man. He was to her as much of an object as he was pretending to be. The money when it was over was the only thing. She would keep the money in mind when she did anything.

She took his genitals in her hands, as though her hands were a serving bowl, lifted the flaccid mass and was a bit suprised by their weight. She squeezed them gently and every so often purposely let them know one or the other of her fingernails. He didn't respond.

She would, she told herself, have to suck him. Men always wanted her to suck them because of her full lips. She believed she was good at it and she usually enjoyed doing it, except when a man was large. And this one would be extremely large when he was hard. She had no choice.

She knelt, made sure of her position, and began. She expected that he would enlarge in her mouth, but he stayed the same. No matter what oral tricks she resorted to, he stayed the same. It was embarrassing for her. It angered her. She persisted, until . . .

Again, for a moment, there was that resonant ringing sound.

Ernestine wondered what she should do next. Should she masturbate? Should she go to the end of the bed and spread her legs and do herself? That seemed so obvious. These were complex people. No mere fingering, writhing, and moaning would satisfy them.

She sat on the side of the bed only to be off her feet. She crossed one leg over the other and bobbed her foot nervously. Let him think up something, she decided.

Again that resonant ringing sound.

Wintersgill came over to her, stood close before her, presenting his genitals to her.

Ernestine's hand lashed out at them.

Caught them with a sharp slap.

Struck them with two more slaps.

She was surprised by how swiftly he hardened. She was both infatuated and frightened by his enormousness.

On the wall opposite the foot of the bed was a recess flanked by silk brocade portieres. It accommodated a Régence daybed. The recess was in shadow. It was impossible to see Libby. She was fully clothed, seated on the daybed with her legs drawn up under her. The wine goblet in her hand was nearly empty. She had sipped some and spilled some, neither out of excitement.

It was boring for Libby tonight. She felt removed, unable to concentrate and use it. And this after she'd saved herself erotically for two whole weeks.

Wintersgill wasn't the problem. Nor could the girl be blamed. The girl was everything Townsend had said she would be. Actually, that cock-slapping business of hers was rather fresh.

Libby yawned.

She considered lying down, possibly curling up on her side with her back turned to them. Instead, she decided she would wait until Wintersgill put his cock into the girl. During the commotion that would cause, it would be easy for her to leave unnoticed. They would be players without an audience. Now, that *was* an entertaining thought.

Libby lifted her wine goblet, signaled them to get on with it by flicking her fingernail against its delicate, ringing rim.

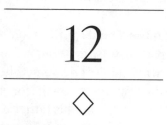

12

The rest of that week went by swiftly for Springer. He sailed through it as though levitated.

He pridefully informed Mal of the big chunk of business he'd picked up from Libby. Never had Springer & Springer gotten a single order of such magnitude. In one swoop four times as much as the firm did over a normal year.

Springer figured the dozen twenty-five-carat stones Libby wanted would each cost anywhere from eight hundred thousand to a million two. Say a million, on average, twelve million altogether. That would leave three million, out of which Townsend would get his expenses and charges for the setting. How much could Townsend charge? A hundred thousand would be exorbitant, more than that unjustifiable. Thus, Springer & Springer stood to make close to three million on the deal. All those zeros kept going off like explosions in Springer's head.

How sudden the change, he thought. From the dregs of Seggerman to the quintessence of Libby in the same day. And to think he'd been avoiding meeting Libby all these many months. Her largesse notwithstanding, he still wasn't sure which Libby he should believe— the slasher or the charmer. He wasn't vain or foolish enough to accept that his winning ways had brought about the difference in her, as Audrey contended. Libby hadn't begun merely dubious of him and been won over. The lady might well be as engaging and hospitable and generous as she'd turned out to be, but Springer felt sure that between the slasher and the charmer was . . . the stone.

He owed the stone.

He sat alone in his office Tuesday afternoon with it the only thing on his white sorting pad. It was, he thought, so damn inanimate. If it was so remarkable why didn't it do something, give him a sign of some sort, perhaps roll over on its own, not just lie there? He reviewed what he knew about it, what his father had chosen to tell him as one of his indoctrinating stories:

In February of 1958 Edwin Springer had, as he regularly did, attended the sights of the Consolidated Selling System in London. At his appointed time he showed up at 11 Harrowhouse Street and received his box of rough diamonds. Edwin was informed beforehand of the price The System had placed on his box. Two hundred and ten thousand dollars, a formidable sum for those days.

The amount delighted Edwin. He took it to mean he was to be more favorably treated by The System. Up until then the value of his boxes had never been more than a hundred to a hundred and fifty thousand. Evidently, The System had decided to allot him more goods or better goods or possibly both.

He broke The System's hardened wax seal, undid its blue grosgrain ribbon, and opened the box. In it was the same sort of medium-to-good grade material in approximately the amount he was accustomed to getting. The only additional thing was a piece of rough that weighed 56.41 carats, for which he was being charged one thousand dollars a carat.

Edwin looked into the stone with his loupe, realized immediately that it was rife with internal inclusions. He'd be lucky if even a few clean half-caraters could be cut out of it. He knew better than to protest. He paid up without a word.

The reason Edwin received such treatment became known to him shortly thereafter in a roundabout way and, assumedly, only because The System wanted him to know. It seemed that while in London for the previous January sight Edwin had sat at a table in the lounge of the Savoy for a drink with a fellow diamantaire, a mere acquaintance who openly expressed criticism of the obdurate way The System conducted business. Edwin had listened and made no comment, but his silence was overheard. The 56.41-carat piece of dreadful rough at a thousand a carat was his penalty for not having spoken up in defense of The System.

Edwin considered chucking the stone down the gutter drain opening outside the Savoy. On second thought he kept it. He kept it on his dresser at home in a shallow silver dish that also held his collar stays, shirt studs, and cuff links. Where, each morning when he dressed to go downtown to the office, he would see it and be reminded of what a dirty business he was in. That was why he called it his reminder stone. It remained in that silver dish for twenty-two years, until Edwin died. And even for several years after that when it was in Janet's possession.

And now there it was, Springer thought, gazing at it: not a diamond at all according to Joel Zimmer.

To bear out his recollections regarding the stone, Springer had Linda go into the old ledgers. Edwin Springer, like most diamond dealers, did much business off and around the books, but it was to the firm's advantage to record a transaction such as this. It was an expenditure, a considerable one that could be honestly carried forward as inventory.

To search that far back Linda had to go into the sealed cartons that were stored in a special room in the basement of the 580 Fifth Building. Fortunately the records were in chronological order. She pulled out the page that showed that particular bookkeeping entry and, as well, The System's invoice.

The stone was referred to as a separate lot: 588.

That was The System's method of numbering. It meant the stone had been sold from its inventory in 1958 and it was the eighth such lot.

Stone 588.

Blessing in disguise, Springer thought.

Despite his sitting there challenging the stone to prove itself in any supernatural way, Springer's attitude toward it had changed considerably. He was not swayed, at least not entirely, by the possibility that he was about to benefit because of it. The claims that Janet had made for the stone, and then Libby, had him really leaning. He realized now that he had experienced Janet's healed mind just as he had experienced Libby's healed hands.

Still, there might be room for a medical explanation.

He phoned Norman in Washington, intending to tell him about it, but he knew as soon as Norman was on the line it wasn't something for long distance.

"I'll be down there this weekend," Springer said.

"Business?"

"I need your professional smarts."

"Something to do with your health?"

"No."

"Money?"

"No."

"This isn't a good weekend for me."

Norman sounded more harried than usual.

"I'll only need a couple of hours, Norm, maybe less."

"Don't be so fucking mysterious."

Springer almost told him he hadn't heard anything yet. "You'll understand when I talk to you."

"Coming with Audrey?"

"And Jake."

Wednesday morning, true to Libby's word, Springer received written notification from the United States Trust Company of New York that an account had been opened on his behalf. Would he please accommodate the bank by dropping by at his earliest convenience to attend to some minor details?

Springer was there within a half hour: At 11 West 54th Street.

It was not an ordinary bank. It occupied a six-story Georgian-style townhouse designed in 1896 by Stanford White. No counter here. No slow-motion apathetic tellers. No hardhats or beehives or leather jackets standing in line. Instead, a prevailing quietness that assured the sort of confident efficiency needed for the personal tending of numerous millions. Oak-paneled walls, Sarouk oriental rugs, period antique furnishings.

Springer assumed the computers were somewhere out of sight and hearing range. The banker who served him, a Mr. Leeds, shook his hand with precise firmness. Mr. Leeds sat behind a mahogany knee-hole desk and made it seem that Springer was doing him a favor by filling out a signature card. He explained in a voice as soft as his silk Dunhill necktie that Springer could draw on the account immediately if he so wished. Up to fifteen million. For some reason, in this place and the way Mr. Leeds said it, it didn't sound like so much. Springer helped himself to a couple of the foil-wrapped chocolate-covered mint wafers that were on a footed sterling dish on the corner of Mr. Leeds's desk. Altogether, while there, Springer said only about ten words, one of which was "thanks."

The following day Springer got a call from London. Though an excellent connection, it did not immediately register that the voice on the calling end belonged to the elderly diamantaire from whom he'd bought the Russian melee. Arthur Drumgold.

"I've some money for you," Drumgold said.

"That's a great opener." Springer reached for his memorandum ledger. He paged through and found the outstanding memo signed by Drumgold acknowledging consigment of four stones, altogether 9.52 carats at $48,100.

"I was wondering how and where you preferred to receive payment," Drumgold said, "cash, cashier's check here or there, or what?"

"I guess you did well with those goods."

"Anyone could have."

"How's that?"

"Do you have your memo there?"

"Right in front of me."

"All right then, first there's the matter of the forty-eight thousand one hundred outstanding. On top of that you've twenty-three thousand eight hundred coming."

"All you owe me is forty-eight thousand one," Springer said.

"And twenty-three thousand eight, which sums to seventy-one thousand nine. I believe that's correct."

"I don't know where you're getting the twenty-three thousand eight."

"I've got it. Those four stones went as a lot for ninety-five thousand seven hundred."

Springer was scribbling the figures on his sorting pad. He realized the $23,800 was a half split of Drumgold's profit. "Oh, no, you don't," Springer said.

"Oh, yes, I do. You know damn well you undercharged me for those goods, probably let me have them at your cost."

Denying that would be insulting Drumgold's intelligence, Springer decided.

"So, how do you want your money? Cash would be no problem."

"Hold it for me," Springer told him. "I'll pick it up when I get to London."

"When will that be?"

"Next week. Wednesday."

"Where will you be stopping?"

"The Connaught." That choice was a compromise, rather than the Savoy or Libby's Chester Terrace townhouse.

"I'll ring you up there. Be nice to see you again. You're coming for the sights, I assume."

"But not only for that reason." Springer and Mal had agreed that Springer might as well attend to the sight on his way to Antwerp, where he hoped to locate the diamonds for Libby.

"Well," Drumgold said, "if I can in any way be of help to you, don't hesitate."

It struck Springer like a hunch. The favorable way things had been going he had to follow it. "Do you know of anyone who wants to sell some particularly fine goods?"

"To what extent fine?"

"D-flawless."

"Investment goods are what you're after, I suppose. One- and two-caraters. Not much of that around anymore, since The System decided to be stingy with it." In the late seventies, when most currencies were unstable, investors bought large amounts of D-flawless diamonds of one and two carats, the most easily salable sizes. The investors stashed those diamonds away at such a rate The System had misgivings. It foresaw a time when those top-grade goods would come pouring back onto the market and raise hell with its price structure. To prevent such a possibility, it began holding back on D-flawless material.

"No," Springer told Drumgold, "I'm looking for stones in the twenty-five-carat range."

"Would you mind repeating that?"

Springer repeated it.

"Cut goods, twenty-five-carat D-flawless?"

"Yeah."

"Not exactly what most people peddle around, is it?" Drumgold commented, amused.

"I need twelve stones."

"Do you now?" Wryly.

"All twelve must be identical, perfectly matched."

"What shape?"

"All rounds or all cushions."

"You're bloody serious, aren't you?" Drumgold said, incredulous.

Calmly, Springer told him, "It occurred to me that with your many connections—"

"Have you considered Russian goods?"

"Not really," Springer fibbed.

"That would be your best bet, I believe. You know, of course, you're talking about an enormous amount of money."

"Isn't that the beauty of it?"

"Quite."

A long, silent moment over the 3,471 miles. Springer could practically hear the old boy's blood racing. "Naturally," Springer said, "if you can help on this there'll be a commission."

"Pardon?"

"I was saying there'd be a commission."

"I was thinking of how best to go about obtaining Russian goods of that size."

"What are the chances?"

"Numerous." Implying risky.

"Regarding the commission, how does two hundred thousand sound?"

"Dollars?"

"Dollars."

"Make it two hundred thousand and one," Drumgold said.

"Why?"

"So I can say I haggled."

13

◇

The following Saturday was a rainy one in Washington, D.C. Not an on-and-off rain but a steady, fine drizzle with no sign of letting up. It intensified the color of the grass along the Mall, polished the cars and the black-topped streets, and subdued the mainly white government buildings. All the American flags hung lank.

Springer, Audrey, and Jake hadn't come prepared for rain but they weren't about to let it handicap their day. Instead of running from it as though it might melt them, they welcomed it. A nice friendly summer rain was what it was. Springer bought a huge black umbrella at a men's store near the hotel, and off they went: down 15th Street past the White House to the Washington Monument. After having gone only that short distance, their clothes were soaked and stuck to them and their feet were squishing in their shoes and the umbrella wasn't really doing much good. They voted unanimously against going up the obelisk, just stood at its base and looked up, squinting as the rain struck their faces.

Jake felt he was too old to go piggyback, but when Springer squatted and offered his shoulders, Jake climbed aboard. With Audrey hugging Springer's arm and Jake riding high holding the umbrella they had a good time singing a Streisand song and strolling along like three rain-loving crazies across the open grass to the Lincoln Memorial.

"What do you think?" Springer asked Jake as they stood at the bottom of the steps taking in the huge statue of Lincoln.

"He was a great president, huh?"

"Sure was."

Jake studied the statue—reverently, Springer thought, until Jake said, "He looks to me like a guy sitting on his porch moping because he's got to go mow the lawn."

Springer would have stifled his laugh if Jake hadn't been so right. The brooding Abe with his hands placed tentatively on the arms of his chair. Probably it would have amused him, Springer thought.

"Out of the mouths of," Audrey said cryptically.

"I'm no babe," Jake contended.

"He's too fast for us," Springer said proudly.

They walked back the way they'd come, continued on along the south side of the Mall, passed up the old Smithsonian Castle, and entered the National Air and Space Museum. Jake was interested in the moon rock, the rockets, and the space capsule but much more in Lindbergh's plane, the *Spirit of St. Louis,* that was suspended from the ceiling as though in flight. Jake stood at the railing of the second-floor balcony where he was eye level with the plane, as close to it as he could get. He read aloud word for word the glass-enclosed caption and had Springer lift him so he could see better into the cockpit. It was as though he understood and could easily accept the existence and functions of the rockets and other space things, but this vulnerable little plane astounded him.

From there they crossed the Mall to the National Gallery, where they were subjected to visual overnourishment. While appreciating a Gauguin, for example, they were unable to keep their eyes from hurrying to its neighboring Monet. Neither Jake nor his attention wandered off, and Springer thought that outstanding for an eight-year-old. He had a fleeting fatherly projection of a future Jake as a successful artist.

They took the underground passageway to the Annex and went up to the restaurant there. Were lucky enough to get a table that offered an overview of the main gallery area. They appreciated how innovatively the architect had arranged the various open levels and steps. A huge Calder mobile hovered like a colorful insect.

Audrey ordered a bacon cheeseburger, a Coke, a slice of black-bottom pie and a slice of peach pie à la mode, vanilla please. Jake said he'd just have the same. Springer shot Audrey a look. She smiled contritely and told the waitress to bring the Cokes immediately, they were thirsty. Springer was torn between the beef-stew luncheon special and the scallops. Over his menu he glanced at Jake and made up his mind. "We'll all have the same," he said.

By the time they were into the desserts it was three thirty. Springer was to meet Norman at four. He'd see Audrey and Jake back at the hotel. He got a black-bottom-flavored kiss from each of them and left them the umbrella.

He arrived at Norman's office at 21st and L street five minutes early. There was no one in the waiting room. The nurse receptionist buzzed him in and led the way. The place smelled medical. Norman was out from around his desk and coming at him when Springer entered the room. They hugged man hugs instead of handshakes. Norman was in shirt sleeves. He told the nurse to bring coffee. He sat in one of the leather armchairs his patients usually occupied, so there was no obstacle between him and Springer, who sat on the matching leather-upholstered Chesterfield sofa. Norman appeared genuinely happy to see his brother, although his smile was a bit strained. When they were settled and through the preliminary small talk, Norman asked, "Now, what's this all about?"

It took about twenty minutes for Springer to tell him about stone 588, including a rundown on Joel Zimmer's analysis. Norman didn't once interrupt, just listened with his interest focused the way he did when he was hearing out a patient. Springer expected Norman might break into a laugh or, at least, a knowing grin.

Of course he remembered their father's reminder stone. Had Springer brought it along?

Springer handed it to him.

Norman rolled it between his fingers, looked at it thoughtfully. "What's Janet doing now?" he asked.

"She's cramming," Springer replied. "Taking an accelerated course for her high school diploma. That way she'll finish the couple of years she missed in just a few months. She wants to go to Princeton and be a physicist."

"Looking that far ahead, huh?"

"She's convinced physics and metaphysics are converging."

Norman glanced at his watch.

That miffed Springer a bit. From what Norman had said he had anticipated a jammed waiting room. The nurse receptionist brought the coffee, two heavy hospital-style mugs of steaming black. She placed Springer's on the side table next to a life-size human heart encased in a cube of clear plastic. Macabre, Springer thought. "That real?" he asked.

Norman smiled. "Possibly. A representative of one of the drug companies gave it to me for Christmas."

"How's your number-one patient?"

"Who?"

"The current father of our country."

"Oh, fine. Couldn't be fitter." Norman took a sip of his coffee, scalded his lips. He appeared nervous. Unmindfully, he tossed the stone from one hand to another. "The idea of precious stones being able to heal or protect people has been around for ages," he said. "The Egyptians, Greeks, Romans, Jews, Christians—what-have-you —all put a lot of stock in their various amulets. In fact, no less a man than Aristotle credited certain precious stones with the ability to cure. So did Theophrastus, St. Hildegard, Bishop Marbode, and a lot of others."

Springer had never heard of those three fellows.

Norman went on. "The emerald, for example, was supposed to

offset lasciviousness, which may be why it wasn't so popular with a lot of people. It also shooed away demons, strengthened the memory, and made an emerald owner good at arguing. Rubies were the thing for syphilis. And sapphires were useful against scorpion and snake bites." Norman paused to measure Springer's interest. Assuming he had it, he continued. "Did you know, when a diamond was held in the mouth of a liar it helped him speak the truth? A topaz would neutralize any liquid that had poison in it, and a pearl tucked in the ear would get rid of a headache. Pericles . . . you've heard of Pericles."

"Yeah."

"Smart fellow he was. Wore a piece of rose rock crystal around his neck to keep him from getting sick."

"Did it work?"

"He died in his prime of the plague."

"I can only go by what I saw," Springer said. "And I'm positive of what I saw. Libby's hands—"

"Imagine, if you can, how many incredible things *I've* experienced over my years in medicine. People dead—I mean getting cold, rigor-stiffening *dead*—coming back to life as though they'd been pushed back, refused. Hopeless cases, incurables left to die, doing a sudden turnaround, rallying, and eventually walking away from their death-beds."

"Are you saying you believe it's possible that the stone—"

"Wouldn't that be something if it were true! A real first-class wish, that." Norman fisted the stone and underscored his conviction with the fist, although he spoke calmly, recitatively. "It is my belief, dear brother, that in every such instance there is a scientific explanation. Elusive at the moment, perhaps, but nevertheless there. The medical miracles of a hundred years ago—hell, fifty years ago—are today's common practices." He scratched the side of his nose and shifted verbal gears. "You know, Phil, autosuggestion can be a powerful influence."

"I haven't got that much imagination."

"There was a doctor in Boston that I knew. He used to chase ambulances to accidents. If he got to the victims while they were still conscious he'd use hypnosis to keep them from going into shock. Saved a lot of lives."

"I was not hypnotized by myself or anyone," Springer insisted.

Norman sat forward. "Okay. I believe you. I believe in the power of this stone. Now, does that make a difference? You came here wanting a logical explanation, I've given you one, and you don't want to accept it."

Springer felt like a man with two pieces of rope not long enough to be tied together.

"In the sixteenth century," Norman said, "when Pope Clement the seventh was sick his doctors gave him powders made from various precious stones. Over a period of two weeks or so, they had him ingest a fortune in diamonds. Which is probably what killed him."

How do you know so much about the subject?"

"When I was at Cornell I exercised my Latin by reading a book about the origins and virtues of gems called *Specimen de Gemmarum,* as compiled by an Englishman named Robert Boyles in the seventeenth century. Big thick book, entirely in Latin. I've been interested ever since. No offense meant, but it helps remind me how gullible people are."

"Did you know for years Dad took some kind of ground-up emerald concoction for upset stomach?"

"No shit?"

"Mattie told me."

A knowing grin from Norman. "Mattie believes in anything she can't see."

Springer's coffee was cold. He drank some anyway.

"How's Jake liking D.C.?" Norman asked.

"Okay, I guess."

"I've depressed you."

Springer didn't deny that. Now he wished he'd just gone on being close to convinced of stone 588, not come to Washington.

"Tell you what," Norman said offhandedly. "Let me keep this thing overnight. See if I get a different impression." Before Springer could consent, Norman had dropped the stone into his shirt pocket.

* * *

When Springer got back to the suite at the Madison he found Audrey and Jake lying on the floor with their bare feet up, digging into a carton of Cheese Tid-Bits and watching MTV. They stayed as they were but invited hello kisses, which Springer knelt to deliver. They'd both bathed and changed. The skin of their feet, Springer noticed, was still pale and puckered from having been wet all day.

"We saw where they print money," Jake said.

"Really?"

"They were only printing ones. They only print ones when people are looking. A guy there told me they print the hundreds at night."

The suite consisted of a sitting room between two bedrooms with baths. Springer's and Jake's things were in the bedroom that had twin beds. Springer went in, removed his wet clothes, and took a warm shower. The shower felt good, but drying off felt better. He put on a pair of jeans and went out to the sitting room, flopped down on the sofa, and read some of the *Washington Post,* mainly the classified ads. It was Springer's theory that the way to get to know what a city was really like was to imagine your way through the help wanteds, lost and founds, personals, and real estate ads.

They had a room-service dinner that smelled and tasted like a room-service dinner, and, of course, they ordered too much. Jake helped push the dining table and leftovers out into the hall. Then Audrey watched while Jake and Springer played gin rummy with a deck of Eastern Airline cards. Springer threw away gin hands to let Jake win but he was very careful about it. Jake was a much better than average gin player for his age. Springer had no idea Jake was breaking up gin hands trying to let him win. Only Audrey, the kibitzer, knew. She loved them both for it.

Time for bed.

Springer and Jake went into their room. Springer didn't get under the covers, said he wanted to read awhile: a paperback edition of an Elmore Leonard novel, fast and tough.

From the other bed, Jake said, "That was a lousy dinner."

"Sure was."

"Better than having sushi, though."

"Thought you liked sushi."

"Enough is enough."

Was he talking about Japanese food or Gayle? Springer wondered. The mother gets custody, the father gets to have a visitor. That in Springer's opinion could only be a fair decision half the time.

Jake raised his right leg and massaged it vigorously just above the knee.

"Got a cramp?" Springer asked.

"Something."

"We walked a lot today."

"The doctor mom took me to said I've got growing pains."

Growing pains, Springer thought, Gayle has been having those all her life.

"The guys in the park say I'm the best digger," Jake said. A digger in volleyball is one who goes after the hard downward smashes of the ball, tries to get his hands under it before it touches the ground. Often it requires a self-sacrificing elbow-scraping dive.

"What about your spiking?" Springer asked.

"Not so hot, not tall enough."

You will be."

"Think we'll every go play again with Mr. Malo and Mr. Bueno?"

Springer promised they would. Malo and Bueno were not the real names of two exceptional volleyball players, Brazilians who hung out up in Highbridge Park. Some of the best volleyball in the city was played up there. When Springer felt the need for a challenge and a serious workout, that was where he went.

"You're as good as Malo and Bueno," Jake said.

"No, I'm not."

"Almost."

"Thanks."

"You think I'm scared, don't you?" Jake said.

"What makes you say that?"

"I mean you don't think I can sleep in here alone."

"It's not that."

"I thought I was going to have my own room."

Springer was sure he was being manipulated. He pretended to be absorbed in the Elmore Leonard. Nothing more from Jake. Apparently he'd dropped off to sleep. It had been a long day with the flight down and all the traipsing around. After half an hour Springer clicked off the light and got up, quietly. When he was going out, Jake told him, "Shut the door."

Springer went in to Audrey. "I got thrown out," he said, as she surrendered one of the pillows and propped it for him. She had only a sheet half over her. Springer took off his jeans and climbed under next to her. His hip scraped something crinkly. "What the hell is that?"

"My malt balls," she said matter-of-factly, retrieving the brown paper bag of candy and placing it on her bedside table. Close to the foot of the bed the television was on: a Fred Astaire with the volume so faint the songs and dialogue couldn't be made out, only the taps.

"I forgot to tell you," Audrey said. "Libby invited us up to Penobscot next week."

"Can't."

"I know. I told her."

"Was she upset?"

"Only disappointed. She adores you."

"Who doesn't?"

Audrey gave him an elbow poke and then a conciliatory malt ball.

"Who exactly is Wintersgill?" he asked.

"I told you. He's the Director of the Hopkins-Hull Foundation. He okays everything."

"Does he ever not okay something?"

"If Libby wants him to."

"What's his background?"

"Old money—or, rather, old *depleted* money. His ancestors were among the original Dutch settlers. They once owned half of New York and a third of Pennsylvania. Now about all Wintersgill has is a fairly impressive apartment on East Sixty-eighth. And the name, of course. For fifteen years he's been trying to persuade Libby to marry him."

"She ever been married?"

"Once. For a few months when she was twenty. To a Polish count. She brags the marriage cost her half a million dollars a week and even more per orgasm. Her words, not mine."

"Why won't she marry Wintersgill?"

"Why should she? She already has all the benefits of him and none of the inconveniences."

"You might say that of me."

"My ears have never once heard you mention marriage."

"Perhaps I'm afraid you might run."

"To or from?"

"I love you," he told her.

"I know."

A brief kiss was taken and given for further reassurance.

Astaire was flipping his cane around and his tails were centrifuging.

"Libby is not my real aunt, you know," Audrey said.

Springer had asked Audrey about her family but she'd always parried the subject.

"I'm adopted," she said.

"Someone left you on Libby's doorstep."

"You might say that."

Springer, considerately, backed off. It was up to Audrey to reveal more or not. Following some pondering silence she told him, "My mother was Libby's personal secretary: one of those I-must-go-where-you-go sorts. Her name was Gillian Croft. Pretty name, don't you think?"

"Very."

"As I understand it, she was extremely bright and beautiful and well paid. She and Libby were quite close. For one thing, neither she nor Libby had any family still living, and I suppose to a great extent that influenced the attachment. They raised a lot of hell, among other things, all around the world. As Libby puts it, 'We scorched the south of France and the north Long Island shore and melted most of the Swiss, French, and Italian Alps.' "

"Anyway, my mother became pregnant and for whatever reason waited too long to do anything about it. She never told Libby who the father was, just wouldn't. Perhaps because, as Libby contends, it was someone highly social who was already married. They were carrying on wildly in Palm Springs around that time. Closer to the truth, I believe, is my mother simply couldn't be sure whom to point her tummy at.

"No matter, Libby stuck by her. My mother had me. She died having me. She's buried in Greenwich in the Hopkins-Hull Crypt. I go there every so often and think how much her presence must perturb those bluenoses lying around her."

"Does it sadden you to talk about her?" Springer asked.

"Not really. Perhaps that sounds callous, but I never knew Gillian Croft, never grieved over her. To me she's just a name, an image in some snapshots Libby showed me. As far as being illegitimate is concerned, I believe it's rather romantic. A child of passion, that's me."

She popped another malt ball into her mouth and extended her nude body to the television set. She turned up the volume for the music that Astaire was now soft-shoeing to.

The following day was a sunny one.

Not a cloud.

Springer, Audrey, and Jake spent the morning watching Ling Ling the panda sit cutely on her hairy rump and with delicate deftness peel and devour bamboo shoots. In the early afternoon they browsed Georgetown shops up Wisconsin Avenue. Several times Springer stopped at pay phones and dialed Norman's number, was told each time by an answering service voice that the doctor was not in, had not called in, and his whereabouts at the moment were not known. Springer felt it was damn thoughtless of Norman, knowing they were in town, not to leave word.

They returned to the hotel at three. Their flight reservations were for four thirty. Norman was waiting in the hotel lobby. He had arrived just moments earlier. Springer noticed immediately that Norman needed a shave, was wearing the same clothes, shirt and all, that he'd had on the day before. He took it as evidence of a tough night spent doctoring and lost his intention to come down on him.

Norman drove them to the airport. On the way he paid a lot of lighthearted-uncle-type attention to Jake and flirted with Audrey.

He was a terrible driver. For him the traffic he could see out the windshield was all that mattered. Whatever was alongside or behind was not yet to be reckoned with. He parked the car with its MD plates in an airport NO STANDING zone and went with them to the boarding gate.

There he took Springer aside and gave him the stone. "Hardly more than an ordinary pebble," he said, stressing its inconsequential-ness with an amused smile.

"For sure?"

"I thoroughly checked it out . . . on a couple of cases. Believe me, it's nothing."

Springer accepted that with a nod. He pocketed the stone and went aboard the flight. Norman waited at the window while the 727 undocked and pulled away. He searched the plane's windows for their faces, smiled, and waved in case they were seeing him.

14

From the airport Norman drove to O Street in Georgetown. The houses along there were three to five stories, red brick and white trim. Narrow older houses side against side, long ago done with their settling. It was a charming, choice area. Mid-block on the north side of the street was where Tom Longmire lived.

Longmire answered the door before Norman could ring the bell. Must have seen him coming. A longtime acquaintance, Norman closed the door after himself and took off his suit jacket as he followed Longmire up the narrow carpeted stairs to the third-floor study.

The study was in the rear of the house, its tall federal windows nearly brushed by the topmost leaves of a lacy locust. It was a small room, given character by a clutter of books and memorabilia. Framed photographs—none really personal, mostly Longmire with recognizable politicians past and present, one with Margaret

Thatcher, another with Giscard d'Estaing, a few with movie stars—hung on the walls or were propped around like spectators. The warmth that all the books and mementos should have created wasn't there. The atmosphere was transient, cool. Dust coated all but the most frequently used and obvious surfaces, giving away a slapdash housekeeper. A worthwhile mahogany table served as a bar. Its gold-tooled Moroccan-leather top was discolored by alcohol.

Norman poured himself an ample drink, peeked into the lidded brass ice bucket.

"No ice," Longmire said. "I forgot to put the trays in." He had a tall red drink in hand that appeared to be a Bloody Mary but was plain V-8 juice. He said he'd just returned from a jog along the canal, had on a gray sweat suit with a black towel wrapped around his neck. He didn't look as if he'd jogged much. If at all. The getup might have been merely to impress Norman, his doctor, who had recommended aerobic exercise.

Longmire was an Assistant Secretary of State. He had been with the Department for thirty years and doubted he'd ever go higher. Now the reward was a matter of how much importance was placed on him and, of course, from how high up the well-dones came. When he wanted he could be a very proficient scene stealer. He gave the opposite impression. An ordinary appearance was one of Longmire's stocks in trade. He was a medium person: medium height, medium weight, medium everything down to the width of his shoes. He usually wore frameless eyeglasses. For the past two years he had been assigned to make announcements to the press—when, for instance, one of America's overseas embassies had been bombed or one or more of its diplomats assassinated. Longmire didn't consciously wish anyone ill, though if there were more of that, more of the television lights and firing of questions, more opportunities to look the world right in its camera eye and say, "No further comment will be made at this time," he would have enjoyed it.

Now, ambidextrously, left fingers to left foot, right to right, he tugged loose the laces of his running shoes and paired them precisely on the floor beside his chair. "They'll probably give you a citation. Secret, of course."

A sardonic grunt from Norman. He gulped Scotch.

"At the very least, from now on you should be having dinner at the White House twice a week," Longmire said lightly. "By the way, what *was* the diagnosis?"

"Acute gastritis."

"On the record."

"That's it."

"What about the other medical records, the ones that were being kept?"

"Destroyed."

"You saw them being destroyed?"

"I handed them over to McDermott and he said they would be."

"EKGs and all?"

"Yeah."

"Every scrap?"

"Every scrap."

"What about the film?"

"I assume McDermott—"

"McDermott's reliable. But perhaps you should have shredded or burned everything yourself."

"Then *my* trustworthiness would have been questioned," Norman remarked.

"You're bitter about it, aren't you?"

Norman didn't reply. He knocked down the Scotch in his glass and went for a refill.

"Reputation is a commodity," Longmire said.

"As is pig iron." The Scotch was getting to Norman. All he'd had to eat was a pear and a few grapes about three that morning—from the bowl of fruit the President's wife had arranged.

"You save the life of someone who is not just someone and can't take credit for it. Must make you feel like shit."

"I feel like shit, but that's not the reason."

"Credit should go where's it's due."

"Exactly," Norman said ambiguously.

Longmire knew he would have felt just as embittered under the circumstances. He'd do his best to pull Norman out of this funk, be more genuinely sympathetic. He got up and clicked on the stereo player, chose a cassette at random that turned out to be Liszt's Piano Concerto No. 1 in E-flat Major. Just right, lively. He adjusted the volume so the music would be dominant over their voices. That way Norman might tire of complaining a bit sooner.

Norman was again at the bar. "No more Scotch," he said, inverting an empty bottle. He dropped it noisily into a metal wastebasket and twisted open a fresh bottle of Wild Turkey.

For the next half hour Longmire tried to counter Norman's mood with various irrelevant topics, ranging from the sexual compulsions of an elderly high-echelon French diplomat to the reminiscences of a time during the previous summer when Longmire and Norman had happily caught huge bass in the private pond of a wealthy South Carolinian. Norman offered few words to the conversation. He just sat there finishing off drink after drink. At times, he looked as though he might erupt, fling his glass through the window. At other times he seemed on the verge of tears. Longmire told himself that was the last thing he needed, a self-pitying drunk. He was expressing his inclination toward buying a getaway place on the island of St. Barts when Norman broke in.

"What a fucking travesty."

Longmire sighed and impatiently told him, "What the hell. For what it's worth, Norm, you can be sure everyone on the inside will be acknowledging your bows."

"My what?" Drunkenly rankled.

"Your curtain calls, so to speak."

"What faith are you, Longmire?"

"Printed on my T-shirts or privately?"

A loose shrug from Norman.

"Episcopalian, I believe."

"How about down in your balls?" Norman asked.

"When I get to dying I'll cover myself and be everything." Longmire thought that true and amusing enough to repeat some other time.

Norman used the under edge of his chair to remove his shoes. He kicked them aside as though they represented him. His mouth was slack, his hands floppy.

It occurred to Longmire at that moment that Norman might be strongly tempted to disclose the situation. "What do you think the chances are of the truth getting out?" he tested.

"Which truth?" Norman slurred.

"Even if there is a leak it won't make any difference. Not now. We can deny everything, can't we?"

"The funny fucking thing is I won't tell even more than you won't tell."

"Right. We're of one mind. No reason to cause any economic quakes. Do you have any idea how many points the market would have dropped tomorrow if it hadn't been for you?"

"I'm hot shit."

"When will the President be able to leave Bethesda?"

"Couple of days."

"That soon? You mean a couple of weeks."

"Day after tomorrow he'll walk the fuck out, climb into the chopper, and land ass at the White House to meet the chief Staffs of Joint like nothing happened."

Drunk talk, Longmire figured. There had to be a fairly long recuperative period.

"All our Prez had was a little upset tummy," Norman said facetiously.

"But we know better."

"I know shit." Norman made a face to go along with his self-depreciation. He snapped his head up to Longmire, asked, "You think I'm a good doctor?"

"The best."

"As they go, I suppose, as they go," Norman grumbled.

Longmire was getting bored with it. He thought he'd go down to the kitchen and make some coffee, leave Norman with the booze. Maybe by the time he came back Norman would have passed out.

"But!" Norman blurted out of his thoughts and went on. "There's one thing I could tell you that would knock you flat on your State Department ass."

That mildly alerted Longmire. "Nothing would surprise me."

"You shouldn't be so fucking smug."

"I've seen and done it all," Longmire baited him.

Norman felt as though his forehead were unfolding. Any moment his brain would eject and plop against the wall.

Longmire was an expert at baiting and drawing out. Norman, especially in his drunken condition, was no match for him.

Besides, it was merely a professional reflex reaction that had caused Norman to promise himself he would never reveal what had actually occurred. It had shaken him right down to his Hippocratic marrow, diminished his respect for the knowledge he had worked so hard to glean for so many years, belittled his methods. Once he started letting it out, it all came. Some of it Longmire already knew.

Sunday night a week ago. Norman had been called from Bethesda Naval Hospital and told to get out there on the double. The President had been brought there by chopper, was actually in the air on his way back from the weekend at Camp David when he began feeling not right. The Secret Service men on duty with the President got him into the hospital swiftly and clandestinely, and as that was often the way he went in and out of places, anyone who happened to notice did not believe it irregular. Somehow, with the Secret Service close around, supporting him, he managed to walk in. For all anyone knew he was there for one of his normal two-to-three-day physical checkups.

The President was placed in the third-floor wing that he usually occupied and tight security measures were immediately put into effect. That part of the wing was virtually sealed off from the rest of the hospital.

By the time Norman arrived three other doctors, specialists who cared for the President, had recognized the symptoms, agreed on a general diagnosis, and taken preliminary measures. They had him hooked up to an electrocardiogram and blood pressure monitor with audio and visual components, and, of course, he was receiving glucose intravenously.

The other doctors backed off. Norman took over. Norman was the heart man, and, according to the President's complaints, he was who was needed. The President informed Norman that his symptoms were worse now. It felt as if an elephant were stepping on his chest, both arms had an electrical current running down them, and he was about to vomit. He couldn't get a deep breath. Not mentioned was the fact that he was sweating profusely, had already soaked the sheets.

The symptoms were classic.

Acute myocardial infarction. Heart attack.

Norman knew by memory each phase of the President's normal electrocardiogram. The readout he now looked at was drastically changed.

Abnormal Q waves, elevated ST segments, and inverted T waves.

Blood pressure 100 over 60.

Respiration rate 20 a minute.

Norman injected intravenously 15 milligrams of morphine sulfate into the President's arm and 10,000 units of the anticoagulant sodium heparin. He put nasal cannulas on the President, inserted one into each nostril, and adjusted the flow to 5 to 6 liters per minute to allow 50 percent oxygen. This made breathing easier. The President's respiration rate dropped to 15 and steadied, and by then the morphine had eliminated much of the pain. It hadn't, however, cut the fright. The President's eyes asked Norman if he was going to die.

Norman didn't have the answer.

The danger of ventricular fibrillation and sudden death was always greatest during the first few hours. Norman went about making sure that the defibrillator, the machine used to administer electrical countershock, was in ready order. He checked its electrodes and paddles. If the President's heart went racing out of control—or stopped—countershock would be vital. Norman preset the machine at 300 watt seconds (joules) and saw that there was an ample supply of electrode paste on hand. He uncapped one of the tubes of electrode paste to save even that much time. He saw to it that syringes containing digitalis, verapamil, and quinidine were in place on a nearby tray. Also a syringe containing epinephrine—Adrenalin—in case it got to that. He had to be ready for anything.

He stood at the foot of the bed with the President's eyes upon him. He watched the variations on the electrocardiograph monitor, had, from experience, a fairly accurate idea of what was happening within the President's body. He tried to picture it exactly, and the impossibility of that reminded him, as it had numerous times before, of his limitations.

Blood was drawn.

The laboratory rushed for results.

They told Norman that the serum enzymes in the President's blood were already above normal range. Serum creatine phosphokinase was up, as was the level of serum glutamic oxaloacetic transaminase. Already elevated and they wouldn't peak for at least another 12 to 35 hours. They indicated damage to the heart muscle tissues.

How much damage up to now?

How much more to come?

It looked bad, morbid.

The only way Norman could decide what steps were best to take, even if they were futile steps, was for him to know what he was up against. He reminded himself who this patient was, but immediately his better judgment warned him not to be overcautious. If he lost the President it wouldn't matter whether he'd done too much or too little. The mark would be on him either way. That went with the territory. Worse within himself, however, would be to have done too little.

When, after three hours, the President's pain increased, Norman decided on coronary angiography.

He himself performed the procedure.

The President was strapped to a rotating x-ray tilt table. Electrocardiogram and blood pressure monitoring was connected and a direct-current defibrillator stood nearby.

An incision was made just above the bend of the President's right arm, exposing the right brachial artery. The artery was opened and into it Norman inserted an 8-French woven catheter with a special top that tapered to 5-French diameter. Steadily but carefully, feeling for any resistance, Norman fed the catheter up the artery. He was able to view this progress through an image intensifier equipped with closed-circuit television. Pressure on the catheter tip from a narrowing or closing off anywhere along the arterial walls was measured and recorded by a Statham P-23 D-G strain gauge.

Norman extended the catheter into the orifice of each coronary artery and, in turn, injected through it a 70-percent solution of Hypaque, a substance that would make the arterial courses appear opaque, thus defining them. His foot pressed the activation pedal of the 35mm motion picture camera that was connected to the optical periscope system above the table. Eastman Double X negative film recorded every phase. Norman worked the table, tilting controls, automatically changing the President's position, rotating him as much as 60 degrees one way and then the other to get both right and left anterior oblique views. The Hypaque passed into all branches of the coronary tree.

Next, Norman manipulated the catheter so it traveled across the aortic valve and into the heart itself—the left ventricle. He opacified that cavity with 40 milliliters of a 9-percent solution of Hypaque. He exposed film to cover that, withdrew the catheter, and sutured up the brachial artery and arm.

None of these procedures were new to Norman, yet when he removed his surgeon's gloves and gown he felt as though his torso was too great a burden for his legs. He hooked his thumbs into the waistband of his trousers to conceal the tremble of his hands. He drew in several deep breaths because he had been breathing shallowly for so long.

The President was returned to his bed and again hooked up to the monitors there, apparently no worse off for the risky measures he had just been put through.

There were two rooms off the one the President occupied: one for the President's wife and family, the other for the attending doctor, in this instance Norman. Norman was in his bathroom in the middle of taking a much-needed piss when McDermott walked in on him. McDermott gave no thought to the fact that Norman was cock in hand as he gave Norman chapter and verse regarding confidentiality. McDermott was the presidential Press Secretary, an appropriately agile-minded, assertive fellow in his mid-thirties. He told Norman that until there was an *eventuality,* as he put it, it had been decided that the President's condition be kept in strictest confidence. By no means should Norman respond to any questions put to him by the press. Surely, McDermott said, Norman could appreciate the sensitivity of the circumstances. The Soviets or who knew whatever bastards would very possibly take advantage during this time of weakness. Foreign policy and national security were involved. He could count on Norman, couldn't he?

A weary Norman zipped up his fly and nodded.

At dawn Norman viewed the angiographic films. They were clear, well-exposed pictures that showed beyond a doubt that the President was suffering myocardial ischemia. Portions of heart muscle were dying from a deficiency of blood caused by the narrowing of the arterial channels. Distal radicles of the President's coronary artery tree as small as 100 to 200 microns in lumen diameter were visible. Larger, major branches were easily distinguishable. Nearly all were being affected to some extent. At various points the buildup of plaque along the walls of the arteries was so severe the flow of blood was clogged. All those years of political campaign luncheons and dinners, all those occasions that were made special, calling for fancier, richer food because of the President's presence, were now being paid for.

Norman had hoped the angiography would tell him what helpful measures to take, perhaps indicate the feasibility of one or more surgical bypasses. However, the atherosclerotic problem was so widespread and segmented and had already caused so much damage that these prerogatives were not open.

Norman realized he was going to lose this patient. It could happen at any moment or a week from now. The most he could do was keep the President as comfortable as possible on his way to death.

Throughout the recounting of all this to Longmire, Norman stumbled drunkenly over words, slurred entire sentences together, digressed and often repeated himself. Longmire listened with moderate interest but heard nothing that would, as Norman had said, knock him on his State Department ass.

Norman changed verbal gears with a couple of gulps of Wild Turkey and went on.

He told Longmire about his father and his father's so-called reminder stone. Told of how yesterday his brother, Phillip, had come down from New York bringing along the stone and stories of its power to heal. Norman gave a secondhand account of what the stone had ostensibly done for Janet and Libby. He told Longmire how, merely patronizing his brother, he had intimated possible interest and kept the stone. Honest to God, he'd had no other motive.

As soon as Phillip left Norman's office, Norman had hurried back to Bethesda. The President's condition was the same. Inevitably the electrical system of his heart would go haywire and there wouldn't be any more beats. For the moment he was sedated, his pain masked. Nothing Norman could do but wait.

In the adjoining room he lay on the bed and thought about his medical impotence. When it came down to the mortal bedrock, he was as useless as this stone.

He took it from his shirt pocket, looked at it indifferently. He had no intention of trying it at that point, although it must have been then that his mind, or whatever, had made such a suggestion.

Chalk it up to fatigue, but it was almost as though another person went into the President's room and, making sure the President was sleeping and no one else was there, taped the stone to the President's left side, up near the armpit where it wouldn't be easily noticed. He then returned to his own room and bed.

Fell asleep.

Awoke four or so hours later and went in to the President.

The first thing he noticed was the President's heartbeat. A steady, strong 70 a minute. The EKG readout indicated a drastic change. For the better. Normal Q waves; the ST segment wasn't elevated, nor were the T waves inverted. He was looking at the EKG of a healthy heart. It wasn't possible.

He drew blood.

The laboratory results showed all serum enzyme levels within normal range. The muscle tissue of the President's heart was no longer being damaged.

Just like that.

Norman had to be certain. He performed another angiogram, repeated all the procedures, and exposed a lot of film to cover every angle. While going through the various steps, Norman felt his anxiety growing, his hope pulling him on. No time for skepticism or questioning.

The developed film showed a highly efficient functioning heart and arterial system. The lumen diameter of the coronary arteries was more than sufficient for full force circulation of blood. Even more amazing, wherever the heart muscle had been damaged there was now no sign of that, not even any scarring. It was as though something had cleared out the arteries and made everything right within the heart.

That morning the President sat up on the side of his bed and had a large breakfast. He was lauded for his recuperative powers, was told the diagnosis had been evasive, extremely tricky, but had turned out to be not what was feared, not serious at all. He was most willing to believe that. He remarked that later in the day he thought he would walk around the wards and shake some hands, which was customary for him. He glanced at Norman for an objection.

Norman saw no reason why he shouldn't.

Longmire chuckled.

So did Norman.

Longmire asked if Norman had spoken of this to anyone, McDermott or anyone?

No.

Had Norman removed the stone from where it was taped on the President's side?

Of course.

Unseen?

Naturally.

So where now was this remarkable stone?

Norman told him.

Longmire, caring friend that he was, said Norman had had quite a time of it over the past several days, must be pooped. Why didn't he crawl up on the couch there and get some well-deserved sleep?

Norman took the suggestion.

Longmire waited until Norman was sleeping deeply before he went to the stereo and removed the cassette. When Norman had gotten to the truly interesting part of his monologue, Longmire had casually gone over and pressed the proper switches. All of what Norman had said about the stone and its effect on the President was recorded over Liszt's Piano Concerto No. 1.

Longmire went downstairs to the kitchen. Put on some fresh coffee and sat at the kitchen table. He imagined the impact of such a stone as Norman had described, the influence it would have over certain instrumental people, people in power whom we wanted to have see things our way. What a persuasive side benefit it would be to any agreement. *And you will have access to our stone* would be the offer. Our entire approach to international diplomacy would be changed. Hell, our entire foreign policy. A stone with such power would be the most prized thing in the world.

Later, Longmire would set up an off-the-record meeting with George Gurney, head of State Department Intelligence. Gurney was a former CIA man, but in his present position with State he resented having to answer to the CIA. Like the heads of the other intelligence branches, the DIA, National Security Agency, and others, Gurney was caught up in the intramural competitiveness of the U.S. intelligence community.

He'd go to any extreme to gain an edge such as this.

15

◇

"Is it Madame or Mademoiselle?"

"Neither," Audrey replied, just to be perverse.

That stopped the stall owner, a short, narrow-shouldered man with a florid face. He lowered his chin and, over his glasses, studied what sort of person this customer was. He knew for a fact that at least half the more beautiful prostitutes who worked the boulevards around the Étoile were depilitated young men in dresses, believably chic down to their enameled toenails. And adept at doing what they did, too. But this, he decided, was not one of those. "I assure you" —he went on selling—"this painting is seventeenth-century Flemish, early seventeenth century. *Regardez.*" He exhibited the painting's back side. Its canvas did indeed appear to be old enough, and the wood of its stretchers was shot with worm holes.

"Who do you say was the artist?" Audrey asked neutrally.

"Jan van Ravenstyn."

"Never heard of him."

"A contemporary of Rembrandt. They drank together. It is said that Rembrandt learned much from van Ravenstyn. The similarity of technique is quite obvious, *n'est-ce pas?*"

The painting was medium in size, a dark-grounded portrait of a plump woman up to her neck in an overly wide starched white collar edged with lace. It was an exceptionally fine copy. The stall owner had sold two like it each year for the past eight years.

"How much are you asking for it?"

"Asking?" the stall owner said with average French condescension. "The price is an inflexible eighty thousand francs."

Audrey reached into her sling carryall.

The stall owner's palms itched. Again his philosophy, *chose qui plaît c'est demi vendu,* a thing that pleases is half sold, had proved to be true.

Audrey brought out her pendulum. Unraveled the twine that had the large emerald bead on one end, the chunk of ivory on the other. She instructed the stall owner to place the painting face up on the floor. He complied reluctantly and watched with dismay as Audrey held the pendulum above the painting. The emerald bead went from a standstill to a rather energetic left-to-right swinging motion.

A madwoman, the stall owner thought. But she appeared to be a well-off madwoman. He would not yet ask her to leave.

Audrey gathered up her pendulum and dismissed the painting on the floor by stepping over it.

"May I hang this back in place?" the stall owner asked.

"By all means."

The stall was on allée number 1 in the Vernaison section of the Marché aux Puces. Audrey and Springer had eye-shopped nearly all the allées and cross-connecting passageways that were lined with stalls offering for sale everything from odd pieces of chipped faience to chateau-quality chandeliers, potholder scraps of seventeenth-century needlepoint to massive architectural remnants.

Neither Audrey nor Springer had bought anything, hadn't even touched. They'd noticed and commented on how the tourists, numerous on this pleasant summery day, compulsively fingered whatever object their eyes caught upon, as though in that there was a gratuitous satisfaction. Audrey had seen a few things that sparked ideas for future Bergdorf windows. Springer saw nothing he wanted.

His mind was too involved with stall 39 there on allée number 1. Both times they'd passed by, that stall had been closed. Springer hoped there hadn't been a mix-up. Drumgold had said stall 39 Tuesday afternoon. Springer was certain of that. Drumgold's contact in Antwerp might have gotten signals crossed. No special time in the afternoon had been mentioned. If he had to, Springer would wait it out until the flea market closed, then call Drumgold in London to find out what went wrong. Drumgold had gone to a lot of trouble to line up the deal. During the week, he'd made quick trips to Antwerp and Moscow, picked up a couple of his longtime personal due bills, and, no doubt, squeezed through some very narrow openings. He downplayed it, said it was all in the run of business.

Of course it wasn't. This deal required sneaky discretion. They couldn't just descend on Antwerp and put out word that a dozen twenty-five carat round-cut flawless Russian stones were wanted. That would have caused troublesome attention from the dealers of Pelikaanstraat. Once given the scent they would scurry to show their better, more expensive merchandise, and, although some of it would have been Russian, it was highly unlikely that twelve stones of that size would be gleaned.

Then, with the word out, within a half day Almazjuvelirexport, the Soviet diamond selling office, would arbitrarily raise the asking price of its larger goods as much as 20 percent. At the same time or sooner, The System in London would hear about the pending transaction and put their security people on it. The way The System had its network of informants organized, there would be no way to keep it from learning that Springer was involved. Needless to say, The System would take a dark view of the matter. For going around The System and encouraging the Soviet's direct selling of diamonds, Springer would be struck from the list of the chosen. There'd be no more sights, no more boxes of rough. Like Drumgold, Springer would be an outcast.

Still, Springer had thought Antwerp would be where the deal

would be made. Not Paris. Paris wasn't particularly a diamond city. Which was probably what made it ideal in this instance.

Springer stood just inside the entrance of stall 38 and looked across to stall 39. He overheard fragments of Audrey's exchanges with the stall owner. Compared to most others the stall was large. It sold only paintings. They were hung on every vertical surface, floor to ceiling.

Audrey now considered one that was hung disadvantageously low near a corner. Not even framed, a small painting about 7 by 10 inches, frayed where it was crudely tacked to its stretcher.

"What's this?" she asked.

"C'est rien."

A landscape so dulled with dirt and years it was difficult to tell which way was up.

Audrey placed it on the counter and held her pendulum above it. The emerald bead on the end of the twine swung to and fro. "How much for this?" Audrey asked.

"Please, *c'est un objet de rebut.* I have been meaning to throw it out. It is not worthy of consideration by a person of your taste."

"How much?" Audrey insisted.

The stall owner grudgingly accepted that he'd misjudged this customer. "Five hundred francs."

"Will you take three hundred?"

"Three hundred," he agreed accommodatingly. He would have let it go for half that. The small satisfaction of such profit turned to pain when he caught a glimpse of the thick sheaf of brand-new thousand-franc notes from which Audrey plucked one.

At that moment Springer saw across the way a woman unlock the entrance to stall 39. A middle-aged woman with an inverted nest of hair dyed a carrot color. She switched on the lights inside the stall and carried out a display table that had a glass-enclosed compartment. She placed the table to one side of the entrance and arranged various items in it. She was not the sort of person Springer had expected. He hadn't been given a name, merely the stall number, and for some reason it was set in his mind that he'd be meeting a man —certainly not this dumpy woman in a cheap faded yellow dress and baby-blue rundown sneakers.

She was done with the display case. She locked it and went back into the stall.

Springer crossed the allée and entered.

It was one of the smaller stalls. Its specialty was jewelry, mostly gold-plated costume stuff, a lot of garish, faceted paste. The woman and her merchandise were well suited.

Springer pretended he was earnestly looking around.

"Monsieur?" the woman asked.

Eyes to eyes, Springer told her, "I'm interested in some unusual buttons."

"Small or large?"

"Large."

"Perhaps you will find what you want among these." The woman brought up a shoe box containing hundreds of odd buttons, placed it on the counter. Springer rummaged through them and finally found what he was required to find: a cut paste button about the diameter of a quarter. He held it up, told the woman, "Twelve of these."

"Twelve, you say?"

"Yes."

"I do not have that many on hand. In fact I doubt that I have even another like this."

Springer wondered if the woman was telling him the deal was impossible. Her expression had not changed throughout. He couldn't read her.

"I might, however, be able to locate what you want and send them to your hotel," she said.

"I'm not staying at a hotel."

"No matter. Leave me your address and I'll see what I can do." She offered Springer a stub of pencil and a tear of brown bag paper. He wrote the address. The woman looked at it and handed it back to Springer. She would rely on her memory.

"When?" Springer asked.

The woman smiled. Every line in her face deepened. "Tomorrow or the following day." She turned off the smile and in place of goodbye said curtly, *"Merci, monsieur."*

* * *

Springer and Audrey went home in a recklessly driven taxi that badly needed new shock absorbers. For quite a while after the long, chattering ride over Paris cobblestones they felt as though their bodies were still vibrating. Even tightly hugging one another didn't help. Springer recalled having once experienced a similar sensation after operating the old tractor all day on the family place in Sherman.

Audrey was delighted with herself because of the little painting she'd purchased. She propped it on the bidet so she might look at it while she took a bath. In Springer's unexpressed opinion the stall owner had been right. The painting was a murky globbed-on attempt worth about forty dollars less than the forty she'd paid for it.

Springer undressed down to his undershorts and sat before the open French windows on the fourth floor. He was glad now he hadn't insisted on staying at a hotel. It was the peak of the tourist season, and when, from London, he'd called the Crillon and gotten a brusque turndown, Audrey hadn't let him try elsewhere. Why should they bother when Libby's place on the Île St. Louis was so convenient?

Libby's place was a five-story, twenty-room private townhouse, the sort the French call a *hôtel particulier.* Located on the Quai d'Orléans, it gave a splendid view of Notre-Dame and the Seine. The house dated back to the sixteen hundreds and, according to Audrey, had at times belonged to various full-fledged and near members of nobility. They were most remembered for their extreme libidinal ways. Perhaps, she suggested, they found the proximity of Notre-Dame ideal—all the swifter to get to daily confession and afterward resume their indulgences with a clean slate.

When Libby bought the place she'd had it done over, cleaned up, and repaired. The interior designer she hired had installed modern conveniences with minimal sacrifice of old elegance. As well, nothing had been done to chase the spirits of the former inhabitants, Audrey claimed. The essences of their salacious souls permeated every inch of the place, occupied the very air, got breathed in. Didn't Springer sense their influence?

It seemed he did.

Since he and Audrey arrived the previous afternoon they had made lengthy assorted love four times.

Now, seated alone before open windows, Springer watched the barges plying up and down river, took in the spires of Notre-Dame that appeared ethereal in the way the late sun backlighted and wrapped rays around them. From the traffic congested on the Pont d'Arcole it seemed the inhabitants of the Left and Right Banks were struggling to exchange banks. Directly below on the quai, Springer saw two very pretty girls strolling hand in hand. That, he thought, was seldom seen in the States: grown girls, close friends, walking together with hands held. It represented a more mature, less self-conscious attitude toward such platonic relationships. The girls were sharing a cassette player, Springer noticed; both had on head sets like little orange earmuffs. They stopped abruptly, turned to each other, and also shared a long, passionate kiss.

Springer decided not to mention the incident to Audrey when she came into the room wearing one of her loose silk kimonos and carrying a tray of things to eat. She placed the tray on the Savonnerie carpet and sprawled down next to it.

There was a *tarte aux quetsches,* a wreath-shaped loaf of crunchy crusted bread called *couronne d'épines,* a *crème renversée,* two bottles of chilled Normandy cider, and an economy-sized jar of Jiffy peanut butter with a silver spreading knife jabbed down into it.

An average, substantial Audrey meal, Springer thought. He joined her on the floor. She was already tearing at the bread, slathering it with Jiffy. "I'm so pleased with my painting," she said.

"Where did you get the peanut butter?"

"Fouchon carries it. Ten dollars a jar. And worth every penny when you're over here sick to death of *pots-au-feu, quenelles, rôtis,* and all that stuff."

Where, Springer wondered, was he when she was tiring of those things? He spooned up some of the caramel custard. "Ever consider that you have a blood sugar problem?"

"Hell, no. I'm blessed. Sugar may be a problem for some but not for me."

"It'll catch up with you."

Her perfect teeth severed the tip off a wedge of plum tart. "That, lover darling, is why I'm getting such a huge head start."

For the next day and the day after, Springer was a prisoner of the house, waiting to be contacted as the Marché aux Puces button lady had promised. He went out only once, left a note on the door saying he would return within the half hour. He crossed over the bridge to the Île de la Cité. Along the quai there in colorful contiguity were the flower vendors. Springer bought anenomes, two dozen purple/blue and two dozen red. They were fresh and shy, their faces still tightly hidden. They were for Audrey's bedside table, would open for her.

Audrey went out several times on errands. She told Springer a surprise was forthcoming. She bought him a pair of black alligator loafers at Hermès and an antique walking stick that had a carved ivory whippet's head. The shoes fit him perfectly and he liked them, though he doubted he'd ever be so much of a dandy he'd use the walking stick. Neither of those was the surprise Audrey had mentioned. On Thursday afternoon she came home with that.

Her little painting.

She had paid a restorer four times his going price to hurry it for her. He had removed layers of grime and varnish and paint to get down to what was there. Not a landscape at all. A portrait of a young girl, an idealized ingenue in a prim blue blouse that accentuated her bluer eyes. Blond hair painstakingly painted swirling around her placid, meticulous face. A direct, guileless gaze, a devoted mouth. Perhaps the artist had projected such ingenuousness, captured it, and then was betrayed by reality. Why otherwise would he have buried her under such drab layers? It was easy to say, looking at the painting now, that the artist had loved his subject. The painting was a Eugène Boudin, signed and dated 1864. A precious find worth a thousand times what Audrey had paid for it.

"How did you know it was there?" Springer asked incredulously.

"The pendulum," she replied matter-of-factly.

Springer recalled the arrogant manner of the stall owner from whom Audrey had bought the painting. Served him right. But Springer didn't believe the pendulum had had anything to do with it. A coincidence, that's what it was. Audrey had gotten lucky. Of course, for the sake of harmony, Springer didn't tell her that.

Thursday night at eleven the sounding of the front door buzzer turned out to be a man who introduced himself as Igor Bitov and said he was delivering some buttons. When he was seated in the salon with a tumbler of vodka in hand, he stated that Igor Bitov was not his real name and let it go at that.

The man was wearing a summer suit and a winter tie, Springer noticed, and black, round-toed, thick-soled shoes. He kept tugging down his shrunken shirt sleeves. His complexion was sallow, a bit jaundiced-looking, and his eyes were set so deep the skin around the sockets appeared bruised. He had black hair combed straight back, long hair. Combed forward it would have covered most of his face. He spoke English with a British accent.

Bitov made some preliminary small talk about Paris and the dispositions of the French. He glanced in Audrey's direction and then back questioningly to Springer.

"My partner," Springer explained.

Bitov reached down and fussed with the right cuff of his trousers. From the inside hem he withdrew a small folded square of chamois that he handed to Springer. It contained a single diamond, round cut.

"That is ten carats," Bitov said.

"I specified—"

"For quality only."

Springer examined the diamond with his loupe under the light of a nearby table lamp. He saw no flaws but couldn't possibly determine the diamond's color. Every lightbulb in the house, no doubt in keeping with Libby's wishes, was the diffused, flattering type. Springer remarked about the light. He blamed himself for not being prepared for such an eventuality; he had thought any evaluating would be done in the daytime.

"The kitchen," Audrey suggested.

They went back through the house to the kitchen and, indeed, there, illuminating the white tiled counters, were daylight-type fluorescent bulbs that allowed Springer to ascertain the diamond's true color.

It was a dazzling ten carats with that unmistakable clear-frozen Soviet quality. And cut to perfect proportions. There was no way Springer could negotiate by opening, as was customary, with some depreciating point. "How much?" he asked.

"This size?"

"This quality, twenty-five carats."

"This size would not satisfy you?"

"Why? Can't you supply twenty-five-carat goods?"

"It is not that," Bitov said calmly. "I merely wanted to make sure you know what you want."

"Twenty-five-carat goods."

"Fifty thousand a carat."

It was as though Bitov was reading the balance in Springer's new bank account. Twelve stones of twenty-five carats each would be three hundred carats. Fifty thousand a carat would come to fifteen million. "Too much," Springer said.

"I agree," Bitov said, as though someone else had set that price. Springer told him, "I have in mind thirty thousand."

"Not enough."

"I'm buying twelve stones, remember."

"All the more reason thirty is not enough."

"How much then?"

"Forty-seven."

"Forty."

There came a time during any negotiation when the next figure stated would be the making or breaking. Springer knew that point had been reached.

Bitov tugged at his shirt cuffs. "Forty-five," he said with a firmer voice.

"Done," Springer said. He'd hoped to get the goods for forty a carat, which seemed a fair price; however, as Drumgold had reminded him, these were not ordinary, readily available stones he was after. A premium price was justifiable. Springer had reduced his take more than half. After Drumgold's commission and Townsend's fee he'd now come out with only a million one. Some "only," he thought. "When can you deliver?"

"Where?"

"London."

"One week."

Springer didn't really want to take delivery in London, would only if that was how it had to be. It would mean his having to find some way of getting the goods into the States that circumvented customs. The fixed import tax on all Soviet goods was 10 percent. An honest declaration in this instance would cost him one million three hundred and fifty thousand. Everyone in the deal would make out except him. He'd even end up losing a couple of hundred thousand.

Fuck that.

The alternative was to carry the diamonds through customs. Be nonchalant. The risk was if he got shaken down by the customs officials the diamonds would be confiscated and he'd owe Libby thirteen and a half million. He couldn't imagine owing anyone thirteen and a half million. Plus interest, probably. Even if he died older than just old he'd still be paying.

"How about delivery in New York?" he asked.

"No problem," Bitov said casually.

A million-one answer. Springer wondered if his relief was apparent. "When in New York?"

"Nine, ten days at most."

"You understand I want twelve identical flawless stones. They must match exactly in color and cut."

Bitov nodded, a bit detached now that the deal had been set.

"And," Springer specified unequivocally, "they must be Soviet goods, equal in quality to this ten-carat piece."

"From Aikhal," Bitov assured him.

"How will you want to take payment?"

"The person who delivers the goods will tell you that. You will be contacted in New York." Bitov folded away the ten-carat diamond, put his foot up on the edge of the kitchen counter, and inserted it into the hem of his trouser cuff. He was anxious to leave, declined another vodka, went out, and walked swiftly down the Quai d'Orléans as though late for another appointment.

"Good for you," Audrey told Springer and gave the back of his ear a congratulatory kiss.

"Maybe," Springer said. It had been both the largest and most nebulous piece of business he'd ever done. No money had changed hands, nor any goods. He didn't even know the man's real name. The so-called Bitov had not once even intimated that he was a Soviet official of any sort, which was untypical. If he'd been with Almaz-juvelirexport or whatever, wouldn't he have established that? Springer decided this man was a go-between. Needed because the diamonds would be coming out of Russia underhandedly. The better-grade large stones from the Yakut were cut and then somehow skimmed, put aside into a secret hoard, and sold off carefully to the West. No ordinary comrade would be able to pull that off. It would have to be someone with weight and leverage. And courage, considering the consequences if found out. Possibly several such someones were, in the milieu of Soviet bureaucracy, in positions to protect one another while they salted it away outside the Curtain. How did they get the diamonds out of Russia and into the United States, for example?

It didn't matter to Springer, as long as he got his.

16

◇

In New York City at that hour, Mal had just set the alarms and locked the office. Outside, the rush from work was on, and the midtown streets, thronged with all the simultaneously released people, were like rapids deep and surging, requiring a certain kind of aggressive swim.

It would not be much of an endurance contest for Mal. He had a standing arrangement with one of the radio-dispatched cab companies to pick him up at five thirty every weekday afternoon unless he notified them to the contrary.

He came out of the 580 Fifth Building. Through the hurrying crosscurrents he glimpsed the yellow of his cab waiting at the curb.

He also saw the woman.

The back of her.

She was at the open window on the meter side of the cab, bent over, talking in to the driver. She probably wasn't aware of how provocative her stance was, the way it shaped her buttocks and featured her legs. She was wearing pale peach, a straight fitted skirt and a sleeveless blouse. Her blond hair was wound and pinned into a chignon.

Mal gave that back view of her a high rating but doubted the front half would measure up. More often than not, when they looked that sensational from behind they turned out to have beaks and overbites. He cut across to the cab, opened its rear door, and got in. The driver acknowledged him and told the woman, "Now you believe me?" Then, to Mal: "My roof light ain't working right. I been trying to tell her I already got a fare."

The woman apologized, withdrew her hand from the cab as though it were hot. She stepped back and sighted up the avenue for another one.

Mal realized now what a total beauty she was, a young one. He hadn't yet closed the door of the cab. The driver was waiting for that. "Are you by chance going uptown?" Mal asked the young woman.

She ignored him.

"I can drop you wherever you want."

She waved at a couple of cabs, unoccupied but also on their way in response to radio calls. Futility tightened her face. She expressed a little fury by stomping the pavement with the heel of her pump. Her eyes continued to search the traffic that had a lot of taxi yellow in it but none available. She glanced at her watch and then at Mal, weighing his offer. Diffidently she asked, "Would Third Avenue and Seventy-eighth be possible?"

"No problem," Mal said, smiling his best reassuring smile. He patted the seat. "Come on." He moved over to offer her plenty of room. She got in, careful about the arrangement of her skirt.

"Give me that address again," the driver said. He was rankled by the delay. Every minute was a dollar.

"Third and Seventy-eighth," Mal said firmly, and when they were under way he remarked, "People should share cabs during the rush hours. There aren't enough to go around."

The young woman didn't comment. She sat with her knees together, as far from Mal as possible. Her mind appeared to be even farther away. She kept her eyes straight ahead.

That allowed Mal to enjoy a more thorough look at her. He didn't steal, was straightforward about it, and she must have known his gaze was on her. She had a showgirl's body—rangy, slender, and tight. In that regard she reminded Mal of a girl he'd done just about everything with twenty years ago, a dancer in the line at the Tropicana in Las Vegas. Donna something or other. The outstanding erotic episode of Mal's life.

This one in the cab with him now looked as though she'd be even better than Donna. For one thing she didn't have any of the usual showgirl brittleness that came from being constantly propositioned and from relying too much on makeup. Mal particularly noticed her hands, impeccable and well cared for. Her long, tapered fingers looked as though they could dance. He was stirred by the thought of their possibilities. She wasn't wearing a ring. No jewelry other than ear clips of single baroque pearls set within a swirl of gold, the practical kind of ear clips a woman would buy for herself.

The traffic was thick on Third. Nevertheless the blocks were swiftly wasting for Mal. He started in neutral. "Where are you from?"

"Here," the woman replied without looking at him.

"What about before here?"

"Phoenix."

"I used to go to Phoenix often. Still do now and then."

"A lot of old people there," she said.

Perhaps she wasn't really putting him in his place, Mal thought. "I usually stay at the Biltmore."

"My uncle just finished building an enormous house on the Biltmore grounds. Right on the golf course."

"Nice place to live."

She almost smiled. "He built it for someone. He's a contractor."

"You miss Phoenix?"

"I think what I miss most is not being able to see Camelback Mountain from everywhere. Have you ever stayed at the Camelback Inn?"

"No."

"It's more relaxed than the Biltmore. I worked there part time and summers when I was in high school. Try the Camelback next time."

She was letting her eyes in on the conversation now. They were dark brown. Nice honest eyes, Mal thought. "How long have you been living here in the city?" he asked.

"Six, almost seven months."

"I would have bet no more than two."

"I give the impression of being such a bumpkin?"

Softly, after a tactical beat, Mal told her: "Just unspoiled."

That got to her. A hint of high color came into her cheeks. She covered her self-consciousness by fussing with the fine hairs on the nape of her neck, stroking them upward with her fingers.

By the time they were approaching Seventy-eighth Street first names had been exchanged and they'd caused one another to laugh several times. She was Marcie, which suited her.

"Near or far corner?" the driver asked.

"Either will be fine," she said. She took three dollars from her purse and insisted on splitting the fare. When Mal wouldn't accept the money she dropped it over onto the front seat for the driver.

Her hand went to the door handle.

Mal couldn't accept that either. Too much was undone. In another moment Marcie from Phoenix would be among the never-knowns and the night would be lonelier than he'd foreseen, no matter who of his licentious larder he chose to spend it with. Out it came. "Are you in a do-or-die hurry?"

"Why?" Somewhat guarded.

"Most nights I stop in at the Stanhope for a drink. Now, please . . . I realize how ulterior and obvious it must seem . . . but I find you such enjoyable company. . . ."

Mal's well nourished air of appeal hung on Marcie's ambivalence. . . .

An hour later, at an outside table beneath the Stanhope's white awning, he was on his third vodka martini and the ice had melted in her second wine spritzer. She'd told him a lot about herself, divulged freely the way reticent people often do when they're convinced of someone's interest.

Her last name was Newkirk. She had a brother and sister, both older and settled. She was her father's favorite and he, most definitely, was hers. To such an extent her mother was jealous. Imagine? Her father was a realtor in Scottsdale, did well. These days nearly every realtor in Scottsdale did well. She had been a mere plane ticket away from giving up on New York a number of times but no longer felt so displaced. She worked at Smith Barney, the stock brokerage firm, as a secretary. Was Mal married?

Never was he more glad that he could answer the question with a truthful *no.*

Her eyes said she was wondering whether or not to believe him.

That she was interested enough to wonder was encouraging to Mal.

She told him that for a while she'd been seeing only one fellow, an account executive with Grey Advertising. That was definitely over now. There were plenty of single men around but most were either light of foot, so to speak, or too young for her taste. The advertising guy had turned out to be insensitive and, even worse, cheap. He'd given her a ring for her birthday and then, when they broke up, demanded she give it back. Outraged, she'd thrown it at him and it had sailed out the window and he'd rushed down seventeen stories hoping to recover it.

"Did he?"

An indifferent shrug. "I'll buy my own rings from now on," she vowed. "In fact, that was why I was on Forty-seventh Street this afternoon, shopping around."

"What kind of ring do you have in mind?"

"Something simple."

"A diamond?"

She laughed. "It would have to be teeny."

"How about a solitaire?"

"I don't know. Sounds lonely."

Mal explained that a solitaire is exactly that: a ring set with one stone alone. As a rule, a diamond had to be a good one to stand on its own like that. Solitaires were especially popular during the twenties and thirties, the favorite gift of the sugar daddies.

"How do you know about such things?"

"It's my business, diamonds."

"You're kidding."

Mal gave her one of his cards.

"Lucky you," she said.

He agreed.

"You probably get to travel a lot . . . Africa, India, all over."

"Yes."

"I suppose you're the last person I should say this to but, frankly, I'm not all that wild about diamonds. They're just not essential."

"You have the hands for them."

"I don't know how I should take that. Diamonds make a woman's hands look greedy."

"Depends on the woman. It wouldn't apply to you."

"What a nice thing for you to say." She veered from the topic by turning away and gazing across Fifth Avenue. The Metropolitan Museum had its linear fountains gushing white. Boys were riding bikes around them, rearing them like stallions. A man was playing a violin to his cap on the sidewalk at his feet. Another, with an invisible bouquet and a tear-painted cheek, was performing a love-lorn mime. The thought Marcie came back with could have just occurred to her. "This afternoon," she said, "I was shown some synthetic diamonds. They were pretty. Don't you think it would be just as well if I got one of those?"

"I absolutely forbid it."

The next day was Friday.

Mal told the receptionist to leave an hour early. Linda had been gone since noon, getting that much of a lead on the droves who would be headed for the Hamptons.

Alone in the office Mal stripped to the waist and went into the washroom. He clicked a new blade into his razor and shaved for the second time that day. It was important that he not be bristly around his mouth and chin. He flossed and brushed his teeth, washed beneath his arms, sprayed on a scented antiperspirant.

Getting ready was always a pleasant part of it for Mal. He enjoyed being honed by anticipation, his intentions. He used a pair of round-ended scissors to snip hairs from his nostrils, tweezers to yank out a few wild white ones from his brows.

So far, he thought, he'd played it right with Marcie. The previous night he hadn't pushed for dinner and a longer evening. When Marcie first halfheartedly mentioned that she should be getting home, which was, of course, his cue, he had promptly paid the check and hailed a cab. On the way he implied that he was late for a business engagement, preempting the possibility of being asked up to her place for a drink. It was easy to see she was disappointed, had wanted more, a whole night of it. At the entrance to the high-rise apartment building where she lived she was reluctant to part, sat silent for a long moment giving him the chance to change his mind. She kissed him on the cheek, a bit lingeringly and close to the corner of his mouth, and when she went in, her walk, the sensual left–right undulation of it, was for his benefit.

She was really some piece of work.

Now, for her, he put on a fresh shirt and a new fifty-dollar tie he'd bought at Sulka while he was out for lunch. He took extra care with the tie because it was silk that would easily crease. Got it right first try, a perfectly shaped soft knot with both ends matching in length. He considered that significant.

Marcie was due at six. Ostensibly she was coming to the office so Mal could help her choose a small diamond. Indeed they would go through with that. There would be a show of diamonds. However, as agreed, afterward they would have dinner. Mal had made a reservation at La Cirque. In case she came too casually dressed he'd made a back-up reservation at Trastevere 84. Of the two places he preferred Trastevere 84 for this night. It was noisy, hurried, not conducive to bullshitting over coffee and snifters. Possibly they could be at his apartment or hers by ten at the latest. He was best early.

Phillip's office, Mal decided, was neater and more impressive than his own. Also more convenient because the safe was there. He went in and adjusted the Levelor blinds, reduced the intrusiveness of the city to a vague atmosphere. He sat in Phillip's swivel chair.

Twenty minutes to go.

He'd like it if Marcie showed up early. Not that he required any further emboldening from her. Short of coming right out and saying it, she couldn't have made it more obvious that she was obsessively attracted to older men. The way Mal saw her, this want was one that had probably ached her for some while and frightened her. He doubted she'd ever given it to it. It was going to be like having a virgin without all the pathos. There was so much to be done to her, so many ways to spoil and addict her.

At five to six Mal heard the outer door open and close. He went out to the receptionist's desk and through the small bulletproof window saw Marcie standing in the vestibule. The vestibule, a confined space, was part of the security system. Nearly all gem dealers in the district had the same sort of setup: an outer door off the corridor that could be freely entered, then the vestibule and a solid inner door. Unless the outer door was closed the inner door could not be opened; an electronic circuit prevented it. This would keep an armed thief from making a dash in from the corridor during the instant when both doors might be open. The inner door was kept electronically bolt-locked. A switch beneath the receptionist's desk released the bolt and allowed the door to be opened.

Mal reached down under the desk, pressed the switch.

A buzz, a click, and in came Marcie, smiling, complaining lightly. "Couldn't find a cab again. I gave up and hiked it."

"I could have called and had one sent to you."

A sigh. "I wonder if I'll ever learn to get around in this town."

"Just remember you're too pretty to chance riding the subways," Mal advised. An unoriginal line he'd used numerous times.

Marcie glanced around merely to familiarize herself with the surroundings. They went into Springer's office. "For some reason I imagined a lot of people would be bustling about," Marcie said.

"Not on a Friday afternoon in summer."

"I'll bet you're a marvelous boss."

"I can be."

Marcie sat in one of the client chairs in front of the desk and dropped her handbag on the floor beside her.

Mal was tight in the windpipe, he hyperventilated. His face and neck felt flushed. She, no doubt, was the cause. More radiant than his memory had pictured her. Today her hair was liberated. Straight, heavy, healthy hair, it reached nearly to her shoulders, had a swishing liveliness to it. Her dress was summery. Cotton in a pale, very becoming blue. A scooped-out neckline with a narrow, rounded collar framing it. Ample sleeves that puffed up at the shoulders and buttoned four times at the wrists. It was, Mal thought, the type of dress an English schoolgirl might wear on a barefoot scamper across a country field. To complete the illusion, all that was needed was a bonnet and some streaming ribbons.

"You don't mind being alone here with me, do you?" Mal asked.

"No," she replied, settling back.

"Are you sure?"

"My father always says we never really do anything we don't want to."

"I suppose you thought about not showing up."

"Well, I'm a shy person at heart—trying to not let it show, of course. It's hard for me to be as forward as I should be. That keeps me good but it also keeps me lonely. Isn't it strange how most people will admit almost anything except that they're shy?"

"You can admit anything to me."

"I feel that."

"Good. Shall we relax a while longer or look at the diamonds?"

Marcie shrugged.

Mal went to the safe, turned its handle, and swung the heavy door open. He knelt on one knee with his back to Marcie, pretended to be searching through the contents of the safe while he kept an eye on Marcie in a small strip of mirror inconspicuously attached to the wall there. Ordinarily, during a sale when Phillip left goods under consideration on his desk and went to the safe for others, the client was watched in that mirror. The switching of stones, a synthetic diamond for an identical real one, only took an instant and was not unheard of.

That, of course, was not Mal's reason for observing Marcie. He merely hoped to view her unaware. It was his theory that often a few seconds of such observation allowed him to know more of the craft and subtlety of a woman than he could ever gather face to face or even body to body.

Marcie, he saw, remained faithful to her impression. The only thing she did was pull back her cuff and glance at her watch, which Mal translated as an act of impatience in his favor.

From the safe he brought a small red leather case. He placed it on the desk and unsnapped it. In it were briefkes, about thirty, each letter coded in pencil on its upper right-hand corner.

"Let's see what we have here," Mal said. Actually he was familiar with every diamond in the case. They were his personal goods: some European cuts, stones extracted from old settings, and some bought from freelance thieves or fences along the street, some extra stones that had been thrown in to sweeten deals. He had accumulated them especially for such situations as this. Thought of them as his ammunition, called them that, and sometimes Linda or Phillip ribbed him good-naturedly about them. It never fazed him. The fact was, his ammunition seldom missed.

He riffled through the briefkes, selected one, and unfolded it. "What about this?"

Marcie pulled her chair up, placed her forearms on the edge of the desk, and leaned forward to see the diamond that lay crown up in a crease of the paper. Mal juggled the briefke to cause scintillations.

"How large is it?" Marcie asked.

"Close to a carat."

Marcie examined it intently. Mal surmised that in spite of her claim that diamonds were unimportant to her she was already warming to their fire. "Keep in mind," she said, "I only have so much to spend."

"How much?"

"Maybe five hundred."

Mal couldn't count the number of times he'd heard that from women. Why was it always five hundred? He folded the briefke, put it away, and chose another. In it was a fairly clean carat-and-a-quarter diamond with a visible yellowish cast. It had cost him three hundred.

"It's larger," Marcie said after looking at it, "but not as pretty as the other one. Sort of yellow, isn't it? Is yellow good?"

"You have sharp eyes." Mal folded that diamond away and again fingered through the file of briefkes. Doing his routine. "Oh!" he exclaimed as though having made a discovery. "Here's one for you!" He unfolded another briefke to expose a one-carat diamond that immediately welcomed the light with brilliant flares. He concentrated on Marcie's eyes, was sure he'd struck home. "That's beautiful," she said reverently and, after some silent appreciation, "I'm sure it costs more than I can afford."

"That doesn't mean you shouldn't have it."

"What better reason?"

"*I* want you to have it." Mal thought she might cry. Her eyes looked watery. With a special pair of tweezers he picked up the diamond by its girdle. He took it around the desk to her. "Hold out your hand, fingers together."

She extended her left hand, palm down, and he placed the diamond in the crease between her second and ring fingers. She moved her hand about, admiring the diamond, evidently very taken with it. "It's really a good one, isn't it?"

"Yes."

"Not too large and not too small. It really doesn't make my hand look greedy."

"It's yours."

"For how much?"

"From me to you."

She got him eyes to eyes, dead serious but tender. "Mal, I'm touched, I truly am, but I didn't come up here for you to give me a diamond. It's important to me that you know that."

"Okay." Mal still didn't believe it.

"Now tell me the price."

"A thousand," he said offhand.

"Honestly?"

"Yeah, an even thousand, no tax." The diamond was worth five thousand. It was the best of his ammunition. A throw-in with a lot he'd bought for the firm only six months ago. It was, now that he thought of it, miraculous that he'd been able to keep it this long.

Marcie placed the diamond in its briefke and reached for her purse. She took out a white business-size envelope and, from that, ten one-hundred-dollar bills. She counted them out on the corner of the desk. "I went to the bank this noon," she said. "I was uneasy carrying this much cash around."

Mal was at a loss for what to say. It had never gone like this.

Marcie must have sensed it. She remained seated, held her hand out to him. He took it. "The diamond was one thing," she said, "you and I are another." She drew him to her, wrapped her arms around his hips, placed her cheek against his abdomen. A tight hug. There was at that moment a duality to her. It was little-girl-like the way she was hugging him, and at the same time he half expected she would unzip his fly and go down on him.

Finally she let loose and offered up her face. He lowered his to hers. His hand went beneath her hair to the back of her neck. He tried to kiss her tenderly but she wouldn't have it. His lips were at once encircled by the openness of hers. Her tongue pried and probed in. It was a long kiss that released and resumed again and again, causing Mal's back to strain stiff, bringing him to his knees before her.

She cupped his face with her hands. "Do we have to bother with dinner?" she asked, breathless.

"No."

"I'll tidy myself up and we'll go." She stood. "Is there a wash-room?"

He told her where it was and she went out to it, leaving him on the floor. He felt incapable of moving. The swiftness and intensity of it had him erotically paralyzed. His senses were confused, some sharpened, some dulled. His ears felt plugged. That was why it didn't immediately register that he was hearing the outer door being opened and closed. He jumped up and rushed from Phillip's office.

Marcie was at the receptionist's desk, her hand beneath it.

A buzz, a click, and in they came.

Two of them.

They both had guns.

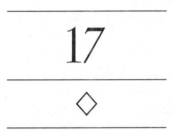

17

Air France Concorde Flight 001 touched down at Kennedy International Airport at 8:45 A.M.

According to Springer's watch, that was two and a quarter hours earlier than it had taken off from Paris DeGaulle. When he mentioned the fact to Audrey she remarked that to that extent their lives and therefore their love had been extended.

Their long weekend in Normandy had been a lazy, voluptuous disappearance. Out of touch with everyone but one another from early Friday to Sunday late. They stayed at an inn that was once a watermill a few kilometers from the painful-sounding village of Conches-en-Ouche. Around there they were brought to earth by bony-hipped black-and-white cows that returned their regard with bewildered wisdom. They also lay on the warm painted boards of a flat-bottomed boat, calmly floated the river Rouloir, and pretended for an hour that they were married by having a foolish spat. They walked the high grasses in the orchards in the daytime so they would know their way at night.

Now it was another land.

Cruel chrome and restrictions.

It took them an hour to pass through customs and forty minutes more to get into town. Audrey had a change of windows scheduled, would stop at her apartment for only a moment before going on to Bergdorf's. Springer went straight to his office.

It was like plunging into unexpectedly cold water. A finger print specialist from Midtown North Precinct was there blowing dust onto all the likely places, making a mess. The detective assigned to the case was moving about passively as though the circumstances and its setting were routine. Springer knew the detective by sight but not by name, had seen him around the street. The card he now gave to Springer said he was Dennis Fahey. He was less than medium height and not athletic looking. Too many complimentary meals prevented him from being able to button the jacket of his wrinkle-proof suit. Fahey had seen it all when it came to the diamond district. From cowboys firing silenced .22 calibers into the ears of gem dealers in the middle of the day to the apes with grappling hooks and ropes who, twelve stories up, swung from rusty fire escape to rusty fire escape across a forty-foot-wide airshaft to gain access to the rear of the 47th Street buildings in the middle of the night—especially on Jewish holidays.

"We'll be out of your way soon as we can," Fahey said, obliquely empathetic.

Springer nodded resignedly. He went in and looked at the open safe, imagined the greedy swiftness with which it had been emptied. He went into Linda's office. She was sitting on her desk with her legs crossed, facing the window. Smoking a cigarette. Springer had never seen her smoke before.

"How did it happen?" Springer asked.

Linda started to say but gave up on where to begin. She handed him a Xerox of several typewritten pages stapled together.

Mal's statement to the police.

The whole story was there, beginning with the Thursday taxi-ride encounter with the young woman Marcie to Saturday morning, when Mal had gotten his adhesive-taped hands free and dialed the police. While Springer read, he asked, "Where's Mal now?"

"Somewhere in Pennsylvania. He left right after he dictated that statement. Said he was going to a retreat where he couldn't talk or be talked to."

"I hope he stays there." Springer was seething.

"Claimed he was going to have himself neutered."

"I even hope he does that."

Mal's statement was not merely factual. It contained numerous subjective descriptions and confidences. There was a confessional ring to it, a mix of boast and shame. His signature on the bottom of each page lacked the usual undecipherable overflourish, was cramped and erratic.

Springer imagined the compound fracture Mal's ego was suffering. Do Mal good, he thought, perhaps limp down his perpetual hard-on, although it was difficult to picture Mal different from what he'd been over the many years. Without all the chasing and humping around he'd be a better businessman probably, but a lot of the color and spirit would be missing. Surely at that moment he was hang-head, feeling failure, doubting he'd ever recover or be able to make amends. The poor, cunt-hungry old fool, Springer thought. Not that he was about to forgive Mal. It was too big a thing and too soon for that. However, he couldn't help but feel sorry for him.

"Steiner was by earlier," Linda said. "He wants you to call him." Steiner was the firm's insurance broker.

"They got everything, I suppose."

"Except what was out on memo." Linda handed him several more Xeroxed pages: a typewritten list, lot by lot, of what had been stolen. "You know," she said, "maybe now would be a good time to get out of diamonds and into colored goods." It was something they'd discussed but never seriously.

"Could be."

"The market is right for it. How did your trip go?"

"I don't know for sure yet."

"Want me to stick around here?"

"Where's Lucille?" The receptionist.

"She came in for an hour. I think the police and everything rattled her. Probably out looking for another job."

"Someone ought to be here."

"I'll stick around."

Springer went out to Detective Fahey. "We need your finger-prints," Fahey told him. "We got everybody else's."

"Why?"

"Just so if we come across a print that shouldn't be here we'll know it." Fahey was tolerant, detached and possibly friendly. While the specialist inked Springer up and took his prints, Fahey said of course no Marcie Newkirk worked at Smith Barney. Nor did she live at that high-rise on 78th Street, had just made it look as though she did by walking in and out. The Scottsdale, Arizona, stuff was all a lie too. The only helpful thing was the cleverness of these people. They had something good going and they would probably keep working it until they slipped. That was how it usually went. The bastards could have a closet full of money and suitcases crammed with flash and still go out and try for another score. The stealing was what they needed, Fahey said. He also recited the litany about not getting hopes up of recovering any of what had been stolen. Goods were goods. For a final routine consolation he promised they'd keep on it.

Springer went into his office and sat with his back to the safe. His anger wouldn't let him look at it. He had never stolen anything in his life, and, although that was no reason to expect dispensation, it did make robbing him seem unfair. Fortunately he had insurance. He telephoned his broker, Bob Steiner.

"I just got through talking to the company again," Steiner said.

"There's a problem?"

"At this stage they call it a consideration."

"They don't want to pay."

"They never *want* to pay. Who the hell *wants* to pay?"

Springer blew. "For twenty years we pay their fucking premiums. We don't even bitch when they raise their rates . . . and now when something happens they're reneging."

"They may settle. I'm trying to work out a figure with them."

"Fuck that! I want what our policy covered. We had it all covered, every carat."

"Insurance is a tricky business."

"Yeah . . . *now* it's tricky."

"The way the company sees it there's negligence. If they can prove negligence they're not liable."

"What negligence?"

"Mal wasn't conducting proper business when it happened. He brought it on himself, as much as admitted so in his statement. That's what they're basing it on."

"A loss is a loss."

"It's an out. They thrive on outs."

"I have to sue?"

"Blame Mal. He should have talked to me before he said anything. He didn't have to go into it like he did. It was a big mistake."

"Four million," Springer said bitterly.

"Four million three is what I put the claim in for. I assume you've got the books to back it up."

"You do a lot of business with this insurance company, don't you, Bob?"

"Springer, I understand what you're implying, and because I like you and know you're under a lot of stress right now I won't take it as an insult."

Springer apologized.

Steiner accepted.

"So, what comes next?" Springer asked.

"They'll make an offer to settle. Not today or tomorrow, but eventually."

"How much of an offer?"

"I'm begging for half."

"Jesus."

"Depends on how much they want to lay out to keep their credibility in the district. That's what I'm betting on, bad word getting around."

Springer held back from erupting again. "Bob, don't let the bastards stiff me."

"I'll do what I can and a mile extra. Know that."

After hanging up, Springer sat there silently for a while. Perhaps it was the voltage of his anger; he had a strong sense of his father's presence in the room. His father was everywhere: on the other side of the desk, over by the safe peering into it, even crowding to occupy the same chair Springer was in. Sympathies and reproaches buzzed Springer's ears.

He phoned Danny.

They arranged a meet.

And a few minutes later Springer was walking west on 47th. The row upon row of diamonds in the display windows taunted him. He loathed them, every one of those hard little hunks of shit. He tried not to look at them, put on mental blinders all the way to the corner of the Avenue of the Americas, where he crossed and turned north. He was never comfortable on Avenue of the Americas. The black and glass corporate buildings loomed oppressively, each reflecting the might of the next. It certainly wasn't an avenue for losers, and Springer was sorry now he'd chosen it for the meet. At 49th was the Exxon Building. It had a perfectly engineered waterfall in front to testify to its altruism. Springer stopped there, sat on the raised edge of polished black granite that felt slippery hot to his haunches. He glanced up. The sun ricocheted off Exxon and pitilessly struck his eyes shut.

Make a million, lose two, he thought.

He glanced to his left where, seated on the same hot granite edge just a few feet away, a secretary on an early lunch hour was bringing a marijuana roach to her lips with her cerise-enameled fingernails, so short a roach and so much of a toke Springer caught the smell of lacquer burning.

He spotted Danny on the other side of the avenue, watched him cut across through the killer taxis like a matador. A different Danny Rags in work clothes: worn-shiny cheap black gabardine slacks, white shirt unbuttoned two down, sleeves rolled up to the elbows. His hands, Springer noticed, were dirty from acid and gold. With his eyes and a slight flick of his head Danny asked what was wrong.

Springer told him.

Danny's expression went cold, the same icy anger Springer remembered of Just John. "Anybody hurt?" he asked.

"Four million hurts."

"Fucking thieves."

Such hypocrisy was typical of the Street.

"I figured you might have heard something," Springer said.

"Wasn't around this weekend or I might have. Took my kids to the Jersey shore. What was it, a break-in?"

Springer let him read Mal's statement.

"They were put onto Mal by somebody," Danny said. "Some other broad who'd been with him, knew his pitch."

"From Mal's descriptions do you make anyone?"

"Not right off."

"How about this Marcie?"

"Sharp the way she didn't lead with her cunt."

"Either way Mal would have gone for it."

"Easier to trust a beautiful broad like that, though."

"Maybe somebody will be around offering my goods."

"Could be in-and-outers, came into town just to make this hit."

"That's possible."

"None of the people I do business with were in on it," Danny said. "At least none of my regulars."

"What makes you sure of that?"

"They wouldn't take from you."

"Why not me?"

"You've got immunity."

"Oh?"

"As a favor to me you've got it."

"Otherwise I would have been hit before now?"

"Probably." Danny looked away to get off the subject. "What say I buy you lunch?"

"I'll pass today."

"Got to be getting back anyway. You should see what a guy brought me. A statue of a cat, like a real cat, that big. A swift on one of his teams swagged it from a house in Westbury. On the way out just because it's sitting there and looked good. Turns out it's solid eighteen K, almost five thousand pennyweights. A pair of matching chrysoberyls for eyes that'll go at least twenty-five carats each. Fucking statue's got to be worth a hundred large. Shame to melt it."

Springer wasn't in the mood for stories. "Find out what you can for me," he said glumly.

"Look, if these people were sharp enough to pull off such a finesse they won't suddenly turn into assholes. They'll deal out the goods a little at a time here and there. Shit, some of your diamonds may come in to me an hour from now, but how am I supposed to know they're yours? Goods are goods."

Again goods are goods, Springer thought bitterly.

"And even, let's say down the road a way, we make these people and get on them. All you'll get is the satisfaction of breaking their bones. That what you want?"

No reply from Springer.

Danny went on. "As a matter of fact, if you can see it from their side it's not easy to blame them. For them it was nothing personal. They were just taking care of business. Think of all the trouble they had to go through to set it up, the chances they had to take to make the move. Understand what I mean?"

"Not yet."

"Okay," Danny said. "I'll ask around." He smiled, hoping it would prime the same in return from Springer. It didn't.

They went in opposite directions. Springer continued on up the avenue, realizing along the way how dimensionally off-register he, now a major victim, felt toward everything and everyone. He had a tinge of the delusion that he could walk right through things, and several times people had to dodge aside at the last moment because he wasn't about to give way.

He told himself it would wear off.

When he got to 58th he went east. About mid-block he paused to be a deliberate audience of one for a just-up hooker who was curbing her Great Dane. She had a clear plastic sandwich bag like a mitten on her right hand, used it to grab at the mound of grainy turd the huge dog dropped. Didn't get it all but as much as she could. She inverted the bag so it contained the turd, spun its neck, and secured it with a wire tie.

Love, Springer thought.

He resumed moving along the street, which was shadowed and dingy because the buildings were high on both sides. There was the sour smell of garbage where it came daily from the service entrance of the Plaza Hotel. Near the end of the block the street opened and assumed an appropriate Manhattan air. Flying from poles above the entrance to the Plaza were the flags of France, Japan, and Sweden, acknowledging the dignitaries of those countries who were staying there. Limousines were triple-parked.

On the corner was Bergdorf Goodman. Its display windows were covered on the inside by stretches of unbleached muslin, except for a six-inch space along the bottom and the area above eye level. Springer bent down and peeked in through three windows before he saw any living feet, and still another before he saw the toes, arches, and ankles that he recognized as surely Audrey's. He tapped on the window with a fingernail, a code of three fast and two slow so she'd know it wasn't just anyone.

Audrey depressed the upper border of the muslin and looked down at him. Because he didn't have a smile she lost hers. She removed the muslin. With a playful bow and a flourish she presented her work.

It was four female mannequins in an indigo environment. Three were adorned with summer-white party dresses: a silk organza, a crepe de chine, and a silk faconne. Layered, bloused, sashed. The manipulatable forms of those three were situated to the left. Their similar attitudes conveyed conspiracy. Each possessed a weapon, identical nickel-plated ivory-handled .32 caliber automatic pistols. Thus, to the frolic, the frou-frou, the almost promlike innocence, there was a touch of devastation. A gleaming pistol was not quite concealed up a sleeve, another was insouciantly inserted in a sash. The mannequin in the silk faconne was most prominent. She'd been put into a wide stance, chin up, arms at her sides. A pistol hung resignedly from her limp grasp. A wisp of something that remembled smoke, probably that Christmas stuff called angel's hair, trailed upward from the muzzle of the pistol. Scattered and gleaming around the mannequin's white sling pumps were several spent cartridges.

The fourth mannequin was in a black dress. She was on the floor off to the right sprawled in a contorted position, her back to the street, her face not visible. Thousands of tiny faux rubies streamed from beneath her, creating an irregular crimson pool that spotlights made the most of.

Springer supposed the statement Audrey sought to make had to do with innocence and competition. She looked out to him for approval. He mimed applause. Having tried before, they knew it was impossible to hear through the window glass, so now Audrey exaggerated her lip movements, hoping he might be able to read her words. He couldn't. She gave up on it, resorted to a black felt-tipped Flair pen that she had in one of the deep pockets of her work apron. No paper handy, she printed directly on the window glass, printed backwards and in so doing made a few childish-looking errors.

WHAT ARE YOU UP TO? her letters asked.

Springer replied with sign language, said he was up to above the wanting-to-breathe level by indicating the bridge of his nose with the edge of his flattened hand.

YOU LOOK PISSED she printed.

Springer scowled, nodded.

AT ME?

He smiled a fraction, shook his head no.

From another deep pocket of her work apron Audrey brought out one of those shiny .32-caliber pistols. She offered it grip first to Springer.

That broke him. He had to laugh. He pointed his first finger to his temple and worked his thumb several times like a pistol hammer.

Audrey printed HANG ON ANOTHER HOUR.

The antics of this speechless conversation were disregarded if not unnoticed by those who happened to be passing by. Not because as New Yorkers they were blasé or uninquisitive. Rather, they believed it was safer to give as little eye as possible to any stranger in the throes of acting strange.

There were, however, two men who were especially interested in

Springer's every move. Across the street near the perimeter of the Plaza fountain, standing in the dapple of a plane tree. They'd been on Springer since that morning, when he'd entered the 580 Fifth Building. They had followed him to his meeting with Danny and would be staying on him.

Fred Pugh and Jack Blayney.

They were State Department, two of George Gurney's men.

Blayney was the taller and heavier. His round face and splotchy complexion gave him the look of a career bartender, the sort who might be pouring and drawing at P. J. Clarke's or O'Neal's. A couple of weeks ago Blayney had turned forty. That bothered him. His legs felt different, not as strong or dependable, and it occurred to him that the spots on the backs of his hands weren't actually freckles. He was nagged by the numerical recognition that he was no longer on the count up but the count down. Such thinking *did* cause a change in him. Made him meaner. The morning that Blayney woke up forty, at the very instant when he'd opened his eyes to forty, he felt something click sharply in him. His meanness was being turned up. He'd always been a bully during all his fifteen years with State, a lethal one; was now all the more so. He didn't look it, though. Surely didn't, standing there by the Plaza fountain sucking the syrupy flavor from a paper cupful of Italian ice he'd bought from a street vendor.

Pugh was more distinguishable.

Less than slight, Pugh's shoulders hunched inward, hollowing his chest, exaggerating his narrowness. He had an elongated face, very close-set eyes, and a sharply bridged nose. His meager mouth had a natural purse to it, seemed on the verge of whistling. All in all Pugh looked as though he'd been forced to suffer many of his thirty-eight years squeezed in a press.

Today Pugh was wearing a blue-and-white striped seersucker suit, a lemon-colored necktie and new, black, wing-tipped shoes with thick soles. There was nothing in bad taste about the shoes as far as he was concerned. The sales clerk at Florsheim had suggested white loafers with little fringed tassels and Pugh had tried them on and almost gone for them but decided they were faggoty.

"What's the asshole saying now?" Blayney asked.

"He's got his back to me," Pugh replied, as, like any tourist, he sighted through the viewfinder of the Canon 35mm camera that hung from his neck by a woven plaid strap. The lens on the camera appeared normal, but it had been internally adapted to the telescopic power of a 500mm. Thus it served Pugh as well as a pair of binoculars while allowing him to focus unobviously on his subject from a distance.

Pugh read lips.

Seventeen years ago, when he'd started with Central Intelligence, he'd noticed that most of those people who were kept on for any serious length of time had things they were best at. Best at Middle Eastern disguises, inducing authentic heart attacks, Cambodian geography, things like that. Just being generally trained and loyal wasn't enough. Even the most nerveless sorts came and went.

What Pugh's specialty would be came to him in 1970 in Marbella, Spain. His assignment there was to snoop on an American NATO diplomat who had taken up with a limp-wristed Rumanian political strategist. The two men were suspected of selling secrets through one another and having a luxurious affair with the pooled proceeds.

That appeared to Pugh to be the case, though he'd observed nothing solidly incriminating, just the exchange by the two men of barely perceptible thrown kisses across their dinner table and, while on the beach, all-done pats to one another's ass cheeks after applying suntan lotion.

On the beach one afternoon Pugh watched them rise from their spread towels and walk to the surf. They waded out to deep water. Only their heads were visible, bobbing in the swells like a couple of children's playballs. Pugh sighted them with his binoculars and believed, according to the proximity of their heads, they were within easy reach of one another. No telling what their hands were busy at beneath the water. He'd probably know if he were able to hear what they were saying at that moment. He could see their lips moving. What an advantage it would be to know how to read lips!

It struck him.

A few days later the American and the Rumanian must have had a rending tiff. They took somber breakfasts at separate tables and that afternoon flew in different directions. Their case was placed in the inactive file and Pugh was ordered home.

He went right to developing his specialty. Spent every spare hour and all the time he could steal from Langley at the Library of Congress. He found numerous illustrated volumes that dealt with the positions of the lips and the corresponding facial muscles during speech. There was, he learned, a science of sounds in language called phonology, which, depending on dialect, included thirty to forty contrasting sound units. These units gave each word its particular shape.

Pugh was glad to know it was all so nicely arranged. He was encouraged enough to think that learning to lip-read wouldn't be difficult. Then, for a while, he thought it impossible.

He kept at it, sought out a school for the deaf in Alexandria, and talked his way into being permitted to attend classes. For homework he watched television with the sound off. As he gained confidence he plugged his ears with the sort of malleable wax plugs that light sleepers use to shut out noise and tried to carry on conversations.

He got better and better at it.

After two years he let his superiors at Langley in on it. He claimed he was the best not-deaf lip-reader around. To demonstrate he had them listen with earphones to that day's episode of *Days of Our Lives* while he lip-read the dialogue.

He didn't miss a syllable or sob.

His superiors were professionally amused. He was given several other tests. His accuracy impressed them. He indeed had a specialty. It would, he was assured, be put to important use. For his incentive he was upped a grade.

Pugh's first assignment after that was in Santiago, Chile. It involved snooping on a troublesome leftist leader. The setup was ideal for Pugh. From the vantage of the building across the street he could see into the apartment where the leftist and his key people met. Powerful binoculars brought their faces close enough for Pugh to easily see the movements of their lips. However . . .

The fuckers were speaking in Spanish.

Pugh didn't know Spanish.

Nor for that matter did he know Russian, German, French, or Arabic.

Thus he was only a limitedly useful lip-reader.

On some of many tedious afternoons he would accompany his Langley bosses to Bowie racetrack over in Maryland. Before each race Pugh hung around the paddock area where the trainers gave last-minute instructions to their jockeys. He read the lips of the trainers and reported to his Langley bosses what had been said. Knowing the various strategies of a race gave them an edge. At the very least they would never waste a bet on a horse whose trainer had him running merely for the conditioning or experience.

Often the information lip-read by Pugh practically guaranteed a sure thing: when two or more horses were being sent out to try to go wire-to-wire with their speed, and in the rest of the field there was only one legitimate closing horse—hopefully a long shot. The front-runners burned up their energy staving off one another, the closer came on strong in the stretch, and the Langley people cashed in their winners.

Pugh resented having to put his hard-learned talent to such playful, lusterless use.

So in 1979, when George Gurney went over to the State Department to head up its Intelligence and Research Bureau, Pugh went with him.

That bureau was, of course, not as large or limelighted as the CIA. Never would be. However, Gurney intended to make up for lack of weight with shiftiness. His would be a cadre of people gifted with abundant sleight and little, if any, conscience—which was, after all, what intelligence work was all about, what had been lost under the years and years of politicking and the pile-ons for power. Ambitious to the bone, imaginative enough to put stock in leads others might dismiss as ridiculous, Gurney foresaw a time when his outfit would no longer be seated below the salt.

Fred Pugh liked working for Gurney. He felt Gurney honestly gave a damn, appreciated him. Gurney found consequential ways to utilize Pugh's lipreading, and at the same time he encouraged another dimension out of Pugh.

Pugh had never done any wet work, any killing. His psychological tests when he was indoctrinated into Central Intelligence had indicated he wasn't suited for wet work. However, under Gurney he'd killed five times, and after the first, as Gurney had predicted, he'd been hardly bothered.

In fact, Pugh was looking forward to the next.

18

There was Moe Bandy on the stereo:

"He's a rodeo Romeo,
Cowgirls and bulls are his life,
He loves what he does
And he does what he loves every night . . ."

Audrey sang along with it and two-stepped improvisingly around the room. A crisp bob of her head, a reaching glide, a tight turn—and, often, a stumble when the high heels of her maribou-covered mules caught in the pile of the rug. Other than the mules she had on only a pale green silk charmeuse teddy, loose and fluid, and a pair of briolette-cut emerald earrings.

She wasn't quite dancing alone. Her extended hands held a Brigette Deval doll that she had bought a month or so ago at Ludwig

Beck. For $2,500. Not only the price made the doll more than a plaything. With its genuine ringleted hair, hand-stitched empire-style dress, and walkable patent leather shoes it was the closest thing to an adorable breathing two-year-old. Especially convincing was the poise of its lifelike fingers, the astonished expression on its paradoxically waifish, little-rich-girl face—and the lovesome way Audrey danced it.

> *"He'll hit the dance halls,*
> *Flashing the girls his best smile,*
> *He's burning both ends of the candle,*
> *Rodeo Romeo style."*

Springer appreciated Audrey with his eyes but his ears loathed her. Not even all that country-western twanging and picking could make up for how off-key she was. Why the hell didn't she leave the singing to Moe? Springer was tempted to convey as much by sticking his fingers in his ears. He didn't only because she was trying so to cheer him up.

She had tried all through their early dinner at Lutece. Ordered a bottle of Bollinger Tradition RD 1973, kissed his glass with hers, and said brightly, "To having been robbed." When he grunted, annoyed, she'd told him that she thought being robbed was probably the next most exciting thing to robbing, and anyway it didn't happen to one every day so it was sort of an event.

Springer begrudgingly drank to it.

He wasn't interested in his dinner, poked at it. They skipped dessert and coffee and went back to her apartment at the Trump. She urged him quickly out of his clothes and got him into a vinegar bath. Two cups of apple cider vinegar added to the bath water. To get rid of all the negative energy he'd picked up, she explained, and, by balancing his acid-alkaline ratio, put his body in a healing state.

Springer went along with it. He didn't say so but he felt bloodlessly wounded, in need of healing. When he was immersed up to his chin the vinegar fumes made his eyes run and stung the inside of his nose. To get thoroughly detoxified he had to soak for at least twenty minutes, Audrey said. For good measure she poured in what vinegar remained in the quart bottle, ignored his protesting moans. She didn't tell him time was up until a half hour had passed.

While they were both drying him off with big towels he remarked that he felt better after the bath because he was no longer in it. Audrey didn't rise to that, except to increase the pressure of her rubbing from brisk to harsh.

She had a lightweight cotton robe laid out for him. And a pot of peach-pit tea. Whenever they ate fresh peaches she saved the pits. Even when either of them had a peach out at a restaurant she'd wrap the pit in a napkin and tuck it in her purse. She placed the precious pits incongruously on her elegant window ledges to dry in the sun. With them she brewed up a vile-tasting tea that she claimed was a sure way to purify the blood and thus increase one's sense of well-being.

Over the months Springer had surreptitiously poured gallons of miraculous peach-pit tea down the sink or the toilet. This day he didn't give a look to the cup on the bathroom counter, went downstairs to the mirrored bar for some Usquaebach Scotch, neat, in a double old-fashioned glass. Usquaebach was his Scotch of choice. Very few bars stocked it, and Springer didn't like to ask for it out because he thought it sounded affected. Usquaebach ran about $60 a fifth and came in a glazed earthen jug, which was probably why it seemed to taste better.

Three Usquaebachs nailed Springer to the roomy chaise longue diagonally opposite Audrey's bed. For nearly an hour he salted his wounds with the pages that listed lot by lot what had been stolen.

Moe Bandy was through now.

Audrey sat the doll in a comfortable position importantly among the antique crystal and silver jars and atomizers on her dressing table. She dabbed some of Libby's personal Guerlain (doled out to her) at the back of each knee before going to the stereo to replace Moe Bandy with Brahms. Tender French horns at the start, woodwinds meeting them midair. Piano Concerto No. 2.

She had the urge to go over and give Springer a rough, emphatic hug. Instead, she flopped down onto the puffy heap of elegantly shammed pillows on the floor at the foot of her bed. Her usual flopping place, preferred by her over the chaise. She fell right into an unintentionally alluring pose, the long dips and rises of her enhanced by the various swellings of the pillows beneath her weight and the way they served as soft backdrops. Her right arm was extended. The lower half of her face was concealed by the round of her bare shoulder. Over that shoulder her eyes vamped Springer, willed his attention. When he looked her way she playfully overworked her eyelashes, trying to draw at least a small smile from him.

He remained glum, but he winked.

"Did they steal that special stone?" she asked.

"Yeah." Lot number 588. He'd noticed it designated and described that way on the list. But he hadn't considered its loss as important as other lots. Such as twenty-six internally flawless D- to F-quality round-cuts totaling fifty-eight carats.

"That's a shame." Audrey sat up abruptly as though reacting to a call. "Whoever has it may never realize what it is."

The Brahms was now tempestuous.

Springer allowed the pages of listings to drop to the floor. It wasn't the loss of stone 588 that made him say, "I think I'll quit the business, get into something else."

"Like what?"

"I don't know."

"Sloth seems to have a future. I know many who've done conspicuously well at it. Could you get into sloth?"

"Possibly." He grinned.

As though considering it she cocked her head and studied him. "You don't have any experience," she decided.

Continuing seriously, he said, "At least what I might do is close the office. Get all that shit off my shoulders." The blasphemy caused a shiver in him. He defied it. "There'll never be a better time to do away with the office."

"Better excuse?"

"Better time," he maintained.

"Where would you do business?"

"Out of my pocket and in my head. I'd freelance around, build up a private clientele."

"Like Libby."

"Sure, why not."

"If she threw you just a few of her sparkling friends you'd have it made. Incidentally, Libby invited us up to Penobscot again."

"When?"

"She called me today at the store."

"Call her right now, tell her we accept."

"You really want me to?"

"No."

Audrey reached for her carryall shoulder bag on the floor nearby. From it she brought out her pendulum. And a bag of strawberry licorice whips. She separated one of the three-foot-long candies from the rest, put just the end of it in her mouth. From then on it required no hands. She fussed with the pendulum while the pink sweet went into her inch by inch.

Springer was in no humor to indulge her pendulum crap. He squinted to eliminate everything extraneous, to be seeing only the aspects of her and what she was about. Audrey, his love, sitting there cross-legged amid the pillows, preoccupied with a toy and chewing up a make-believe snake. He reassured himself that she was as mature as her body, not retarded. Maybe, he thought, that was one of his reasons for loving her—because she was so foie gras *and* Baby Ruth. He certainly wouldn't be as attracted if she were entirely foie gras. Oh, well. . . .

Audrey finished with the pendulum. She dropped it in her bag. She'd also had enough Brahms. She got up and put on Aretha Franklin's "Sweet Bitter Love."

Springer thought that Audrey, now she was up, would come snuggle on the chaise with him. But she returned to her pillows and selected a couple of books from those stacked on the floor by the bed. Wild bird feathers that she'd found served as her bookmarks, so she was able to turn right to her place in *The Secret Doctrine, Volume 2, Anthropogenesis* by H. P. Blavatsky. She'd been nibbling on it for well over a year and was about two thirds of the way through, on a section that was headed "The Law of Retribution."

After intense concentration on a page and a half Audrey resurfaced, said without looking up, "We're going to get it back."

"Get what back?"

"Stone Five eighty-eight."

"So says your pendulum, I suppose."

"It was very definite about it."

"Did it mention the rest of my goods?"

"Pendulum doesn't mention, it answers. You know that. Anyway, I only asked about Stone Five eighty-eight, would we or wouldn't we."

Springer exhaled some of his peeve. Part of the rest of it came out with "You are a fucking whacko."

She hard-eyed him. "Want to fight?"

He really didn't. "Not with you."

"We ought to have some knock-downs and drag-outs once in a while," she said. "Fights are the bread and jelly of a relationship."

"You ever wanted to punch me out?"

"Sure."

Springer wondered when those times had been. Whenever, he must have sailed unaware right through them. Was he that insensitive? "Why didn't you?" he asked.

"I didn't want to hurt you," she said, and closed the subject by closing Blavatsky and splitting open another book to any page. After a moment: "If you were on your own there'd be less or more time for us?"

"You'd like more?"

She felt anything so obvious didn't deserve an answer. "Libby adores you," she said. "She'd go out of her way to help you get a running start."

The old time-fighter traipsed across the front of Springer's mind, waving her hands. "I guess Libby's okay," he said.

"We should make a point of getting together with her . . . often."

"I don't want to be such a user."

"There are users and losers," Audrey cautioned.

"Also sinners and winners," was his cynical retort.

Audrey considered that, agreed with a nod, and went to her book. In her spendidly accented Foxcroft and Wellesley French she asked, "How does *Lièvre farci à la Périgourdine* grab you?"

"What is it?"

"Stuffed hare." She spelled the homonym.

"Ever had it?"

"Not that I was ever aware of. Listen." She read. " 'Take care to collect all the blood when drawing the hare; break the bones of the legs that they may be easily trussed; clear the legs and the loins of all tendons, and lard them. Chop up the liver, the lungs, the heart' . . . God, it's gory!" The book was *The Escoffier Cook Book for Connoisseurs, Chefs, and Epicures.* She flipped to any other page. "*Supremes de volaille,*" she read and raised her eyes to Springer. "Chicken breasts. The French have about two million different ways to fix chicken breasts."

He realized what, in a roundabout way, she was saying to him. Up to now a tuna salad sandwich had been an accomplishment.

"Next you'll probably be thinking I want to get pregnant or something." She laughed. "Anyway, there's a self-serving motive in my wanting to learn to cook."

"Oh?"

"I figure, hell, I can't expect you to keep up your sexual hardihood for the next fifty or so years on a diet of Almond Joys and pepperoni."

Springer told himself if it hadn't been for the robbery and all the uncertainty it had caused, he would have at that moment asked her to marry him. He met her gaze, told her, "You're a lulu of a lady."

"*Your* lulu of a lady," she said courageously, not letting out any of the feeling that she'd just been turned down. She returned to Escoffier, pretending to read.

Springer stood and went across the room to one of the windows. The view it gave was down Fifth Avenue. The traffic, mainly a scattering of taxi yellow, appeared Lilliputian. Beyond the reflection on the window glass, out there in the perpetual aura of the city, he saw the 580 Fifth Building. Nine blocks away and oddly inconsequential from this vantage. He picked out the windows that were

Springer & Springer easily because he'd done it numerous times before from that spot. What would it be like, he wondered, to never again feel obligated to that space and all the proprietary pride that had occupied it? How absurd, even bizarre, that its reason for being was particles hardly larger than specks clawed up out of the earth and declared precious? We hadn't come much of a way from the grunting prehistorics who bludgeoned one another to a pulp over certain prettier pebbles and animal teeth, had we?

Springer used his wrist to rub away a little itch on the side of his nose. The pungent smell of his skin surprised him. His rancor seeping out? He remembered the vinegar bath.

He had spoken of closing Springer & Springer, of going it alone. He'd thought his words were merely words, empty threat to whatever power was determining his circumstances. (Smile upon me or else.) However, now the idea was taking the shape of an earnest alternative. Audrey was right. With only a few of Libby's friends as clients he could do better than ever. He might even become another Winston or Townsend. Townsend had built his business with social stones, using charm and regretted confidences for mortar. Townsend had always dealt a highly lucrative few notches above the wholesale level. For Townsend the divorce or death of a client invariably meant money to be made.

The safety deposit box was registered to a corporation so it would not be included in her personal estate. The day after the funeral the primpily attired eldest son, who had authorized access, went to the bank, emptied the contents of the safety deposit box into a Mark Cross shopping bag, and proceeded directly to Townsend's. He didn't have an appointment but Townsend was expecting him.

"Sell these off for me, Gilbert."

Bracelets, necklaces, rings, tiaras: diamonds, sapphires, rubies, emeralds. Dumped upon Townsend's desk like so much junk.

"On the Q.T., of course."

"Do you have prices in mind?"

"Whatever's fair."

Springer might become what Townsend appeared to be.

But never what Townsend was.

Those Russian diamonds for Libby would be a nice beginning, though Springer doubted that deal even more now that he was back on familiar ground. The so-called Igor Bitov and his brief visit in Paris seemed a figment. The man had been so casually agreeable to delivering the diamonds in New York because he knew the whole thing was impossible. And Libby—perhaps she'd invented the opportunity in the first place just to make Springer jump and fail. When Igor didn't come through, that fifteen million would go back to Wintersgill, keeper of the great green funnel. Interest too.

Something gave Springer a sharp mental poke.

What a fucking pessimist he was getting to be, he thought. A mope, a brooder, a wallower, and after just this first big setback. Shit, he knew guys who had suffered worse three or four times in their lives and were still outlooking with spirit. Drumgold, for example. Springer almost laughed aloud at himself.

He turned, unaware that Audrey was standing close behind him. She didn't *give* ground, she closed it.

"I have a kiss for your stiff upper lip," she said and gave it to him.

His body would insist that she take small steps backward. Her legs would come to the edge of the bed and she would allow herself to fall onto it. He would drop upon her, but lightly, supporting most of his weight with his elbows. She would spread her legs. The loosely leg-holed teddy would accommodate. And, as they often jested about how his cock without assistance was able to find where it was wanted and wanted to be, it would.

The telephone rang.

They let it ring itself out.

Within the time it took for someone to redial it began ringing again.

Audrey answered it, told the caller to hold on. She placed the receiver down and walked away from it, saying, "It's your ex-wife."

Bad enough he was so often subjected to Gayle and her bitchiness at the office. This was new and worse behavior on her part. When

213

he got on the phone he felt justified to come down hard on her. "How the hell did you get this number?"

Audrey's number was not even supposed to be listed among the unlisted.

Gayle told him. "The doctor had the police get it from the operator."

19

◇

Between 67th and 68th streets on York Avenue.

Memorial Sloan-Kettering Cancer Center, the largest, most comprehensive facility of its kind in the world.

Springer and Audrey went in and up a flight on the escalator to the spacious main waiting room. Regular visiting hours were over; only a few people were there, seated, it seemed, as far apart as possible. Gayle was in one of the plastic upholstered chairs by the window overlooking York. The way she was facing, Springer and Audrey were in her line of view as they approached, but she wasn't noticing them or anything at that moment. They didn't register until they were no more than a dozen feet from her. Then she stood, as abruptly as if she'd been jerked up by a magnet.

Springer realized immediately that this was a different Gayle from the one he'd been disliking. Crisis and grief had subdued her; she appeared physically smaller, easily breakable. Her face was drawn pale, the color of fright, and the lids of her eyes were inflamed from crying. She tried to smile but only managed a twitch of the corners of her mouth. Her upper arms were tensed against her sides. Her hands were palms up, cupped, as though asking for someone to put any crumb of meaningful comfort in them.

Springer didn't hesitate, overcame any unsureness of the moment by putting his arms around Gayle. They hadn't touched in more than two years. Gayle gave in to it, let herself be entirely held. Over Springer's shoulder her eyes connected with Audrey's. The two women had never met, only knew of one another.

Audrey reached out and stroked Gayle's hair back from her forehead, a sympathetic caress.

"They told me I might as well go home," Gayle said. "Twice I got as far as First Avenue." She sounded out of breath. Her voice had little hoarse cracks in it. She clung to Springer, drawing from him, and after a short while she was fortified enough to pull away. She raised her chin, sniffled twice, blinked, and widened her eyes to untighten them.

Observing her, Springer thought at least now she was farther from crying.

Gayle glanced around to make sure the chair was still there before she sat down on it. Springer and Audrey moved identical chairs into position so they'd be facing her.

"I called Norman," Gayle said.

"When?"

"While I was trying to reach you. He's flying up tomorrow morning."

That was good, Springer thought, Norman to back him up. A doctor to get more from the doctors and, out of close personal concern, make certain whatever course decided upon was best.

"He's taking an early shuttle," Gayle said. "I wrote it all down." She dug into three pockets of her jeans before she found the slip of paper. She gave it to Springer.

"What else did Norman say?"

"Just that we could count on him for anything . . . and . . . to keep the faith. I most remember him saying to keep the faith." Gayle was on the edge of her chair. She settled back but immediately sat forward again. Fidgety, she rocked left and right, inserted her hands flat beneath her buttocks. To keep her legs still she locked her ankles. She was wearing well-scuffed blue Topsider moccasins. The white leather lace of one was undone, dirty where it had been stepped on. "I've had too much coffee," she said, merely stating the fact.

"When did you last eat?" Audrey asked.

Gayle didn't reply.

"There has to be a deli close by. I'll go out and get you a sandwich or something."

Gayle was oblivious to the offer. She told Springer, "If you want to go up to see him it's all right. Even though it's late they said it would be all right."

"I'll go up in a couple of minutes. First, fill me in."

Gayle started to speak. Her mouth was forming the first word even as her mind retracted it. Her memory was like a tape being rewound. Finally, she began with: "April. It was in April—or possibly March —anyway it was around that time . . ."

She told it recitatively in a monotone, pretending as much as possible that it was the story of someone else so she could get through it. About how she had gone to Dr. Landon, their family doctor, for no reason other than a checkup. Jamie—Jake, she changed it to Jake with a small glance at Springer—went with her, which was not unusual. He enjoyed the waiting room magazines: *Sports Illustrated, Town and Country,* and particularly the one called *Human Sexuality.* She was aware of this precocious interest but thought whatever Jake might discover in the good doctor's office couldn't possibly harm him. Anyway, that day, after her checkup, Dr. Landon saw her out to the waiting room. He made a bit over Jake, asked him how he was. To the doctor's surprise, Jake took the cordial inquiry literally and replied that his leg hurt a little.

This was the first Jake had mentioned it, so Gayle thought he was merely trying for some extra attention. It wasn't like him, but she thought that had to be it. Dr. Landon, between patients, took him into one of the examining rooms. Jake indicated rather unsurely where he claimed his leg hurt a little. A few inches above the right knee, in there somewhere, he said. Dr. Landon pressed and poked and asked if when he did that did it hurt more? Jake said nope. Dr. Landon feigned a concerned frown, told him what he had was a bad case of . . . growing. And that he had years of growings ahead of him. To that, Jake scrunched up his nose and remarked what a pain.

Gayle was quite sure the truth of it was that Jake had injured his leg playing volleyball, badly pulled a muscle or something. He so often came home with knees and elbows scraped bloody, and once even his chin. He was such a toughie when it came to pain, no wonder with this he hadn't complained enough.

A few days after he got back from the trip to Washington she noticed he was favoring his right leg and asked him about it. With playful insolence he told her to stop overmothering him. It was just that he was growing, he said, *growing*. Oh, so that was it, she thought. He was acting out Dr. Landon's words. Well, like so many other affectations he'd picked up from watching MTV and movie heroes and whatever, this too would soon get used up and pass.

What should have been obvious to her was that he'd stopped playing his beloved volleyball. His clothes had told her. He returned from the Park looking as tidy as when he'd gone out. Imagine how much it must have hurt him to have to stand off to the side and watch the play.

Last week he began limping. Couldn't walk a step without limping.

Jake had agreed with her then that he must have hurt his leg at volleyball. He didn't remember when exactly, so it must have happened during some hard, fast play. Some fellow probably got him with a knee, Jake said. He knew from sports commentators on television that athletes frequently suffered what they called deep bruises, even so much as bruised their bones.

At that point Jake's leg just above the knee was somewhat swollen, reddened and warm to the touch. Gayle had him soak it in Epsom-salted water as hot as he could stand and she put the portable Jacuzzi whirlpool in the tub with him, thinking that might help. She massaged the area and applied some Ben-Gay ointment. All this was stoking her irritation with Springer and she intended to give him some of her usual ex-wife hell for encouraging Jake at a sport that could be so rough. She was of a mind to call Springer right then and melt the lines but he was somewhere in Europe.

The soaks and Ben-Gay massages didn't help. By Friday Jake's leg was visibly worse: redder, swollen more, and hotter. She gave him double-strength Tylenol for the pain. He hobbled around the apartment using the furniture for support. When she phoned Dr. Landon she was told that he was away for the weekend. The doctor covering for him was offered. She decided against him, imagining incompetence. She requested an appointment with Dr. Landon for early Monday morning. Was it an emergency?

Yes.

Dr. Landon examined Jake's leg and immediately ordered x-rays. Even before the doctor had seen the x-rays Gayle sensed his gravity. She had thought what she'd be hearing at worst was that Jake had an infection of some sort and would have to take an antibiotic. However, Dr. Landon advised that Jake be put in the hospital for more comprehensive tests—a thorough workup, was the way he put it. He mentioned the possibility of osteomyelitis with a tinge of optimism in his voice, which Gayle thought was a strange way of looking at it. Osteomyelitis, as she understood from having read about it somewhere, was a serious infection of the bone. Certainly nothing to be hoped for.

Dr. Landon's attitude became a bit less enigmatic to her when she overheard him call and arrange for Jake's immediate admittance to Memorial Sloan-Kettering.

Other than osteomyelitis what else could it be? she wanted to know.

Dr. Landon was careful not to unduly alarm her, said he was merely being cautious. He referred her to a Dr. Stimson.

Dr. Stimson was a pediatric oncologist.

From then on Gayle had the feeling that everything was happening too fast while time dragged. It had been just this morning, only about twelve hours ago, that Jake was put to bed in a private room there at Sloan-Kettering. Nurses and interns and various hospital personnel moved about in white cotton jackets and coats with the

Sloan-Kettering insignia on them: a thin sky-blue cross with three transverses, resembling somewhat a papal cross but probably not with any relative intent. Dr. Stimson showed up almost immediately. A man in his early forties with a harriedness just below his considerate manner. The sort of doctor who was much more do than show. He examined Jake, made no comment, had him wheeled on a stretcher down to the second floor for x-rays. Gayle tried to get an opinion, any crumb of an opinion, from Dr. Stimson then; however, he put her off. The x-rays would tell him what he should tell her, he said.

An hour later she was with Dr. Stimson in his hospital office, an almost cubbyhole of a place cramped all the more by stacks of accumulated information. Jake's x-rays were clipped onto the light panel on the wall. The chief radiologist and Dr. Stimson had already studied them—various views of the lower section of Jake's right thigh. Some included the knee.

The troubled area was easily distinguishable. It was where the bone appeared to bulge out, an area about two inches in diameter that deviated from the straight line of the rest of the femur. Dr. Stimson called Gayle's attention to the outermost covering of the bone, which he told her was the periosteum, and the mass of compact bone just beneath it. He patiently pointed out the difference between the affected area and where the bone was healthily normal. As though she already knew the implications, he told her that it was often extremely difficult to differentiate osteomyelitis, a bacterial infection of the bone, from something more serious.

Such as what more serious?

Osteogenic sarcoma.

Cancer of the bone.

Gayle had a sensation like a parachute opening inside her, a plosiveness. She silently told the x-rays that Jake was only eight years old. A plea and protest.

Dr. Stimson explained that osteogenic sarcoma was usually a young person's cancer. It occurred mainly in eleven- to thirteen-year-olds but younger cases were not uncommon. He must have sensed her reeling inside, her needing to be steadied, because he quickly added that to assume the worst in this instance would be jumping the gun. He was not, he said emphatically, on just the basis of these x-rays, ready to make a diagnosis of cancer. Osteomyelitis was still a possibility, and there were other possibilities as well. A favorable thing was that the articular capsule did not appear to be involved. He pointed out Jake's knee joint in the x-rays.

Holding nothing back, putting kindness entirely aside, what was really the chance of its being something other than bone cancer? Gayle asked.

Dr. Stimson turned away from the x-rays, as though self-conscious that they might hear him tell her that he'd say the chance was fair. Then his beeper had sounded, saving him from being further pressed for hope—that tenuous commodity he was incessantly asked to dispense.

That, Gayle told Springer and Audrey, was more or less how it had gone. She paragraphed the moment by pulling her hands out from beneath her. She immediately laced them in her lap, so tightly her fingertips showed bright pink. "They've scheduled a biopsy tomorrow morning," she said. "We'll know more for sure then."

Springer stood.

Audrey told him, "I'll stay here with Gayle."

He gave Gayle's shoulder an encouraging pat on his way to the reception desk at the far end of the waiting room. A pleasant-mannered gray-haired woman provided him with a visitor's pass and directions. He had to show the pass to the uniformed guard in the corridor before he was allowed to take the elevator to the fifth floor. He hadn't expected the pediatrics department to be so vast. A nurse on duty there verified his pass and indicated the way to go. Springer believed he could have found the right room without directions from anyone, by merely relying on the instinct of needing, during crisis, to be with his own.

Down the beige corridor.

Past entrances of room after room, all the way to the last one on the left.

Dimly, indirectly lighted. A small room but adequate.

Springer paused to take it in. The stillness made him feel an intruder. He walked noiselessly to the bed, stood at the foot of it. Springer's own boy was lying on his side, covered up to his chin by a sheet. The head section of the adjustable bed was slanted up and he'd slid down to where it angled. In Springer's eyes he looked too small for the bed. Displaced, Springer thought. He had the notion to take him up in his arms and carry him away, to anywhere, to happy circumstances. God, if only it could be that easy.

For twenty minutes Springer stood there silently communing. A part of him suggested he sit in one of the visitor's chairs and keep an all-night watch. Another part of him advised that he had better go rest for the demands of tomorrow. He was about to turn to leave when his son came awake, didn't stir up out of sleep gradually, was at once abruptly conscious, as though influenced by Springer's presence, feeling him there.

"How's my Jake?"

"Not half bad."

"Are you hurting a lot?"

"They gave me something. With a needle. Ouch."

They must have also given him a sedative, because he was barely opening his lips, having to push the words out.

"I got here as soon as I could," Springer told him, moving around to the side of the bed.

"I figured you'd be along. Where were you?"

"France."

"With Audrey, huh?"

"She sends you a kiss."

"So give it to me."

Springer lowered a kiss to Jake's lips. Jake's mouth had never felt so small to him. Funny, he thought, how much he'd lost sight of the child that Jake actually was. Jake's dependencies, lack of adequate defenses. The boy's reaching out so early and eagerly for maturity had had a lot to do with it, of course.

"What do you think of this place?" Springer asked, to measure Jake's frame of mind.

Jake thought a moment, evidently deciding which reply to make. "They give you room service you don't even ask for," he said and laughed a little, lazy, back-of-the-throat laugh.

"Like the Ritz in Paris."

"Never been there."

"I'll take you."

"Double promise?"

"We'll sit by a tall window that can be opened by a golden knob, and we'll eat all kinds of fancy cakes and pies. . . ."

"Audrey will eat most of them."

"So we'll order more."

"We'll have some croak monsters."

For years they'd shared a just-between-them joke about Croque Monsieurs, those melted cheese and ham sandwiches the French sell at nearly every bistro. Their joke involved a nearsighted bartender and a frog.

"Maybe we'll even have some croak madames," Springer said.

"That's after we get back to the hotel from a long walk around seeing everything."

"A long, long walk around."

That future prospect hung in the air.

"I see you've got a television," Springer said.

A set with a seven-inch screen was fixed to the end of a manipulatable elbowed arm. Attached to the wall, so it could be swung out of the way or down before the eyes of the patient in bed.

"They don't have cable. I felt like watching some MTV but I couldn't get it. Instead I just watched the bridge."

"The bridge?"

"Out there."

The window blinds were drawn down and closed tight. Springer went over and parted a couple of the flexible metal slats to peek out. It was a south view featuring the Queensboro Bridge. Floodlighted, the gray-painted intricacies of the span had a blue cast, a clean almost baby-boy blue. Twin reds of taillights were animate embellishments.

"Dad?"

"Hmm?" Springer returned to the bed.

"What are they going to do to me?"

Springer couldn't answer honestly, couldn't say he didn't know. "Nothing bad," he said. "But it's okay if you're afraid. Don't be ashamed of being afraid."

"If you say."

Springer took Jake's hand. It was fisted. He held it, enclosed it within both his hands, felt the shape and the bones of it. It was like he'd captured a little creature that he loved. "Maybe," he said, "you'd better be getting some sleep."

"Everything's Jake, right?"

"Yeah, everything's Jake."

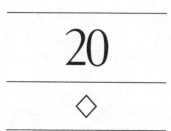

20

$\diamond$

Early the following afternoon Springer leaned against a mail reposi-
tory box on the corner of 67th Street while he kept an eye on the
York Avenue entrance of Sloan-Kettering.

He didn't want to be in there, not anywhere within the walls of
the hospital, when he got word. In there was where cancer concentrated, came to do battle, and he felt the news he awaited had a better
chance of being good if it was brought out to him. It was, he realized,
the sort of intuitive reasoning Audrey or Mattie might have used and
that he would normally indulge.

Also, waiting outside alone allowed him to air his thoughts more
clearly. The problems of yesterday, the robbery loss and all that, had
been preempted. They were still sorry facts of life but were now far
back in his line of concern. Diamonds and the perpetual scramble for
them were inconsequential. He doubted that diamonds would ever
again be as important to him as they had been. He was sure he was
changed, humbled.

He'd waited an hour. It was another half hour before he saw Norman come out of the hospital. Norman paused, glanced upward as though to verify the sky. He armed out of his suit jacket, slung it by a hook of finger over his shoulder, and walked in Springer's direction.

From half a block away Springer tried to read Norman. Did Norman's slouch and unhurried pace signify that he was burdened with regrettable information, or could it be taken as easygoingness because the findings had been favorable? Was that a glimmer of smile on Norman's face, or merely the squinting of his eyes against the day's brightness pulling up the corners of his mouth?

Although there was no traffic coming, Norman waited for the WALK light before he crossed 67th Street. "Let's have a beer," he said.

From that Springer surmised the worst. But he had yet to hear it. It would come soon enough. No need asking for it.

They bought Heinekens from the cooler case of a nearby delicatessen. Went across York Avenue and down a block to the wide paved walkway situated between the FDR Drive and the East River. They sat on one of the benches and yanked the pull tabs from their beers.

"Osteogenic sarcoma," Norman said.

"For certain?"

"Positive. I saw the biopsy report, was even allowed a look at some of the tissue specimens. Anything I didn't understand Stimson explained to me."

"Tell me what you saw."

"Why?"

"I want to know. I don't want anything to be happening to Jake that I don't know about."

Not an unusual attitude, Norman knew from his doctoring. Often, seriously sick patients and, just as often, those closest to them wanted as much information as they could glean. He'd known people who had become lay experts from trying in this way to make up for their feelings of futility.

He told Springer, "I viewed several slides under a powerful microscope. They were sections—that is, very thin slices of tissue excised from in and around the tumored area of Jake's leg. Some of the sections were purposely taken from the edge of the tumor so they included normal tissue for comparison. Are you sure you want to hear all this?"

Springer nodded.

"What I saw was an average number of osteoblasts in the normal tissue and far too many of them in the tissue of the tumor. Those in the tumor were deformed one way or another, lopsided, missing membrane or something. They were also dark and angry-looking, and reproducing like sons of bitches. I could see them in various stages of replication: growing two nuclei, stretching out into spindle shapes, separating."

"What did you say they're called?"

"Osteoblasts."

"Cells . . ." Springer muttered vaguely.

"The kind that form bone tissue. Osteoblasts aggregate within the matrix of a bone, where they become osteocytes, which in turn connect and harden into compact bone. Up until the time when the body has completed its growing—say, at about age twenty—there are lots of osteoblasts doing their constructive work throughout the skeletal system."

Springer grabbed that. "Jake's still growing."

"But in that one area on his femur too many of those cells are being reproduced. Remember, they're ugly tumor cells, enemy cells. I once saw a motion picture of such cells. It was astonishing how fast they multiplied, almost too fast for the eye. Like they had a vengeance."

Springer visualized the enemy.

"What happens is they multiply so fast there's not enough room for them. So they make room, pushing through whatever happens to be in their way: soft tissue, bone, blood vessels, nerves."

Springer wondered if Norman had brought out to him even a scintilla of hope. "What," he asked, "makes those cells behave like that?"

"The person who answers that will get a Nobel, will deserve a hundred Nobels. From what I understand, the theories are narrowing down and pointing more and more toward something genetic. Seems we all have the potential of cancer in us but about twenty-five percent of us are short on the genetic material that provides the necessary immunity. There seems to be little doubt that the immunological system is involved. Now that some of the taboos have been lifted from the field of genetic engineering, someone will probably hit on the one little thing that will do the trick."

Norman paused, swigged, got back to Jake. "This tumor he has is a nasty sort. It's unquestionably malignant. Left unchallenged much longer, its cells will get into his bloodstream and start doing their dirty work elsewhere in his body. It happens quickly."

"They can be stopped?"

"Slowed down, killed off to some extent with chemotherapy. The objective is to diminish the cancer, shrink it, and then cut it out. Hopefully all of it. It's not uncommon that in a case like Jake's it means having to amputate."

"So unless Jake gets chemotherapy he dies."

"Short of a miracle."

What Norman omitted was that even if everything went well with Jake's chemotherapy treatments and the operation, there were very likely to be morbid complications later on. Once malignant osteoblastic cells got into the system, they tended to clump and hide in some niche in the body for months or years. Then, suddenly, as though giving in to some whim of fury, they exploded into action, began replicating mercilessly, building bone tissue where it didn't belong. There would be little chance of stopping it. The five-year overall survival rate for what Jake had was only about 20 percent.

Springer sat forward on the bench. The river, he noticed, had a bilious look to it. The day was warm, the tide running out. The water smelled putrid. The river in any condition was usually a forgivable fact of the city. Today it was a personal affront. An incongruously clean seagull hovered for a handout. A Tropicana orange juice carton drifted by, and so did a filmy something that appeared to be a condom but could have been a plastic sandwich bag. Springer thought: Jake with a leg and a half was better than no Jake.

A car on the drive chose that moment to drop its muffler. There was a sharp, punctuating clang as the muffler struck the pavement, an instant before it smashed against the car behind and was slung by its speed at the windshield of another car driven by an elderly man who overswerved reflexively. Then, not just one sound but a brief, full orchestration of screech and scrape and killing metallic impacts.

Springer and Norman heard the accident, but it was out of sight up the drive a way. In all lanes traffic backed up, stopped. Impeded drivers, irritated, glanced around for a way to go on.

Norman got up from the bench. He leaned on the fat iron railing, over it and out, as he would aboard a ship. That the rusted railing was staining the sleeves of his shirt didn't matter. A well-dressed green and black tug passed by, headed for the harbor. Norman's gaze didn't follow it. His eyes were fixed windows, and the tug merely something that traversed their frame. The wake of the tug sloshed against the river wall and, it seemed to Norman, against his thoughts.

Nothing had been the same for him since the President's crisis in Bethesda. He felt primitive, at times inept, and the bodies of his patients, geographies he'd believed familiar, had turned foreign. Listenings with stethoscope, observations of blood pressures, measurings of cholesterol levels, interpretations of electrocardiograms—all seemed little removed from the applying of leeches. What *was* medicine? He found himself asking himself at every tack of his professional routine.

The government insiders had mistaken his preoccupation for modesty and made his quandary all the worse. Their covert kudos, the hushed, private gratitudes from the highest level had to be endured. He hated the dissemblance. Every thank-you he'd said in return for congratulations had been like a hook torn from his mouth. He'd succeeded in not allowing it to affect his daily efficiency, but he felt he was a changed man, a changed doctor. The nuclei in him were as surely divided as those he'd looked at in the cells of Jake.

"Chemotherapy," he said to the situation, drawing the word out and losing part of it to the sound of a siren.

Springer said, "What?"

"Maybe Jake shouldn't be given chemotherapy."

"What the hell are you talking about? You just got through telling me he'd die without it."

"And what I'm telling you now is go another route."

"I'm open to whatever's best for Jake."

"Then use the stone."

It was so far from Springer's thoughts it took a while to register.

"The stone you brought down to Washington for my opinion," Norman reminded.

"And that you said was nothing more than an ordinary pebble."

"I intended to tell you different. At the time I couldn't. I was . . . anesthesized, dazzled beyond belief. I didn't know whether I'd been tricked or privileged, whether I'd experienced something I should fend off or embrace. Even now I don't have a single clear excuse."

"Why?"

Norman ran it down for him. The entire Bethesda scenario, all its inexplicable medical aspects and his personal reactions. He said it was the first he'd spoken to anyone about it. Evidently his telling to close acquaintance, patient, and Assistant Secretary of State Thomas Longmire was forgotten on the other side of drunkenness.

Springer heard Norman out and then put it to him pointedly. "Do you believe that stone was the reason Janet got well?" He looked Norman squarely in the eyes, saw reluctance but no doubt.

"Yes," Norman replied.

Springer added it up: His sister Janet's remarkable recovery, the transformation of Libby's hands, the miraculously healed heart of the President. He asked himself, Was it only now, desperate, that he was vulnerable to believing such things? Outweighing that possibility was Norman's conviction. Norman was the most practical-minded man Springer had ever known, always looking ahead to where his next step should be placed, never venturing out on a limb that was even slightly shaky. If one word described Norman, it was judicious.

Again a siren sent its red blade of sound into the atmosphere. The exhausts of the idling cars on the drive were a collaborative contamination.

If he had stone 588 at that moment, Springer knew, he would run with it up to that fifth-floor hospital room and clasp it for as long as was needed in Jake's hand.

But he didn't have it.

21

◇

For the next couple of days, Springer and Audrey spent most of their time at Sloan-Kettering with Jake. Springer's mother and sister were down from Connecticut, staying at the family apartment on East 72nd, so at times there was only standing room around Jake's bed. Janet, Springer observed, was still a newborn adult, rational, light of heart, and glowing. Not a sign of her old seesaw mental illness. Springer was now certain her abrupt recovery came from stone 588.

"Have you found out anything new about that stone of Father's?" Janet asked, while she and Springer were out in the hospital corridor.

"It's everything you thought it was," he told her, and when he saw her eyes moisten, he was glad he'd chosen not to mention that the stone had been stolen.

"Perhaps it might do Jake some good," she said.

Springer agreed and Janet took that to mean he intended to give it a try.

When they went back into the room they found Mattie and Audrey doing some healing, standing on opposite sides of the bed with their hands extended above Jake's malignant thigh. Their hands were flat, palms down, layered one above the other like a metaphysical stack of pancakes. Their eyes were closed to enhance their connection to whatever power they were drawing from. Jake remained tolerantly still. Springer stood off to the side and watched, alert for any discernable change in the atmosphere. After ten minutes Mattie and Audrey broke their healing trances. Both shook and snapped their hands vigorously, as though ridding them of a filthy substance.

"Surround yourself with healing white light . . ." Mattie advised Jake. "The God light." She also told him that his name was at that very moment in thousands of prayer baskets all over the world.

"How about in Paris?" Jake asked.

"Even in Paris," Mattie said unequivocally.

Springer suspected she was fibbing but he loved her for it. Since he'd accepted the efficacy of stone 588 he was seeing Mattie differently. He no longer loved her despite her eccentricities. He loved her more because of them. He understood now the plain generosity of her nature and was a bit ashamed of how narrow-minded he'd been. He rightfully blamed some of that on 47th Street. Its ways had compressed him, intensified his dubiousness with its cold, mean realities.

While Mattie and disciple Audrey did their spiritual best for Jake, Springer comforted him on less abstract levels. He lugged a new nineteen-inch Sony television to Jake's room. Also a Sony video recorder. Jake's having mentioned there being no cable TV at the hospital had created for Springer the opportunity to please. He phoned around and located a store on Third Avenue near 96th that had an extensive selection of video cassettes. Springer bought a whole day's worth of rock videos. Twelve cassettes, two hours each. Stints by Van Halen, Sting, Foreigner, Springsteen, and a lot of Jake's other favorites. From his own collection Springer brought a cassette of the 1984 Olympic Gold Medal volleyball match between Brazil and the United States. He hooked up everything, including earphones, so

Jake could listen anytime, even in the middle of the night, as loud as he wished.

Jake could use all the support and distraction he could get. On Wednesday, the very next day after his biopsy surgery (which was not all that minor, considering an incision had been made all the way to the bone and even a "window" of the bone excised), Jake was put through a battery of tests to evaluate his condition for chemotherapy. A technetium-99 bone scan and a CT scan of his chest determined that the tumor had not yet spread. A trispiral tomograph further verified this with a dimensional "sound picture" of his chest. Other tests measured the function of his liver and kidneys.

The hurry to have these evaluations done was not arbitrary. Whenever a tumor such as Jake's was cut into, the malignant cells took advantage, ran rampantly into the bloodstream. They had to be chased down with chemotherapy as soon as possible.

Thursday would be Jake's day for that.

First, because it was essential that his system be alkaline, he was given intravenously 50cc of sodium bicarbonate solution. Then, over a period of four hours, 10 grams of methotrexate in a 5 percent glucose and sodium bicarbonate solution was dripped into his veins. Methotrexate, a synthesized chemical substance, is a very potent poison, 10 grams of it enough to kill a dozen men. Methotrexate literally tricks the body. Its molecular makeup resembles folic acid, one of the vitamins in the B-complex needed for healthy cell division. The resemblance of fatally poisonous methotrexate to harmless folic acid is, in fact, so close that the body misidentifies it and readily admits it into the system.

Jake also received injections of three other aggressive chemotherapeutic agents: bleomycin, cyclophosphamide, and dactinomycin.

At six o'clock Thursday morning he was "rescued" from deadly methotrexate by being given calcium leucovorin. Thus he was poisoned one day and given the antidote the next.

He had to drink a lot of water.

He had to have intravenous fluid going into him constantly.

He had to take allopurinal pills to prevent the cells that were being killed by the chemotherapy from creating uric acid and causing him to have gout.

He had to remain alkaline, have every pee litmused.

By Thursday noon Jake was just about out of cooperation and courage. Springer, who was more sensitively in tune with Jake's feelings at this time, detected as much when a laboratory specialist came to draw blood and Jake begrudgingly stuck out an arm already badly discolored from previous punctures. Springer remembered he'd promised Jake that nothing bad was going to be done to him. He hoped Jake didn't feel betrayed.

When not at the hospital, Springer spent some time at the office. The box of rough from the sight he'd attended while in London required going over. It consisted of an average number of pieces of average quality goods, indicative of The System's merely average opinion of him.

He tried to give the new rough the scrutiny he would ordinarily give it, but his spirit wasn't in it. He handed the task to Linda. She would sort and classify the stones and see that they were sent off with instructions to the cutter in Antwerp.

Some of the goods that had been out on memo at the time of the robbery were trickling back into inventory. Other out-on-memo goods had been sold and payments for it received. Springer & Springer was reviving, just stirring but nonetheless showing signs of getting back on its feet.

"I think I'll sue," Springer told his insurance agent, Bob Steiner, during a phone call.

"Don't. They've got lawyers who are cousins to God."

"A million what?"

"A million eight. They balked at that figure. One five was their firm top. I warned them that you were an influential force at the Diamond Dealers Club."

Springer belonged to that club by tradition, hadn't been to it more than a half dozen times in as many years.

"The company assumes you'll be continuing with your coverage," Steiner said. "Of course, your premium rate will be automatically higher."

"They're worse thieves than those who robbed me."

"Better thieves," Steiner contributed.

"When can I expect a check?" Springer asked.

"The company has ninety days. It's in your policy, ninety days from the time an adjustment is agreed upon. Look for a check ninety days from tomorrow."

"Just to make me wait."

"That's not it. They figure even a day short of ninety would be a waste. Ninety days' interest on a million eight is roughly fifty thousand."

Well, at least that was settled. Not to Springer's satisfaction, but done with.

On Thursday afternoon, Springer arrived at the office to learn from Linda that he'd been called twice by someone named Karinov, who hadn't left a number, would call again. At five o'clock, just as Springer was about to leave, the same party called again. It was a woman. Using a pay station phone. Traffic sounds backgrounded her voice.

"You were in Rome last Thursday," she said.

"I was in Paris last Thursday," Springer corrected.

"A diamond was shown to you, an eight-carat diamond."

"Ten carats."

"A square cut."

"A round cut."

Evidently that was verification enough that Springer was her man. "Your material has arrived," she said. Her Russian accent had a British accent.

"That's good news."

"I wish to put it in your hands as soon as possible."

"You name it."

"Tomorrow morning would be ideal."

They made an appointment for nine o'clock the next morning at his most recent bank, the United States Trust Company of New York at 11 East 54th Street.

Karinov, who said her name was Nessa (Springer believed neither) turned out to be a Valkyrie type. A straight-haired blonde, about thirty, strong-boned and rangy. She was handsome more than pretty. Her eyes were a vulnerable blue but quick, cautious. A true maiden of Odin, bored with merely helping war heroes find their way to Valhalla, she'd gotten herself into a much more precarious game. Springer found it rather easy to imagine Audrey in her place.

At the bank, Mr. Leeds served Springer again. At Springer's request he led the way to the second floor and an office intended for the use of clients. It suited Springer's purpose well, had a tall window that faced north.

There, in privacy, Nessa impassively lifted her skirt and held it up by its hem with her chin, while she undid a compartmentalized cloth belt from around her waist. She sat at the desk and from the compartments of the belt removed twelve small chamois pouches, then, from each of the pouches, a round-cut twenty-five-carat diamond. She lined up the diamonds on the beige desk blotter, handled them perfunctorily, as she might had they been merely backgammon pieces. She raised her eyes to Springer, silently giving him permission to touch them.

He left the diamonds as they were for the moment, scanned them bare-eyed. No doubt they were Aikhal goods, they had that distinctive colder-looking blaze. From his jacket pocket Springer took out his loupe, a stark white business envelope, and the small leather case that contained his set of master stones. The master stones his father had given him when he was a boy.

He tore open both ends of the envelope and placed one of the diamonds in the crease of the long fold that remained. Turning to the window he examined that diamond with his loupe. The white trough of the envelope cut down on whatever extraneous light might be affecting the color of the diamond, allowed its true uninfluenced color to be viewed. Even the slightest hint of yellow, devaluating yellow, would be detectable. It was a little testing trick his father had shown him early on, usually done with a once-folded business card.

Springer placed the D-color diamond from his master set close beside the Russian stone. His master stone was much smaller, of course; however, it served for comparison. Springer placed four of the Russian stones side by side in the white trough of the envelope.

Compared them, shifted them about, and compared them again. He examined all twelve stones in this manner.

Satisfied with their color, he next looked into them for flaws. He would not forgive even the most minuscule speck, but he saw none. Nor were there any feathers or clouds, graining or knot lines. As for the cut of the stones, he believed he'd never seen finer.

Throughout the procedure, which took a good hour, Springer and Nessa had not spoken a word. Now, he looked into her eyes and nodded almost imperceptibly. Springer kept close watch of Nessa's fingers, as she put the diamonds back into their individual chamois pouches. No sleight of hand. The pouches remained on the desk.

"I understand you're to tell me how to make payment," Springer said.

"To this account." On a note pad Nessa jotted down from memory: *Bank Gallar and Cie., Bauhofstrasse 93, 8022 Zurich, Switzerland, account number PR-200819.* She checked to make sure it was correct.

Springer used the phone to summon Mr. Leeds. He instructed Leeds to send thirteen million five hundred thousand dollars to the Swiss account Nessa had designated. Springer signed the required documents for a wire transfer from account to account. Leeds treated it routinely, unfazed by the amount of the transaction. He said it would take approximately an hour.

Nessa said they would wait for verification from the other end. She'd been through this before.

While waiting, Springer wondered how it had been pulled off, swiftly and precisely as ordered. Surely it wasn't mere coincidence that someone in the Soviet Union just happened to have on hand a dozen perfect diamonds of that size. Perhaps they had hundreds like it, equally flawless, hundreds of every significant size. Perhaps it was true—the rumor that the Soviets had more diamonds than The System, more diamonds than they knew what to do with, evidently so many diamonds that whoever was supposed to be keeping track of them could easily skim. Sweet deal. Dangerous but sweet.

Springer was right. But he would never know that the diamonds had been included in the diplomatic pouch put aboard an Aeroflot plane at Sheremetyevo Airport in Moscow. Three diamonds in each of four 14-ounce tins of Imperial Caspian caviar bound for the Soviet installation in Glen Cove, Long Island, New York, and the palates of the upper-echelon Soviet diplomats assigned to the United Nations and the Consulate in New York City. The Glen Cove place was a sumptuous estate in an area of sumptuous estates. With swimming pool, tennis courts, and all such decadent amenities, it was preferred, especially in summer, over the somewhat austere apartment house on East 67th Street that served as the Soviet Mission.

The so-called Nessa Karinov was one of the staff at the Glen Cove installation. She was a chef, a specialist in French cuisine, had been sent for three years to learn at the École de Cordon Bleu in Paris. As a chef, naturally she saw to the caviar.

She also saw to the diamonds that sometimes came concealed in it. Dug them out from the huge choicest-of-all sturgeon roe and washed them in warm water sudsed up with a squirt of lemon fresh Joy detergent, rinsed them with hot, dried them, and dropped them into her deep apron pocket where she always kept a few extra cloves of garlic.

"Do you like being in New York?" Springer asked her just to break the silence.

"Very much."

"I suppose you miss Russia."

"Very much."

Springer had recently read somewhere that the Russians had 900 people stationed in New York. He'd bet that Nessa was less talkative then the other 899.

Leeds returned with verification that the money had been credited to the Swiss account. Nessa went over the verifying printout carefully before saying, "Done." She asked to have returned to her the slip of notepaper upon which she'd written the name of the bank and the numbered account. To destroy it, Springer surmised.

Nessa left the bank. It was her day off. She would shop Alexander's for a while and go to an early movie.

Springer decided that while at the bank he might as well take care of Drumgold. He had Leeds transfer Drumgold's commission to an account at a bank in Nassau that Drumgold had stipulated should the deal go through.

Two hundred thousand dollars. And one.

Out on the street with the diamonds safely pocketed, Springer's first thought was that he'd drop them off at Townsend's, only a block and a half away up Fifth. Hadn't Libby said that was how she wanted it? He'd get a receipt from Townsend, of course.

Springer's second thought was that he shouldn't be so hasty about that.

He returned to his office and phoned Wintersgill at the Hull Foundation to ask him how he believed the matter should be handled. He was somewhat surprised when he was put right through.

"Why don't you just bring the diamonds over to me and I'll see that she receives them," Wintersgill suggested amiably.

"Would that be putting you out?"

"No bother at all. Can you be here within the hour?"

Springer was a breath away from saying *sure* when some part of him told him he was about to step out onto a wrong bridge. "What I'd prefer," he said, "is to deliver them to Libby myself. I guess I'm a bit proud of them."

"As you wish," Wintersgill said, changed to curt.

Springer couldn't blame the man for that. He was probably sitting there surrounded by importance wondering why the hell Springer had bothered to call.

22

At noon the next day when Springer came out of Sloan-Kettering, that dark brown Daimler limousine of Libby's was at the curb. Attending it was the same big chauffeur named Groat. For a moment Springer had the notion to ride up front, but then he wasn't sure Groat would approve. So he sat where he was supposed to, in the back sunk in the plush.

He'd spent the morning with Jake. The boy was giving his bravest best; however, the chemotherapy had really gotten to him, sunk and dulled his eyes, sallowed his coloring, made him nauseated and dizzy and sapped. Several times that morning Jake had been on the verge of tears. So had Springer.

Tomorrow, Jake would be allowed to go home, Dr. Stimson had said. That would be better. But in four weeks he'd be due back in the hospital for more chemotherapy. It might take as many as six treatments. Six months of such misery for Jake before they'd take a slice of him, then more chemotherapy to make sure. And that was if everything went well.

"Every positive thought is another for our side," Mattie had said.

Springer tried now for a positive.

The best he could do was a neutral as he gazed straight ahead through the separating glass at Groat's bullish neck and thought, Groat takes at least a size twenty collar. He caught Groat's glance in the rearview mirror. Three times, before Groat put on aviator-type dark glasses, and that was that.

At one o'clock precisely Springer was looking at another equally massive neck: that of the butler, Hinch, who preceded him along the ground-floor main hallway of Libby's mansion in Greenwich. All the way to an extremity of the south wing, where doors like a triptych decoratively painted in the manner of Fragonard were folded back, giving to a garden room. It was a large semicircular room enclosed all around and high above by small framed glass panes. The panes were frosted so everything was bathed in a flatteringly soft light.

Including Libby.

She was on one of a pair of facing white-lacquered sofas: arranged on it, was Springer's impression. No doubt she'd been notified of his arrival the moment he'd gotten out of the Daimler and there was no possible way she hadn't heard his and Hinch's footsteps on the marble floor of the hall, yet she remained preoccupied for a long moment before she glanced up to be pleasantly surprised.

Her initial smile broadened.

She offered her hand and drew Springer down to her face with it for welcoming cheek kisses right and left. Springer got a whiff of her, an extravagant scent that was not just her perfume. The rich smell different, he'd once quipped to Audrey at a playful, erotic moment, and that applied now.

Springer sat on the sofa opposite, which was what Libby had planned. There were unfolded blueprints on the cushion beside her. She picked them up and flung them over the back of the sofa.

"Plans for a new boat someone wants to build for me," she said. "The best, of course, are built in Bremen, outfitted in Southampton, and moored almost constantly in Monaco. I'll bet you're one hell of a sailor."

"I get seasick."

Springer believed he discerned a hint of I-would-have-thought-as-much in her expression, or perhaps that was only because he was looking for it.

"I can take an average sea," she said, "but there's nothing I detest more than being out when it's heavy. All that energy wasted just trying to move about. The most deplorable thing about a heavy sea is you can't just turn it off. I don't for the likes of me understand why some people enjoy being out there, tossed about to the point of upchucking. Perhaps they're closet bulimiacs." She laughed at that, as though it was the first time she'd said it.

Springer saw that she'd taken considerable care with her appearance. The pale pastel floral-printed dress she had on was of that finest cotton called lawn, with an amply pleated skirt and oversized sleeves. Considerably less casual than such a Saturday afternoon called for. Her makeup was by no means slapdash. The various layers of hues on her lids, the gradually edged dominance of blue that shot from her lashes out and up to her impeccably tweezed brows, the blushing concavity of her cheeks, the red slicks that helped her mouth—all had required time. And motive. Her only jewelry was a ring: a thirty-carat Burma sapphire of a very unusual intense lavender shade. Springer thought of it as a stone with a dilemma, one that could not make up its mind whether it should be a sapphire or a ruby.

"What will you have to drink?" Libby asked.

Too early for his Usquaebach, he decided; what was she having?

The open bottle on the table between them was a Chateau La Conseillante 1966. A white-jacketed servant came forth as though his cue had been said. He was another large man. Perhaps, Springer thought, this one, Hinch, and Groat took turns butlering, driving, and waiting on.

"Thank you, Fane," Libby said automatically as he poured fresh glasses and set down a doilied silver tray bearing tiny crustless sandwiches. Fane soundlessly gathered up the soiled glasses and napkins and was gone. Springer couldn't see where. Well-trained orange trees in bleached white tubs were lined along the perimeter. There were numerous other plantings, some with huge leaves and undoubtedly tropical. Two or three enormous ficus almost reached the ceiling, their containers softened by legions of primroses, day lilies, dahlias, and ranunculus. Fane was hiding somewhere in the bushes, Springer thought: Fane and probably a few others equally formidable. What would happen, he wondered, if he responded to Libby's flirtatious manner? At what point, what temperature, would they skulk away? Had they been told? He had a mind to turn and see if he could catch sight of them. Schubert's Ninth Symphony began as though its time had come, but at a level that would not interfere. An orange dropped from one of the trees and landed on the marble floor with a thump soft as a final heartbeat. Springer gazed upward. Among the hundreds of perfect glass panes he found one that was cracked. He looked directly at Libby, tried to magnify, to determine any of the cosmetic surgeon's tiny incisional lines that he knew were there. Why was he so ready to notice, trying to find, mistakes? With an air of lighthearted reproach Libby told Springer, "You're incorrigible."

"Why?"

"You were in London and didn't take me up on my hospitality."

"I thought it best not to impose."

"Nonsense. What do you take me for, one of those bourbon-brained Southerners who invite irrepressibly and then are at a loss when someone shows up?"

"It wasn't that—"

"You're practically family," she reasoned and blotted wine from her lips with her napkin.

Springer tried to appear appropriately contrite.

Libby did a simultaneous moue and a smile. "I'm chiding only because I'd enjoy seeing more of you. You really should come up to Penobscot."

"What's there?"

"Our own island."

"How large?"

"About two miles long and—oh, I'd say a half mile across."

"I'm not partial to islands," Springer said, having decided to give her some of her own. "They bore quickly. You know what I mean, they're so limited."

"Our Penobscot place is craggy around the edges, very Maine-like, but soft in the middle with many beds of pine needles and moss."

Her tone was insinuating, caused Springer to suspect Audrey had confided their alfresco love-making penchants to her. He imagined such woman-to-woman dialogue on the subject. More boastful than anything, so how could he mind?

Springer looked away. His eyes aimed into the peach-pink bell-like face of a nearby day lily but he wasn't seeing it. He absently sipped wine. His thoughts were on Jake.

Sensing the cloud that had come over him, Libby said, "Audrey told me your son is ill."

"Yes."

"Is it as serious as she said?"

Springer nodded.

"If there's anything I can do, anything at all, please . . . let me know."

"Thank you."

"I also understand that your miraculous little stone was stolen."

"A week ago."

"That's a shame. You have no idea who took it or where it is?"

"No."

A deep, dreary sigh. "I wasn't kidding when I offered to buy it, you know. You could have named your price."

"A hundred million?" Springer asked casually.

"Yes. I might have hesitated and wanted more of a demonstration, but yes."

"Really, a hundred million?"

"That amount would leave a hole in any fortune," she said. "However, great wealth does have a way of swiftly replenishing itself. You might say it grows out of control."

Malignant osteoblastic cells came to Springer's mind. "Would you like to see your diamonds now?" he asked.

"Not yet," Libby replied quickly. "Once I've been shown the

diamonds you'll have no other excuse for staying. Or will you?" she asked, bold-eyed.

Springer was reminded of Lady Irith, his initiatrix at the Savoy in London so many years ago. Where was she now? Flourishing, he hoped. Had his intimacies with her really been as delirious as he remembered? How much had he embellished? Clearly he recalled how Lady Irith with words and reactions had made him feel the exceptional lover, manful. He was grateful to her for that and, as well, grateful to his gullibility.

A Doucai bowl painted with lotus flowerheads and scrolling foliage that would have been a treasure to any collector of things oriental was on the table, filled with salted cashews. Springer put a couple of the nuts in his mouth, chomped on them.

"How much in love with Audrey are you?" Libby asked.

"How much is too much?"

"She's my pet, you know." And after a shrug: "Well, not actually mine. I suppose she told you?"

"She did."

"There isn't a chink anywhere in the adoption papers. I made sure of that. Should any of Gillian's forgotten relatives come pestering with a claim, hoping to be bought off."

A leather-bound volume of Stendahl's *On Love* lay on the floor near Libby's foot. Springer noticed a red wildbird's feather marked a place. How many other similar things?

"Gillian," Libby said, as though she were announcing the title of something she was about to recite, "was a marvelous person to be around—to have around. She and I both had the same low threshold of ennui. It was uncanny in a way. No matter where we were we never once disagreed about whether or not to stay or leave. She was, I must admit, a bit more of a daredevil than I, loved being in over her head, waiting until the last possible second to shoot the charging tiger. Metaphorically speaking, of course. There's never been anyone in my life like her."

That, Springer knew, was not entirely true.

"Gillian had her faults," Libby went on, "but none too messy to put up with. She was an incurable tester, if you know what I mean.

246

Every once in a while she'd do something dreadful just to find out if you'd love her in spite of it. Put a lot of people off with that, and I suppose I was the object of it more than anyone, but I never fell for it. She used to get absolutely livid when I just allowed her to get away with things. We'd laugh about them later."

Libby drank what wine remained in her glass. Fane appeared to refill: Springer's glass as well.

"Anyway," Libby said, "Audrey has never wanted for anything."

"Then what is it I'm supplying her?" Springer asked, a bit insubordinately.

"Good question. Do you foresee marrying Audrey?"

"It's being mentioned."

"Why the wait?"

"I don't know."

"Perhaps you're trying to wear one another thin."

That could very well be it, Springer thought, and if it was he knew Audrey was failing at it. For him every experience with her was the adding on of another strengthening layer.

"You're aware, no doubt, that Audrey stands to get all the Hull money someday."

"I'll never dislike her for that," Springer promised straight-faced.

Libby smirked sardonically. "Broadminded of you."

Springer agreed.

"Be warned, however," Libby said with a glare too suddenly cool to be believed, gracefully pointing a beautiful finger at him, "I plan to live to be over a hundred. Well over."

Fighting words, Springer thought. She was indeed a tenacious time-fighter.

"Now"—she sat forward—"let's see those diamonds."

He placed the twelve little chamois pouches on the table. She looked at the diamonds one at a time. Held each up for a moment before returning it to its pouch. The diffused light was disadvantageous, most diamonds would have suffered tremendously in it, but these had blaze to spare.

Libby was merely pleased, not enthusiastic. "Nicely done," she said.

Springer reminded himself that neither the diamonds nor the appreciation of them mattered, only the money. "Do you want me to get these to Townsend?" he asked.

"No." She stood abruptly and instructed: "Bring them along."

Springer gathered up the diamonds and followed her out of the room, along the hall, and down a flight of stairs to a lower level that was not at all dank. There at the end of another passageway was the wide and tall blackened steel door of a vault. Off to one side was an electronic panel consisting of ten buttons numbered one through zero, much like the dialing face of a touch-tone telephone. Probably it worked on the same principle.

"Only I know the combination," Libby said, "and it's something I'd never divulge."

Springer politely faced away while she touched off the combination. "The day, month, and year of your birth," Springer guessed and knew he'd hit it right when he turned back and saw Libby's disconcerted expression.

The vault door clicked open, a thick heavy door but evidently well balanced, for Libby easily swung it open. It was a walk-in vault, actually a small, brightly lighted room. Nearly all the space of the wall directly ahead was taken up by a pair of handsome Louis Seize mahogany cartonniers, each with fourteen numbered drawers faced with tooled leather. As with all such cartonniers, it was impossible to pull any of the drawers open without first unlocking and folding back the narrow hinged panels that ran vertically along each side. That was no problem, of course, when the keys were in the escutcheons as they were now.

Libby pulled open a drawer.

Springer dropped the twelve chamois sacks into it, giving in to his 47th Street nature and counting them aloud so there would be no misunderstanding.

"You did so well with this," Libby told him, "I'm going to have you handle something else for me."

"Thank you. What?"

"I'll think of something." Even though they weren't cramped for space, she seemed very close. She lavished her softest smile on him.

"I'm going to recommend you to Wincie Olcott," she said. "The poor thing was broken into a month or so ago. I know she especially misses a certain bracelet, a chunky all-diamond piece that was at least a hundred carats. You could have it duplicated using the insurance photographs, couldn't you?"

"No problem."

"The impression I get is you're much more ambitious than Townsend and, God knows, more attractive to deal with." She paused, reminded of another consideration. "Although I must say Townsend *does* come up with some lovely things." Her tone was ambiguously edged. "Let me show you. . . ."

Out they came. From drawer after drawer. So many, so swiftly, that Springer couldn't adequately take them all in. No sooner had she placed one in his hands than it was replaced by another equally dazzling.

A diamond necklace that had belonged to Empress Eugénie. Another that had belonged to Empress Alexandra Feodorovna, and another once owned by Princess Marie Louise. Tiaras, diadems, bracelets, brooches that had belonged to this or that grand duchess, this or that Hapsburg, one princess or another. There were pieces that had adorned the necks or wrists or hands or ears of Du Barry and de Pompadour, Consuelo Vanderbilt, the Duchess of Marlborough, Elizabeth Morgan, Sarah Whitney, Caroline Astor. Marian Davies, Mary Pickford, Pola Negri, Wallis Windsor: Libby chanted off the names of the famous former owners with nearly an auctioneer's rapidity. She knew each piece well. There was no doubt in her mind which had belonged to whom.

Springer was astounded by the precious jewels that shot before his eyes, a veritable deluge. While being shown some Czarist bibelots that would have put La Vieille Russe to shame, he asked, "Doesn't keeping all these things here in the house make you a bit nervous?"

Libby scoffed. "They're perfectly safe here. And a hell of a lot more convenient. If I kept them somewhere in bank deposit boxes I know I wouldn't wear them nearly as much. Certainly I wouldn't get to play with them as often. No, I feel they're safe. I have an alarm system and enough people here to form a cordon around the place if it ever came to that. Quite capable people, and very loyal, I should add."

Springer wondered how she knew they were capable, as she put it, and why she was so confident that they were loyal.

Perhaps she sensed his doubt. "Wintersgill finds my people for me," she said, "recruits them and screens them intensively." She placed a necklace that she'd said had belonged to the Duchesse de Noailles back into its fitted leather box and its drawer and told Springer, "Naturally, I'm not one to flaunt. I don't allow just anyone down here."

Springer held back telling her he knew the psychology of jewelry —90 or more percent of the joy of owning it was letting people know you did.

"Is it possible that I might induce you to stay for dinner?" Libby asked.

"I'm meeting Audrey."

"Sometimes impetuousness can be very rewarding," she said predictably.

Even if Springer had been more strongly tempted he wouldn't have stayed. Danny had phoned him yesterday late and arranged a meeting for tonight, had been very cryptic about it, wouldn't say why. Only rarely did Springer and Danny see one another on weekends.

Libby waved her hands before her face, dismissing disappointment as though she were shooing away gnats. For a further countermeasure she dug into one of the drawers and came out with a small cobalt-blue enameled gold box, edged with a crust of diamonds and diamond-monogrammed with an R. Unmistakably a Fabergé creation for Czar Nicolas II.

"When and if you get your precious little stone back," she said, handing him the Fabergé, "this should be nice to keep it in."

23

◇

On the return trip from Libby's, Groat was surprised when Springer told him he wanted to be left off at Arthur Avenue.

Springer was surprised when Groat, without consulting a street map or asking directions, took him right to it.

Arthur Avenue is the aorta of an Italian section in the mazed heart of the Bronx. A short unimportant-looking street, actually. About three blocks of it is commercial, store next to store, and it is here that the bosses and underbosses in the churchlike hierarchy of the Mafia come to replenish their larders. From their large, illicitly earned houses in Larchmont or New Rochelle or Orient Point they come (usually on Saturdays) to confidently leave the keys in their double-parked cars while they get the *real* romanos and provolones, veal and sausage as it should be, olives authenticated by the stenciled wooden barrels they're ladled out of, and olive oil that makes those sold at Grand Union taste like something better used in an old engine. Too, here, only here, the bread of all breads can be bought, crackly crusted, sprinkled with sesame. And always a few evocative anise-spiced cookies to munch on the way home.

The larders of their egos also get replenished on Arthur Avenue. Elsewhere these family executives are mere successful businessmen. Here, however, the way is parted for them. The sidewalks are water to be walked upon. They exaggerate their heights, float their heads, and fix their mouths with a smile of proper friendly disdain. For Sicilianos gathered in front of the fish store, seated there on empty milk crates. And the Neapolitanos down the way in *their* place, close up to a store that sells produce. Each group maintaining the understood distance from the other, and each wondering if this will be one of those times when a capo's nod will be conferred.

"He tipped his hat."

"He wasn't wearing a hat."

"With his eyes he tipped his hat."

"It was to me that he did it."

"Why only you?"

"I was not always a fucking shoemaker." Said with mystery and a hard mouth.

Thus, Arthur Avenue in its own way is consecrated. Borne out by the fact that it has the lowest incidence of crime of any neighborhood in the city.

Springer got out of the Daimler on Arthur Avenue and by only an inch missed stepping on a glob of rotting tomato. He leaped over a pool of milky, detergented water to gain the curb and went into the Vesuvio Restaurant.

It wasn't a cozy place. About forty white cloth-covered tables. On a ledge along each side were plaster quarter-scale copies of classical Italian statues. Almost nudes. The walls were hung with Italian townscapes oil-painted straight out of the tubes. The lighting was indecisive, neither dim nor bright enough. Hardly anyone was there at that early hour. Waiters outnumbered customers. The waiters stood in the back, anticipating the tips of Saturday night, fresh white napkins on their forearms.

Danny and Audrey were at a table for four midway along the wall on the right. They didn't notice Springer enter. Audrey was listening intently to whatever Danny was saying. Springer got a possessive welcoming peck of a kiss from her. He and Danny were beyond shaking hands.

Danny ordered a drink for Springer.

Audrey urged Danny to go on with what he'd been telling her. When Danny didn't, Springer guessed it had been a story he'd already heard that Danny was self-conscious about repeating. Must have been that because Danny went on to a different one.

He told about two swifts who hit a mansion over in Jersey, Short Hills or Far Hills or one of those Hills over there. A really big, luxurious house. The people, who weren't at home, were obviously rich but there was no flash lying around the way there should have been, on the dresser tops and places like that. Also, there was nothing worth stealing in any of the drawers or anywhere. It didn't figure. Then one of the swifts comes across a safe in the back of a closet in the master bedroom. Not a built-in safe but a regular heavy little bastard. About a five-hundred-pounder.

Anyway, the swifts hadn't come prepared for it, and the safe seems to know that, the way it stands there among the two-thousand-dollar dresses like it's enjoying the situation. The swifts figure since they found nothing anywhere else in this fat house, everything has to be in the safe. It has to be loaded with jewels and a lot of cash.

They can't pass it. They decide to take the safe—with them. They heave and shove it along inch by inch. It takes them an hour just to get it out to the second-floor landing. They let it go crashing down the stairs. Three hours it takes them to get it across the lawn and into their van. Their shins are bleeding, their toes and fingers are mashed, they've thrown their backs out—but it's in the van, and pretty soon it's in the garage at the house of one of the swifts.

It doesn't seem so smug anymore, the safe doesn't. For one thing, it's standing on its head. Like most safes of that kind it's got an easy bottom, just skin and concrete, and that's where the swifts cut and peel it and chip it open.

Inside the safe is—you guessed it—nothing. It doesn't even have dust in it. If either of the swifts was alone he'd cry. Not only because after breaking their balls they've come up empty—now they've got to get rid of the safe, and that means more sweating and struggling with it.

That night they're dumping the safe in a ditch somewhere up in Putnam County. A state trooper comes along and nails them. No way can they explain the safe. It gets identified. For breaking and entering they each pull down three to five in Trenton.

"The safe won," Audrey remarked.

"It was a lock," Danny punned in street talk, meaning it couldn't lose. A line he'd probably used before to cap the story he'd just told, Springer thought.

Danny was up and smoother, as he usually was when in Audrey's company. Part of it was his male Italian disposition responding to her, his need to erotically overstate and let her know how close he was to being helplessly aroused. He was mindful, of course, to keep his wooing oblique; nevertheless, there were instances when it seemed he was only a breath away from being direct.

The other part of it for Danny was his reaction to who Audrey was, the element she represented. It was in her hemisphere, so evidently removed from his own, that Danny believed the better things were simply the way of life. Just being in Audrey's presence elevated him. Anyway, it was closer to the upper league than his kind usually got.

Audrey found Danny fascinating for the same reasons in reverse.

Springer, because he knew them both so well, just sat back and let them play at it.

Danny ordered dinner. This was his territory, he knew what was best. He also knew quite a few of the people who came into the restaurant, especially the men in mohair suits who took off their jackets and with dandyish care hung them over the shoulders of their chairs, the ones who looked like they'd just come from their barbers. Most were *made* guys on the same level as Danny. He acknowledged them casually. A few others he greeted with an almost grim respect.

Once during dinner Danny excused himself and went over to speak with an older man, alone at a table, who was taking his food seriously, sort of growling at it before it went down into him. A man with a heavily creased face, wearing a short-sleeved summer-weight white shirt with his undershirt showing through.

Just John.

Springer almost didn't recognize him.

Crime sure ages, Springer thought.

It wasn't until after dinner over anisette and espresso that Danny got around to the other than social reason for this meeting. He moved his chair sideways to the table so he could cross one knee over the other and be closer to Springer without having to lean to him.

"I was wrong," he told Springer.

"Yeah?"

"Your goods."

"Someone brought them in to you."

"No, the whole package went to one party."

"A private?"

"Someone in the trade."

"You know who?"

Danny nodded.

"Then who?"

Danny hesitated. "I won't be doing myself a favor by telling you . . . and I don't think it'll be doing you any good either."

"So why even mention it to me?"

"You've got to understand. I do business with this guy off and on. For years we've been doing business."

Springer twisted a sliver of lemon peel above the surface of his espresso, saw the blue oily film it made, stirred it away with a little spoon. He glanced around indifferently as though he'd already dropped the subject. He knew the best way to press Danny was to not press him.

Danny again heavy-lidded his eyes at Audrey. She winked at him to defuse him. He got back to Springer, told him, "Townsend."

"You're shitting me."

"No."

"The same man by that name that I know?"

"He goes for swag now and then."

"The fuck."

"Just one of many," Danny said. "Actually he goes for swag more often than now and then."

Springer wouldn't have been nearly as surprised had the goods not been his own. Nor as angry if the buyer had been anyone other than Townsend. He reminded himself that Townsend had no way of knowing the swag he'd bought was from Springer & Springer. Thieves never said, buyers never asked. Townsend wouldn't know. Goods were goods. Swag was swag.

Except . . .

Except for that one stone, stone 588. The one Springer so desperately wanted back. Townsend had seen it. That night at Libby's he'd had a good look at it, would recognize it the moment he saw it again. Sure, Townsend would see it and know exactly whose stolen goods he'd bought. He had seen Libby's hands, seen what the stone could do. No matter how much he doubted that part, he couldn't dismiss it entirely. Too much in it for him if the stone wasn't bullshit. Townsend would find a way of proving it out. Then he'd offer it to the highest bidder. Just that afternoon Libby had seriously said she would have paid a hundred million for it. Someone else might make it two hundred million.

What irony.

A dirty diamond that wasn't a diamond, a stone The System had forced on Springer's father as punishment, that his father had probably come close to throwing away in disgust, probably would have if there hadn't been a tax advantage in keeping it in the inventory, that his father had drawn hardening caution from each day when it lay in that little silver tray on his dresser top among mere collar stays —now, as it turned out, point for point, carat for carat, it was by far the most precious thing in the world.

A measure of that, Springer thought, was how much he himself now needed it for Jake.

Perhaps, Springer wildly suggested to himself, he could go see Townsend. Appeal to him. Come right out and tell him why he had to have stone 588 for a few hours. Promise him whatever it took. Leave a million cash deposit. Even pay him a million just to rent it for that long. Townsend, of course, would simply deny any knowledge of the stone, act offended.

Then perhaps what he'd do was get in to see Townsend on some pretext. Put a gun to his ear. Demand the stone. Tell the fuck to keep all the other goods, just come up with that one stone. Would he kill Townsend if he didn't comply? Springer pictured himself being led away in cuffs and Townsend, indignant and shaken, telling the police his omissive but credible side of the story as he filed charges.

So what should he do? What other option was open to him? It galled Springer to know at that very moment the stone was in Townsend's vault only a few miles away, just lying there. Like Jake, just lying there. Somehow he had to get the two together.

Audrey ordered zabaglione and berries.

Springer another espresso, his third.

Danny loosened his tie slightly and undid his collar button. He'd said hardly anything for the last couple of minutes, letting Springer ease himself down. He figured from the silence that was what Springer was doing.

Springer placed his forearms on the table and leaned forward to ask Danny in a hushed tone, "Can Townsend's place be taken?"

"What are you talking about?"

"Townsend's."

"Depends. What's he got, a house, an apartment, or what?"

"His business place on Fifth."

"You're out of your fucking mind."

"I mean it."

"Nobody takes a place like that right on Fifth. While you're at it why don't you also knock off Tiffany and Cartier and Winston? Shit."

"Has anyone ever tried?"

"Who enjoys being in the joint that much? Do yourself a three-to-five-year favor and forget it."

Audrey stopped eating her zabaglione, that taken with what she was hearing. "I think it's a superb idea," she said.

Danny smiled. He liked the way she'd said *superb.* Not great or wonderful but superb. He told her, "Stealing is dangerous."

"I'd be disillusioned if it wasn't," she said archly.

"Amateur hour," Danny said. "You just don't know."

"But we're more than willing to learn." Audrey, wide-eyed, hung on Springer's shoulder conspiratorially, not about to be left out of this.

Shades of Gillian, Springer thought. His teeth were on edge and he couldn't keep his hands or arms still. He blamed the espresso. Eyes to eyes, unequivocally, he told Danny, "It's what I've got to do."

Danny's face soured. "I never realized you were such a bad loser. Tell the truth, I'm ashamed of you."

"Not for the goods. I've got to do it for Jake."

"I don't get it."

Springer was reluctant to tell Danny about stone 588. He was sure he knew how he'd react to it. Danny's perspective had always been street level, where not much was ever left to the imagination. People like Danny believed only what they saw and, even then, only after their hands were on it.

Springer told him as briefly and credibly as he could.

Danny got up and went to the men's room.

Couldn't blame him, Springer thought. It wasn't easy to tell a longtime friend he'd jumped the tracks.

Danny took his time coming back to the table. He picked up his anisette glass, shook the coffee bean from it into his mouth, ground the bean with his back teeth. His expression was blank. He could do that to his face whenever he wanted or had to, make it absolutely unreadable.

"There's an old lady," he said, "lives a couple of blocks from here. Named Mrs. Perella. She pours salt on a black Formica table, just salt, ordinary salt. Makes circles and lines in it and then tells you what's going to happen. Half the guys in this room go to see her, wanting to know if they should make this move or that move, but mainly wanting to know whether or not they're going to live another month."

"You ever go to see her?"

Danny smiled. "Some months twice." He went on about Mrs.

Perella, said she also had *jettatura,* the evil eye.

Springer patiently listened to how a certain capo hired Mrs. Perella to sit in the courtroom every day of his trial so she could hex the federal prosecutors with her black glance. Everyone on Arthur Avenue swore that was how the capo got acquitted.

Finally, Springer put it to Danny. "What do you think, is there any chance at all that Townsend's can be taken?"

For whatever reason, Danny's attitude was considerably changed. "Maybe not," he said, "but like we always say, anything is possible when you've got the right people."

Also at the Vesuvio Restaurant that night were Fred Pugh and Jack Blayney, the two State Department spooks. Blayney liked spaghetti but he wasn't very good at winding it and getting it to his mouth without dripping red sauce on his tie or fly or somewhere. Pugh was more sensible. He had veal piccata. Their table was about twenty feet from Springer, Audrey, and Danny, so they weren't able to overhear anything. That didn't matter with the angle Pugh had.

He saw every word they said.

24

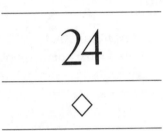

Walter Strand.

Sat on the concrete bench and enjoyed the gusts of the wakes of the cars that sped past on Connecticut Route 37. He could have taken the bus into Danbury. They had provided a bus, and Strand now wasn't sure he shouldn't have taken it. Not that he was impatient. He'd always been long on patience; it was one of the things that had helped see him through.

He was too warm just sitting there. Nothing, not a leaf or a cloud, was between him and the sun, and the white shirt he'd put on fresh less than an hour ago was wilting on him. The suit Patricia had brought up for this day when she'd last visited in March was the wrong suit. Right weight for then, wrong for now. A hard wool, gray. It probably hadn't occurred to her it would be wrong. Strand didn't want to believe she hadn't cared enough to have it occur to her. Anyway, the tie she'd chosen went well. Felt good to have a tie on again.

He wished he was going to be with Patricia rather than be picked up by these people. It was too soon for these people, no matter what. That had almost been his answer to Danny Rags, would have been if Patricia had waited. He didn't blame her, though. Didn't like it but didn't blame her.

Strand looked across the road to the Texaco station. Clean, well-kept station with a modest white frame house in back. Someone in business for himself and doing well enough to be satisfied with that illusion, Strand thought, aware of his own bitter-edged perspective. He heard the sharp, compressive shots of a grease gun, saw the station owner in the repair port servicing a car that was up on the hoist.

A Ford pickup pulled in for gas.

Strand observed the transaction.

After the truck was gone the station owner wiped up some oil droppings. He glanced across to Strand, greeted him with a raise of his hand. Decent of him, Strand thought. No doubt, being right there across the road, he knew what Strand was. Strand vetoed the notion of going over and talking with the guy.

His wrist watch told him eleven thirty-four. He was early. He was early, and probably these people would be late. The wrist watch was an 18K vintage Vacheron & Constantin that required winding. Strand could never look it in the face without being reminded that it had come from the hit of some house out on Long Island. Part of the first package, right after he'd bought the team. He'd never been able to convince himself that the watch was his, and numerous times he'd considered going into one of those Madison Avenue stores and overpaying for a watch just so he would feel he really owned it. He never got around to doing that. Even when he was looking in the shop window and the shop was open, he never got around to it. An infectious point of view, takers keepers.

Strand smoothed his hair in back, an unconscious habit triggered early and still going off because of the cowlick he'd always had. That tuft contributed to the impression that Strand was younger than forty-five. So did the shade of his hair, a variegated sandy brown with blond in it rather than gray. The natural tendency of his hair in front was to grow forward, also a bit boyishly, concealing his hairline and cutting down on his ample, nearly perpendicular forehead.

The right half of Strand's face was the dominant half, although anyone would have to be interested to notice. His nose, well indented at its root between his brow ridges, was straight and narrow enough, but it had a ball at its tip. His left eye was smaller than his right. The irises of his eyes were a blue-gray, so striated it was as if baguettes were set around his pupils. He had wide-open, alert-looking eyes, but there was deliberation and caution in the unhurried way they shifted from one thing to another. It seemed he was always anticipating what he would be seeing next, was never surprised. The most telling barometer of Strand's temperament was his chin. When he was angry or passionate the cleft in it deepened; when calm or pleased it was hardly perceptible.

Starlings were perched on one of the telephone wires that ran overhead. Strand counted the birds. Eleven identical black shapes against the sky. Why were they just sitting up there? Gossiping about which and which had spent the night together, or were they making arrangements for the night to come? Where, Strand wondered, would *he* be spending tonight? He had to stop thinking about Patricia. Distance and circumstances that excluded were also penitentiaries.

Strand got up.

He walked down the roadside, crunching pebbles beneath him. It took him only a couple of minutes to reach the vegetable stand, an outside-inside place selling from tilted bushel baskets. He bought one large tomato and asked the woman minding the place if there was anywhere he might wash it. She washed it for him. Gave him a bit of salt and a section of paper towel. He appreciated how thoughtful it was of her.

It was going to take time for him to get used to extra things like that.

On his way back to the bench he walked alongside the native stone retaining wall that bordered the grassy slope of the prison grounds. It was a steep, expansive slope and the prison structures were situated over its shoulder, out of sight except for the shiny peaks of a couple of roofs and a water tower. A concrete plaque inset into the wall was the only way of knowing a prison was up there. FEDERAL CORRECTIONAL INSTITUTION the plaque read.

Strand hadn't known anyone in there who was being corrected.

The three years he had done inside were part of a five-year possibility. Two off for good behavior. Neutral behavior was more like it. From the first day in, Strand had socialized as little as he could, and once the other inmates realized that was how he was going to be, that was what he needed to be to make it, they didn't get on him about it.

He was quiet. He didn't laugh much. He didn't work. He could have made a dime an hour just going through the motions of stabbing up litter around the grounds or a dollar fifty an hour painting cell blocks or whatever, but he hadn't needed the money or the therapy. He kept his body up by jogging a few miles three times a week and in between doing no-strain workouts with weights. Each week, without fail, he solved the Sunday *New York Times* crossword puzzle. Did a part of it each night, rationed it to himself so he'd still have twenty downs and twenty acrosses yet to do come Saturday night.

Thus Strand put himself in limbo, a sort of animate cryogenic state.

He hadn't appealed his three-to-five-year sentence. He knew he was going to have to do the time, so he figured he might as well do it and get it over with. They had him cold. Receiving stolen goods and transporting them across state lines. The state lines part made it a federal offense.

That he'd been caught by accident was something he sometimes found amusing. It had been on a Saturday night. He was driving his purposely modest Chevette up to Stamford to show swag to one of his regular buyers, a private. About five miles beyond the Greenwich toll station there was a tie-up: cars inching along as far as Strand could see. An accident, he thought, and resigned himself to the delay.

Actually it was a roadblock by the Connecticut State Police, checking for drunk drivers. They would stop Strand, not even ask him to get out of the car, just prompt him to say a few words to get a whiff of his breath and detect any drunken slurring. He hadn't even had a beer, so there wasn't going to be a problem.

The problem was the unhappy woman in the Honda Prelude behind him. She'd been crying into bourbon-Sevens since afternoon. She stalled her car and had some trouble restarting it. When she finally did get it going she stomped down on the accelerator, smashed into the rear end of Strand's Chevette, knocked out its taillights, and sprang open its trunk.

A state trooper came. He surveyed the situation and the damage. He also got a look into Strand's trunk. Part of the swag was a pair of six-arm Georgian silver candelabras that the buyer had expressed interest in. Really large, heavy ones. And some other silver pieces. Over a thousand ounces altogether. Strand had them wrapped in newspaper and packed well in cardboard cartons, but the impact of the Honda had scattered them.

The trooper spotted the silver but didn't say anything to Strand. He radioed. Two other troopers arrived. They put a few roundabout questions to Strand and then some straighter, to the point, and although he gave plausible replies, it all soon became quite obvious.

He was promised he'd only do a year if he gave up his people, Scoot and the others, but he didn't go for that. He liked to think Scoot wouldn't have gone for it either. The thing about it that pissed Strand was that none of the fences he knew had ever done a day of time and some had been dealing for twenty-five years. And here he'd been into it for only four years.

Before then he'd been straight.

Well on his way to being a master jeweler.

He had apprenticed in Chicago and New York and also in Paris with the old, prestigious firm of Chaumet. It was his Chaumet experience that landed him the position with Townsend. A prize of a job, the Townsend job. Only a rung from the top, and Strand was already professionally capable of taking that step.

He knew every phase of fine jewelry making. Given the materials, the chunks of gold or platinum and the precious stones, he could fashion a piece entirely by hand no matter how complicated: every detail graceful, every mounting snug. It got to a point where some of the custom pieces he'd made were known for having been done by him. The owner of a magnificent ruby and diamond suite, for example, was proud to be able to say it had been executed by Strand. That fact was mentioned as an attribute for a number of pieces that appeared in the catalogues of important jewelry auctions at both Sotheby's and Cristie's.

In 1979 Strand had every reason to feel secure and sanguine about his future.

On a midmorning in the autumn of that year a well-known actress and prodigal customer huffed into Townsend's. Townsend met with her in his office behind closed doors. After about a half hour Strand was summoned. He was shown a diamond bracelet and asked if recently he'd been responsible for seeing that it was cleaned and all its settings checked—something Townsend advised all his customers have done periodically with their important pieces.

Strand remembered the bracelet well. It was made up entirely of pear-shaped one-carat diamonds. He also recalled, as they were shown to him, two diamond necklaces, another channel-set bracelet, and several brooches and clips belonging to the actress that had been in for service at that same time a few months previous.

Townsend brusquely requested that Strand examine each piece closely. Did he see any discrepancies?

Strand couldn't say that he did. He was, naturally, looking more at the structure of the pieces than their stones. And the trouble was with the stones. Someone, the actress claimed, someone at Townsend's—it couldn't have been elsewhere because the only other places the pieces had been were in her bank strongbox and on her body—had replaced many of the stones with synthetics. She had discovered the fact quite by chance when a personal acquaintance who happened to be a wholesale diamond dealer remarked about them and, as a favor, checked them out. She'd never in her life been so taken aback as when she learned many of the stones were fakes. She'd never been so taken period, she said. She was furious, genuinely, not playing a scene.

Strand was allowed to take the pieces upstairs to the work floor where he could better examine them. He returned within a half hour to report that indeed quite a number of the stones that were supposed to be fine diamonds were cubic zirconium. Someone, one of the setters perhaps, must have switched those stones. Strand could offer no other explanation.

The actress threatened to sue.

But not only to sue.

She would, as she so graphically expressed it, drag Townsend's reputation through shit six feet deep. She would expose the entire affair to the press, appear on every news and talk show. She detested fakes of any kind, she said pointedly.

Townsend knew how to handle her. This was the man who had charmed treasured tiaras off imperial heads. He commiserated, as though he himself bore no blame. He soothed her with unctuous sympathies accompanied by perfectly timed compliant nods, shrugs, little distressed coos. He told her that of course he would personally see to it that her missing stones were promptly replaced.

Not enough, she told him.

And, he added, for her trouble she might want to choose any emerald bracelet from those he had in stock.

She was a lioness at feeding time.

He threw her Strand's head.

It didn't have to be Strand's. A lesser head would have pacified her, but Townsend wanted to give himself plenty of margin. It didn't matter that Strand had had nothing to do with the stone switching, Townsend let him go.

Ruined him.

Townsend saw to it that word of Strand's dishonesty was smeared throughout the trade, here and in Europe. He could have played it down, dismissed Strand quietly and squelched any rumors, but he must have been harboring a jealousy of Strand all along, felt his own spotlight threatened. Townsend even went so far as to invent the slander that other instances of such stone switching had been brought to light, that evidently it was something Strand had been doing for years. Thank God, Townsend said with an air of blessed relief, the rotten spot had now been pared from the fruit.

Strand's good standing was knocked flat. It made no difference how exceptional his work was, no one would hire him. It was said no stone was safe in his hands. That those in the trade so easily believed such things about him, that many were even smugly delighted by his fall, was additionally disillusioning for Strand.

He considered taking up a different line of business and floundered for a while trying to decide on what it might be. Jewelry was all he knew. There was no room in his head for anything else. An opportunity came up for him to get into the illicit underside of the trade.

Strand didn't jump at the chance, but he soon reasoned that he might as well live up to the unfairly imposed level of his reputation.

He bought the team of swifts, Scoot and the other two, from a fence with a suddenly bad heart who wanted to move to Fort Lauderdale. It was not an unusual transaction. Fences often sold their teams of thieves for one reason or another, as though they were chattel.

The arrangement between Strand and his newly acquired team was traditional. The swifts would sell whatever they stole only to Strand. In turn, Strand agreed not only to buy all their swag but also to look after the team in other ways. Advance them fucking-around money when there was a dry spell, see that they had a good lawyer on their case should they ever be caught, and, while they did time, provide for their dependents.

As deviative as the underlife was for Strand, in some ways he was well suited for it. He was an expert at removing stones from settings without damaging them, could pop them out in seconds. He was also experienced at handling precious metals. For a few hundred dollars he set up a portable electric smelter in the kitchen of his apartment. After he stripped a piece of all its stones he tossed the setting into a crucible and melted it down. A setting was identifiable, incriminating, but transformed into a lump of gold or platinum it was salable by the pennyweight without risk.

Other aspects of the underlife were not so easy. It took quite a while for Strand to learn the people and how they expected him to deal with them. There were codes held as inviolable as federal statutes, and certain cautionary measures it was assumed for everyone's sake he would adhere to. On the whole, in Strand's opinion the underlife people were no worse than many of the straights he'd formerly dealt with, particularly Townsend.

The hours were another thing.

The team made their hits at night, but at any time of night. Usually around 3 A.M. they would call from a pay phone and say they were on their way to him. When they arrived they dumped their flash in a pile on his kitchen table. Their part done, it was up to him to say what it was worth. They wanted the swag gone and cash in their hands as quickly as possible. Sometimes they were in such a hurry they accepted his approximate estimate of the entire package. Other times they weren't satisfied until he'd weighed every tiny gold chain, calculated every five-pointer, listed and gone over the package with them piece by piece. It could take several hours.

There were times when in their eyes a piece was worth more than he'd quoted. For instance, a single-stone diamond ring.

"How the fuck much did you say?"

"Three five."

"No fucking way, man. Not this time."

"Three five is fair."

"Any asshole can see it's the pick of the package."

"It's a spread."

"The stone will go five carats."

"It's just cut to look five. Thin table, large crown. A spread."

"We don't need you teaching us about stones, man. We know stones."

"A dealer down on Canal will give seven for it."

"You shopped it?"

"We think you're fucking us, man. You been fucking us an inch at a time."

"Yeah, and it's starting to hurt."

Such friction was more dramatic than crucial. Eventually it was always Scoot who leveled off first and brought the others around to being reasonable. Strand realized it was merely their way of confirming that he was sharp and strong enough to keep them in line, but at four or five or six in the morning it was nonsense.

Month after month of such indeterminate routine took its toll on Strand. His circadian clock refused to be reset. He never adjusted to having to sleep during the day, and a night when he got four undisturbed hours was an event. He was so run down that every flu bug passing through New York called on his body.

Well, he'd certainly caught up on his rest while in Danbury prison.

Now, on the morning of his release day, he returned to sit on the concrete bench by the side of Route 37. An engine began growling: a trusty was power-mowing the grass of the prison's slopes. Strand couldn't make out who the trusty was at that distance. Most likely, Strand thought, it was one of those politicians doing a token year for what would be a hundred years for anyone else, and whose grass at home was being tended by a well-paid gardener. Strand ignored the noise. If there was one thing he'd taught himself while inside, it was how to cut out noise.

He held up the tomato he'd bought.

Not to admire it but to determine where he would bite into it.

He wet the tomato with his tongue so some of the pinch of salt he sprinkled on it stuck. He felt the taut, tissuey skin puncture under the pressure of his front teeth. Like some not entirely helpless creature retaliating, it squirted juice and seeds, spoiled the taste of Strand's first bite by staining his shirt cuff.

At that moment a BMW 745i pulled up.

Strand assumed it was the one but he waited until he heard his name asked by the man on the passenger's side. He placed the mortally wounded tomato on the bench where birds were sure to see it. Did a quick study of the man in the car while he wiped his hands on the paper towel. Taking up his satchel from beneath the bench, he got into the rear seat.

When the car was under way Springer introduced himself and Audrey. The situation was awkward. There was common ground for conversation, actually a lot to be said, but Springer felt it would be wrong to get so quickly to it. What should he say? *How was it in prison? How does it feel to be out after three years?* What?

Strand wasn't about to take the initiative. He gazed out at the Connecticut countryside, which along there wasn't all that attractive: split-level houses with moats of pine-bark chips.

"Ever been up this way?" Springer asked. They were headed north on 37.

"No," Strand replied conclusively.

Springer was at a disadvantage because Strand was seated directly behind him. There could be no eye contact unless Springer strained around and looked over his shoulder. Just as uncomfortable for Springer was having the eyes of this stranger fresh out of prison fixed on the back of his neck. No matter that Danny had thoroughly briefed him on Strand's background, Springer didn't believe anyone could spend that much time locked up and not come out angry.

Concerned with that he hadn't noticed that Audrey was driving, as usual, too fast. The blacktopped road was unshouldered and excessively patched where each winter had heaved it up. The BMW skittered on a curve and grazed the turbulence of an oncoming twenty-ton Mack truck loaded with gravel. Actually it wasn't as close a call as the whirled air made it seem. Springer gestured to Audrey and she let up some. The last thing they wanted was to give Strand the impression that they were foolishly reckless.

Going slower accentuated the lack of conversation, but after a mile or so they were passing through a town and that helped.

"What's this place called?" Strand asked.

"New Fairfield."

A one-stoplight town, Strand observed to himself. Takes a certain kind of person to settle for a one-stoplight town. A lot of people, like Patricia, who were wrong about themselves thought it was what they wanted. Half dying early was really what it was. Fuck that. But what did he want in the long run? The three years in limbo hadn't clarified that for him. If anything, all the thinking he'd done had depleted his possibilities.

One thing for certain, Strand thought, he wasn't ready for these people. Danny had said, *Just listen to what they have in mind. As a special favor to me,* Danny had said, *special* implying a due bill. Honest to himself, Strand doubted that he would have consented had he been getting out with someone to go to. In a way these people were surrogates, all he had, and that was a hell of a lonely thing to admit. A couple of straights with a scheme, that's what they were. They were a ride to the city.

Audrey glanced into the rearview mirror and into Strand's eyes. She smiled at him in a way that Springer couldn't.

Strand smoothed his cowlick.

Springer turned to Strand. "What I thought we might do is stop someplace for lunch. There are a couple of nice places over on New York Twenty-two."

"I want to get into the city."

"Okay. We can talk on the way."

An hour and twenty minutes later the BMW pulled up where Strand said he wanted to be left off, a prewar apartment house on East 75th Street between First and Second Avenues.

"I'll give you a call," Strand said.

"You can reach me day or night at one or the other of those numbers," Springer told him.

"We'll be waiting to hear from you," Audrey promised.

Strand slammed the car door harder than necessary and entered the apartment house.

Audrey went east on 75th. As she approached the corner of Second Avenue, Springer had her pull over into a hydrant area. From there they looked back at the apartment house Strand had gone into.

"You were really selling," Audrey commented.

"I overdid it?"

"I don't know if you had to go into it as much as you did. Maybe to him it sounded like a sob story. Anyway, what do you think of him?"

"He's a good listener," Springer said sardonically.

"I'll pendulum him when we get home."

The two minutes they waited there at the curb seemed longer. Possibly even longer for Strand. He came out with his satchel still in hand, walked to the corner of First, and hailed a cab.

25

For the next five days Springer was as edgy as an actor waiting word about a part he'd auditioned for but wasn't entirely sure he wanted.

Audrey helped him cope with his ambivalence.

Drawing from her enthusiasm in favor of the robbery, she bolstered Springer's reasoning that it was the only choice left open to him. She neglected to say how much it appealed to her own penchant for putting everything on the line, as Springer had expressed it. In her mind there was not a grain of doubt that the robbery was possible, would be pulled off by them without a hitch. After all, the pendulum told her precisely that, every time she asked it. She looked forward to all the chancey moments, the stomach-hollowing, the adrenaline-rushing the robbery would involve. Surely it would put to shame such dabbling things as placing phony automatic pistols into the hands of store-window dummies.

To offset Springer's restlessness she kept him occupied. She asked

Wintersgill to get video cassette copies of all the current films. Wintersgill contacted a bootlegger who for a premium price regularly supplied well-offs with such copies even before the films were released.

Audrey and Springer went through the stack of cassettes, watching triple features until they'd used up half a bottle of Visine. Only a few of the films were worthwhile. Included were a couple of somewhat attractively soft hard-cores Audrey had requested. They served their purpose but really weren't needed. In that area Audrey dipped into her wellspring of artifices and came up with some variatious. Not elaborate, obviously staged productions but such feasible things as having a shipment of lingerie coincidentally arrive from Paris at the very same hour that Ferragamo delivered two dozen of their latest spike-heeled evening sandals for her selection. She needed Springer's opinion, she said, and had him get comfortable while she did quick change after quick change.

Camisoles *sans* panties, panties *sans* camisoles, chemises, step-ins, teddies—and her, striding and turning about with the detached insouciance of a Givenchy runway star.

Needless to say it took Springer's mind off all else.

Another sort of therapy was what she called centering him. As Springer understood, it was a way of keeping his body and spiritual self well balanced, very important especially in times of stress. All it took was his cooperation and her hands. He lay supine and nude on the rug. She poked around until she located this or that contact point. (Evidently she knew one when she felt it, but when Springer asked her how she changed the subject.) Maintaining contact with slight finger pressure, she closed her eyes and allowed healing white light to course through her and into him. So she claimed.

Since the wonderworkings of stone 588, Springer was ready to believe just about anything was possible. He told Audrey that he felt considerably better, stronger, clearer-headed after one of these centering sessions. Only because it made her happy to hear it.

Audrey also had him take *bhasmas.*

Without Springer knowing, she located an Ayurvedic physician who had quite a number of patients in the East Indian community in Queens.

Dr. Shayama Chakravarty.

He suggested that in order to ensure the medicine he prepared for Springer was of superior quality Audrey should obtain several fine rubies, the finer the better, and a thirty-inch braid of 15 millimeter natural oriental pearls. He had Audrey observe while he burned the rubies and pearls and stirred the ashes (the *bhasmas*) into a mixture of alcohol and glycerine and a drop or two of red cake frosting coloring. He transferred the mixture to an 8-ounce medicine bottle. Wrote SHAKE WELL and PITTA/KAPHA on the label.

Dr. Chakravarty, a soft-spoken man with two unfortunately placed purplish moles below his left eye, explained to Audrey that Pitta and Kapha were two of the three known Doshas, the three forces of energy, inertia, and harmony that are in every cell in our bodies—in fact, in every atom of all other existences as well.

Audrey asked why the doctor hadn't prescribed the third Dosha. Why only two?

"From what you have told me, there is no need for Vayu."

"What's Vayu?"

"Harmony," the doctor replied matter-of-factly.

Audrey didn't see how anyone couldn't use a bit more harmony.

Before Springer would take the *bhasmas,* Audrey had to tell him what it was and how she'd gotten it. She told him honestly that she'd bought the rubies at Cartier's and the pearls at Seaman Schepps.

"What will it do for me?" Springer asked.

"All sorts of good things," Audrey said with a tinge of innuendo.

"Is this an indirect complaint regarding the quality of our sex life?"

"Hell, no."

To patronize her Springer gave the bottle a vigorous shake and took a swig of the syrupy stuff now and then. Often he stuck his tongue in the neck of the bottle and pretended to be swigging. If it had been prepared as Audrey claimed, it was the most precious (though not necessarily efficacious) potion of all time, Springer thought. He suspected that the procedures of Dr. Whateverhisnamewas were faster than Audrey's eyes and that the ruby and pearl ashes he was now supposed to be quaffing were not from those Audrey had supplied. Rather than upset her, he never mentioned the possibility.

Frequently during those five days of waiting Springer stood at the south-view window of Audrey's apartment and looked down upon Townsend's place of business. Because it was on Fifth Avenue between 55th and 56th streets, which was almost directly below, Springer, on the thirty-fourth floor, had to press close up to the window glass to see it. From that height the five-story buildings below, including Townsend's, looked like miniatures modeled to scale. Sometimes Springer felt as though he could crush them by taking a single step.

On the afternoon of the sixth day of waiting, Springer decided he needed a more realistic perspective. He had about three quarters given up on Strand, believed Strand would have gotten in touch by now if interested. Anyway, Audrey would be there in case Strand called. Springer went down to Fifth Avenue and across 56th Street to the sidewalk in front of the Steuben Glass showroom. It was a horribly humid Friday. The tourists were hurting. They roosted hip to hip on the short ledge around the reflecting pool outside Steuben. The pool was still as glass, the black bottom of it scattered with coins. Mostly pennies but quite a few quarters and half crowns and francs. Springer wondered how it started, this paying for wishes. One night a couple of summers ago he had happened to be passing by there when the police were having a hard time apprehending a panhandler who was up to his crotch in the pool, diving to get enough for a bottle in a bag. The panhandler claimed he was merely baptizing himself.

A Japanese man *without* a camera vacated his place on the ledge. Springer was fast to claim it. On either side of him were young out-of-town lovers hanging on as though the city might steal them from each other. Springer fixed his attention on the buildings across the way. First, on the corner of 55th, was the Fifth Avenue Presbyterian Church, constructed of brownstone and with a steeple and a half where two must have been originally planned. Adjacent to the church was an attractive six-story building and next to it another of three stories. The kind of turn-of-the-century European-influenced structures that the New York City Landmarks Commission was trying to save.

Next came Townsend's building. It, also, was turn-of-the-century but simpler in line: five stories with a flush, almost unornamented natural limestone facade. Its twelve upper windows (three to each floor) had identical shades, decoratively scalloped and tasseled. At street level the arched entrance was flanked by two display windows only about three feet high and half as wide. These were strategically lighted in much the same manner as Winston's windows three doors away. Even from across the wide avenue, Springer could see the scintillations of the diamonds they displayed.

Second floor front was Townsend's private office. Perhaps, Springer thought, the prick was up there that very moment, sitting at his desk with stone 588 the only thing on the surface before him. Gloating over it. Springer focused intensely on those second-floor windows, as though he were capable of transmitting some sort of lethal hate beam.

Buses.

Six of them lumbered down the stream of the avenue like behemoths in single file. Their advertisement-bearing hulks interrupted Springer's point of view.

More likely, he told himself, stone 588 was tucked securely away in Townsend's vault and the man himself was gone to some country place such as Libby's.

Springer tilted his head back and sighted up the grouped black shafts of Trump Tower, evil and powerful looking and so tall they threatened to topple over on him. He estimated just about where up there Audrey was. She would throw gold pieces into wishing pools, he thought. He leaned forward, forearms to knees, glanced down the avenue.

At first he didn't recognize Strand.

Strand looked so different in a short-sleeved cotton-knit sport shirt and casual slacks. He also had on wraparound wire-framed sunglasses. But there was no mistaking the cowlick. Strand was about thirty feet away in front of the Coca Cola/Columbia Pictures Building, using a brass Siamese automatic sprinkler outlet for a seat. How long had Strand been there? Springer wondered. More important, why was he there? Strand's gaze seemed to be fixed upon Townsend's across the way. Possibly he hadn't even noticed Springer.

Springer got up, went across the wide sidewalk to the curb. Stood diagonally facing Strand. He did everything but dance trying to get Strand's attention, even took a couple of quarters from his pocket and pretended to drop them accidentally. After about five minutes of such antics, when there was no way Strand could have possibly not seen him, Springer walked away.

He didn't look back. Either Strand was following him or he wasn't. He crossed over and went east on 56th to the atrium of the IBM Building. In there he sat at one of the small stationary marble-topped tables.

Strand came and sat across from him.

"Nice place," Strand commented, glancing around and above. "I remember when they were putting it up."

The atrium, courtesy of IBM and certain city building codes, was spacious and public. Clusters of bamboo grew thirty to forty feet tall. Bowl-like containers five feet in diameter held thriving ranunculus. High-ceilinged and open, with no music and only muted conversations, the place had the atmospheric quality of a public library.

Springer told Strand, "I was about to give up on you."

"I had things to do."

After three years who wouldn't, Springer thought.

"A guy I knew in the joint . . . his wife was having a problem with her Jody. I promised I'd see if I could straighten it out."

"A problem with her what?"

"Her Jody. It's what they call the guy a woman is with while her man does time."

"Must be frustrating as hell, being jealous and unable to do anything about it."

Strand smiled at Springer's normal assumption. He thought he'd let it go at that but then, merely for the talk of it, decided to explain. "It's not a matter of infidelity," he said, "it's an accepted arrangement. And quite practical, all things considered."

"Oh?"

"Not many guys have the wherewithal to support a woman while they do time. Also, it's self-deceiving to believe she's not going to have to be taken care of sexually."

"So a Jody provides, huh?"

"Yeah."

Springer tried to imagine himself in prison and Audrey with some Jody. He'd be chewing the bars.

"Have you spoken to Danny?" Strand asked.

"Not for a couple of days."

"I had a few words with him this morning."

"What have you decided?"

"Nothing."

"Okay then, which way are you leaning?"

"I like the project. Not enough yet to say I'll get involved, only that it has its attractions."

"Why do you like it?'

"Someday maybe we'll discuss that."

"Danny told me the shit Townsend pulled on you."

"That's one reason."

Strand got up. So abruptly Springer thought he was offended and leaving. Without a word Strand went to the refreshment bar at the other end of the atrium. He returned with a tray bearing wedges of cream-cheese poppy-seed cake, chocolate mousse cake, and chocolate walnut pie and two glasses of fresh orange juice. He placed the tray in the center of the table and told Springer, "Help yourself."

Springer thanked him for one of the orange juices.

Strand drew the tray to himself and began on the desserts. He favored the cream-cheese poppy-seed cake but didn't slight the others.

"You and Audrey should really hit it off," Springer remarked.

"I want to ask you about her. Is she in this all the way or just around for you before and after?"

It was by no means a mere loose end. When Springer had told Audrey he didn't want her taking part in the actual robbery because it was too dangerous, she scoffed and told him to skip the movie hero obligatory speech to his girlfriend, when both knew, according to plot, she was going to be with him up to her ass in danger throughout. When Springer again mentioned he'd feel better if she wasn't so deeply mixed up in it, she didn't argue, didn't put it to him in the form of an unequivocal, eternal ultimatum. She just silently stood her ground, and from her stance and the look in her eyes, Springer knew if he insisted on holding his line she was going to be miserable, and therefore he was going to be miserable for a long time to come. "Audrey is in it all the way," Springer told Strand.

Strand grunted rather disagreeably with his mouth full of chocolate walnut pie. He pushed his sunglasses up so they were atop his head. "If this move is made it's going to take quite a few people, figure six to ten."

"That many?"

"They won't all be shareholders, of course, but there'll be things that will have to be done. Danny said he had some guys who would do without wanting to know why."

"I'm sure I can count on Danny."

"In return Danny wants first on all the goods."

Springer was disappointed that Danny's offer to help wasn't unqualified, but then he *was* trespassing Danny's livelihood, and no doubt Danny had to answer to others. "I wouldn't have any problem with that, would you?"

Strand shook his head no. He finished off the last of the chocolate mousse cake. It sure beat the hell out of raspberry Jell-O, or jail-o, as the guys in the joint called it. He scraped the plate with the side of his fork, got every last crumb. From the rear pocket of his trousers he brought out a once-folded legal-sized envelope. He held it open, offering its contents to Springer. Several folded pages. "Those aren't in my handwriting, nor are my prints on them anywhere," Strand said. He tore the envelope into small squares and dropped them onto one of the chocolate-smeared plates. "Even if I don't make it a joint venture—shit, that's an unfortunate choice of words, isn't it—anyway, I'm sure you'll find those helpful."

Springer thanked him with his eyes. He put the pages in his pocket. "Let me ask you just one thing."

"No harm asking."

"You know the place. Can it be done?"

"Depends."

"On the people?"

"And on what some call luck and others call perfect timing." Strand slipped his sunglasses down into place. "C'mon, let's take a walk."

They went west on 56th, down Avenue of the Americas, east on 55th, and up Fifth. Around the block counterclockwise. Three times around. The first time they said nothing, walked slowly and took things in. Second time around they called one another's attention to possibilities. The third time they culled.

On the corner of 56th and Fifth outside Winston's, Strand had had enough, was anxious to be elsewhere. "I'll give you a call," he said.

"That's what you told me last time."

"Call *me* if you want. I'm at the Helmsley Palace."

"Really?" Dubious Springer.

"Room service loves me." Strand grinned, turned, and hurried to make the light.

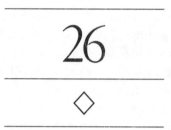

26

◇

Springer unfolded the material Strand had given him: eleven neatly hand-printed pages, including drawings of floor plans, overhead and side views.

He and Audrey read slowly and passed the pages to one another while sprawled head-to-foot and foot-to-head in the deep lap of an obese sofa.

It was obvious that Strand had spent a lot of time preparing the information, hadn't given it just a half-interested lick. He was very thorough in describing Townsend's as he remembered it, the particulars of the building and all the security measures that protected it. The drawings, though freehand and not in proportion, made it easier to visualize. Even approximate measurements were indicated where they might be helpful.

Now Springer and Audrey were brought to realize what they were up against.

Townsend's building.

Twenty-seven feet wide and from its front on Fifth Avenue about one hundred twenty feet deep. Its main structure was beam and brick, circa 1906.

The rear of the building and its roof were thought to be most vulnerable, so those areas were intensively protected. The rear shared an enclosed space, a littered and unkempt sort of inner courtyard, with the backs of other buildings of the block. Access to that space could be gained through any of those other buildings, and someone wanting to break in would be able to work undetected there for hours. For that reason, disregarding the city fire laws that require at least a second unimpeded exit, the rear door and windows of Townsend's had been sealed, filled in with brick to present a sheer wall five stories high. For additional security a downward-aimed television camera was mounted a third of the way up.

The roof of Townsend's was flat. It was on a level with the flat roof of the building next door to the north. To prevent merely stepping from one roof to the other, two steel mesh fences were spaced three feet apart. Not ordinary steel mesh fences. The first fence was woven with sharp barbs and topped with spikes curved well outward. The second fence was electrically charged. It was not known exactly how much voltage ran through it; however, it was said and believed that merely placing a hand to it would knock a man down.

A pressure-sensitive alarm was integrated throughout the surface of the roof. Weight in excess of fifty pounds anywhere upon it would activate the alarm.

Four television cameras were installed up there. Two covered the roof itself with wide-angle views. The other two overlooked the roof of the adjacent building to the south. Because that building was two and a half stories lower, it did not pose a threat as a way of access. Anyone on the roof of that building looking toward Townsend's would be facing an uninterrupted brick wall thirty feet straight up.

Although it was unimaginable that an attempt might be made to break into Townsend's from Fifth Avenue, all twelve of its sash-type front windows were permanently closed and equipped with both contact and vibration-sensitive alarms. The archway entrance was closed off after business hours by a roll-down steel gate. The front door had two heavy-duty deadbolt locks as well as a contact alarm.

So much for Townsend's from the outside.

Intermission.

Audrey went to the kitchen for a heap of pistachios in a proper silver bowl.

Springer got on the phone, dialed the Helmsley Palace, and asked for Mr. Strand. He expected to be told no one by that name was registered, but he was put through and on the second ring a woman picked up. She said hello three times and then Springer heard Strand's voice in the background asking her who it was. Springer hung up feeling slightly encouraged.

He and Audrey resumed their reading positions at opposite ends of the sofa, the bowl of pistachios within equitable reach. Springer used his thumbnail to split apart the pistachio shells and get at the kernels. Audrey, valuing her nails, popped the pistachios into her mouth shells and all, three or four at a time. She stored them in a cheek while using her tongue to maneuver one into position for her front teeth to find the crack on the seam of its shell and force it open. She kept the empty shell halves in her other cheek until it was bulging, handicapping her oral dexterity. Springer, afraid that Audrey might get her storing and cracking and chewing and swallowing and breathing out of sync, was always ready to apply the Heimlich maneuver.

Back to Strand's pages.

The inside of Townsend's.

The three top floors were partitioned into workrooms of varying size. Up there was where goods, rough and finished, were graded, and where the phases of jewelry making, the polishing, setting, and finishing, were performed. Two faceting machines were on the fifth floor, a couple of designer studios on the third. Nothing extraordinary.

Townsend's office, second floor front, was separate from the vault but adjacent to it. The vault was actually a walk-in armored strong room that measured eight by ten feet with a seven-foot ceiling. It was installed in 1975. Purportedly out of nostalgia, actually as a matter of thrift, the interior of the prior vault was kept intact. The walls, floor, and ceiling were made of steel-reinforced concrete with a solid steel skin two inches thick. A copper alloy lining was sandwiched in the steel to keep anyone from cutting through it with a torch. Heat, dispersed by the conductivity of the copper, could not be concentrated to a high enough degree in any one spot.

The door of the vault was four-inch-thick case-hardened steel. It had eight solid cylindrical bolts one and a half inches in diameter. When the vault door was locked, the bolts extended five inches into the seamless steel jambs left and right of the door.

A computerized timing device controlled the bolts. At the end of a business day, once the vault was locked, the bolts would not retract and allow opening under any circumstances until 9 A.M. the following morning. The timer was also programmed for weekends and holidays.

The vault had a ten-digit electronic combination. It was Townsend's secret, set by him. He was so cautious about it he didn't seem to even trust himself, changed the combination frequently.

Another television camera was concealed in paneling opposite the vault, and there were pressure alarm pads underneath the wall-to-wall carpeting right up to the vault door.

The interior of the vault was about five feet by seven. The floor was covered with black vinyl; on the ceiling, two fluorescent lighting fixtures and a circular air vent that was nine, maybe ten inches in diameter. In case anyone got locked in.

On the wall opposite the door was a black velour-covered table.

On the walls left and right were the drawers that contained Townsend's goods.

The drawers were steel-faced, had knob pulls, and were etched with numbers, 1 through 100, so there must have been about fifty on each wall. They were arranged in vertical courses, much like the card catalogue in a library, starting a foot from the floor and going up to five feet or so. The drawers were identical in size: say, six inches wide, five inches deep, and twelve inches long. A few were wider, about ten inches, to accommodate larger pieces such as tiaras and parures.

When a Townsend employee removed something from the vault

he was to pull out the drawer entirely, place it on the velour-covered table, and go into it there. He would note the number of the lot, sign the Goods-Out sheet, and return the drawer to its proper slot. Townsend wouldn't stand for having drawers protruding from the wall where they might be accidentally knocked out, their contents scattered. A stone or two had been lost by such carelessness, Townsend claimed. He had a remarkable memory when it came to his stock.

The alarm systems at Townsend's were connected to Reliance Security Services, Inc., which was as close as any business could get to being hooked up directly to the Midtown North police precinct on West 54th Street. Other security outfits such as Wells Fargo, Pinkerton's, and Holmes were larger and better known; however, Reliance offered the advantage that it was owned and run by a group of retired Midtown North detectives who were wiser to the ways of city swifts. Reliance had connections at the precinct that it could count on for more than plain old cooperation. Quite a few guys still on the force moonlighted at Reliance. In fact, some daylighted, so to speak.

Townsend's alarms ran to an electronic console at Reliance that was continuously watched. An alarm set off showed up at once. A closed-circuit television channel monitored view after view of what the various cameras at Townsend's were picking up. Trial runs of break-ins were conducted twice a year. On the average, Reliance officers and Midtown North precinct police with guns drawn reached the Townsend vault in four minutes.

One last thing: A backup alarm was situated behind a panel of boiserie on the south wall of Townsend's office. All alarm systems and television cameras were connected to this backup. It was battery-operated and, in the event of a power failure, could be switched on.

Springer got a pistachio that had no accommodating crack to its shell. It refused to be opened.

He let the last of Strand's pages drop to the floor.

"Shit," he said futilely.

Audrey pulled up the corners of her mouth. "Perhaps that's only an amateur's opinion," she said. She moved up to be in the cave of Springer's arm, comforted herself there before suggesting, "Why don't we get really dressed up, black tie, everything, and go out somewhere snazzy to eat?"

"Snazzy?"

"You know how good dressing up is for the mopes."

"Not tonight."

"Then let's just go out somewhere for dinner, walk and discover. We haven't done that in a while."

"I'm not hungry."

Neither was Audrey.

They remained there on the sofa while, suitably, the day also drained away. No need to discuss the robbery. It would be foolish to give it another thought. They couldn't get close enough to Townsend's vault to throw something at it, much less get into it. And a fence that fries, and half the most frozen-hearted ex-cops in the city just waiting to pounce.

Forget it, Springer told himself. If he was to get back stone 588 for Jake it would have to be some other way. Giving Townsend the muzzle of a pistol for a hearing aid again came to mind.

In the gloom of only the light reflecting from the city, Springer gathered up Strand's pages. He thought he'd keep them as a souvenir of folly, or a reminder not ever to underestimate the invincibility of people of Townsend's ilk. He took the pages up to the dressing room and put them in one of the drawers designated for his things, beneath his socks and underwear.

Audrey took a long bath.

Springer disliked himself in the mirror and thought of growing a beard like Balzac's.

Audrey meditated. For an hour sat tranced with eyes closed, palms lying open on her lap.

Springer was glad when she'd had enough of that, was back with him and his give-ups.

"I love you," she said from across the room.

"I know you do."

While he read a John Updike and merely saw the words, Audrey sat on the floor among her pillows and buffed her legs. Springer had never seen her do it before. It fascinated him, the way she applied some special lotion and, like polishing boots, used a length of flannel cloth to put a shine on the skin of her lower legs and thighs. He'd wondered on occasion how her legs got their slick finish. The tricks of women, he thought, a bit more depressed than amused.

At one o'clock they tried for sleep.

At two dropped off.

At three Springer came stark awake. He didn't toss, not to disturb Audrey. She was on her back eyes closed, one hand beneath her head. Apparently having peaceful dreams. Then, without any thickness or mumble, as though continuing a conversation, she said, "Tomorrow, what we should do is indulge, go out and buy one another something ridiculously extravagant."

"What is it you want?"

When she didn't reply, Springer thought she might be mentally going over some long list. As for himself, all he wanted was a miracle or two.

At seven o'clock he got up and padded nude down to the kitchen for coffee. He was too bleary to bother with anything more than instant. Audrey called down that she wanted some hot chocolate. That supplied him with a little purpose. He made it extra rich with heavy cream.

At five to eight Springer decided he wouldn't wait until nine to call Strand. It didn't matter that it was a bit early, he was only going to tell Strand that the move was off—because of impossibility. It had occurred to Springer during the night that probably the reason Strand had come up with the information on Townsend's was to have him reach that realization.

Springer was reaching for the phone when it rang.

It was Strand.

After apologizing for calling so early he said, "This project of yours. I've given it some thought. I believe we should go ahead with it."

"Good," Springer heard himself say.

"Do you know someplace where we can get together for a few days to work it out?" Strand asked. "Someplace quiet and out of the way."

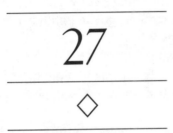

27

The country house in Sherman.

Springer and Audrey arrived there just as Mattie was driving out in her mechanically slighted and rarely washed Audi 5000.

Mattie stopped to say a goodbye hello. She was bound for a Psychical Society seminar being held somewhere in Maryland, cheerily looking forward to a whole ten days of being around no one other than sensitives and believers. Springer and Audrey would have to fend for themselves. The fridge needed restocking, Mattie said, and she thought but wasn't certain she'd changed the linens on their bed a few days ago. "Pick the raspberries" were her last words before she shaped her mouth into a kiss and threw it at them. The wheels of the Audi spun up pebbles and dust as, with Maryland in mind, she took to Route 37.

The house was as welcoming as ever. The huge chairs in front of the fireplace and by the side windows seemed to be begging to be sat in. It was impossible to be in any room and not be within reach of a challenging book or magazine. There was a two-month stack of *Manchester Guardian*s by the commode in the main floor bathroom. Now serving as a stop for the kitchen door was a sizable new brook-polished speckled black rock, Springer noticed. And Buddha was gone from the top of the piano. Was he in disfavor this month or gone for good to one of the consignment shops down on Route 7? In his place was a frosted Lalique vase that contained wild phlox. Picked that morning but already dropping. Many tiny blossoms had sown pink on the black mahogany surface.

Audrey and, especially, Springer should have known by now what a loving fibber and surpriser Mattie enjoyed being. The refrigerator with many of their favorite things in it told them she'd shopped that morning, and when they went to their room, that done-over former slaughtering shed they called the *boucherie*, they found their bed freshly made and folded open neat and clean as a new envelope. The room was well aired and wildflowers, expecting to be appreciated, were here and there in cut glass containers. For Audrey, on her bedside table, a new supply of bookmarks: feathers blown loose by the wind or the vigorous rufflings of flickers and cardinals and jays.

Mattie's efforts, thoughtful as they were, did nothing to ease Springer's self-conscious feeling about using these surroundings to plan a burglary.

At seven o'clock Strand and Scoot drove up, in a five-year-old Mustang that Scoot had borrowed from a girlfriend who was so straight he was 95 percent sure it wasn't stolen. Strand's driver's license had expired while he was in prison, and neither he nor Scoot had any credit cards that were really their own, so it had been impossible to rent a car.

Springer showed them up to their bedrooms. Like most old New England houses, the second-floor ceilings were lower and, although there was ample clearance, Strand and Scoot moved about hunched down. They appeared out of place in their suits and white dress shirts. Their leather-heeled black shoes clacked on the bare wide-board floors.

Springer believed from the size of their satchels they couldn't have brought an adequate change of clothes, an error commonly made by those unfamiliar with country life. No doubt tomorrow he'd be digging up some proper rough wear and some mucking-around shoes for them. No problem. Springer left them seated on their respective beds, checking out the quality of the mattresses with small bounces.

A quarter hour later they came down to the kitchen, changed. Now they had on faded blue jeans, chambray shirts, Puma sneakers. What Springer hadn't known was how compactly they could fold and roll up such clothes, part of the respect for space they'd acquired while living in cells.

Audrey asked if they were hungry.

They said they'd stopped at a place called Schubie's on the way up, had a couple of great burgers and fries.

"Okay," Audrey said, "you guys go find wherever you want to sit, and I'll bring coffee. But you've got to promise not to discuss anything important until I get there. Otherwise I'll stop playing woman." Her eyes let them know she damn well meant it.

Strand and Scoot followed Springer out onto the wide screened-in back porch. The porch faced west but already the sun was gone behind the hump of Connecticut hill across the way, and much of the color, the greens especially, was gone from everything. They sat in white-painted wicker chairs that creaked and caused Scoot to regard his chair dubiously. He kept glancing down at it as though expecting it to collapse.

Actually, Scoot should have been less concerned than anyone. He was a naturally gaunt five-foot-ten, weighed at most one thirty-five. He had thick, coiling, sandy hair and the mealy pale complexion of a full-blooded Irisher. His real first name was known to the authorities and hardly anyone else. His last name was Healy.

"Where are you from?" Springer asked Scoot just to make conversation, naive to the code that under the circumstances it wasn't something to be asked.

"Kansas City," Scoot replied because it sounded knock-around.

"You live in New York now?"

"Detroit."

"Never been to Detroit."

"Me neither," Scoot said pointedly.

Strand was amused. He explained to Springer that Scoot had been one of his team of swifts: in fact, more or less its leader.

"I ain't worked except here and there for six months waiting for Strand to get out," Scoot said.

"I don't know why, but I assumed you and Strand were in Danbury together."

"I've only done time in two places," Scoot told him. "Greenhaven and Dannemora."

"Dannemora has the ring of a nice little Irish village," Audrey remarked brightly as she brought sweating glasses on a tray. "I changed our minds and made iced tea," she said and served around. She chose the chair next to Strand's to offset the possible feeling of factions.

Strand spooned six heapings of sugar into his tea and stirred it methodically. "What we ought to first get settled is the split," he said.

A surprise to Springer. Why at this stage deal with anything so far down the road? It made good sense to Audrey, however. First thing anyone starting a new job wanted to know was how much it paid.

"What would you say the goods in Townsend's vault are worth?" Strand asked Springer.

"I don't know. I suppose the amount varies substantially."

"Give or take a million," Strand prompted.

"Take," Audrey quipped.

Springer told Strand, "You're more qualified to know."

Strand agreed. He was merely plumbing Springer's expectations. "Then let's just work out what kind of cuts would be fair. It's your thing. It's up to you."

Springer wasn't ready for it. He hesitated.

"All we have to decide on is two chunks," Strand said. "I'll take care of Scoot out of mine and you and your lady . . ."

"Audrey," she put in.

An apologetic nod from Strand. ". . . you and Audrey probably already have some kind of arrangement."

"Yeah."

"So, you tell me."

"Well, as you say, it's my thing. I brought you in."

"How about sixty-forty?" Strand suggested.

"Why?"

"Because I think even if we go at it all night that's where we'll end up."

"Who's the sixty?"

"We're the forty," Strand assured him, as though that was obvious.

Springer looked thoughtfully into his emptied glass, tilted it up, and got the melt from the ice cubes. He felt Audrey's eyes on him. "I only want one stone," he said.

Strand believed he'd misheard.

"One particular stone," said Springer.

"Danny mentioned something about that."

"The rest is yours."

Strand looked to Scoot with amused incredulity.

"You think I'm some kind of case," Springer said.

"No," Strand told him, "What I think is when it comes down to it you'll change your mind."

"What about me?" Audrey contended, "How about what I might want?"

"How much?" Strand asked her.

"You offered him sixty-forty."

Are you saying you want sixty?"

"Maybe I'm saying I want to be offered sixty," Audrey said.

"I was under the impression that he was speaking for you."

"He was . . . to a point."

Strand smoothed his cowlick. "I don't know about sixty. Perhaps thirty."

"Tell you what." Audrey leaned forward, elbows to knees, fingers loosely laced, a bargainer. "If you guys will promise not to be at my elbow, so to speak, not to concern yourselves with helping me up or helping me down or any of that other chivalrous shit, I might go for thirty."

Strand decided he liked her a lot. Springer was lucky.

"And," she went on, "if during this thing you don't hold back swearing, I could even knock off the thirty."

"We're to forget you're a woman?"

Audrey tossed her chin in Springer's direction. "Except him at times," she said, shamelessly forthright.

"So what would be your split?"

"One stone," she said. "Just any old stone. For a souvenir."

By then the sky was indigo to mauve to vermilion, as though the sun had rolled into a cave. The moon, a slivery scallop, was taking its turn. Darkness pressed the sides of the porch.

Springer lighted a glass oil lamp, adjusted its wick.

Instead of another round of iced tea, Scotch was accepted. Springer broke out a bottle of Usquaebach. They had it, as he suggested, neat in thick glass tumblers. They toasted to the success of the thing they were in together.

Strand, with the luxurious Scotch sliding like a molten gold wire down into him, thought how far he was from Danbury cell 328. He could, he told himself, finish the drink, say thanks and good night, and go sixty miles an hour away from this thing. He had four hundred thousand cash in a safety deposit box, along with another hundred thousand or so in loose stones. Wouldn't that much do? There was no use manipulating himself; he was in this for more than the take. He had to wonder, though, why it wasn't something that had occurred to him. Probably it had. Probably it had been crouching there in some lair of his mind for six–seven years. For some reason it was always easier to get into someone else's idea, as though that way there was partial exoneration.

Strand had a sudden catch inside at the possibility of more years in a cell. That same moment Audrey was laughing at a remark Springer had made. For Strand her laughter was catalytic. He tried to recall the sound of Patricia's laugh and couldn't. The paid-for company over the last few days had been inadequate, not even a fraction of what he'd needed.

They didn't discuss the burglary that night. The mood was wrong for it. And so was the place. Strand was too used to having snitches around, and the exposure of the porch made him uneasy.

Springer topped their drinks.

Audrey asked Scoot why he was called Scoot.

"Because I can run and still look like I'm just walking," he said. "It comes in fucking handy, believe me."

That got Scoot started. It wasn't usual for him to open up so quickly. He had a near infallible antenna when it came to people. He liked Springer and Audrey even though they were straight. Besides, they wouldn't be straight for long.

"Shit, man," Scoot said, "I've hit rich-looking houses that turned out to be so fucking poor inside, instead of me stealing from them I felt like I should leave *them* something."

He was on.

"I get into this apartment and I'm about to shake it down when I hear the people coming in the front door. Must have changed their minds about going to a movie or something. I jump into this closet that's there. I leave the door open a crack. One of the people notices it's open and shuts it. I can't get out. I spend the whole fucking night on the floor in this little closet. I don't sleep. I can't sleep. Not because I'm nervous but because there's no air and there's all these mothballs. I'm close to passing out. I don't know if I'm fucking dizzy or not in the dark, know what I mean? I'm close to banging on the door and taking the fall. Shit. Better than dying. I'm in fucking solitary, man. I'm in there until two o'clock the next afternoon when finally all the people leave. I bust out. I'm weak. I stick my head out a window for ten minutes to get my breath. Then, of course, I clean the place. I remember there were these nice five-carat pear-shape drops and some other stuff hidden in the most likely place, a douche bag."

Springer's watch told him quarter after ten. He glanced at Audrey.

She did a yawn and blamed it on the country air. She gathered up the glasses and carried them into the kitchen.

Strand asked Springer would it be disturbing anyone if he stayed up and watched television? Sleep was the last thing he needed.

Springer led Strand inside to the den, turned on the television set, adjusted it, and apologized for the poor reception. "By the way"—

Springer tried to sound offhand—"How much do *you* think the goods in Townsend's vault are worth?"

Strand told him. "Counting loose stones, finished pieces, everything, I'd say . . . in the neighborhood of two hundred and fifty million."

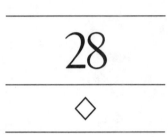

28

◇

The next morning, Monday morning.

As soon as the sun had dried the dew, Springer, Audrey, Strand, and Scoot went out to be in the meadow. They sat in a spot about two hundred feet from the house. The grass, waist-high and thick, was like a springy net beneath them. There was huge headed purple clover in it and spindly buttercups and seedy horsetail rye that stood around and swished approvingly.

Audrey had brought along a large sketch pad and a fistful of felt-tipped pens. And Strand's pages of Townsend information.

All morning and on into the early afternoon they went up against Townsend's many alarms and other security measures. And got nowhere. They became mired in complexities. Just when they thought they might have a way to beat one alarm, there was another to contend with. It was disheartening.

They took a break.

Audrey went into the house and made sandwiches, hunks of toasted peasant bread slathered with sweet butter and globs of a Fortnum & Mason jam called High Dumpsie Dearie. Springer would have preferred liverwurst and mustard on rye instead of this sweet plum, pear, and apple concoction. Strand, however, gobbled it up, and he and Audrey had a playful verbal battle over the extra sandwich, which they ended up dividing.

Audrey got a big purplish High Dumpsie Dearie smudge on her sketch pad. There was nothing useful on that sheet anyway, just a lot of doodles such as her and Springer's names lettered various ways and combined by design into a corporatelike logo.

Audrey tore off that page and began afresh.

They went at it differently, tried a simpler approach with disregard for the alarms for the time being. They imagined their challenge as a mere box within a box: Townsend's building one box, Townsend's vault another. To be examined for a weakness from all sides and top and bottom, from outside and in.

Springer suggested what might be a way into the building. Not easy but less difficult. They went to work on it: took turns playing devil's advocate, really kicked it around, were careful not to be misled by enthusiasm. By late afternoon they had settled on it. It felt good, right to them. The one box, the building, was possibly solved. Nearly as important, the spirit of collaboration had set in.

The following day they returned to that same spot in the meadow grass. Because of the previous day's success they considered the place conducive, even providential. At noon they had more High Dumpsie Dearie jam sandwiches, not to change a thing.

Springer skipped lunch. While everyone else was licking their sticky fingers, he stood up and stretched. Using his hand as a visor above his eyes he caught upon a high hawk doing aerobatics for the fun of it. It was then that the idea came to him, right out of the blue. The way perhaps into the other box, the vault. He tossed it out for consideration and everyone jumped on it. At first it seemed a bit too complicated, but then the more they thrashed it the simpler and more feasible it got.

For having thought of it, Springer was rewarded with a sweet proud kiss from Audrey, a congratulatory and amiable remark from Strand, and a compliment from Scoot, who said he believed Springer had the sort of mind needed to be a really fucking-good swift.

That settled, they were brought to face the most formidable problem of all, Townsend's alarms and surveillance system. It was agreed that it would be next to impossible to deal individually with all those sonar and contact devices, pressure-sensitive pads, and strategically placed television cameras. Perhaps, Audrey said, they could be lumped. Thinking in that direction, it took all day Wednesday and most of Thursday to arrive at what might be a solution. Something not all that tricky, as it turned out.

Now it was a matter of going over everything, piecing the phases together sequentially, making sure no detail was overlooked, determining what would be needed. Audrey made a list on the sketch pad.

Friday was errand day.

Strand and Scoot went to New York City.

Springer and Audrey went to a plumbing supply company in New Milford. For the quarter-inch pipe. Springer had it cut into foot-length sections, twelve altogether, threaded on both ends. He casually told the plumbing supply man that he was replacing some of the lines of a flower-bed sprinkler system. The man was all for it: He charged for each cut and threading.

While at the plumbing supply place, Springer also purchased eleven straight connecting pipe joints, the ten that he had to have and a spare. And did the man have on hand a flexible joint, the kind that were used in conjunction with brackets of pipe that allowed awnings to be raised and lowered? Rather than describe, Springer sketched it: like an elbow, threaded so two pieces of pipe (an upper arm and forearm) could be attached to it.

The man had exactly what he needed.

From there Springer and Audrey went to a hardware store for the picture-hanging wire, fifty feet of it, more than enough, guaranteed to hold five hundred pounds. Also the six-volt lantern-type flashlights and the two-inch bolt.

On Route 7 at a sporting goods store they found the woven climbing rope and snaps and the new folding-type grappling hook. It was there that they were also able to get the fisherman vests with numerous zippered pockets of various sizes, including a large ample compartment in the back like a built-in pack.

The blasting cord.

They had to go all the way to Litchfield to locate that. Farmers around there still used it to blast apart the inmovable rocks they hit upon when they cleared a field. So it was not extraordinary for Springer to be buying some. With typical twang and irritation, he cursed the rocks, calling them goddamn Connecticut potatoes, as he paid cash and waited for his receipt.

The stereo speaker was next. For that they drove all the way down to Westport. Couldn't buy just the one speaker they needed, had to buy a pair. And they were very expensive. What's more, they had to endure the effete salesman's gibberish of how these speakers were state of the art (what else?) with a woofer system rated at 1.5 kilowatts achieved by use of a military grade accelerometer, and how they incorporated high pass filters, passive and selectable, for the input impedance of a high-frequency amplifier. What blessed relief for Springer and Audrey to step on the gas and be out of range.

Final stop was the Caldor's off Federal Road in Danbury. Springer waited in the car. Audrey went in and pushed a shopping cart around. Bought taupe-colored work trousers and shirts, beige high-traction sneakers, leather work gloves. Two yards of red cotton flannel. A roll of extra-wide sealing tape. She thought it indicative of the sorry state of things when a salesperson informed her that heavy duty work boots were not made for women. *À contre-coeur,* she bought herself a man's pair.

It was so good to get home.

What an excruciating thing it would be to have to shop for a living, Audrey remarked as she collapsed into a chair.

Springer said he didn't know how those stick-legged Park Avenue widows did it. He had newly realized admiration for their stamina.

Strand and Scoot got back from the city about eleven. They'd managed to get everything they'd gone for. Strand had met with Danny, and that end of it was set. All Danny needed to know was when, a few hours' notice would be enough. Strand had told Danny it would be sometime during the next week. They had also taken another look at 55th Street and, from what they'd seen, there was no reason why that shouldn't work.

Audrey was anxious to know if they'd picked up the parcel from the doorman at her apartment as she'd requested.

It was in the back seat of the car.

She hurried out and got it.

Before calling it a night Audrey insisted they try on their outfits, the trousers and shirts, sneakers and fishing vests. Everything fit well enough, but the vests were a dark green and that would never do.

Saturday morning Audrey was up earlier than anyone else. She found an old twenty-gallon metal washtub out in the barn. She held it up to the sun and saw that it was rusted through in a few places but the holes in it were small. She filled the tub with water from the outside spigot on the side of the house. Added a whole gallon of Clorox and threw in the fishing vests. The vests insisted on floating. Audrey poked at them with a broom handle. Finally she had to use rocks to weight them down and make them stay entirely under.

She sat on the nearby steps and thought.

Thought this might be a good quiet time to ask her pendulum a few things.

Thought she ought to wash her hair and even put on a little makeup, tweeze her brows.

Thought maybe she'd go in and cook a batch of pancakes for everyone, although whenever she'd attempted pancakes they'd turned out either too thick and gooey inside or too thin and burned. Only real, pure maple syrup had somewhat saved them. She'd give anything to just suddenly have the ability to one-two-three knock out perfectly light, precisely browned pancakes or, even better, crepes. Wouldn't that be something? She doubted she'd ever conquer the recipes she'd been reading in that cookbook by Escoffier. She was ready to admit, with no reluctance or guilt, that she just didn't have the talent for it. Springer wouldn't give a damn. Theirs would never be a split-level something's-in-the-oven life. Springer might pretend it mattered to save masculine face but it really wouldn't ever be crucial. Besides, there were so many other things she had to offer.

Thought about . . . going to the crypt in Greenwich to make sure the Johnny-jump-ups she'd planted in the spring hadn't gotten too out of hand.

Thought about how happy Springer was going to be when this burglary was over and Jake was well.

Thought, after a judgmental squint at the sun, that it was time anyway for the others to be getting up. She went into the house and tore the covers from four *Town and Country* magazines. Opened the parcel Strand had brought from the city for her. Went out to the far side of the barn.

Socialite Palm Beacher, Santa Barbara heiress, scioness of Houston, Viscountess somebody.

Audrey push-pinned the *Town and Country* covers to the old red paint-peeling barn. In a horizontal row. As though some transgression was about to be committed, a breeze came up suddenly, causing the covers to flop every which way. Audrey considered letting them do that, letting them dodge, but then she decided there was no reason to handicap herself. She wanted to do well right off.

She walked off twenty-five paces, bullying down the goldenrod that was tall enough to get in her way.

She assumed a solid stance, a comfortable one-third crouch, and cocked the hammer of the Detonic .451 magnum automatic. Firmed up her right arm and grasped it at the wrist for steadiness. She got the face of the Palm Beacher in the sights, but knew as soon as she'd fired that she'd been tentative, a bit shy of the imminent explosion and the leap of the pistol. After all, it had been how many years? At least five since she'd had any sort of gun in hand.

She walked to the barn and, as she expected, the Palm Beacher was unscathed. Six inches off to the left was a splintery hole in the barn siding. No matter, Audrey told herself, a hit would have been only luck anyway. She went back to the spot from where she'd fired.

Again in her shooter's stance she got the Palm Beacher in the wide combat-type sights of the .451 magnum. This time she didn't hurry, knew how crisp the trigger was, squeezed it as though she had a baby by the finger. The .451 went off. While the air was still percussive, Audrey returned it to point of aim and fired again. And four times more.

All six shots were hits of a sort.

Two in the hair, two in a cheek, one nicked an ear, the other got the corner of the mouth and altered the Palm Beacher's smile. Nevertheless she was still smiling.

Sorry, sweetie, Audrey said sardonically and almost aloud. She wasn't satisfied with the grouping of her shots: all over the map when they were supposed to be literally on the nose. She liked very much, however, the feel of the .451. Its wraparound rubber grip was short and suited her hand, enabled her to keep a good tight hold. The *feeling* she got from this more powerful gun was also something that appealed to her, having that much force on the end of her arm, the hard, serious heft.

Why was it, Audrey had once wondered, women of wealth usually had fewer compunctions about guns than women of poorer circumstances? A housemaid seeing a gun left on a bed wouldn't dare touch it, while her mistress would just snatch it up as though it were as benign as a hairbrush and toss it in a drawer.

Audrey had never been squeamish about guns. Even before her Foxcroft years, when horses were prerequisite and shooting a personal elective, there had been guns.

In her nine-year-old hand there had been Libby's little nickel-plated .25 caliber automatic with Libby showing her how to be careful with it and how to load it and come close to hitting an empty Piper-Heidsieck bottle from across the bedroom. There had been skeet shooting from the fantail of Libby's yacht, with a custom sized-down pump gun. Audrey's exceptional young reflexes were seldom fooled by the clay targets, no matter how rapidly or unexpectedly they were thrown. She had embarrassed numerous experienced skeet-shooter guests and Libby had won wagers on her. Only three times that she could recall had Libby told her to let her opponent outshoot her. She assumed Libby still won, though in a different way, on those occasions.

A sixteenth-birthday present from Libby had been a .32 caliber automatic, as sweet as a gun could be, silvery with a mother-of-pearl inset grip and her initials engraved on the housing in Spencerian script. Along with it, a carte blanche to carry it anywhere in the world. "If ever a situation gets down to a dreadful bind," Libby told her, "don't blabber threats as they do in movies, just pull the goddamn trigger and we'll clean up the mess later."

Fortunately it had never gotten to that. Although once on a dove hunt in Spain she'd come as close as another thought to blowing the balls off an excessively macho marquis who had her cornered.

The sixteenth-birthday automatic had been stolen from beneath her mattress during her first year at Wellesley. She neither told Libby nor replaced it.

Now, with the .451 magnum in her grasp, she wondered how and why she'd done without it. The .451, in its own way, was as capable as life or death as her heart.

She reached down into the parcel that lay at her feet and brought out a silencer, a newly developed, snubbier kind, only about an inch long but with the same silencing compression as the fatter, longer sort. It's compactness allowed it to be kept on even when a pistol was in its holster. She'd never shot with a silencer but had thought, considering the stealth that would surely be required for this thing, it would be best. There had been some question about being able to legally obtain one; however, Wintersgill, as usual, had managed.

Audrey screwed the silencer onto the muzzle of the .451. She was shoving a new full clip into the magazine well when Strand and Scoot came hurrying around the corner of the barn. And then Springer. Awakened by the shots, Springer was barefoot and bare from the waist up. The fly of his jeans was unbuttoned. He stopped short and stood well back off to the side, as did Strand and Scoot.

Audrey, with not so much as a good morning, continued with the .451. Now that she had an audience, and two thirds of it professional, she was even more set upon shooting her best. She chose a fresh target, fired off the entire clip in rapid succession. The empty casings flew hot from the .451 and the odor of gunpowder spoiled the air.

Audrey sauntered nonchalantly to the barnside. Springer, Strand and Scoot followed behind her.

They saw that the nose of the Santa Barbara heiress was blown away. All six shots had hit within a two-and-a-half-inch radius. The men didn't say anything, were that impressed. Audrey acted as though what she'd done was commonplace. All business, she went back to the parcel, ejected the spent clip, inserted another full one.

"What kind of gun's that?" Scoot asked.

Audrey told him.

"Never heard of a four fifty-one mag," he said.

"With hundred-and-eighty-five-grain bullets like these I'm using, it puts out a muzzle velocity of thirteen hundred feet per second," she said, remembering what she'd read in the manual that had come in the parcel.

Scoot did a bullshitting nod, as though he understood.

"That's as much stopping power as a forty-five," Audrey added. She offered the .451 to Scoot. "Squeeze off a few."

Scoot took a couple of steps back, shoved his hands into the pockets of his jeans.

"Don't worry," Audrey quipped, "you can wipe off your finger-prints."

Scoot and Strand just looked at her.

Audrey thought perhaps they were feeling what so many men do when it comes to a woman with a gun: that instinctive, nervous bristling that the combination caused. A woman psychiatrist Audrey had chanced to meet socially in Gstaad had referred to it as the Macomber reaction.

Audrey asked Scoot and Strand, "What kind of pieces do you carry?"

"We don't," Strand said.

"What do you mean you don't? Never?"

Scoot indicated the .451 Audrey was casually holding pointed groundward. "What you've got there is four years," he said. "Four of your best fucking years."

Strand explained. "This Townsend thing is a burglary, that's all, just a burglary. If we get nailed you'll be able to negotiate and do one to three years at the most. But if we get nailed and even one of us is carrying a piece it's armed robbery. You *and* Springer will each do five to seven."

"Strand and me, we got priors. We'll do twenty-five." Scoot told her.

Audrey dropped her gaze. She felt foolish for having made such an amateurish assumption. It also wasn't good to have the atmosphere filled with such negative possibilities as Strand and Scoot had just expressed. Best to get off the subject. "I just think," she said, "we're going to be in a hell of a helpless fix if somebody starts shooting at *us.*"

No argument on that point from either Strand or Scoot. They just left her standing there, went into the house for coffee.

Springer remained. He'd been transfixed by the sight of Audrey and her easy way with that gun, astounded by the demonstration of how good a shot she was. He'd had no idea. There she was now, his sensitive, softhearted love, with lethalness in her hand. His concept of her had shifted.

"I had Wintersgill also get one for you," she said, taking another identical .451 from the parcel. She tossed the pistol to Springer. He caught it gingerly.

His and hers, he thought, like coffee mugs and bath towels. "You heard what Strand and Scoot said. We won't be carrying guns." Springer was firm about it. *"None* of us."

"I quite agree. However, I think when this is over with, you and I should always have guns on us."

"Why?"

"And plenty of spare ammunition."

Springer saw she was serious.

"It's a philosophy," she said.

"Hitler's?"

She disregarded that. "Before there were guns there were swords. No one ever thought of going anywhere without a sword. They'd be caught dead without one. Probably even when they were chasing one another around bare-ass they still had their swords on. And before swords, everyone—and I mean everyone—carried at the very least an enormous, hard club." She combed her hair back with her fingers. "I don't know where people get off these days thinking we live in such a sane, civilized, nonviolent time that we can go around defenseless. Shit, what a delusion!"

Springer thought about mentioning that we have laws and police, but he was sure she was ready to jump all over that. He shrugged a bit concurringly, looked at the .451, weighed it with his hand. "Did it come with a special holster?"

"Silencer and everything."

"Maybe," Springer remarked, "we ought to also wear bulletproof underwear."

Audrey laughed. "Not unless they make it really flimsy."

She turned to the barn and let the Viscountess somebody have it.

Later that morning Springer dismantled one of the stereo speakers and removed the magnet from the electrical coil of its woofer. Then Scoot did the welding. Audrey and Strand laid out everything on the grass, all the tools, equipment, and gear, in the order that it would be used. They checked each item against Audrey's list. Where were the surgical gloves? Audrey had forgotten them. She'd run into New Milford for them later. She printed GLOVES on the palm of her hand with a felt-tipped pen, not to forget. What about the fishing vests? They were hung over the fence and dry by now. All the green was bleached from them. They were now various shades of buffs and beiges, mottled because of the way they'd been bunched up and rocks placed upon them during the bleaching. Strand thought Audrey had somehow purposefully camouflaged them and he complimented her on it, said the vests were now a good Townsend color.

During the afternoon they did several run-throughs. There was no way of duplicating the circumstances they'd actually be up against; however, they made do with the second story of the barn and some old metal filing cabinets that were out there.

They also tried out the blasting cord. None of them had ever worked with it before. Springer knew a little about it from twenty years ago when he'd watched the dairy farmer up the road use it on a stump. There was nothing complicated about it. It resembled ordinary quarter-inch clothesline but with a core of a gel-like substance running through it made up of a cured resin and nitroglycerine.

They took a length of it down the slope to where the land was wet and chose a swamp maple, one that was leafless dead but still standing solid. Springer fastened two turns of blasting cord around the trunk of the tree, which was nearly two feet thick. The others stood a safe distance away while he ignited it. The explosion was sharper than they had anticipated. It cut through the trunk. The tree crashed down. The blasting cord would more than do.

Back at the house they greased the threads of the twelve sections of pipe and the connecting joints. Audrey wrapped them individually in red flannel. They packed those in the large back pouches of two of the fishing vests, and then packed everything else so the loads were about equal and they would all have their hands free. The zippers of the various pockets and pouches were stubborn from having been soaked, so Audrey sprayed them with silicone and worked them back and forth until they were easy. They memorized which pocket and pouch contained what so there would be no searching and fumbling. They tested one another on it and got it really down. At least they'd have control over what they could. There would be enough things left to chance.

For Saturday night dinner Springer charcoal-broiled some steaks and Audrey threw some potatoes in the oven. As a celebratory gesture she baked a cake. Not from scratch, but she followed exactly the directions on the Duncan Hines mix package. When the layers had cooled she spread them with icing out of a can, sprinkled on a generous amount of shredded coconut, and there it stood on a pedestaled glass cake dish, all fancy white and sweet-looking. What a triumph! It was glorious to her eyes! To hell with Escoffier, she thought, there was hope for her yet.

As she sliced into the cake rather proprietarily, she was reminded of the wintry night when she and Springer had met; the white coconut cake she'd devoured at that narrow Greek coffee shop while suppressing the impetuous urge to then and there devour *him*. Strange, she thought, how the past returns time and again to delight in its presentiments.

Springer told her the loving fib that it was the best cake he'd ever had.

Strand came back for thirds.

Audrey sang "Night and Day" as off-key as ever while she did the dishes.

They watched the late television news on channel 7. There was the usual warehouse fire in New Jersey and hospital workers on strike, a passé movie star had died and was suddenly loved by everyone again, and the Yankees had been clobbered by Detroit. The weather was the best news. According to the five-day forecast there would be two days of sun but a very low low was headed up the Atlantic seaboard and was expected to arrive in the area Tuesday morning, bringing heavy showers.

29

◇

The van was stolen.

Tuesday morning from the Con Edison garage at Avenue C and 16th Street.

The guy who stole it, one of Danny's people, could have taken two or three if he'd had to. Dozens of vans were there, all lined up with the keys in them, just waiting for somebody like him to waltz in and drive them away. Big money company, Con Edison. He'd chosen to steal that particular van because while he was casing the place he'd seen it brought in and, using his head a little, he figured nobody had yet gotten used to seeing it around. He even gave the wave to a couple of Con Ed guys when he drove it out. He left it legally parked on First Avenue between 84th and 85th, as he was told to. The easiest three hundred he'd ever made.

Now, around eleven, the van was headed down Second Avenue in traffic that was stopping and going more than usual because of the rain. Audrey was driving. Not only because she wanted to. It was thought that if they were stopped by a cop for running a light or something, Audrey would stand the best chance of charming out of it, unless, of course, the cop happened to be a woman. Springer was in the passenger seat. Strand and Scoot were squatted on the floor in the enclosed back.

The rain couldn't have been worse and therefore couldn't have been better: almost tropical the way it was so densely pouring down, large close drops that the van's windshield wipers weren't efficient enough to cope with. Any rain, but surely one such as this, would be an edge, they thought. While people were caught up with trying to keep their heads and feet dry and find ways of fording the curb-deep swamps at every corner, they weren't likely to be so closely noticing incidental things.

Audrey swerved the van—but failed to avoid one of the city's more notorious potholes.

She was having trouble driving in the heavy steel-toed work boots she had on. Her feet felt out of touch with what they were supposed to be doing. Most of the time she couldn't tell whether she had the brake or the clutch, and she couldn't feel the gas pedal at all. Damn boots were clunky, so much too big that six pairs of thick woolen socks wouldn't have filled them. For some reason, possibly her attitude, they hadn't seemed nearly so large when she'd bought them.

Springer leaned forward and squinted through the animate film of water on the windshield, trying for a better look at the truck that was just ahead of them. An open flatbed truck stacked with a dozen or so large rectangular boxlike objects that were individually covered by quilted moving pads and securely tied down. Coffins bound for imminent occupancy.

Audrey declared emphatically that those were not to be taken as an omen. Nevertheless, at the very next intersection, which happened to be 70th Street, she hung a right.

Springer slouched, wedged his knees up against the dashboard, hummed a fragment of any song, and, to further demonstrate how loose he was, cocked his head at Audrey, put on a proper crooked smile, and told her, "You're a swell looker."

"You just like my chapeau," she said affectedly, raising her perfect chin.

"I sort of thought it was more than that, but"—he nodded—"that could be it."

She cut him playfully with a glance. Every move of her head caused the yellow hard hat she had on to slip awry, down over an eye or an ear. It had been one of those found in the van among the equipment and she hadn't had time to adjust it to her size. It was almost as much of a bother as her boots.

"I love you, Springer," she said seriously to him and the situation.

Springer nearly responded in kind but felt it more loving on his part to just let her have *her* say.

They proceeded along East 70th until it ended at Fifth Avenue, went left there, and continued on downtown. Approaching 56th Street Audrey got the van over into the extreme right lane. Midblock between 56th and 55th she stopped a few feet from the curb and cut the engine.

Almost in front of Townsend's.

Strand and Scoot opened the double rear door and jumped out. The bright yellow ponchos they wore were immediately slicked shiny by the rain. They each had a manhole-lifting key, a T-shaped steel rod about two feet long with a blunt hook on its end. Scoot knelt to the manhole cover. He used a screwdriver to dig the compacted grime from the notches along the outer edge of it, opposing notches about an inch square and an inch deep.

With the notches cleaned out, Strand and Scoot were able to fit the blunt hooks of the keys into them. They stood facing one another, got good holds on the T ends of the keys, and lifted.

The thirty-six-inch cover weighed about five hundred pounds. Not an easy heft, even for both of them, but they lifted it clear and, stepping awkwardly because of the dead weight and shape of it, placed it aside out of the way.

Next to deal with was the inner seal of the manhole, a seven-inch-thick metal-coated fitting like a plug. Its purpose was to prevent surface water from seeping in. Strand and Scoot got it with the lifting keys, drew it up and out.

Meanwhile, Springer and Audrey had put a sawhorse barrier in place up the avenue about twenty feet from the rear of the van. It had glowing orange stripes and reflectors. They stuck several orange plastic pennants on it and ran a string of those pennants from the barrier to the van, setting the boundaries of the work area. Buses were already hating it, having to swing out into the center lanes to get by. That, of course, put the squeeze on the taxis and other cars. All the way up beyond 59th Street, circulation was beginning to suffer. There at 56th it was practically coagulating.

Audrey was sure so much anger and impatience was in the air and directed at them that it was dangerous to breathe.

Springer experienced it differently. Now, as he surveyed the avenue, he understood the sense of power Con Ed and New York Telephone workers derived from causing such disruption: the wasting of precious time out of people's lives, the spoiling of strictly scheduled business deals. Springer assumed the role-appropriate attitude of enjoyable indifference and went about his chores.

An orange plastic tarpaulin was rigged from the rear of the van and extended out loosely above the manhole. A metal railing-like barrier was positioned around the opening to prevent anyone from accidentally stepping into it. Some ropes that had seen considerable underground service were slung over the barrier, along with a few other things just for show.

While Strand and Scoot were in the van starting the generator, Springer had a moment to look in the direction of Townsend's. From where he stood, the entrance to Townsend's was only about twenty-five feet away. His view was somewhat oblique, but he could see in through the ornate brass grillwork. Lights were on in there but Springer didn't see anyone moving about. Of course, it wasn't the sort of store that encouraged just anyone to walk in off the street to browse. A nattily attired man always stood inside tending the door. The same man for two decades, he not only knew well the face of every Townsend client, he was also infallible when it came to sizing up a stranger who wanted to enter. Perhaps it was instinct as much as years of practice that allowed him to instantly tell a tastelessly dressed tourist from an indigently dressed socialite.

Springer glanced up to the second floor. The lights were also on in Townsend's office. Townsend was up there, no doubt, doing some slick business. Springer wished Townsend would come to the window so he could see that face if for only a second, the arrogant, censorious expression as if nothing smelled quite right. To see it today, Springer thought, would supply just that much more to go on.

Two heavy-duty utility cords were plugged into the generator and run out to the manhole. On the end of each was a three-hundred-watt bulb within a protective bulb-shaped wire cage. One of the lights was lowered into the manhole, so Springer could see where to step.

His feet found the steel rungs of the narrow ladder. Like a ship's ladder, it went straight down, deeper than Springer expected. He had to be careful, be sure he had a good solid foothold on each rung, because the ladder was dripping wet, slippery. The light was lowered along with him. Finally, after descending fifteen feet, he reached the bottom—and stepped from the ladder into water up to his shins. He was thankful now for the knee-high rubber boots they'd found in the truck.

He saw that he was in a chamber about twelve feet long by seven feet wide, with an overhead clearance of a foot or so. The walls and ceiling were constructed of concrete brick. They were wet with seep. The floor was level, probably a concrete slab. The atmosphere was dank, oppressive. Springer had the eerie sensation that he was trespassing in a tomb.

At one end of the chamber stood a transformer with power cables running in and out of it. The walls were crowded with cables, not all coiled up snakelike but an organized arrangement. Strand had shown him a six-inch section of cable like these. Each cable was an inch and a half in diameter, contained a hundred copper circuits embedded in rubber with a thick outer casing of neoprene. Brackets were bolted to the walls. These supported the junctions that the cables were connected to. The junctions were the type Con Edison people referred to as seven-way sevens, because they had seven connecting points on each side.

To Springer they looked like huge, black, fourteen-legged spiders clinging to the walls. And they were all around.

GERALD A. BROWNE

He saw how from the junctions the cables went to circular openings in the walls, ducts. He could not see, but imagined, the ceramic
pipes that ran underground with the cables in them, thus distributing
electric power to the buildings in the vicinity. The cables were identical. So were the ducts. They bore no designative markings. There was
no way to tell which serviced Townsend's. Thirty or more ran in that
general direction. It didn't matter.

Scoot came down the ladder.

Several wire baskets containing tools and other things they would
need were lowered by a rope.

They started to work.

Above, on the avenue, Strand and Audrey didn't pretend to be
busy. Characteristically, they just stood around. Every so often Audrey shined a flashlight into the manhole and peered down. She saw
only murky water and heard sloshing.

To pass time and neutralize their nerves, Audrey and Strand
talked about anything. About the fascinating contrariness of the city.
About the deceit of abstract art. Why, really, women had resorted
to exaggerating their shoulders and pumping iron. How beautiful
was the Burmese belief that a person at the moment of death becomes
an invisible butterfly. Audrey brought up the subject of bilocation,
the metaphysical ability of some sensitives to be in two places at the
same time. Strand was commenting on that, saying that over his last
three years it would have come in handy, when he stopped mid-
sentence. From his pocket he brought out the stub of a chewed-up
cigar and stuck it in his mouth. He closed his right eye into a
vacant-looking slit.

Audrey thought for a moment that she was being allowed the
comical side of Strand, but then she too noticed the baby blue and
white of the police patrol car that had pulled up.

Strand went over to it.

The cop on the passenger side had the car window down only a
few inches, not to get wet. He was an older cop with a perfunctory
attitude. "How long ya gonna be?" he asked out to Strand.

"I don't know," Strand replied through his teeth that had the cigar
clamped.

314

"Ya got everything fucked up for ten blocks."

Strand quivered his slitted eye. Rain was running off his hard hat like a veil. "A couple more hours maybe. We got a wet transformer."

Duty done, the cop closed the window. The light rack on the top of the patrol car was turned on for a few flashes and a sharp fragment of wail intimidated the traffic to make way.

Strand returned to Audrey beneath the tarpaulin. "No problem," he assured her. There wasn't any reason for the cop to suspect an authentic blue, white, and dove-colored Con Edison van. And even if there was some blowback later and that cop stepped forward with the incident, what he would remember was the bad eye and the cigar. It was a little something Strand had learned from a wise-guy in the joint.

A short while later, Springer and Scoot came up for a break. Being on the surface again made them realize how claustrophobic they were becoming down in that chamber. It was unnerving, to say the least, to be messing around with all that voltage while standing shin-deep in water. Their faces were smudged and their hands grimy. They said they had a bit more to do.

Audrey hurried to the corner of 55th to a shiny vending cart that had a red and yellow umbrella over it. There wasn't room for her beneath the umbrella, so, while the vendor put the works on four hot dogs and got four Yoo-hoos from his cooler, Audrey waited in the rain.

Her yellow poncho kept her from getting wet but the drops drumming on her hard hat were something she wouldn't want to suffer for long. She carried the hot dogs and drinks back to the van and presented them to the others like a surprise treat. Like most such hot dogs these were mostly bun, but they had that unbeatable street-corner taste. Springer forgot to shake up his Yoo-hoo, so his last few gulps of it were thick and awfully sweet.

He and Scoot went back down to work.

For nearly an hour.

They emerged from the manhole then and said they'd done as much as they could and maybe it was enough. Strand and Springer with the lifting keys put the inner seal and the manhole cover back in place. The tarpaulin was taken down. The ropes, the power extension cords, the strings of pennants, everything was put neatly into the van. Last was the sawhorse barrier. Even before Strand and Scoot could get it disassembled, a bus was reclaiming that lane of the avenue, honking insolently and threatening to run them over.

By four o'clock that afternoon the van was unstolen.

One of Danny's people just drove it into the Con Edison garage at Avenue C and 16th Street, parked it among all the other identical vans, and casually walked away.

It hadn't been missed.

30

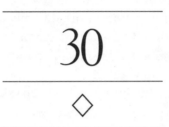

It was nearly night.

The rain had wind with it now, vagrant gusts that blew it into sheets.

The sidewalks were deserted. The few taxis and cars were like strays. A lot of fifty-dollar theater tickets would go unused, restaurants would suffer no-shows. The high-rises were decapitated and the bag ladies had taken to the deeper doorways.

Vince Fantuzzi, driving a white 1977 Chrysler with a stolen New Jersey license plate, waited for the light at the intersection of Fifth Avenue and 55th Street. On green he hung a right and about a third of the way down the block pulled into the Star Parking Garage.

A sign that Vince's eyes couldn't miss told him to turn off his engine and leave his keys. He did as he was told because he was doing what he was told. He was one of Danny's people, a knock-around guy whose hard and fast rule was Ask no questions, need no lies.

A parking attendant came out of the office, grabbed the top ticket from a stack that was on a small shelf below a punch clock. He'd done it so many times he didn't have to look when he inserted the ticket in the slot of the clock and—*chunk, chunk, chunk*—imprinted the hour and minutes on it in three places. He tore the ticket, put the main part of it under the wiper on the wet windshield of the Chrysler, handed the stub to Vince, and asked, "When ya goin' out?"

"If I get lucky not until morning."

The attendant came as close to smiling as he ever did, but then it occurred to him this guy could be on his way to only a card game.

Vince put the parking stub in his shirt pocket where he was less likely to lose it. He didn't have a raincoat or an umbrella. He wasn't the sort to own an umbrella. He pulled up the collar of his jacket and walked out into the downpour.

The parking attendant started up the Chrysler and pulled it ahead into the industrial type elevator. He closed the elevator gate and took it up to eleven. The Star Parking Garage was fourteen floors. Which floor a car was put on depended upon how long it was going to be in. The cars that were going to be in for only a couple of hours were put on the lower floors so they were easier and faster to get to. The overnights and others were put higher up, where they'd be out of the way. A few cars had been up there four or five months. At what came to about a dollar an hour the parking bill on such cars was more than their worth. Usually it turned out they were stolen, either that or whoever owned them had disappeared or died one way or another.

The attendant parked the Chrysler on the back side of the building where there weren't any windows. Left it dripping. On the way down in the elevator he thought about the slow night ahead. There was no ball game to watch on the small black-and-white television in the office. Later maybe he'd try a few trunks and glove compartments. Week before last he'd scored a complete set of nickel-plated German-made tools from the trunk of a Mercedes. Once, from a Pennsylvania car, he'd gotten a woman's Rolex watch and nothing had ever been said about it. He was always getting sunglasses.

By the time the attendant returned to street level two cars had come in. A blue Pontiac Bonneville and a gray Olds Cutlass Supreme. The manager had them already ticketed, so all the attendant had to do was take them up. They were both overnights. He arbitrarily put them next to one another on nine and took the elevator back down.

An estimated five minutes were waited, four hundred pulse counts.

On eleven the only sound was the rain dripping from the Chrysler, contributing to the puddles beneath it.

Then the contradicting sound of its trunk lid popping open, released from the inside.

Springer pushed the lid up. He and Audrey climbed out. They glanced around to get their bearings. The place was dark, had a strong automobile smell to it, every inch of every surface permeated with carbon monoxide. They knew from the elevator ride that they were on one of the upper floors of the garage but they didn't know exactly which. They removed their fishing vests from the trunk of the Chrysler and put them on. The vests felt snugger with every pocket bulging. They also now had on the taupe-colored work trousers and shirts and the sneakers and their work gloves, what Audrey called their burglary outfits.

They listened for the elevator. Its frictional *whir* would warn of anyone coming up. The atmosphere of the garage amplified every little sound, but their steps were close to silent as they went across to the front of the building to one of the windows. There were five windows spaced about ten feet apart. They were narrow casement type, intended merely for ventilation. Each was open to some extent, no regard for the rain.

Springer looked out and down and knew upon seeing the wide ledge one floor below that they were on eleven. The top five floors of the garage building were inset about twelve feet, no doubt for some structural reason, as otherwise it was an irrational waste of premium city space. Springer and Strand, during their street-level reconnoitering, had noticed the tenth-floor ledge created by the inset and it had been the decisive factor in their choosing the garage as a starting point rather than the Hotel Shoreham farther down the block.

All such buildings as the garage were required to have an interior stairway. Springer and Audrey found it and went down to the tenth floor to the rendezvous point at the front windows. Those windows were also open part way, must have been left as they were for years because the geared cranking mechanisms that would allow them to be opened and closed were bound with rust. Not one of the windows was open enough.

The third window from the left had slight play. Springer used force on it, put increasing outward pressure on its metal frame, and, more easily than he expected, the cranking mechanism gave way, snapped off entirely, and the window swung wide open. A strong wind could have done it.

At that moment Strand and Scoot arrived, having gotten out of the trunks of the blue Bonneville and the gray Cutlass and come up the stairway from nine. Without hesitation, Scoot, the veteran swift, climbed out the window. Then Audrey, Springer, and Strand.

It was surely night now.

Even with the rain, the lights of the city reflected on the atmosphere above it and provided adequate visibility.

They paused on the twelve-foot-wide ledge to get used to being out there. Within moments their clothing was soaked through and sticking to them, their hair was plastered to their skulls. At that height there was more wind, and the storm they had thought so prerequisite seemed a dubious ally. After a short while, they accepted that this was how it was going to be and moved left along the ledge to where it abutted the next building.

The roof of that next nine-story building was only about five feet higher. For that very reason it was protected by a six-foot-high steel mesh fence topped by concertina-type barbed wire. It was the sort of obstacle Scoot had opposed and won out over countless times. He toed his sneakers into the mesh openings of the fence and climbed up. Using a pair of snippers he cut the barbed wire at the few points where it was attached to the fence. It hadn't been conscientiously installed. The coiled-out wire sprang back into itself. Scoot continued up and over without a scratch. The others followed.

There was nothing extraordinary about the roof of the next building, nor that of the next two buildings over. All were typical of older New York City apartment houses: tar-black, puffed up in some places, depressed in others. Television antennas, pre-cable relics, were like sky-worshiping mantises. Tubular aluminum patio chairs lay crippled and thus forsaken near the squat, square structure above the roofline that housed the elevator winches and the stairway that gave access.

Separating the three apartment houses were fences that ran all the way from front to rear, expressing the usual mutual distrust. The fences were alike, six-foot-high steel mesh with concertina-type barbed wire along the top. Same as the first that Scoot had so quickly reduced to little more than a schoolyard climb-over. Perhaps all these fences had been put up by the same company—one that knew nothing would stop whoever was motivated enough not to be stopped.

Such as Springer and Audrey, Strand and Scoot. Stealthily, although the pelt of the rain would prevent their footsteps from being heard by the tenants just below, they crossed the first apartment house roof and the second and were crossing the third when they saw the cigarette stub. Flicked from the doorway, it was immediately extinguished by the rain. The superintendent of the building. He'd come up for a solitary moment away from complaints and stopped-up toilets, and had it not been for the rain he would have been out on the roof rather than standing just inside the access doorway.

Strand, who was leading the way, came only a couple of steps from walking right into the superintendent's view. As it was, they were only a few feet from him, huddled against the wall of the elevator housing. If he happened to pop his head out and glance to his left he would be looking right at them.

The roof access door was metal coated yet a bit swollen from the humidity. It scraped on its threshold and required a solid shove to fit into its jamb. There was no doubt when the superintendent slammed it shut; nevertheless, the four remained in place awhile to completely recover from the effects of such a close call. Strand, Scoot, and Springer considered it a matter of fortunate timing. Audrey took it as a demonstration of how fate was determined to smile their way.

They continued on across the roof, to an obstacle more formidable

GERALD A. BROWNE

than a fence: the side of a building four, nearly five stories higher.

It was the annex to the Fifth Avenue Presbyterian Church, where the church's administrative offices, social rooms, and so on were located. The plan had been to go up and over it using the grappling hook and climbing ropes, but they had underestimated, had believed it three stories higher at most. Perhaps, Springer thought, its height was exaggerated because they were standing close up to it. He backed off from the wall and measured it with his eyes and knew he would be fooling himself if he said it was less than forty-five feet. Were they stumped? Was this as far as they'd be able to go? Might he or Scoot be able to toss the grappling hook that high? Even then it would be a hell of a climb.

Scoot had the grappling hook and climbing rope out to give it a try. Audrey, meanwhile, went along the wall to the rear edge of the roof. From there she had an overview of the enclosed backyard-like space formed by the buildings of the block. Below to the right were the roofs of the buildings that faced onto Fifth Avenue. It was easy to make out which was Townsend's. First there was a six-story building, then a three-story one, and then Townsend's. So close it seemed she could take a flying leap and land on it. She stepped closer to the edge to better see the rear of the church annex building, peered around the corner of it. What a blessed gift it would be if there was a fire escape and they could simply walk right down, she thought. Her eyes scanned the rear surface of the church annex building. They caught upon what occurred to Audrey might be an alternative. She hurried back to tell the others, led them to it.

About three feet down on the rear of the adjacent annex building was a ledge. Not a nice, wide, perfectly safe ledge such as the one of the garage. This ledge was barely a foot wide, a mere outcropping that defined a structural aspect, probably a horizontal beam covered over.

Strand shined his flashlight on it, very briefly but long enough to see that it went the entire width of the building. About thirty feet out, the ledge was interrupted by a six-inch exterior metal pipe, apparently a permanent drain. The pipe seemed to run all the way down the rear of the building. Perhaps at the sixth-floor level it ran close

322

enough to that first building that faced upon Fifth Avenue, the one immediately north of the church.

Worth a try?

Audrey thought so.

Springer wasn't so sure. He'd never been one for heights; not phobic about them, but high places, even Audrey's apartment or the Windows on the World restaurant, always caused a slight hollowness in the pit of his stomach. He peered over the edge at the nine-story drop, told himself it made no difference whether it was nine or a hundred stories. He thought of Jake.

Strand was able to be a little philosophical about it. In all things improvisation was seldom without extra risk. That was certainly true here. The step-by-step plan had been to go up and over the church annex and down onto the church roof and from it easily over onto the roof of that first building facing Fifth Avenue. Strand looked at his watch. Whatever was decided, it would have to be soon or their timing would be off.

For Scoot it was just a matter of weighing risk against reward: no different, really, from the terms of any other burglary. There were legends about huge scores that had been easy, but he knew in his light-fingered heart they probably weren't true.

They huddled there near the edge and discussed whether to give up or go on. The thought of giving up was, for their separate reasons, unacceptable. The prospect of what lay ahead brought them to agree on trying the ledge and the pipe. They swiftly devised how best to do it, the mistakes that could be made, the advantages and cautions to be taken. Not the least of their considerations was the problem of being able to get back up.

Scoot felt inasmuch as he had the experience it was his responsibility to be the first to give it a go. A demonstration of his practical knowledge was the way he prepared the climbing rope. It was the type of five-eighths-inch woven rope used by mountain climbers, soft to the hands, lightweight, and yet extremely strong. Scoot arranged the rope into a series of reverse loops, laying one loop upon the other neatly. He threaded the end of the rope into the eye of the pile of loops and pulled it through. The result was magical. A knot appeared every two feet along the rope, accomplished in a fraction of the time it would have taken to tie that many knots individually.

Both Springer and Audrey drew some reassurance from observing that trick of Scoot's trade. It promised others in a pinch.

Scoot secured the end of the rope to a nearby standpipe. Tested how well it was secured by having a brief, vigorous tug-of-war with the pipe, because his life might depend on it. He lay prone with his shoulders and head over the edge of the roof to examine the ledge. He played his flashlight along the ledge, covering every inch of it. He examined the wall and the pipe for several minutes and took another comprehensive look at the ledge. He stood and removed his vest. The bulging pockets and back compartment of the vest was not compatible with the ledge. If he wore it he wouldn't be able to flatten against the wall. The vests would have to be carried for this part of it. Fortunately the armholes were large enough. Scoot put his head through one of the armholes so his vest hung down the front of him. It was awkward. The vest with all its contents felt heavier. It would be all the more difficult to maintain balance.

Improvisations, Strand thought cynically as he took off his vest and slung it around his neck. How much more improvising, additional risking, would there be?

Springer and Audrey did the same with their vests.

Scoot tossed the rope over the edge and then wrapped two turns of it around his forearm. He sat on the edge of the roof with his lower legs dangling over. He extended his right leg, reached for the ledge with it. Slid down until the edge of the roof was beneath his buttocks. His right foot found the ledge, then his left. As gradually as possible he transferred his weight and was standing on the ledge.

The others watched his every move, would try to imitate.

Scoot just stood there for a while to get used to being on the ledge. It was about three inches wider than the length of his sneakers. He knew, and he had told them, the key to it was the head. And the feet, of course. The head had to be kept up, the back of the head in constant contact with the wall. Much of it would be a matter of depending entirely on feel. He felt the heels of his sneakers lightly in touch with the wall.

He took his first step.

A six-inch sidestep with his right foot.

He drew his left foot to his right.

That was how it went. Six inches or so at a time. Nibbling at the distance.

The weight of the vest hanging from his neck seemed to be trying to make him violate the rule of keeping his head up. The pouring rain was a help and a hindrance. The wetness increased the traction of the soles of his sneakers, but at places along the ledge it also slickened the accumulated pigeon droppings. Several times his mind tried to beat him, tried to get him to visualize where he was, how high up he was, the precarious thing he was doing. He knew such thoughts were traps and closed them off, concentrating on the back of his head, his heels, the wall, the ledge, the playing out of the rope around his arm, his little sidesteps.

His right elbow came in contact with the drainpipe before he realized it was that near. The thick pipe was cast metal, sturdy. There was, he found, room enough between it and the wall for his arm. He hugged the pipe with his right arm and let out that deep breath he'd been holding.

Using his right hand he pulled the rope taut and took a turn with it around the drainpipe. At a point about chin level a section of the pipe was fitted into the wider collar of another section below it. It was one of the things he had noticed initially and was counting on. He adjusted the turn he'd taken so it was snug above the collar, took a second turn, overlapping it into a good bite.

Now the rope was dangling in line with the pipe, the down end of it reaching to the third or fourth story.

Scoot committed to the rope, got it with both hands. He faced the pipe now, the rope over his shoulder and down his back. Quickly he scissored the rope between his legs. He raised his feet, placed a foot on each side of the pipe, the toes of his sneakers tucked in behind it, his ankles hugging it, monkeyish. That way he wasn't hanging by his hands with all his weight.

He went down the rope and the pipe slowly, in somewhat of a rappeling fashion, hand under hand, knot by knot. When he reached the sixth-floor level, off to his left was the roof he wanted. Five feet away. He maintained his position on the rope while shifting his upper body, and thus most of his weight, to and fro. From a slight motion the momentum increased and soon he was swinging like the emerald bead on the end of Audrey's pendulum. As he swung left far enough he loosened his grip and slid down the rope and landed well on the roof.

He looked up.

Only three stories, but it had seemed a longer way. It wasn't going to be an easy climb back up, when it came to that. He put his vest on properly, signaled to the others with three shining blinks.

They came as Scoot had: imitatingly, and with a slight advantage as they inched along the ledge because of the rope he'd strung across to the drainpipe. To have it under their chins was reassuring, although had one of them lost balance and grabbed hold of it, it wouldn't have saved anyone for long.

Audrey was the first down, her eyes open a bit wider than normal, breathing almost entirely through her mouth. She peered up into the rain and was still on the ledge, still coming down the rope, until Springer was there beside her.

It was nine forty-three when Strand got down.

They were seventeen minutes early.

They crouched reflexively as they proceeded across the roof to its north edge, where there was a raised facade of about two feet. Kneeling behind the facade they peeked over at their objective: Townsend's, the sheer south side of Townsend's. It was about forty feet opposite and down a floor from them, across the chasm created by the three-story building which adjoined.

They had a good view of Townsend's roof and knew the snare it was with all its security devices. On the front and rear corners were the television cameras, deeply hooded so the lenses were protected from the rain. There was no way of knowing how the wide-angle lenses were set. Perhaps they included this second roof over, even though it was a story higher. Better to be careful, keep down.

Scoot knotted another length of climbing rope and secured it to a standpipe.

At five minutes to ten Springer and Audrey crawled along the facade to the front edge of the roof for a peek at Fifth Avenue. They remained there. At twenty seconds to ten they took another more anticipatory peek. The sweep hand of Springer's watch approached straight up and started around again.

What had gone wrong?

At that moment there was absolute darkness in the Con Edison chamber fifteen feet below the avenue in front of Townsend's. Drips subtly disturbed the surface of the water that had seeped to the bottom of the chamber. Concentric circular wakes were, on their lesser relative level, tiny tidal waves that sloshed turbulently.

There were no beetles, no spiders, no cousins of roaches or strange multipedic creatures in the chamber or in the ground around it. Rats often used the ducts for getting from block to block, but there were none now. It seemed that every such living thing in the vicinity had been warned by its most elemental senses.

The blasting cord.

Springer and Scott had wound it twice around each of the inch-and-a-half electric power cables. They'd woven it along both sides of every seven-way-seven junction. Not knowing which cable was *the* one, they'd included them all. To do that had required stringing the blasting cord back and forth across the chamber numerous times. It looked like so much clothesline.

Taped to the top surface of the transformer was the battery-powered timing device. Simple as an ordinary alarm clock, set to go off at ten. Scoot had set it according to Springer's watch; however, in the past nine or so hours the timer had accumulatively become slow by forty-six seconds.

Tick, tick, tick.

Those forty-six were ticked away.

Current flowed through the detonating wire.

The explosion, though muffled, was tremendous: a powerful grumble, the indigestive pangs of an enormous belly. It shuddered the avenue and the buildings. Several store windows were reduced to shards. The Con Edison manhole cover, all five hundred pounds of it, shot straight up six stories and came down on its edge, gouging ten inches into the asphalt.

Springer and Audrey watched, astounded. They had intended an explosion, but this was overkill. It might take not just hours but days for Con Ed to restore power.

Near the corner of 56th a geyser of water spouted up forty feet from another manhole opening. The quaking had ruptured a twelve-inch high-pressure water pipe. The avenue was rapidly being flooded, water was deepening, flowing down the slight grade of Fifth.

The lights went out for two blocks up and two blocks down. Even Trump Tower diagonally across from Townsend's was without power for several minutes, until its emergency generators could be switched on.

Townsend's television cameras went blind.

Townsend's alarm systems went dumb.

Three blocks away, in the monitoring room at Reliance Security, numerous alarm indicator lights went red and television viewing screens turned to meaningless pointillism, not just those of the Townsend hookup but others as well. At once the men on duty got on the direct line to Midtown North precinct and were informed of the underground explosion. Most likely caused by a leaky gas main, the precinct said matter-of-factly. (There were 4,000 miles of gas-bearing pipe beneath the city, most of it old, much of it leaky.) Had the circumstances, explosion or whatever, been limited to a single building such as Townsend's, Reliance would have been on the run; however, an entire four-block section of Fifth Avenue was affected. The precinct was taking measures. For the time being, Reliance was advised, sit tight.

Strand and Scoot were already down the rope and on the roof of the three-story building next door to Townsend's. Audrey and Springer went down. It was no less than the previous descent but it seemed easier, less perilous.

They crossed over the roof to the wall of Townsend's, the sheer high wall on the south side of the building. It was painted a taupe shade over several layers of waterproofing. From a distance the wall appeared smooth, but close up, and because it was now slicked with rain, the unevenness of the underlying bricks and mortar lines was apparent.

Strand, from memory, paced off where they would go through the wall: a spot about twenty-five feet from the front of the building and about a foot up the wall. Only a foot up because the three stories of the building they were on were equal to about two and a half of Townsend's taller stories. Strand indicated how much of a hole would be necessary.

Springer and Scoot went at it.

With diamond-edged chisels they cut through the wall's waterproof coatings, removed those, and exposed the bricks: regular, fired, red bricks, eight by four by two and a half, about three eighths of an inch of gray-white mortar between them.

Springer and Scoot used hand drills on the mortar. Compact, ratcheted drills with quarter-inch diamond-edged bits so sharp they could cut a finger if merely touched. The bits chewed easily into the mortar. This cementing substance dated back to when the building was constructed in 1906. It wasn't crumbly old, but neither was it hard.

Almost effortlessly Springer and Scoot bored holes through the mortar: hole after hole, spaced no more than a quarter inch apart entirely around one brick and the one next to it and the two on the course below those. Then Springer went to work with a pry bar.

A sledgehammer would have been more suitable, surely quicker, but they couldn't afford the noise of pounding on the wall. Now on Fifth Avenue just three stories below were police and firemen, Con Edison, New York Telephone, and Water Department people. And, of course, television crews of every channel from 2 to 11. Minor catastrophes, and this was certainly that, deserved to be news. The red, white, and blue flashings from so many racks on so many police patrol cars and fire engines caused the falling rain to look like iridescent strings of tiny bugle beads.

Quietly, but with force, Springer rammed the pry bar in. The blade of it dug at the mortar. He concentrated on one particular brick, dug all around it with the bar. The first brick would be the most difficult. Springer kept prying and chewing at it. The brick gave slightly and then he felt it break free.

Scoot got hold of it with his fingers and slid the first brick out.

The second and third bricks were easier, and with those out Springer was able to bite into the mortar with the pry bar, apply some leverage, and snap the others out. He removed eighteen whole bricks and six halves to form a horizontally rectangular hole twenty-eight inches wide by eighteen inches high.

That put them nearly halfway through the wall. There was still another identical thickness of solid brick and mortar to deal with. Most brick buildings of this vintage were constructed double-thick with a four-inch in-between space to allow for pipes and wiring.

Strand and Audrey were just getting started with the drills on this inner wall when they heard an unmistakable roar and clack.

A police helicopter.

It had a pair of searchlights attached to the struts of its landing gear. Adjustable searchlights, powerful enough to beam efficiently from an altitude of eight hundred feet. It was now patrolling the blacked-out area, raking the rooftops with light. Not looking for anything in particular. Just making sure nothing irregular was there. It was surprising how the helicopter's searchlights cut down through the rain.

Scoot and Strand flattened against the wall. So did Springer and Audrey. Their taupe-colored work trousers and shirts had been about the same shade as the wall—when they were dry. Now wet, they were darker, outstanding. The only recourse was to stand absolutely still.

The helicopter hovered directly over Townsend's for almost a full minute. Observed the emergency from its vantage and gave the roofs and rears of both Winston's and Townsend's some extra attention with its searchlights. It then proceeded on its patrol, headed downtown. That was the saving thing, its direction. If it had been on an uptown course its searchlights would have thoroughly illuminated the south wall of Townsend's. Springer and Audrey, Scoot and Strand would have been as visible as featured performers on a stage. Instead, they and the south wall had remained in shadow for all but an instant. The helicopter would be back. Chances were it would come from a different direction.

Strand and Audrey resumed with the drills, more urgently now.

Even before they'd bored all the many necessary holes in the mortar, Scoot crowded in to go to work with the pry bar. He jammed the sharp end of it in insistently, pulverizing the mortar, causing it to break away in chunks. The mortar and the bricks seemed to realize the need for cooperation, testified to whose efforts they favored by coming loose more easily in less time.

The hole in the second thickness of bricks was done.

Now only lathing and plaster remained. The strips of rough pinewood ran horizontally, were spaced close together, providing the plaster with something to adhere to. The plaster was dry from age.

Springer wasted no time with it. He reared back and kicked at it full force with the flat of his right boot. The lathing still had a bit of spring in it, but it snapped under the impact and the plaster crumbled. Nor did Springer waste time shining a flashlight in to see exactly what he was crawling into. It would be somewhere inside Townsend's, and that was all that mattered. In his haste he went in head first. That was a mistake. Where they'd broken in was about four feet up from the floor. Springer grazed the corner of a solid little table as he tumbled in and down among the plaster bits and splinters of lath that were strewn about.

Strand was next in, but feet first.

At once Scoot and Audrey began handing bricks through, thirty-six that were more or less whole and a dozen fairly large pieces. Couldn't have bricks scattered around out there where the helicopter might spot them. Audrey and Scoot also tossed in whatever hunks of mortar they could gather up. The finer sandlike particles had been carried by the rain to the depressed areas of the black roof.

Such patches of white would be obvious from above. There was no way to eliminate them. Even with a broom it would have been impossible. The most that might be done was reduce the white somewhat by spreading it around. Audrey and Scoot tried, with their feet and then with their hands. It was just a lot of futile sloshing. The rain caused the mortar particles to accumulate again in the low spots. Audrey gave the problem at least the benefit of a positive thought: Those white patches wouldn't appear significant to anyone high up in a helicopter.

She removed the taupe-colored upholstery fabric from the back compartment of her vest. When she refolded it to a size a bit larger than the hole, it was six layers thick, all that more opaque. She held it up to the wall, covering the hole with it, while Scoot taped it in place using three-inch-wide beige filament tape. Despite the wet surface the tape stuck firmly. To make sure they applied second and third lengths of tape across the top edge of the fabric and down the sides.

Scoot signaled Audrey to follow him. He lifted the left lower corner of the fabric just enough for clearance and went in through the hole.

Audrey stepped back for a final check on things.

Helicopter!

If she'd been listening for it intently, no doubt she would have heard it sooner. It was already close, approaching from downtown, its searchlights sweeping the rooftops.

Audrey dove for the opening. No time to go in more appropriately feet first. She ducked her head, shoulders, and arms in under the corner flap of the fabric only an instant before the helicopter's searchlights struck the south wall of Townsend's.

It hovered.

Inside, in the dark, Springer and Audrey, Strand and Scoot stood as still as defendants awaiting a fateful decision.

Had the policemen in the helicopter noticed the patches of white mortar on the black roof? Had they made out the fabric taped to the wall? Were they at that very moment radioing to those on the ground that something at Townsend's warranted investigation?

The helicopter moved on.

The whirring and clacking diminished.

Springer switched on one of the six-volt lantern-type flashlights. He cupped its beam with his hand, allowing only dim light. Strand and Scoot moved a table across the room, turned it on its end, and shoved the flat of it tight against the wall, covering the hole. Audrey closed the door to the hallway. Two more six-volt lanterns were switched on, and now they were able to see where they were.

It was a workroom. About ten by twelve. Practically unchanged from what Strand recalled. Along one wall was a high workbench and a pair of swivel-seated stools. The numerous tools for finishing jewelry were arranged on a shallow shelf above the bench. Off to one side was a steam generating unit used to clean away the grease that diamonds have such an affinity for, and situated nearby was a stationary polisher and buffer and its various disks. Trade magazines were stacked in a corner. On the walls here and there were framed full-page Townsend advertisements that had appeared in *Vogue* and *Town and Country* and *Connoisseur.* Surely less inspiring than the labial glistenings of the *Penthouse* centerfolds that the workers probably would have preferred.

Strand removed his vest, hung it over the back of a chair. The others also took off their vests and placed them within reach. They zipped open all the pockets and compartments so they'd be able to more easily get at whatever they needed as they needed it. Strand studied the floor, measured by counting off the nine-inch squares of vinyl tile.

They had discussed and determined exactly where they believed they should go down through it. Strand indicated the spot. Almost in the center of the room.

Springer and Scoot pried up the squares of vinyl. They chiseled at a seam where the floorboards joined. The boards were oak, aged and hard, but the chisels gouged in and bit off curl after curl of the wood until they'd made an opening large enough for Springer and Scoot to use short, narrow-bladed, diamond-toothed saws. With these they cut away an area of the floor about thirty inches square.

That revealed the ventilation duct. Round like a stovepipe, made of galvanized metal, it ran between the joists. Evidently, it was the duct they wanted, but they were about a foot and a half off, had to rip up that much more vinyl and boards to get to the point where the duct served the vault directly below on the second floor.

The squeeze of a bandlike coupling held the curved-down end of the duct in place. Springer loosened the coupling with a wrench and then, straddling the hole in the floor, bent over and got his hands around under the duct and gave it a sudden yank. The entire section of the duct came free so easily that Springer stumbled backward, off balance. Audrey caught him, kept him from falling. She held back a complaint that he'd stepped hard on her toes, just gritted, grimaced, and flexed her toes vigorously inside her squishy soaked sneaker.

There now, where the duct had been disconnected, was the ventilation grate in the ceiling of the vault. Ten inches in diameter. It was made of quarter-inch steel set down in and welded to the thicker, impregnable six-inch cadium-steel ceiling. The uneven ridge of the seam where it was welded was plainly visible.

Strand handed the portable acetylene equipment to Scoot. It consisted of a pair of small capsule-shaped pressure tanks that weighed about seven pounds each. The paired tanks were connected to a mutual fitting. A built-in gauge indicated they were full. The contents of the tanks were premixed in the proper ratio of oxygen and acetylene.

Scoot threaded the flexible hose onto the fitting, tightened it firmly. Springer took a wooden match from a small waterproof container, struck it, and held it to the tapered metal nozzle of the torch. Scoot turned the valve that allowed the gas and oxygen mixture to flow.

With a potent plosive sound that was nearly a *pow!* the torch ignited. Scoot adjusted it, changed its flame from merely hot yellow to more forceful, hotter blue. Over his many years of swifting he had worked often with such torches. He directed the torch to the welded seam of the circular vent grating, kept the 3400 degrees Fahrenheit point of the flame just inside the circumference where the steel was surely no more than a quarter inch thick.

He cut through it.

All the way around.

The grate fell nine feet to the hard vinyl floor inside the vault, landing with a dull ring, like a frying pan being dropped in a kitchen.

Strand had the six-volt lanterns ready, tied by their handles to lengths of climbing rope. He lowered them into the vault one at a time, swung them, tugged, and otherwise maneuvered them to get them placed where they would provide the most light.

Springer looked down through the opening. Saw, on the left and the right, the vertical rows of drawers, not much different from how he'd pictured them according to what Strand had said.

Townsend's goods.

In one of those drawers, Springer thought, would be stone 588, or, as Springer saw it, in one of those drawers, only six or seven feet away but still beyond reach, was Jake's life.

They changed their gloves now, put on the surgeons' gloves.

Audrey got the foot-long lengths of quarter-inch pipe from Springer's vest. All twelve. And the ten straight connecting joints. They'd been wrapped in the red flannel to prevent them from clanging against one another. Audrey laid them out on the floor in the order they would go.

The male threads on the ends of the sections of pipe were well greased, so the female threaded connectors accepted them smoothly. Springer attached six sections end to end in this manner. What he had then was a shaft of pipe nearly seven feet long.

To the end of that he threaded on the flexible joint, and to that joint another section. Last to be connected was that section of pipe to which Scoot had welded the two-inch bolt. Scoot had also welded a steel eye to that last section, close to the end of it near the bolt. And similar eyes were positioned on the third section up from the flexible joint and the sixth.

Springer tied the picture wire to the first eye, making several sure, tight knots. He ran the wire up through the second and third eyes and that was done.

He tried it.

By pulling on the wire that ran up the shaft he was able to work the flexible joint and bring the lower sections of pipe up to whatever angle he wanted. It functioned like a human arm: the long shaft being the upper arm, the flexible joint the elbow, the shorter part the forearm.

Springer had gotten the idea for it by recalling the armlike extension that had held the television set in Jake's hospital room at Sloan-Kettering. While in the meadow in Sherman working out how it would function, they had come to call the device "the reacher," and that had stuck.

The reacher was complete now, ready to do or not do. Except for the one most important thing.

The magnet.

The woofer magnet was not an ordinary magnet by any means. It was made of $SmCo^6$, samarium cobalt, the most magnetic substance known. It was round, three inches in diameter, one inch thick. Inset with threads on one side.

Springer screwed it to the two-inch bolt on the end of the reacher. Now the arm had a hand.

Springer inserted it down through the hole, into the vault. One of his hands held the shaft, the other had hold of the picture wire. He pulled upward on the wire. The elbow flexed. He directed the shaft and maintained tension on the wire. The little practice he'd had in the barn in Sherman had helped.

Slowly, relying greatly on his depth perception, he guided the magnet toward the metal face of one of the drawers.

A crucial moment.

All their efforts might be for naught.

Everything depended on the faces of the drawers, what kind of metal they were made of. If they were stainless steel, nickel or chromium-based steel, the magnet would touch and slide off, unattracted. However, if the faces of the drawers were iron-based steel . . .

It was one of the things Strand couldn't possibly have known, that would just have to go their way.

Springer maneuvered the magnet still closer to the face of one of the drawers. Now it was only eight inches from it. Then three.

When it got within two inches Springer felt a sudden tug on the reacher, like the striking of a trout. He also heard a single definite *chunk*.

The magnet had hard hold of the face of the drawer.

Springer breathed easier and thanked whoever had early on impressed Townsend with frugality. These drawers had been saved from the original vault. Had Townsend chosen to spend for an entirely new vault outside and in, the faces of the drawers probably wouldn't have contained a trace of iron.

Springer now reversed the direction of the reacher and at the same time kept tension on the wire. He had to go a lot by feel. It was somewhat like playing a fish.

The drawer slid out a few inches. Then, with more pressure from Springer, it came completely out of its slot. It was one of the smaller drawers. It weighed about five pounds.

Scoot took charge of the wire, maintained tension on it, as Springer drew the reacher upward, section by section. Held fast by the samarium cobalt magnet, the drawer was brought up to the ceiling of the vault and the mouth of the hole.

Audrey reached down in and removed its contents.

Watches.

Diamond-embellished wristwatches of various styles by Piaget, Le Coultre, Audemars Piguet. About a dozen altogether, lovely and valuable but under these circumstances unwanted. They bore serial numbers on the backs of their platinum or gold cases, were thereby traceable.

Audrey took them over to the workbench to Strand. That was the system they had settled on beforehand. Springer and Scoot would operate the reacher. Audrey would pick up from out of the drawers and relay to the workbench, where Strand would decide on what would be left behind. It had been agreed they would take only loose stones and not even any of those that by their large sizes or special cuts might be identifiable.

After the merest look Strand tossed the watches to the corner of the floor to the right of the workbench. Rougher treatment than they deserved.

Springer reached down in and pushed at the empty drawer, attempting to separate it from the magnet. More than a push would be required to break this magnet's hold. He ended up having to punch at the drawer sharply. It dropped and clanged to the floor of the vault.

The time was eleven thirty-seven.

They had about four and a half hours to work the vault. The sun would rise at a few minutes after five. To be on the safe side they had to allow at least an hour to get up those ropes and across the roofs, and even that might be cutting it a bit close. There were a hundred drawers: ninety-nine now, to be exact. Allowing only three minutes a drawer, Springer still wouldn't have time to get to them all. He probably wouldn't have to, he thought. Stone 588 could be in one of the first few drawers he brought up.

Inspired by his own optimism, he went fishing for another drawer. Not randomly. The drawers closest to the floor had to be first, otherwise, later on, when the empties piled up in the vault, he wouldn't be able to get to them.

He knew now that he had to be precise with the magnet. If it latched onto anything immovable such as the metal frame that formed the slots for the drawers, he might not be able to pull it free. Carefully he maneuvered the reacher, manipulated the wire. The magnet chunked solidly onto the face of one of those bottom-most drawers.

Springer drew it out and up.

This was one of the larger drawers. It weighed ten to twelve pounds. In it were several shallow leather boxes, gold-stamped with filigree and initials. Springer recognized them for what they were: Vintage boxes of the sort leading jewelers such as Cartier, Schlumberger, and Chaumet once used to present their better merchandise. Each box especially made to fit a particular piece.

Audrey gathered them up and carried them over to Strand, and now he had something to get busy on.

Nestled comfortably in the silk lining it had impressed with its exact shape for sixty-some years was a ruby and diamond parure: necklace, bracelet, ear clips, and brooch. The necklace consisted of twenty cushion-cut rubies of seven carats each and a centered, featured ruby of fifteen carats, all intricately surrounded by diamonds, both round and marquise cuts. The rubies were unmistakably Burmese, of finest quality; the diamonds matched and were equally fine.

Strand knew he was looking at four million dollars. The fifteen-carat ruby alone was worth a million and a half. No time to count profit, he told himself, and brought down in front of his eyes a double-lensed magnifier that was attached to a headband. It left his hands free to take up the necklace and a pair of small, very sharp snippers. Magnified three and a half times, the prongs that held the rubies and diamonds in place were easily visible. Strand clipped the prongs away as though he were pruning roses. It was something he'd done countless times. The rubies and diamonds dropped from their settings, tattooed upon the bottom of the Bendel shoe box Strand had found beneath the workbench. When he'd shorn all but the incidental small diamonds from the parure, he tossed the platinum mountings into the corner, the potentially incriminating mountings.

Audrey had already brought him over a case that held a dozen five-carat diamond rings. He had to get going or he'd fall behind.

Up and out of Townsend's vault in a steady flow came the precious things, piece after piece, new and antique, art nouveau and art deco. Diadems and tiaras, lavalieres, tremblantes. Strands of 15 millimeter South Sea pearls, even two strands of that size that were natural black. Opera lengths of Chinese imperial jade. Colombian emeralds, Kashmir sapphires, chrysoberyl cat's eyes and alexandrites.

Hundreds and hundreds of briefkes contained loose goods of various sorts and sizes. Diamonds of every conceivable cut. Some fancy colored diamonds, especially rare and accordingly more precious. One, an intense pink of six carats, was surely worth over a million; another, even more rare, more valuable, was distinctly red. There was lot after lot of diamonds ranging in sizes from one carat to four carats. With those, Strand had merely to unfold the briefkes and let them slide down the crease of paper and into the shoe box.

Every now and then there came a larger diamond. These, Strand knew, were Townsend's most coveted goods, the ones he held back, doled out to favored clients as though at any price he was doing them a favor. Townsend called these stones his sleeping beauties. Although the agreement had been to not take any of these larger, identifiable stones, Strand held them aside. He got two of the bricks they'd removed from the wall and placed them end to end off to his left on the workbench. On the flat surface of the bricks he put the larger diamonds: a forty-seven-carat marquise cut next to a sixty-six-carat pear-shape next to a thirty-five-carat round next to . . .

Audrey thought Strand was probably putting them there just to appreciate them. She enjoyed the progress evidenced by the increasing amount in the shoe box. She considered it an accomplishment when the bottom of the box was covered with a blazing layer. That layer now was at least an inch and a half deep.

But, as yet, no stone 588.

Springer was working at a furious pace with the reacher. The floor of the vault was strewn with emptied drawers. He'd been at it for almost two hours, and his shirt was as drenched now with perspiration as it had been before with rain. He hoped with each drawer he brought up. *This one will have stone 588 in it,* he told himself. It had gotten so he glanced to Audrey at the workbench each time she and Strand were going through the contents of a drawer. He anticipated hearing her say, *Here it is!*

Springer straightened up and stretched his back, rotated his head to release some of the tension that had knotted in his neck. Audrey thought he appeared tired, strained. She sensed his desperation. "Take a break," she suggested caringly. She had a box of Good & Plentys in her shirt pocket. Once, at a much lighter moment, they had decided that the white ones were the goods and the pink ones the plenties. Now she put one of each into his mouth. "At least stop and take a couple of real deep breaths," she told him.

At that instant two floors below Gilbert Townsend had just entered the building. He'd left his limousine up near the Plaza because the streets were still closed to traffic. The policemen at the barrier had let him through on foot only after he'd convinced them of who he was.

Fifth Avenue was no longer a stream. The Water Department people had closed a valve up the line so no water could reach the rupture. A Con Edison crew had pumped out the chamber where the explosion had occurred and was now assessing what would have to be done. Townsend asked when electric power would be restored and was irked when a Con Ed workman told him it would be a day or two. A new transformer had to be installed and all new cable pulled. Townsend was glad to see there were still plenty of police around.

In fact, two officers in yellow slickers and boots were standing in the rain just outside the entrance to his building. They were helpful with their flashlights when Townsend unlocked his outer gate and the heavy glass entrance door.

Now inside, Townsend let down his black umbrella and held it well away from himself as he shook the rain off. He was in evening clothes, just come from a party. He'd learned of the incident not more than twenty minutes ago when his driver had mentioned it. If he'd heard sooner he would have been there sooner, to see for himself that everything was in order. One thing he knew for certain: The battery-powered backup alarm had to be set. It had shorted and been a bother so many times he'd disconnected it years ago. Hell, he couldn't even remember when they'd last had an outage.

Townsend had a young woman with him, an aspiring fashion model and beauty of the night who hoped to appear in his advertisements in *Vogue*. He had asked her to wait in the car but she'd refused, resorted to some rather clumsy guile with her hands and sucked at the skin of his neck and pleaded that she wanted to be with him. He knew, of course, that what she really wanted to be with was the tiny platinum vial of cocaine he had in his jacket pocket.

Like a subservient and hungry pet she followed Townsend across the main showroom, dimly lit from the emergency lights out on Fifth Avenue. Her high heels clicked on the parquet marble floor. She had on the merest short evening dress, might as well have been nude, the confident, careless way her body wore it. At the bottom of the stairs she reached for Townsend, who was a couple of steps up, and tugged sharply at the back of his jacket.

He almost fell.

She laughed, a brief, boiling, malicious laugh. "I need a toot," she said.

"No."

"Don't be so goddamn stingy, Gilbert. What's a couple of toots?" She had a numb nose.

"You're being a cunt," he told her. His saying that stemmed from a mild lecture on deportment he'd given her earlier in the evening.

Evidently she hadn't taken it to heart. "Who's a cunt?" she said, making her beautiful face ugly and defiant. "You're a cunt."

Townsend was above getting really angry with her. Smoothly, he assuaged her. "When we get back to the car."

"Now!" she howled like a deprived cat. Her voice resounded through the building with its tall ceilings.

Townsend walked over to the nearest display case, a glass-topped case with Louis Quinze legs. He tapped some cocaine from the platinum vial onto its glass surface and rolled a brand-new hundred-dollar bill into a tight tube. The beauty used the edge of one of Townsend's business cards to divide the cocaine into four lines. She inserted the tubed hundred into her left nostril, then the right, vacuumed up the lines. What little cocaine was left she dabbed up with her second finger and rubbed on her gums.

Townsend wiped the glass top with the sleeve of his jacket. The beauty pouted when he took the hundred-dollar bill from her fingers.

On the third floor in the room above the vault the one thing that was heard was the howl. It was fortunate that Springer had paused for a breather just then, or else the clanging of an emptied drawer dropping within the vault might have given them away. They switched off the lanterns, covered the hole, and stood still in the absolute dark.

After a long moment Strand noiselessly opened the door to the hall and listened. He heard the voices, realized it was Townsend and a woman. He stepped out into the carpeted hall and moved along to the top of the stairs, crouched there.

Townsend came up to the second-floor landing. He went directly to the vault, stood looking at its reassuring thick steel, its door unchanged from when he'd locked it eight or so hours earlier. He considered opening it for a look but remembered the power was off, the electronic combination not functioning. Well, if he couldn't get into the vault, sure as hell no one else could, he reasoned.

Strand, watching from the head of the stairs on the third floor, saw only Townsend's lower legs and feet, saw them turn and move off in the direction of Townsend's office. After a moment he heard keys rattling and scraping against a paneled wall. He believed he knew what Townsend was up to.

A decision for Strand: Should he take the violent initiative, sneak down and strike Townsend on the head? The woman on the first floor, he'd have to take care of her similarly. He'd never struck anyone, but it might be worth it in this instance. He doubted that he could do it without being seen. He'd be identified. Or should he chance everything on timing?

Townsend made up Strand's mind by hurrying from his office and down the stairs to the main floor.

At the same time, nearly step for step, Strand hurried down to the second floor, his stealth aided by the rug and his sneakers and Townsend's own movements. Strand caught a glimpse of Townsend's back at the bottom of the next flight down. The door to Townsend's office was open. Strand went in and straight to the panel that concealed the backup alarm.

He had to wait.

There was a built-in delay on the alarm that gave whoever activated it sixty seconds to get out of the building. Townsend was well aware of that. How close would he cut it?

On the main floor Townsend picked up his umbrella. The beauty was temporarily satisfied. She wanted to go someplace and play, she said. She complained that her shoes were ruined from the rain. She made a remark about the empty display cases and wanted to know where all the fucking diamonds were.

"Sleeping," Townsend told her and pulled her out the door.

In the office above, Strand waited until he heard the door being closed. The lock on the panel would have been easy to jimmy if he'd been prepared for that. Within the paneled compartment the time delay clock was ticking off the seconds that would cost him year after year.

It didn't matter if he broke every bone in his hand.

He rammed his fist through the paneling.

Whatever noise that caused was lost to the commotion out on Fifth Avenue. Anyway, Townsend surely didn't hear it because it coincided with the racket he made shutting the exterior flexible-steel gate.

Strand tore away the split wood to get to the backup alarm. It was enclosed in a large gray metal box. He opened the box and saw the controls. There had to be an on–off switch, but where the hell was it? Townsend had just turned the alarm on, so why shouldn't he be able to just turn the alarm off? There were two wires, a blue and a red, running together from something to something, and another pair of wire connections elsewhere, a white and a black. He had no idea what purpose they served. He just yanked and tore them all loose.

He beat the timer by half a second.

He went back up the stairs to the room above the vault, merely told the others what they wanted to hear: Everything was okay. They switched on the lamps, uncovered the hole, and got to it again.

Springer tried to cut down on the time required to bring up the drawers. He was more efficient with the reacher now, but instead of taking the drawers as they came, level by level, he began choosing by hunch. A certain drawer would catch his eyes, as though saying to him, *I'm the one you want, choose me, I'm the one that will give you back stone 588.* They were deceitful, these drawers, Springer thought, as one after another they failed to produce that stone. Nevertheless, his hope continued to listen to them.

One of the drawers contained an assortment of rough diamonds, evidently Townsend's ample allotment from the most recent sight in London. They were still in the box they came in, but the ribbon had been cut and The System's seal broken. Several of the stones in the box resembled stone 588, were about the same size, give or take a few carats. Audrey went through these carefully, looking for the telltale tip that was chipped off. One of the stones was almost identical to stone 588 except for the chip. Audrey had an intuitive feeling about that stone.

"My souvenir," she said as she showed the stone to Strand. He shrugged and resumed the more important matter of snipping from their necklace settings twenty-four rectangular-cut diamonds of four to six carats each and forty-eight two-carat pear-shapes. They were, Strand noticed, nicely matched D-color stones and of such fine quality that he would probably have to search hours to find a flaw. The value of these diamonds alone was enough to cause most people to consider retirement.

Naturally, Strand had given thought to what he would do with his share of the take. He couldn't go whenever he wanted or greatly change his life-style because he had two years of parole to do, including regular monthly visits to his parole officer. A requirement was that he get a job of some sort. To rehabilitate himself. As far as he was concerned, this Townsend thing was perfect rehabilitation. It settled a lopsided, long-chafing score and provided him with the wherewithal to do something straight and satisfying. When his parole time was over he would move to Europe, to Monaco or Nice. He would open a small, exclusive business, dealing only in the most finely made merchandise. He would enjoy attending auctions in Geneva and Paris and London, outbidding other dealers when it was a pleasure or profitable to do so. He would never in his life knowingly touch another piece of swag. And sometime, somewhere along the line, there would be a more patient Patricia.

Scoot, too, had his plans. He wouldn't stick around New York. Oh, he'd return every once in a while for a visit, but where he'd live would be someplace like Bermuda or the Bahamas. Not too far from the action, not Tahiti or one of those dry and scrubby Greek islands, but just far enough away that he could come and go and stand less of a chance of running into one of his old cellmates. He would have to get a passport. He'd never had a passport. He would never in his life steal another thing. In fact, he'd probably be the one to get stolen from. Just thinking about such an eventuality pissed him off.

The police helicopter hadn't gone over for an hour and a half.

The shoe box was more than half full.

The gutted platinum and gold mountings were a pile in the corner.

It was five minutes to four.

Strand had accumulated eight of Townsend's sleeping beauties, had them lined up on the face of the two bricks on the workbench. The largest of these special diamonds was a 112.43-carat cushion cut. It was most likely a famous stone. All eight were probably famous stones, for that matter. Even now under these subjugating circumstances, they seemed to flaunt their preeminence, draw strength, blaze from one another. Strand was not without respect for them. He gave them a full minute of deferential regard before returning to the fact that they belonged to Townsend, were, in a way, his professional heart.

Strand took up the acetylene torch, ignited it, and adjusted its flame. Audrey observed, fascinated with what he was doing. She was not aware that diamond is one of the most thermal-conductive of all substances. Heat shot right through it. But at 3400 degrees Fahrenheit, not without causing change.

Strand went from left to right with the acetylene torch, giving each of the eight large diamonds a mere lick with the blue hot tongue— no more than that was necessary to transform the diamonds into hunks of graphite, the same as found in ordinary lead pencils or used to eliminate the squeak from hinges. For Strand it was the coup de grace.

He began picking up, putting things in the pockets and compartments of his vest, preparing to leave.

Springer was still working the reacher. He hadn't gotten to thirty or so of the drawers. Most of those were high up along the rows. It was doubtful that Townsend would have put stone 588 in a drawer so inaccessible. In fact, the drawer Springer was bringing up now contained less valuable pieces and loose stones not nearly so desirable as those before.

"We've got to quit," Strand said.

"A couple more," Springer told him.

And after one of those drawers contained only some low-grade Thai sapphires and the other a few mixed lots of very included Brazilian emeralds, Strand told Springer, "C'mon, it's four o'clock straight up."

Springer didn't seem to hear. He went for another drawer. Audrey knelt beside him, peered down into the vault, saw the drawer that was being brought up by the reacher. This drawer looked promising, had some chamois pouches and fat briefkes in it. Audrey grabbed them up, opened them eagerly, and found aquamarines, citrines, tourmalines, amethysts. She poured them back down into the hole.

"One more," Springer insisted desperately.

The drawer that came up was empty.

He was coming up empty.

Strand and Scoot had to wrest the reacher from his grasp, pull him away from the hole. He struggled with them briefly and then gave up.

They got the lanterns up from the vault, disassembled the reacher, and packed everything into their vests. Changed back to their leather work gloves. They double-checked to make sure nothing was being left behind that might incriminate them. Audrey even retrieved a pink Good and Plenty that she'd dropped an hour ago.

They moved the upended table away from the hole in the wall. Scoot peeked out. They heard a helicopter approaching: from uptown this time. As it had before, it hovered a short while almost directly above the building and then continued on.

One by one they climbed out through the hole. They wouldn't have left the fabric taped to the wall if it hadn't been for the helicopter, the chance that it might come patrolling again and notice the hole and heat up the entire area too soon.

The rain was still coming down hard. It felt refreshing, cleansing in a way. They blinked as it washed their eyes. They crossed to where the climbing rope hung from the six-story roof. They would go the way they'd come. Strand motioned to Springer to go first.

Springer reached as high up the rope as he could, grabbed hold, and planted his feet flat against the wall of the building. The rope was soaked through, but its weave was designed for such inclemency. It wasn't at all slippery, and the knots that Scoot had made in it were now especially helpful. Springer went up, hand over hand, a knot at a time, putting resistance against the wall with his feet, sort of walking horizontally. His arms and hands were tired from having worked the reacher all those hours, but there was a mixture of anger and disappointment in him that potentiated his strength. When he reached the top he rolled up over the edge and onto the surface of the roof and just lay there, face up. He had the sensation that the rain was dissolving him, as it would so much clay. It occurred to him that because of the rain he could give in to crying and his tears would go undetected.

Audrey came up over the edge.

Then Strand and Scoot.

The time was four thirty-two.

Scoot hurriedly gathered up the climbing rope, untied it from the standpipe, and put it in his vest. They went to the rear corner of that roof to make the next climb, another three stories up to the ledge. They transferred their vests to around their necks and proceeded in the same order. From the hand-over-hand upward hauling of the weights of their bodies, the muscles of their arms and shoulders burned with fatigue, and it was a relief to reach the ledge and put the burden on their legs. Because of that and because they had already once safely experienced the danger of it, the narrow ledge seemed less perilous. They sidestepped along it, a few inches at a time, feeling the wall with their heels, mindful to keep their heads up. Their ally, the rain, had washed away the layers of bird droppings so the ledge was no longer slippery.

When they'd reached the nine-story roof, Scoot took in and untied that longer length of climbing rope. They hurried across the roofs and over the fences, one, two, three.

Dawn was coming.

Darkness was giving way to gray.

The rain, as though it knew it was no longer needed, was letting up.

They climbed in through the tenth-floor window of the Star Parking Garage. They heard the industrial elevator of the garage coming up. They ran: Strand and Scoot down the stairs to the blue Bonneville and the gray Cutlass on nine, Springer and Audrey up the stairs to the white Chrysler on eleven.

Springer opened the trunk of the Chrysler. They threw in their vests, quickly climbed in, and got into position on their sides, with Audrey's front pressed against Springer's back, spoon fashion. Springer didn't have time to close the trunk all the way. The parking attendant, who was now approaching the car, would have heard it.

The attendant got into the Chrysler and started it. He drove it onto the elevator and took it down.

Vince Fantuzzi, doing what he was told, was right on time.

The attendant did not bother with exactly leveling off the elevator with the ground floor, so when he drove the Chrysler out to Vince there was a jarring, noisy enough bump.

Click went the shutting of the Chrysler's trunk lid.

Unnoticed.

31

The black waiter in the white jacket came in carrying an ornate Georgian silver coffee server and tray that were worth his yearly salary.

Wintersgill stopped mid-sentence and gazed out from the sixty-second floor. Central Park was a carpet, a wide runner that led to his presence. Yesterday's rain had greened it, plumped the wilt from the blades and leaves. More than ever the park had the quality of a respected London park, Wintersgill thought. By tomorrow or the next day, however, it would again be abused and exhausted.

The waiter poured.

Steam, like a capricious spirit, ascended from the brew that went into the cup.

"Have another scone," Wintersgill suggested.

The man seated opposite flipped aside the white linen napkin that covered the silver latticed basket. He chose the scone that to him seemed most dotted with currants. "You must be in league with my tailor," he said, which was what he usually said whenever he accepted a rich treat.

Wintersgill had already taken stock of the man's suit: a three-piece ready-to-wear not even conscientiously altered. At least unlike so many of his kind he hadn't shown up in a gray hard finish gone shiny in the seat and elbows from too many hours of hard-chair Senate meetings.

The waiter aimed the spout of the coffee server Wintersgill's way. Wintersgill declined by quickly covering his cup with his flattened hand, came within a fraction of tilt of getting scalded. He dismissed the waiter with his eyes.

The "second breakfast" was what Wintersgill called it. He had it every morning he was in the office, shared it with whoever was his ten-thirty appointment. Thus his ten-thirty was reserved for anyone he might want something from or someone he was obliged to thank. Perhaps it was a *peu de chose,* the second breakfast; nevertheless, Wintersgill was sure that it had more than paid for its trouble over the years. It was in keeping with his belief that people came to the Hull Foundation knowing that its business was philanthrophy and therefore would feel slighted if they left without having gotten at least a little something for themselves—even if it were only a couple of Callard and Bowser toffees from the dish in the reception area. Let the other foundations poor-mouth and tight-pocket. With plushness underfoot and wealth on the walls, Hull's generosity was all the more credible.

This morning's ten-thirty was a senator who had recently become the senior from his state because of another senator's demise. He had also inherited the chairmanship of the committee that could either stir or calm the waters of taxation. At the moment he was picking up crumbs from the Hull table linen, accumulating the little doughy dots of scone from around his plate and putting them into his mouth. "As you were saying . . . " the senator prompted.

"I was calling attention to the fact that last year the Hull Foundation gave six hundred and seventy million in grants."

The senator was politely impressed. "How does that break down?"

"I'll get the exact figures for you, but I know offhand about thirty percent of what we gave went to health and scientific projects. For the past few years we've really stepped out in the field of biomedical research. We've been responsible for some considerable advances in the understanding of immunological abnormalities." Wintersgill felt that ten minutes of this would put the senator to sleep.

"The Rockefeller people have quite a few Nobel laureates in their fold," the senator said, as though he'd personally done a head count.

"So do we."

"I've always had the impression that Hull involved itself mainly with cultural matters."

"That, of course, is only the tip of the iceberg, what is generally evident. Actually, we're comfortably diversified here at Hull. Last year, for instance, a number of sizable grants went toward studies in defense policy."

"That's about as close as you get to politics, I suppose."

Wintersgill's nod, they both knew, was a lie. In violation of the 1969 Tax Reform Act, which prohibited foundations from any sort of lobbying to influence legislation, Hull had discreet, hands-around-and-over-and-under-the-law ways of tangibly predisposing certain vital people in Washington. That stipulation of the 1969 reform only made everything seem a little more sensitive and justified the need for Hull to up the ante. Hull really didn't play politics, though. That is, it didn't favor either party or play one against the other. A politician's affiliation was not important to Hull, as long as he knew enough to close his hand when Hull put something in it.

The 1969 tax reform caused a lot of independent foundations to run for other cover. For Hull, however, it only necessitated some mark-time and a slight bit of reshaping. No matter that the act limited the amount of private business enterprises a foundation could own, the Hull-controlled conglomerates merely went on funneling their profits into the Hull Foundation and no one even raised a brow. Never mind the requirement that a philanthropic foundation had to be truly philanthropic, give away a minimum of 5 percent of its assets each year to worthwhile endeavors. As long as the amount granted by Hull appeared to be considerable, who questioned? No one was tabulating, no one came to seriously audit. Hull was never on any congressional hit list, and even if it had been, someone would have seen to it that it was an early scratch.

Now, the senior senator who was Wintersgill's ten-thirty this day added so much heavy cream to his coffee it overflowed. He used his spoon to bail a quarter inch or so from the cup and make it manageable. He blotted the base of the cup on the tablecloth before taking it to his lips. He had a steady hand for a southern drinker. "I hope you haven't gotten the wrong idea," he said. "I'm not here to snoop."

"It never occurred to me," Wintersgill told him.

"I assure you it's meant to be just a visit, more to get acquainted than anything."

Wintersgill's secretary entered with an air of urgency, a sheaf of papers in her hand. She begged pardon for the intrusion and explained that these were grants that required Wintersgill's signature immediately. People were anxious to receive their money, she said, handing Wintersgill a readied fountain pen and separating the sheets to facilitate his signing. "We don't operate like most other foundations," he said, along with the intermittent scratching of the nib of the pen. "By that I mean we never allow ourselves to become mired in bureaucratic nonsense. Our grants are made swiftly. We don't ask for evaluations, reports of progress, or any of that. We don't even look into how a recipient has spent the grant."

"Really?"

"A molecular biologist doesn't want to be encumbered with accounting for every penny. Nor does he function best with someone peering over his shoulder." Wintersgill signed the last of the grants. The secretary hurried out with them, as though a significant world event depended on them. It was a prearrangement, of course, a walk-on she performed for the benefit of every initiate ten-thirty.

Wintersgill sat back, glanced again out the window. To the west a small but angry remnant storm cloud appeared to be stuck between the twin towers of the San Remo apartment building.

"You still subsidize films, don't you?" the senator asked.

"For public broadcasting, yes."

"Would you be receptive to a documentary film about the Navajo Indians? My son-in-law . . . "

God, not another documentary on the plight of the Navajos, Wintersgill thought. He assumed an interested expression and put himself on automatic behind it for as long as the senator's lips continued to move.

Then he said, "Sounds like something we'd be extremely interested in funding. Say no more. My secretary will take your son-in-law's name and address and send him an application for a grant."

That had the ring of a brush-off, the senator thought.

Wintersgill had purposely put it that way so he could mind-fuck the senator a bit. "I *personally* will see that the grant is processed," he reassured him.

Ten minutes later the senator, satisfied, was gone.

Wintersgill was told by his secretary that Gilbert Townsend had called twice.

"Stiff him once more," Wintersgill told her. "When he calls after that, put him through. Meanwhile, I don't want to be disturbed." He removed his suit jacket, hitched up the legs of his trousers so as not to bag their creases, and sat at his desk. Leaning back with eyes closed he took pleasure in the stir of another windfall, this one to come from Townsend's direction.

He had learned of the Townsend burglary on the morning television news. The first report was that the thieves had gotten away with a hundred million. The last word Wintersgill had heard, that figure had tripled. Wintersgill tried to find in himself some sympathy for Townsend, and perhaps there was a speck of it way back in one of his long-lost callow corners, but how could he feel sorry when the timing was so perfect? Hell, if he knew who the thieves were he'd send them a note of gratitude.

He reached down into the black alligator business case beside his chair. Brought out a red kid drawstring pouch. Opened it and shook out onto his desk pad twelve smaller black chamois pouches. Those contained the twelve twenty-five-carat Russian diamonds Springer had acquired for Libby. She had given them to Wintersgill over the past weekend, for him to deliver to Townsend Monday, the day before yesterday. Wintersgill just hadn't gotten around to it. He'd planned on taking care of it today.

He removed the twelve diamonds from their pouches, lined them up girdle to girdle. Libby had shown them to him, but they were much more beautiful now.

His interphone blinked.

Townsend was calling for the second time in ten minutes. Wintersgill picked up. Instead of hello he said, "I've heard."

"I have to see you," Townsend said, his voice an octave higher than usual.

"I'm with auditors up from Washington, been with them since early morning, and it appears they'll be here all day."

"It's imperative that I see you."

"Can't it wait until tonight, or tomorrow?"

"No."

"I understand." Wintersgill sighed to dramatize the pressure he was enduring. "Well, a friend in dire straights takes precedence over all else," he recited. He told Townsend where to be in exactly fifteen minutes, then timed himself so that he arrived there in twenty.

The southeast corner of Central Park, opposite the Hotel Pierre.

Townsend was standing there in the middle of the walk. His eyes were fixed with painful introspect. He was somewhere between shock and catatonia. His jaw was slack. Wintersgill took hold of his elbow to get him going up Fifth alongside the park.

Wintersgill wanted to skip all the details. A robbery was a robbery. But it was looping in the most immediate layer of Townsend's consciousness, detained there because it was still too excruciating for the rest of his mind to accept. He had to unload. In that higher-octave grieving voice, he related how he'd come to his business that morning even though he'd known there'd be no electric power, no lights. How he'd discovered first the smashed-in panel and torn wires of the backup alarm and then the mess in the room above the vault. He described how the mountings with stones extracted were thrown like so much junk in the corner and how his most precious larger stones were depreciated to gray, faceted lumps. He had touched one and it crumbled. He called his security service, the Reliance people, and the next thing he knew police were all over the place. They still were. They didn't have a clue. They hadn't offered him any hope.

Before Townsend could tell it all again, Wintersgill asked, "Actually, how much was taken?"

"Three hundred million."

"Your cost, retail value, or what?"

"Mine."

"And how much is insured?"

"Twenty million. More than twenty would have cost a fortune in premiums. As it is I've been carrying two policies. That's how it is in the trade."

"At least you're going to have a hell of a write-off," Wintersgill said with a light edge.

"I'm in trouble."

"A loss is only a loss."

"Some of the goods that were stolen belonged to clients. Several very important pieces were in on consignment. Others equally important were in for appraisal. One client alone had twenty million worth with me."

"Altogether how much of that sort was lost?"

"Close to seventy million. I can't cover it."

"I gather you're asking for my help."

"Which by no means would be charity," Townsend reminded him gruffly.

Wintersgill was surprised that Townsend had even that much contention left in him.

"You could give me something more on the account," Townsend said.

"How much?"

"Twenty million."

"When would you need it?"

"Already this morning clients were calling wanting to know what if anything had happened to their pieces. I dodged most of the calls, but I won't be able to put them off for long."

"Would tomorrow afternoon be soon enough?"

"Tomorrow afternoon would be most appreciated."

"It will have to be a transfer from account to account in Zurich."

"That will do fine."

"Any particular account you want it put into?"

"Same as last time."

They walked on a way farther, then did an about-face and headed downtown. Mothers or nurses wheeling dark-blue, very expensive perambulators claimed the center of the shaded walk. Ruffian boys came leaping over the wall of the park, uncatchable. There was the smell of the zoo.

Townsend had begun again on the robbery, describing the hole in the top of the vault, theorizing on how the thieves had managed to rifle the drawers, confounded by it.

Wintersgill interrupted. As though it had just then occurred to him, he said, "There is in this an opportunity for you to do me a favor."

"Oh?"

"Actually, not a favor for me but for Libby."

Townsend was not in a position to refuse.

"No doubt you recall the twelve rather large diamonds Libby wanted you to make into a necklace?"

"Libby mentioned last week that she had them. I must say I was surprised that fellow Springer was able to come up with them. Are you certain they're not cubic zirconium?"

"They were within a day of being included in your robbery."

"How fortunate," Townsend remarked, wishing that could be said of his own goods. "I'd be glad to take a look at them if that's what Libby wants, make sure they're authentic."

"Let's assume, Gilbert, that these diamonds were handed over to you the day before yesterday, what record would you have of them?"

"A receipt. I would have given Libby a receipt. And I would have entered them in my computer as inventory."

"Can you still do both?"

Townsend got it. The larcenous side of Libby wanted to write off her diamonds and have them too.

"It must appear as though it was done Monday," Wintersgill said pointedly.

"How much did they end up costing?"

"Fifteen million."

Townsend looked off, frowning as though his thoughts were just barely clearing difficult obstacles. The favor would be a simple matter, but Wintersgill shouldn't know that. "I'll need to be precise about the cut of the diamonds, their quality, how much they weigh."

"They're identical," Wintersgill said and, casually, as though it were no more than a commonplace amulet, from his vest pocket he brought out one of the precious Russians.

A glint from it shot across the avenue, momentarily distracting Fred Pugh, the lip-reader.

By late the following afternoon Townsend had regained considerable composure.

He wasn't his normal, polished self, but the blanch of shock that had jaundiced his tan was gone and about 80 percent of his legs was back under him and again it was somewhat important that his necktie be knotted small but not tight, just so it caused a precise little pleat.

Much had been lost but not all, was Townsend's attitude.

He still had his credit. He'd be able to obtain goods on memorandum. He also still had his contacts for getting swag. No doubt the fences, downwind of his needs, were going to their banks and into their *iceboxes* to decide on what to offer him: pieces they had personally liked and thought they would keep for themselves, pieces that were not yet comfortably cooled. To beat down their asking prices he would use the burglary, the suffering of the loss. Also, from now on, he would be even more conscientious about fucking the sort of people who would never feel it. The Libbys, that crowd. Every antique necklace that came along—not just every other—was going to have a signed and dated certificate of provenance attesting that it had originally belonged to the Marquise de Maintenon or the Comtesse de Polignac or anyone like that who was supposed to have had a historically notable libido. Perhaps, Townsend thought, he would even revive the rumor that he'd cut a discreet deal with the Hermitage to help it sell off more of their Romanoff pieces.

He'd be restocked and back on top in no time.

As long as he didn't come up short now. It was essential that he act gracious, make good every dollar his clients were owed, and, in certain cases, throw in a few dollars extra. He would be able to do that with the insurance and what money he had and the twenty million from Wintersgill. He'd expected that twenty million to show up in his Zurich account today but it hadn't. Wintersgill swore he'd ordered the transfer. Probably the Swiss were using the money for a day, as they so often did, drawing interest for themselves while they held the money briefly in limbo, Wintersgill had suggested.

Fuck the grubbing Swiss!

And the same for Wintersgill, Townsend felt. How transparent was Wintersgill's offhand manner when he inquired about Libby's fishy fifteen-million-dollar loss. Had Townsend seen to it? Townsend already had the receipt made out, with last Monday's date on it, as requested, and a thorough description of the twelve Russian stones. He was only waiting for Wintersgill to ask for it. He had it delivered by hand to Wintersgill. He had also manipulated the inventory in his computer so the dated entry of those stones was correctly included. It was the last thing he did before making a printout of what had been stolen for the insurance people and the police.

The police.

It seemed to Townsend that at least half the force had been trampling all over his establishment yesterday and today. Up and down the stairs, in and out of his office, out on the roof. Smears of their greasy white fingerprint powder were everywhere. They had interrogated and given lie detector tests to the staff. They had, at first, made a lot of the fabric and tape they had found on the outside wall, but as it turned out, the fabric was only a few yards of several mill runs totaling three hundred thousand yards that was spread across the country, and the tape was from one roll out of a half-million similar rolls.

Townsend soon came to realize the reason so many different and high-level police showed up. They came out of curiosity, more than anything, and to add their theory to the many of how the vault had been plundered through a ten-inch hole in its ceiling. There was no concensus of opinion. Precinct captains, lieutenants, and detectives looked the situation over and stood staring incredulously at the hole. Some returned for a second, reverent look, as though visiting a shrine. One commander with a vivid imagination was convinced that the thieves had used some sort of trained animal, a smart little monkey.

Thus, Townsend was made to feel that his was not just a burglary, but an anomaly in the annals of crime, a case for Sherlock Holmes or Hercule Poirot.

Well, at least now, at the end of the second day, the police were gone. Townsend went throughout his building to make sure. Then he locked up, crossed over Fifth Avenue at 56th Street, and entered Trump Tower. It was routine for him to be there at this time of day to close his satellite outlet in the atrium. Cartier had a shop at street level, Winston and Asprey had places on level two, Buccellati on level four. The Townsend outlet was on level five. It wasn't grand but, like Winston's, intimate and extremely elegant. A single, expensively appointed room intended for mere presence, impression, rather than meaningful sales.

Townsend could have taken the elevator up. It would have been faster, but he'd had enough scurry. He went up level by level, riding the grill-like steps of the escalators. He took vague notice of these surroundings: the prevalence of Breccia Perniche marble that was either a pleasing aggregation of various shades of sienna, ochres, and madders or too much the color of dried blood and vomit, the five-story ledgelike waterfall uplighted and tropically accessorized by long trailing vines, the abundance of gleaming brass and gold-tinted mirror. Not many sightseers, hardly any shoppers. No shoppers on level five.

It was seven o'clock.

The manager of the Townsend outlet had already removed the merchandise from the display cases and put it in the floor safe. He reported a bit proudly that sales for the day amounted to fourteen thousand three hundred and twenty-two dollars. Several gold and pavé diamond pieces had been purchased.

Townsend acknowledged the accomplishment with a proportion-

STONE 588

ate quickly on-and-off smile and told the manager he could leave. Townsend put the day's proceeds to pocket and closed the floor safe. As usual, to accommodate anyone who wanted to look in and admire his excellent taste, he left the lights on.

As he was locking the door he noticed off to his right a large red plastic bucket. Overturned. The sudsy water from it was spilled slick across the marble floor in front of his shop. A fat red-handled mop lay nearby. Evidently one of the Trump maintenance people had just had an accident and, for some reason, left it there. It was unsightly and dangerous. Townsend would complain.

His mind was on that when the hand came around from behind. He never actually saw that it was a hand because it was so quick. The edge of the stiffened fingers flicked at Townsend's throat, struck his voice box.

The next thing he knew, he was being lifted from behind by arms around his thighs. Arms so thick and a grasp so strong it was as though he'd been caught up by some brutal mechanism that would have to be switched off before it would let go.

Ten feet to the railing.

Townsend kicked and flailed and wriggled. He was screaming but no sounds were coming out. Then he was where he shouldn't be, above the fat polished-brass railing, passing over it, and, perhaps because of the glimpse he got of the waterfall across the way, his mind told him he was merely diving and he expected the air to be a substance with a surface that he would plunge into and be able to swim.

He was dog-paddling, working his legs furiously, when at 105 miles per hour he belly flopped on the marble lower level seventy-five feet below.

The tabloids, the *Post* and the *Daily News,* gave Townsend's death their entire front pages. It was a godsent follow-up to the boldly headlined play they had given the burglary of his vault earlier in the week. The *New York Times* also positioned Townsend's death on its front page, but below the fold in a single column with most of the story continued on the obituary page, section D.

361

The question posed for journalistic mileage was whether or not Townsend had died by accident or suicide. Both the *Post* and the *Daily News* made a lot of the spilled bucket of sudsy water and the mop, especially when no one came forward and owned up to having left them there. However, photographs of the mop and the bucket intended to illustrate the story were killed before press time by the editors, who knew such things were far below the body-bag and string-bikini interest level.

The *New York Times* account made no mention of controversy. The factual tone of the *Times* was in agreement with the conclusions of the police and the medical examiner. Townsend, with good reason, had been despondent. His death was an apparent suicide. Most of the content of the *Times* article concerned itself with Townsend's business background and prominence, information drawn from the obituary that had been already written and kept on file with the obituaries of other notables, ready to go.

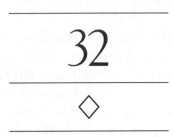

32

◇

Eight days since the burglary.

Audrey hadn't yet come down, thought she never might.

The first morning after, when she'd stood on tiptoe and pressed her
face to a window of her apartment to watch the commotion that was
almost too directly below—all those police going in and out of Townsend's, scrambling and nosing around the rooftops—she'd had the
adolescent notion to jot off a cryptic note, fold it into an airplane,
and send it gliding down to baffle them all the more.

What self-delight! Possibly the largest burglary of all time and
she'd taken part in it. Not just a wait-in-the-car or help-by-loading-
the-guns part, either. She'd been right in the thin of it, putting it all
on the line, making criminal history. How about that, fellow women?

Even when the police were gone from Townsend's and the brick
wall repaired and everything down there appeared back to normal,
Audrey found herself drawn to that window—to visually trace and

therefore to some extent reexperience the exact steps of the adventure: the rooftop fences they had overcome, the perilous ledge they had defied, the walls they had scaled. Each reliving caused a physical sensation in her that was not at all unpleasant, a clenching in the left and right sockets of her groin that could only be described as erotic. Perhaps, she thought, what she was striking was an instinctual nerve connection between sexuality and survival. That would explain her desire for risk. And might it be a two-way circuit, that nerve, so that each orgasm one had was a sort of close call? Didn't the French, who were legendarily wise about such things, call coming *la petite mort,* the little death?

Anyway, the burglary was certainly something to savor, Audrey believed, a high point second only to Springer's entrance into her life.

If only it had turned out better for him. His failure to steal stone 588 back left him frustrated and perplexed. Might it have been in one of those drawers in the vault that he hadn't gotten to? Might Townsend have it in safekeeping elsewhere? But then came Townsend's death and there was no way of knowing, nothing to go on, and Springer gave up on it. He just gave up.

He didn't mope, didn't go around brooding and bitching, just goddamned the circumstances and did his best to accept them. His best was spending a lot of time with Jake. As though driven to trying to compact the sharing of a lifetime in . . . what would it be, a few months or maybe, with luck, a few years? It was excruciating for Springer to know that Jake was on such a short path. Unfair that Jake should have to give up dreaming ahead. What did fate do with such untaken years?

Springer kept these feelings to himself, but with the communion that often exists so sympathetically between father and son, Jake sensed Springer's despair and tried to allay it. His laugh couldn't be the quick, boy-bright Jake laugh, he couldn't hasten his eyes or twinkle them, but there was no way for anyone to see the complaints held back, the whines not whined, the fears unexpressed, Jake thought—and, of course, he was wrong.

Springer and Jake.

Gave one another spiritual transfusions.

With funny stories, some favorite enough to deserve repeating, some new that were now, for some reason, allowed to be a bit risqué. And hand after hand of generous gin rummy competing to see who could let the other win. And just sitting on a fat summer-warmed rock in the park to take turns asking any question and getting cross-the-heart answers, no dodging around with I-don't-knows or you'll-find-out-somedays.

And a trip up to the Bronx to watch volleyball as played by Mr. Malo and Mr. Bueno, who, informed in advance of the situation, put out a lot of extra energy and dazzle. Their one-on-one game was a cross between volleyball and soccer. The ball had to go over the net without being touched by their hands. They had played it on Copacabana beach in Rio many more hours than they'd ever gone to school or worked. Springer and Jake watched and drank Pepsis from the can while Malo and Bueno showed off, went through their entire tricky repertoires. Jake cheered them on, seemed genuinely delighted.

Friday, day after tomorrow, he was scheduled to go into Sloan-Kettering for his second chemotherapy.

Now Audrey sat on the floor among the pillows at the foot of her bed and did her pendulum again. It had never, at least never that she knew of, lied to her. Every day for the past week she'd done her pendulum and gotten the same *yes* from it. Perhaps, she thought, she wasn't doing it right or something contrary was influencing it. Or could it just be that her pendulum was tired? It certainly appeared lively enough now as once again, suspended from her fingers, it swung to and fro, insisting emphatically that, yes, Springer would get back stone 588.

The intercom buzzed.

It was the lobby wanting to know if a Mr. Raggio and another gentleman were expected.

While they were on the way up Audrey hurried downstairs to awaken Springer, who was dozing in the deep of their favorite sofa. He got up, went into the guest bath, and shocked the laggardness out of his face with several splashes of cold water. Audrey checked her face in a mirror and decided it was good enough.

Springer answered the door, opened it, and didn't step aside until his eyes had told Danny that coming here was out of line and Danny's eyes had said he knew that and it didn't matter. They went into the living room. Danny introduced the guy with him as a friend named Dave. The guy didn't have the look of what he was. No broken nose or pointed black shoes. He had on gold wire-rimmed glasses, and his brush mustache was trying to make up for the hair he was losing. Danny was wearing a suit and tie, so Springer surmised this wasn't an impromptu visit.

Danny took a chair before it was offered. Friend Named Dave remained standing, sort of hat in hand without a hat.

Did they want something to drink?

No drinks.

Springer got himself some iced coffee, just to delay the situation to that extent and get a better reading of it. He was barefoot, his shirt badly wrinkled from being napped in. He chose the chair directly across from Danny. He wanted to start off with letting Danny know how pissed he was with this violation of their territorial understanding, and all the more so because this was Audrey's place and the likes of Friend Named Dave didn't belong any closer to it than street level. Instead, Springer asked casually, "What's up?"

"I haven't heard from you," Danny said.

"You were supposed to?"

Danny turned his hands palms up, as though Springer should put something in them. "You tell me," he said, cold.

Maybe Danny was feeling slighted, believed he had some big thanks coming for his help in the burglary, Springer thought. If that was it, it was bullshit. Danny had made the thing business by insisting that he handle all of the take.

"Let's you and me go into another room and talk," Danny told Springer.

"You've got something your friend shouldn't hear?"

Danny's eyes shifted to Audrey and back.

Audrey was trying to fathom why Danny appeared so different to her in these surroundings. It occurred to her that up to now her exposure to him had been limited to restaurants. She felt that she was seeing his real dimensions for the first time. His slickness that she'd thought amusing was now just slippery, his smarts were self-servingly shrewd. There were thick, hard underlayers to his likable toughness in this light, Audrey realized. "Whatever you do," she said archly, "don't pretend I'm not here." She transposed her crossed legs.

Normally that would have evoked Danny's best Italian smile, but now he went right through it, asked Springer, "You get what you were after from the Townsend thing?"

"No."

"Sorry to hear that."

"Yeah."

"You got nothing?"

"Nothing."

"How's Jake doing?"

Springer shrugged, didn't really reply because he felt Danny hadn't really asked. He was right. Danny took it quickly in another direction. "Doesn't figure," he said. "Even when we give it the benefit of the doubt and all that shit it still doesn't figure." He paused, looked off to his right at one of Modigliani's better elongated faces. For a moment it almost seemed he was studying the painting. "Nobody takes a shot like the Townsend thing and comes away with nothing," he remarked. "I ask you, if we could exchange mouths and ears, would you believe it?"

"Probably not."

"My people don't. I don't."

Springer didn't let show how much that affected him. A mixture of anger and disappointment. "I'm holding out on you, kept something aside for myself?"

"That's it."

"If I had kept a little something I deserved it."

"We don't do business like that. We make a deal we keep a deal. Our agreement was for the whole package."

Audrey squirmed in her chair. She combed at her hair with her fingers, settled into a slouch and sat up again.

Why was she so suddenly fidgety? Springer wondered. No doubt, like himself, she'd had enough of this, was anxious to have it over and Danny and Friend Named Dave gone.

"What exactly am I supposed to be holding out?" Springer asked.

"Twelve stones," Danny replied, a sharp eye on Springer's reaction. "The twelve Russian stones you got for a client about a month ago."

Springer had shared with Danny his good feelings about making that deal. He had expressed rather avidly his appreciation for the quality of those Russian goods.

"You fell in love with those stones," Danny said. "Had this chance at them and couldn't pass."

"Why me?"

"It's an amateur move, you're the amateur."

"As far as I know they weren't even in Townsend's inventory."

"They were there."

"They weren't there," Audrey put in staunchly. "I saw everything that came from the vault. I would have surely seen them."

Danny brought out some papers from his jacket pocket. About a dozen pages. They were copies of the computer printout listing Townsend's inventory. The same that Townsend had submitted to the insurance adjuster and the police. Each item or lot that had been stolen was so indicated and boldly circled. Halfway down one of the pages convincingly included and encircled was the lot of twelve Russian stones. They were described in detail and in the far right column was their worth. A fifteen million loss.

Springer passed the printouts to Audrey and waited for her to finish reading that particular entry before he told Danny pointedly, "Never saw them."

"Neither did I." Audrey's chin went up a defiant notch.

"Possibly he was using those stones to pad his loss," Springer suggested.

Danny scrunched his face, an ugly no. "Townsend, like everybody, fattened up his loss. By about twenty, twenty-five percent, we figure. We're allowing that much from the package. But that fat he put on was goods out of his head, not goods like this Russian stuff that we know are for real."

Good Friend Dave had left his spot, was now wandering around, looking at things. He picked up a Galle cameo glass vase and held it up to the window light to better see its lavender to deep purple treescape.

Springer was afraid if he told him to put the Galle down he'd drop it on purpose. Safer, probably, to ignore the bastard. Springer sat forward on the edge of his chair for emphasis. "I don't give a fuck how your people see it," he said. "I don't have those stones." Springer found himself hoping Danny wouldn't say he believed him.

Danny didn't say anything.

"While we're at it, is there anything else I'm supposed to be holding back?" Springer asked.

"Just those," Danny said. His eyes had turned suddenly icy lethal.

Exactly like the never-forgotten eyes of Just John, Springer realized. He stared right into them, told them, "You're wrong."

"That your stand?"

"That's my stand."

Danny got up, gestured to Good Friend Dave.

They didn't wait to be shown out.

Springer didn't know when he'd be seeing Danny again, but, whenever, it wouldn't be the same.

Audrey quickly bolted the front door. She waited time enough, then called down to the lobby and asked if the two gentlemen had left. Told that they had, Audrey did a blithesome, pivoting, arm-floating Isadora Duncan accompanied by her hums and trills of laughter twice around the living room. She finally dropped into the sofa with her throat arched and the rest of her body contrived in a graceful pose.

Springer was also glad the unpleasantness with Danny was over, but not to the extent of dancing. Audrey, for some reason, was overreacting, he thought. He went to the sofa, stood above her. He knew from such previous playfulnesses the rule was she wouldn't break her pose until he acknowledged it in some active loving way. His Galatea.

This time he ran a single tender finger along the line of her throat, from her chin all the way down to that tensely defined little cup between her collar bones.

At once she came to life, came up to him, brushing his lips with her own, implying that more of a kiss was imminent. She kept her face close to his, the tips of their noses nearly touching. Now she was his beautiful Cyclops. At that range she asked, "Do you have those Russian diamonds?"

"No," he replied. "Do you?"

"Nope."

She felt that her mind was wide open and he, of all people, should be able to read it. When, after a long moment, he didn't say anything about what she was thinking, she stood abruptly. "I'll be back in a breath," she promised and bounded up the stairs two at a time. Went through her bedroom to her dressing room to one of her dressers. Third drawer from the top. She disturbed the tranquillity of neatly layered lingerie to get at something in the deep corner of that drawer.

A black, truly silk stocking.

With its foot stuffed and tied off with a knot.

Like a homemade sachet.

She hurried down the stairs with it, twirling it around her head as though it were a bolo. On her way she got a large pair of scissors from her writing desk in the study.

Springer was where she'd left him, seated on the sofa. She swung the stocking before his eyes, back and forth as she would her pendulum. It was teasing. He couldn't get a good look at it. What the hell was she up to?

She knelt beside the glass-topped table that was in front of the sofa. Holding the stocking above the table she used the scissors to snip it just below the knot.

They poured from the stocking.

To the glass top of the table.

(Causing Springer to recall at that instant, but only for an instant because it only circumstantially applied, Seggerman and his hooker that day at the Parker Meridien.)

Bounced, scattered in all directions, piled up. Many hopped off onto the rug.

Diamonds.

Rubies, emeralds, sapphires too.

Round cuts, fancy cuts, every conceivable cut, ranging in size from a single carat to fifteen carats.

About forty million worth.

Springer was stunned.

In mimicking mobsterese Audrey explained. "What we got here, lover-boy, is Townsend's fat." Meaning, of course, the twenty-five percent Danny and his people assumed Townsend had tacked on to his loss. Thus conceded, these goods would never be sought.

Springer now understood why Audrey had been so edgy in Danny's presence.

She anticipated his question. "While you were so desperately fishing in the vault, Strand took a couple of handfuls from the shoe box and put them in a pocket of your vest. I guess he didn't believe it was fair, your coming away with nothing."

"Strand, huh?" Springer said thoughtfully, picturing Strand's generous moment, liking it. "And I suppose you had nothing to do with it."

An ever so slight evasive shrug from Audrey. She shifted the aim of her eyes to above Springer's head, then to the left and to the right as though spotting something in the air. "Remind me to burn some sage to get rid of all the negativity," she said. "God, but they brought in a lot of negativity."

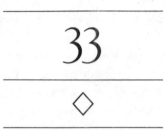

33

Libby gave a graceful little tug to each fingertip of her pale yellow gloves. She hardly ever wore gloves any more; however, when she did she enjoyed gradually peeling them off, having someone anticipate the emergence of her hands.

She shoved the gloves anywhere into her handbag, as though they were now used, discardable things. She brought out a platinum Tiffany case, popped it open for a cigarette. Cancer fear had influenced her to quit smoking fifteen years ago. That, along with becoming a believer of a highly regarded dermatologist who claimed that smoking strangled the capillaries and thus hastened aging. Up until then she'd averaged twenty a day of a blend especially concocted to suit her taste by Dunhill in London. Wherever in the world she happened to be, Dunhill had seen to it that she was freshly supplied. Just recently they'd been notified and resumed shipping to her.

She held the cigarette between her index and middle fingers, poised about four inches from her mouth.

Wintersgill was quick with his lighter.

Libby's first inhale was a deep one. "Brooke Edgerton died yesterday," she said.

"So I understand," Wintersgill said. "Will you be going to her funeral?"

"Don't be macabre." Libby sliced him with a sharp side glance. "Who would you say will be her executors?"

"Doesn't she have a son?"

"He was drowned sailing or something years ago. I know because she seldom called unless it was to tell me her tragedies, large or small. At least this is one she can't unload on me."

"Right off I'd say Loomis, Hird and Longstreth will be handling her estate."

"Seems I've met Longstreth, haven't I?"

"Very likely. I've played squash with Loomis any number of times, but not for the past year or so. He's gone to fat."

"Can Loomis be gotten to?"

"Possibly. Why?"

"Brooke owned a Whistler portrait that I've always coveted. One of those subtly washed, rather incomplete-looking things Whistler did while in his Japanese spell. As soon as the Freer Gallery or the Glasgow Museum hear they'll pounce on it. I thought we might be able to get the early inside track."

"I'll see what I can do."

Libby waited a moment before remarking curtly, "You didn't write it down, Thomas."

"It's not something I would forget," Wintersgill contended.

"That doesn't matter. Up until now you've always written things down, and I prefer that you continue to do so." Her words came from her mouth with smoke around them. She liked the effect.

Wintersgill took out his little note pad and pretended to scribble on it.

They were at the River Club, as far east as anyone could go on 52nd Street and just about as far as anyone could go socially. The

Whitneys and the Astors belonged. So did the Vanderbilts, Hitch-cocks, and Mellons. Libby had been a member of the River for more years than she cared to admit and, like so many well-bred well-offs she covered her social flanks by also belonging to such other private clubs as the Brook, the Colony, and the Union.

Libby didn't use the River much. She never attended the Thurs-day night buffets that for so long for so many had been both enter-taining and convenient, inasmuch as Thursday by tradition was cook's night off. In fact Libby hadn't even been downstairs to the bar in over ten years. She found most of those in her caste (she never used the word *class* in that context) to be bloodless bores. Being a snob was one thing—there was a certain give-and-take amusement in snobbery—but to be a bore and remain a bore when one had been told one was a bore was inexcusable, Libby believed. There was one particular New York City club that she referred to as Menopause Manor.

Libby used the River mainly to fend off impositions in a nice way. When acquaintances she didn't want to entirely ignore came to the city, she counterbalanced whatever excuse she invented for not being able to see them with arranging for them to be put up at the River. She also used the River for business tête-à-têtes with Wintersgill, such as the one she was having now.

A table had been set up for tea in the bay window of the library, a sofa pushed out of the way to accommodate it. Libby's own linens and silver were used. Also her own early eighteenth-century Meissen tea service, a brocaded Imari pattern with an elaborate floral border and cartouches of gold phoenix birds. Libby had acquired the tea service from Baroness Eugène de Rothschild. The tea caddy alone had cost seven thousand. When not in use it was kept there at the River, locked in its own special box.

The tea had steeped enough.

Libby poured, filling Wintersgill's cup before her own. As a cour-tesy in return, Wintersgill waited for her to take first sip. The tea tasted a bit off, Libby thought. She was as fussy about her tea as she was about anything. It had to be Oolong Extra Fancy from Formosa. The sort known as a "handkerchief tea" because the precious little that was grown was picked with great care and carried from bush to plantation in a silk handkerchief.

Lifting the lid from the Meissen tea caddy, Libby reached in for a pinch. The large white-tipped leaves were definitely her Oolong Extra Fancy.

"Also make a note to replace what's here with some fresh oolong," she instructed Wintersgill.

Again he pretended to scribble.

Libby gazed out the bay window to the small but conscientiously manicured terrace four stories below. In the days before the F.D.R. Drive was constructed, members had been able to bring their yachts right up to where that terrace was. It had been a pleasant convenience. There should be more attention given to the preservation of pleasant conveniences, Libby thought, as she watched the cars, many of them dreadful rattletraps, going up and down the drive.

"Do you have any opinion about selling the Penobscot house?" she asked Wintersgill.

"Is that what you want to do?"

"I ask for an opinion, I get a question. What the hell is going on with you, Thomas?"

Wintersgill apologized. He didn't care if the Penobscot house sunk into the bay. "Large summer places such as that are not in demand. They require too much heat and help."

"No matter. I suggest we list it with Sotheby's. Let them worry about getting a price." Libby broke the corner from a fan of Fortnum & Mason shortbread. Eating it made her mouth want another cigarette. "That about does it from my end of the court," she said. "What do you have for me?"

Wintersgill transferred the cup and saucer from his thigh to the table. Went into his business case. "We had a bit of unfortunate timing. Those twelve Russian diamonds you had me give to Townsend were lost in his burglary." Wintersgill showed Libby his copy of Townsend's computer printout and Townsend's receipt. "As you can see, I gave him the twelve stones a week ago Monday, as you requested. They were stolen the following day."

Libby let that bother her for a few seconds. "Oh, well." She sighed.

"*Tant pis.* I suppose we can use the write-off."

Wintersgill nodded. He knew her, knew those twelve diamonds were now out of her mind, as if they'd been washed from a slate. She'd never give them another thought. He was over that hump. Now for the next. "As you surely recall," he said "a week ago today after speaking to you on the phone and getting your permission, I made a payment on account to Townsend. I thought you might want to see the receipt of transfer."

Wintersgill handed it to Libby. It was, indeed, an official bank receipt indicating that twenty million dollars had been transferred from one of Libby's accounts in Zurich to account number 3083W1820 at the private bank of Starzenegger et Cie in Vaduz, Liechtenstein.

Libby read the transfer carefully. It seemed to be in order. "I wasn't aware that Townsend had an account in Liechtenstein," she commented. "I thought he always relied on Zurich and Geneva."

"You know how Gilbert was. Whenever anyone even mentioned that the Swiss were being pressured to end their secrecy, he was ready to take his funds elsewhere."

"That's true." Libby pursed her lips and exhaled a funnel of white. "How do you feel about this loss?" she asked.

"Fate could have been a day or two kinder to us," Wintersgill replied.

"I'll keep this for a while," Libby said as she folded the bank transfer receipt and tucked it into the zippered pocket of her handbag.

Wintersgill didn't like that. He had expected she would dismiss this matter as easily as she had the other, and all the others previous. He wasn't alarmed, but it did make him uneasy. She had no way, at least not that he could think of offhand, of finding out that the Liechtenstein account was his, a shell that he'd had and activated last Wednesday with the twenty-million deposit.

"Don't you have any *good* news?" Libby asked.

"I assume you still don't want to see any annual reports of Hull corporations?"

"Hell, no. A forty-page annual report is like a man taking an hour to open his fly."

Wintersgill laughed a bit too heartily.

Libby merely grinned at her remark, as though she had uncountable others.

"As usual I've prepared a summary of quarterly earnings and dividends for you." He handed her several legal-sized pages. "They're quite healthy."

Libby scanned the figures on the pages. For those few moments her eyes were serious calculators. Bottom line, she was most satisfied with her income. "Is there anything else?" she asked.

"Might I have more tea?"

A waiter was summoned. He hurried off with the pot and the caddy to brew some fresh.

Wintersgill closed and snapped shut his business case. He smoothed back the parted side of his hair with the heel of his hand. Stretched his neck to reset it within the circumference of his shirt collar. Gently squeezed the soft silk knot of his tie. These were all hyphenating actions, premeditated to set apart the personal from the business.

Wintersgill smiled at Libby, the sort of smile that asked for one in return. "What I wish very much to discuss," he said, "is the matter of us."

"Oh, shit, Thomas, let's not get into that again."

"I haven't mentioned it in nearly a year . . . "

"Seems like last week."

" . . . and at that time you left me hanging on the rather promising note that you would think about it."

"I always say that. I can't believe that you're so dense you don't realize by now that it means *no*—no and no again."

"May I suggest that perhaps you've merely gotten into the habit of saying no? What you might do, for the sake of objectivity, is take a step back, consider what an advantageous arrangement our marriage would be."

"You're a persistent bastard, I'll say that for you."

The tea was brought.

Libby poured.

"I enjoy having you pour for me," Wintersgill remarked romantically.

For some reason the tea was now as it should be: a high amber color with a distinctive delicate taste. "Now that's my Oolong Extra!" Libby exclaimed after her first sip.

Wintersgill got right back onto the subject. "Don't you want me, Libby?"

"I already have you," she said matter-of-factly.

Wintersgill didn't rise to that. "I see beyond your defensive exterior," he said.

A dubious smirk from Libby. She had to admit, however, it was nice to know that *someone* was looking that deep, albeit a Wintersgill.

"You need love," he said.

"Like I need another hysterectomy." She punctuated that with an arched brow and a sip of oolong. "As a matter of fact, it just occurred to me that love between us would *be* rather like surgery. One of us would make incisions while the other pleaded for anesthesia."

"You're playing with me."

"I'm not." She grinned.

"You're behaving badly."

"Then I'm taking a respite from my usual self." She laughed and shifted about in her chair, enjoying, through her silk Givenchy dress, the slicking sensation of her thighs on the leather seat. "Tell you what, Thomas," she said, "let's put an end to this once and for all. You give me the single most convincing reason why I should marry you . . . and I'll tell you one why I shouldn't."

"Libby, damn it, I'm serious and you're making a game of it."

"Winner take all," she said enticingly.

She'd never before allowed the proposal to be taken this far. Wintersgill was encouraged, believed she'd at last shown a chink in her wall. What he chose to say next would be vitally important, he thought. Why she should marry him? His attractive appearance? His sexual prowess and endowment? His correctly educated mind? His stalwart attitude, tolerant nature, sense of humor? The strong comfort he would forever be? All those attributes went into the making up of his splendid personal portfolio; however, there was one thing, in his estimation above all else, that made him most worthy, that would, when she was reminded of it, sway her.

Confidently he told her, "You should marry me because of who I am. A Wintersgill." It was as plain as that, obvious to him and therefore certainly to her—the unquestionable breeding, the impeccable line of descent he was offering her.

Libby was astonished. A throwback, she thought, that's what he is. At least in this regard. Doesn't he know that these days a lordship or even an earldom that predates the Norman conquest can be bought in England for less than fifteen thousand dollars? That by merely purchasing a run-down estate in Italy one can become an instant marquesa?

She told him so.

He huffed a bit. "That's a far cry from being an authentic Wintersgill," he said. "Besides—"

"You've had your say, now allow me to have mine."

He politely gave way with a nod. Whatever her argument, he felt he would be able to parry it.

"The reason I won't marry you is—you're dishonest."

Wintersgill drew himself up indignantly.

"Exceedingly dishonest," Libby said.

"That's absurd. Where did you ever get that impression?"

"The First Industrial Bank of Philadelphia," she said, as though it were the title of something she was about to recite.

Wintersgill appeared perplexed.

"In nineteen seventy-eight, in cahoots with the chairman of that bank, who happens to be one of your old school chums with a name as old and above reproach as Wintersgill, you arranged for the purchase of one hundred million dollars in stolen securities. You paid the thief two and a half cents on the dollar, only that much because those stocks and bonds were on the hot list, the computerized roster of stolen securities maintained by the Securities and Exchange Commission. You sold the securities to your chum, the banker, for twenty-five cents on the dollar, netting yourself a tidy twenty-two and a half million. The bank was not concerned with the hot list because it had no intention of ever cashing those securities. The question of whether or not they were stolen would never come up. The bank would hold them and year after year include them in its assets, increasing its financial ability to borrow from the Federal Reserve and giving it that much more money to make money with. Such a safe, neat deal. The bonds won't mature until the year two thousand and something. By then everyone concerned will be dead or too feeble to fuck with. I'll bet anything at this very moment those stolen securities are wrapped in plain brown paper and sitting in some corner of the First Industrial's vault. Probably stacked alongside other securities equally stolen, wouldn't you say?"

Wintersgill didn't comment, didn't even blink. Silence, he believed, was his best defense. It was also an admission. Inside he was churning, wondering how she could have gotten her information, dates, and figures so accurate.

"Then," Libby went on, "there's the skimming you've been doing at the Foundation. Like a damn squirrel salting away acorns."

Wintersgill's eyes wavered.

Libby advised herself not to carry this too far. Wintersgill had been of advantageous use and would continue to be. She altered her tone from accusing to condescending. "What I resent most about the skimming is it indicates your estimation of me, as though I'm so lah-dee-dah I wouldn't notice. Hell, Thomas, as long as you don't get overly greedy I don't mind your helping yourself to a bit of the cream."

Her smile was like a suture intended to close his wound.

He'd forgotten that he was still holding his teacup and saucer. He set them down on the table so roughly they rattled.

"Careful with my Meissen!" Libby reproached.

The next thing Wintersgill knew, her chair was vacant and she was outside getting into the limousine. Wintersgill stood, close up to the tall library windows that were right there, level with the street. When the chauffeur, Groat, closed the car door after her and walked around to get behind the steering wheel, his eyes momentarily clicked with Wintersgill's. Then the car was gone and Wintersgill was left in the wake of the unpleasant episode. There were so many angry, humiliated voices in him he didn't know which to heed.

Taking up a silver teaspoon he struck a large chip from one of her Meissen saucers.

He had scheduled appointments with his tailor and to have his hair trimmed by Gio at the Pierre. He didn't even bother to call and cancel, was driven straight home to his apartment on East 68th Street.

It was more of a relief than usual to be there, to take sanctuary in air he felt was his own. He switched on the lights in the wide entrance hallway that served also as a gallery for the portraits of his forebears. They were hung side by side in identical frames, each receiving his share of illumination. They bore such a resemblance to one another that anyone scanning them might think they were the same man in stages of modernization.

One portrait, that of an early eighteenth-century Wintersgill, was awry. The housekeeper, Mrs. Donnell, had again been too hasty with her dusting. Wintersgill had spoken to her about that, but finding that portrait out of place tonight was too trivial a thing to disturb him. He merely corrected it. Left his business case beneath the hall table, bypassed the large formal living room, and entered the study. Rather ritualistically, he made martinis in the Georgian silver pitcher he had long ago designated for that purpose. From a proper glass he drank most of the first martini while standing. He decided he wouldn't, for the time being, think of the problem of Libby. His ability to put things, no matter how bothersome, out of his mind at will was something that had always given him an advantage.

Mrs. Donnell had a roast on, he now realized from the wholesome fragrance that he could have smelled before. He topped his martini just short of the spilling point and, as a test of the steadiness of his hand, carried it into his dressing room.

He undressed.

He would shave. It was not a question of whether he would or not. He normally shaved twice each day, the second time at this hour.

His bathroom was a large area, tastefully designed, done in gray marble, beveled mirror, and polished brass fittings. The gray marble dominated and gave it a gentlemanly feeling. The bathtub was custom made, narrower and longer than standard to better accommodate Wintersgill's height and leanness. The tub was centered in the room, inset so that it was level with the floor. An abundance of dark gray towels from Porthault were stacked beside it; farther off to the side, Régence chaises, a pair of them, were covered in a soft gray flannel.

To shave, Wintersgill used his grandfather's Sèvres mug and badger bristled brush, his great-grandfather's straight razor. He'd heard his father claim thousands of times that no modern safety razor could match the shave this straight razor gave. What total length of Wintersgill whisker had this razor cut away over the generations? Miles of whisker, Wintersgill imagined. Such functional consistency was deserving of high regard, he reminded himself to believe each time he took up this razor. Its handle was yellowed and minutely crackled the way ivory gets with age, its gold inset monogram worn from being so often held, but its blade was untarnished, as gleaming as the day it had been bought in London three generations ago. It took to being honed to a fine cutting edge, as though it presumed eternity.

Finished shaving, Wintersgill respectfully washed and dried the razor and put it back into its fitted red leather case. He showered and dressed, chose to wear beige summer-weight gabardine slacks, a matching cotton crew-neck pullover, and a pair of leather loafers so supple they could be doubled up by the mere pinch of a finger and thumb.

Dinner was ready. He ate very slowly, not consciously procrastinating. After dinner he settled in a chair in the study for his usual *digestif* reading. An 18K bookmark helped him cut to the place where he'd left off in the leatherbound Paris edition of *The Memoirs of Madame de Montespan.* Within moments he was caught up in the personal impressions of this mistress of Louis Quatorze, entertained by the obliquity of her phrases as she described, for example, the four-inch heels, heavy perfumes, and diamond-studded laces worn by the king's brother.

Mrs. Donnell came to let Wintersgill know that she was done for the day. He nodded almost imperceptibly, without even looking at her. However, when she was on her way out the service entrance he listened with his entire attention to her closing of the door, her keys double-locking it—and he nearly believed what he heard.

He sat there in the silence, the book lowered to his lap. The atmosphere seemed changed now that he was alone, the familiarity of it could not be taken for granted. Nonsense, he told himself, he was only sensing the absence of sound. He got up and put on a cassette of Bartok's Violin Concerto No. 2 in B Minor, adjusting the volume in case there might occur other sounds in the apartment that it would be prudent for him to hear.

He went back to Madame de Montespan and was in the third sentence of one of her paragraphs when . . .

Libby intruded.

She'd been tampering all the while with the seal of his mental gate that was supposed to keep her shut up until he was ready for her. It had been his decision that he wouldn't allow her out until tomorrow, not until after he'd had a good night's rest, was calmed, cleared, better able to settle upon what shape he should assume to fit what was now known of him. But here Libby was, sneaking out into his night. He wouldn't allow it. He poked her back where she belonged, prodded her with the pretense that the episode at the River Club had never happened. Hell, he hadn't even been at the River Club that afternoon.

There, that should do it. Gate closed.

On with Madame de Montespan.

Wintersgill's eyes ran the printed words, but the words never reached destination. In the milliseconds it normally took for his mind to recognize each word and connect it with its meaning . . .

Libby interposed.

Came right out the gate.

Where the hell was his gatekeeper, anyway, his guardian of sanity, the chemical thing that saw to whatever was allowed to get in or come out of him? What a terrible time for his gatekeeper to be remiss. Probably Libby had tricked the gatekeeper, bought off the gatekeeper.

Wintersgill closed the seventeenth century, the stretched red leather that the animate Madame de Montespan had been reduced to. He placed the book on the side table, straightened it so it symmetrically coincided with the other books there, demonstrating his confidence that he would be reading it again soon.

He walked the apartment. With Libby. From study to bedroom to living room to study.

The Bartok sounded somewhat screechy now.

Who, Wintersgill wondered, had been Libby's source of information on his stolen bond deal with First Industrial of Philadelphia? Only he and Lawrence Vickrey had been involved, and Lawrence wasn't the sort who was easily shaken, surely wouldn't incriminate himself unless, of course, he'd been hopelessly cornered. Had Libby managed that? How? When had she found out about those stolen bonds? Did she know about the others? She'd intimated as much.

The bitch.

She'd been looking down his throat all the while. That was the humiliating thing of it. A veritable voyeur of his misdemeanors, she'd overseen his every move while appearing to be distracted with extravagances and vanities.

The devious bitch.

How much of him had she exposed? Possibly she knew within a thousand the amount he'd skimmed from the Foundation. He could have been much more clever about it, but her behavior had lulled him. Now it was easy to imagine her keeping tabs on him, a running account of Swiss and Bahamian deposits that, at whim, she'd be able to hold against him.

But hadn't he known all along that she'd known? He must have sensed it. Surely. That would explain why he'd been so insistent about marrying her. By consenting she would have been forgiving.

Do you, Elizabeth Hopkins-Hull, forgive this man . . . ?

That was it. What he'd really been after was neither her social standing nor access to the power of her wealth but, rather, immunity.

The cunt.

The way she'd manipulated his conscience, finessed him into doing things he would never have otherwise done. Those many times over the years he'd catered to the libidinal warp of her, been intimidated into playing the part of her erotic stuntman. All those hard-ons had been hers, not his. And the same went for the comings. She was a glutton for comings. Her own, her rare own, were not enough. He'd been only an implement while led to feel the conspirator. Hadn't had a single quality sensation that he could now remember.

The violin performing the Bartok had become a wounded, beaked thing swooping around. With the flick of a switch, Wintersgill put it out of its misery and out of his own. The silence was such relief that for a full minute he didn't relate it to his being alone.

He went into the kitchen.

It wasn't out of singular distrust of Mrs. Donnell that he checked to make sure she'd locked the service door. That door was, after all, where the apartment was most vulnerable, he believed, and he wasn't about to stake his well-being on anyone's competence. Certainly no one cared as much for his safety as he did.

The door was locked. He saw that. But it didn't matter. He unlocked it and relocked it himself, watching the vertical bolt of the Segal unit snap into place. He inserted the security chain and thought he would unlock and lock the Segal again, but he didn't want to get stuck on it. Not tonight. He wouldn't get stuck on anything tonight.

From the refrigerator he got a tall glass of buttermilk for his bedside because his hiatal hernia might act up. He checked the lock of the front door twice, and, leaving on certain adequate lights, he went into the master bedroom.

His bed was turned down as he expected it would be. His extra pillows arranged just so. The bed linens were immaculate, ready to receive him if he undressed completely, not merely took off his shoes as he so often did. He padded into the bathroom. Brushed his teeth with Elgydium, the French toothpaste whose strong fennel flavor he disliked but felt was better for his gums. As he brushed he avoided looking into the mirror because something in him had suggested his reflection would not be there. When he was through brushing he risked it, raised his eyes, and . . . there he was!

To that extent reassured, he returned to the bedroom. There, awaiting him again, were the three doors, the every night doors and their arbitrary dead bolts. Originally there had been only the one door leading from the main hallway, and that one was still most critical. The only access to the master bath and dressing room was through the bedroom they served, so under normal circumstances there would be no need for doors to them. But in Wintersgill's mind those were places where whoever might want to could hide and wait until he was helplessly asleep. So, for the sake of his nights, he'd had the doors put in and the dead bolts installed.

He looked to see there was water at bedside before closing up. Nothing could more easily set him off than needing something from outside the bedroom once he'd closed up. Beneath the skirt of his bed was an antique English chamber pot hand-painted with roses. Only he knew its purpose was more than decorative. He emptied it first thing each morning.

In the order that his mind required he closed the doors, listening carefully for the confirming clicks of the tongues of their locksets. His whole night depended on his believing his fingers and the dead bolts. He focused intently on them. He didn't feel the small, brass, half-moon-shaped knobs of the bolts. It was enough to ask his mind to accept what his eyes said they saw. As an aid he'd made a red line on the brass faceplate of the knob which the knob was supposed to correspond to when in a locked position. The red line device had worked for a while, until he couldn't depend on believing it.

Tonight he wouldn't need red lines or anything, he told himself. He felt all right about the dead bolts. The bedroom was definitely locked. No one could get to him.

On the surface of his bedside table, next to his glass of water and his glass of buttermilk, he lined up a two-milligram white, a five-milligram yellow, and a ten-milligram blue. At this point he never knew what strength Valium a night might be. This one had the temperate climate of a yellow night, he thought, but in any case he was prepared.

Into bed.

On his back.

The top sheet gently molded against him. His head indented the down-filled pillow with its shape. He would dry-read himself to sleep with the original French version of Brillat-Savarin's *The Physiology of Taste.*

The book was in his hand and he was readying his eyes for it when his mind told him he should wonder about Libby. Where was she? He'd damn well put her in her place. Hadn't he so precisely pegged her for the self-centered manipulator she was that she'd retreated and closed the gate behind her?

Not entirely.

The gate of his mind that was supposed to keep her confined—she was swinging on it. Back and forth, away and diminishing, then forward and dominant. The gatekeeper was fucking off again.

If Libby was motivated and resourceful enough to uncover that piece of Philadelphia business, as close to the vest as it had been, Wintersgill thought, she might very well get to the truth of the twenty million Townsend thing he'd just pulled off. It was conceivable that nothing, no one, was beyond her reach, certainly not some bank officer in Liechtenstein with all the secrets in his head. Libby would have someone have that bank officer open and spilling out in no time.

Wintersgill recalled the smug way she'd folded that bank transfer receipt and put it in her handbag. Obvious to him now that she intended to do something with it, use it to check up on the transaction. And when she found out the twenty million had been deposited into an account that was his, how much deeper would she delve? Might she just recover the money, reprimand or dismiss him, and let it go at that? Fuck, no. She of all people would smell the more that was behind it. It would be hard for him to sell Townsend's death as a coincidence. Surely Libby wouldn't buy it. She'd pry around and pay off until she had him tied to it, and then she'd enjoy having it be up to her whether or not she preferred to make a stink of it.

A Wintersgill indicted for murder.

A Wintersgill in prison.

For him, almost as much hell would be Libby forever holding that possibility over his head. She would thoroughly document the mess with records: facts to substantiate facts, depositions. She'd put it all in a sealed dossier that the Hull lawyers would be instructed to get into whenever she gave them the nod.

Gone then, rendered ineffective, would be the ledger on her that

Wintersgill had been compiling over the years, the privacies he knew about her, had done for her. All those things he'd never brought out but that they both understood were there, keeping them more or less in balance. She'd have him groveling. She'd have him fucking collies on a treadmill twice a week.

The slut.

The pretentious slut. *Elle pète plus haute qu'elle a le cul,* as the French so aptly say of her sort: She farts higher than her asshole.

For the next two hours Wintersgill lay there, his rage ripening. The Libby in him kept at him, and as if she wasn't enough, now there were also Audrey and Springer to contend with. Audrey and Springer came out from another of his mental gates to side with Libby. They ganged up on him, the three of them. Every accusation, every threat from Libby was also from Audrey, and she was inseparable from Springer.

Wintersgill lay there festering.

With too much of a grip on himself. His legs and arms tensed, drawn up as though their tendons were thongs of leather going dry.

The promising bed linens had betrayed him, were now confused, wilted. Every pillow had given up its comforting puff.

He had swallowed the yellow five and the blue ten, but they didn't help with the gatekeeping.

Brillat-Savarin had been dropped spine first to the floor.

Wintersgill, self-sorry, was resigned to having to get up and check the dead bolts. His confidence that they were locked was long lost. The bedroom bolts would only be the start of it, he knew. Once he was up and concerned with those he would also have to do the service door and the front door again, and there was no telling how many lockings and relockings it would take for him to convince himself before he could get back to the bedroom to cope with the locking and relocking there, the fixing of his eyes upon the crack between the door and the doorjamb, anticipating the horizontal movement of the brass bolt as it slid into place, trying to put stock in it.

By time time he would be in such a rising spiral of disbelief and fear he would have to *look* the room. Down on his belly to look beneath the bed and see only floor there but not believe that and have no choice except to continue looking, lifting and lowering the bed-skirt time after time. It wouldn't matter that the bed frame was only seven inches from the floor and that it would be impossible for anyone to squeeze under. So caught up in it, he would have lost his sense of proportion.

He would have to look it all—under the commode, the chest, the chaise. Behind the portiere drapes. Such a traditional hiding place they always gave him trouble, those drapes.

And when, exhausted, he was finally convinced that he believed he had everything locked and looked enough, he would get into bed and try to keep himself believing until he fell asleep.

This would be that kind of night, Wintersgill thought.

Unless therapy helped him.

More often than not after therapy he was able to lock right up and go straight to sleep.

At quarter to one he dialed the number.

An hour later he answered the front door.

"I'm Millicent," she said, smiling impressively and stepping in before she was invited.

Not her true name but conscientiously appropriate, Wintersgill thought. She looked Millicent. Tall and brunette with the good bones of a well-bred. More beautiful than pretty. If she'd been gamine or ingenue or horse-faced he would have refused her.

He led her into the living room.

She walked well, he noticed, and he also noticed that she sat nicely in the large armed chair, not up on the edge of it but deep in it as though such luxury was commonplace for her. Everything about her that he took in was important to him, every little thing. She was wearing a knee-length dress of crepe de chine, a dark blue that was just a bit livelier than navy. At the least a good designer copy. It was long-sleeved, ample at the upper arm, tapering to the wrist. The large square-cut stone of the ring on the third finger of her right hand blazed enough to be imagined a diamond, as did the stones of her ear clips.

"May I offer you something to drink?"

"What are you having?"

"Evian." He'd drunk two glasses while awaiting her.

"All right," she said and stipulated, "Evian *sans gaz.*"

"Ice?"

"No," she said, purposely leaving off the thank-you.

While he was getting her Evian she found the money. Where she'd been told it would be: beneath the most recent issue of *Connoisseur* on the table beside her chair. New hundred-dollar bills, twenty of them. She counted them before putting them into her evening bag.

He returned with her Evian in a crystal goblet so fine she felt, as she sipped, it might shatter on her lips.

His gaze was on her.

She met it for a moment with her strong gray eyes and then glanced about the room. "Quite charming," she said as though she almost approved.

Wintersgill tried not to think that she was probably a passé fashion model who hadn't married well but intended to, who was in the throes of that interim stage of having to depend on what she'd saved, which was only herself, and that barely in the nick of time. Keeping herself above the milieu with wardrobe, with address, was vital to her ends. He tried not to think there was nothing more pathetic and more easily compromised to extremes than beauty desperate for money. He studied her nose, decided it hadn't been pared. There was nothing he detested more than a face overly reliant on a revised nose, a peasant looking to pass.

He gulped his Evian and gave her the conversational openings.

Millicent said, rather credibly, that she'd just returned from the Algarve, adored Portugal, adored the people, their eager humility, so different from the French and Italians and especially the Greeks in that respect.

Millicent said, and it seemed entirely possible, that she'd spent most of last winter being shared by Eleuthera and Steamboat Springs. Had he ever skied Steamboat or Crested Butte? Marvelous snow, and not nearly as stuffy as St. Moritz. Although, of course, the accommodations were not adequately seasoned, never would be.

Wintersgill accepted the quality of her voice, its typical affectations, the way it handled vowels. Only once did she give herself away with an error of speech. He was also grateful for her presumptuous and condescending airs. Yes, he concluded, if anyone would do, it was this Millicent.

Without his verbally suggesting it, they went into his bedroom, through, and on into the bath area.

He relaxed on one of the chaises while she undressed. She had on expensive underwear.

He waited until she was nude before he removed his dressing robe to also be nude. He had the start of an erection, just enough tumescence to make him hang heavier. From anticipation rather than from wanting her.

Using both hands she gathered her dark hair back, glanced at him questioningly. He gestured no and she released her hair, got it more or less back into place by tossing and shaking her head haughtily. "I went to an exhibition of jewelry at Christie's yesterday," she said with characteristic ennui. "Only a few pieces were worthwhile: a Schlumberger emerald-and-sapphire choker, for one. The rest were the usual leftovers, things various people we know have, with good reason, tired of."

She stepped down into the elongated, sunken bathtub. No water in it. She stretched out, langorously.

Wintersgill gave the situation a moment to register sufficiently. He went to the tub, straddled it, stood with one foot on each side of it.

From her point of view he loomed like a colossus, his genitals dominant. He controlled the intention of his huge limp cock with his fingers.

She had been instructed not to close her eyes while he urinated on her. She was to cower and protest, express how repelled she was by it, scream out, flail to almost fend it off, writhe evasively.

Her face was cringing ugly with distaste, as Wintersgill shook his cock and the final few drips fell on her. He put on his dressing robe and left her there. She had only five minutes to cleanse, dress, and be gone, because he needed the experience to be as fresh as possible in his mind.

It was two thirty when Wintersgill heard the front door closing behind her.

At four o'clock he was in his bedroom. On the floor behind a bergère. Rivulets of perspiration running down his neck and back and sides, his heart pounding like some separate creature trying to burst out. He had been looking that corner for nearly half an hour, just that empty *corner.*

And there was still most of the room to do.

34

Dance, diamonds, dance.

So glittery and gleeful looking.

It doesn't matter; 47th Street is still a way of woe, habitually heartsick. Even its most prosperous days are enjoyed with characteristic despondency. Ask a 47th Street dealer how business is, and although it's been only an hour since he made the deal of his dreams, he will hunker his head into the shrug of his shoulders, make a glum mouth, and say things could be a lot better. That's how most 47th Street people are. Wouldn't think of passing up a chance to commiserate, to wail at least a little, to find fault. That fault-finding disposition might very well have a lot to do with the way they're forever looking down into diamonds with their magnifying loupes and nearly always coming up with something wrong.

Naturally, in such an atmosphere any rumor of misfortune is quick to spread. Those men in pairs or threes seen huddled on the sidewalks of the street aren't always in the course of making pocket-to-pocket deals. More often than not what they're up to is putting downside rumors in one another's ears.

One such rumor had been along the street for several weeks. Springer & Springer was going to fold, it was said and heard and said. Springer & Springer couldn't recover from the nearly total loss it had recently suffered. Such a pity. See what could all at once happen to even a solid third-generation firm? *Kaput.*

Springer, by merely tearing the corner off an eight-by-ten manila envelope, squelched all that tattle. Out of the envelope and onto his white desk pad poured some ten million dollars' worth of goods, a mix of colored stones and diamonds. A fourth of what Audrey had dropped from her stocking yesterday afternoon. On his way to the office today Springer had stopped at his bank and put the rest of the goods, worth thirty or so million, into his safety deposit box. He had decided to feed the goods into the firm in reasonable portions, so never at any one time would there be more than ten to twelve million in his safe. Then, if he got hit again (an increased possibility, now that he and Danny weren't on good terms), at least he couldn't be wiped out. Not only that. There were taxes. A sudden forty million into the flow of the firm would be a bit much. No need to rub the IRS's nose in it. Business just reasonably better than usual was how things should appear, and, as usual, like everyone else on the street: one set of books, but another in his head.

The goods made a pretty pile on Springer's sorting pad. It wasn't right for them to be in a haphazard mixture like that. Agitated, the diamonds might bully the not-so-hard rubies and sapphires and especially the even softer emeralds, scratch or fracture them. Springer would feel better when they were all sorted and graded and folded away in their individual briefkes. He and his assistant, Linda, would do that together.

When Linda saw the goods pour from the envelope her legs went. She had to sit. In keeping with the code that the right to handle goods belonging to another is never assumed, she asked, "May I?"

Permission granted by Springer with a casual gesture.

Linda used the side of her tweezers randomly to separate some of the goods from the main pile. By lightly running the tweezers back and forth she spread them into a single layer, then isolated several sapphires, intense pinks and Burma blues in the six- to ten-carat range. With professional deftness, she flipped the sapphires over onto their faces so, one at a time, she could more easily get a pinching hold on their girdles and bring them to her eye. While she examined them through her ten-power loupe the sounds that came from her were similar to those usually drawn out by physical ecstasy. She was too loyal and too knowledgeable about the ways of the trade to ask where Springer had gotten these fine goods or how much he'd paid for them.

"We're going to expand," Springer said.

"Looks like we already have."

"From now on you're in charge of all colored goods."

"I'm what?"

He told her again, explained that Springer & Springer would no longer be dealing exclusively in diamonds. She would make sure that was known by all the major dealers of sapphires, rubies, and eme-ralds. She would be calling on the buyers at Cartier and Tiffany, Van Cleef and whoever, charming orders out of them. She would estab-lish sources in Bangkok and be going there at least once a year, and to Bogotá, and probably even more frequently to Paris and Geneva.

It hit Linda's dream so squarely on the nose she had to tell herself it would be awful if she cried. She always looked as though she had an eye infection when she cried. Now was a moment to be at her best.

"Regarding salary," Springer said. "Triple what you're making, and we'll work out some sort of commission."

Linda knew graduate gemologist assistants such as herself who felt trapped in the trade, who had practically given their eyesight, and in some instances much more, to their jobs, and in return received only twenty-five-dollar raises and a spritzer of Estée Lauder for Christmas. This was her break, the helping hoist over the hump. "I'll still be answering to you, won't I?"

"Only when I ask," Springer said lightly.

She thanked him. Three times. Was tempted to get gushy about it. She sent him her most purely grateful look and then, to ease the earnestness of the moment she added a smack of her usual dalliance. "Damn that Audrey," she declared, smiling, which, of course, expressed all the otherwises. She pincered up one of her new charges, a six-carat ruby that she would get no less than twelve thousand a carat for. While momentarily lost in the ruby's blood-red atmosphere, she told Springer in a by-the-way manner, "Mal's here."

"Here in the office?"

"Came in about an hour ago. To get something from his desk, so he said. He's been just sitting in there."

"Do me a favor. Go in and let him know I want to see him."

"Want to or would like to?"

Within a couple of minutes Mal appeared in the doorway, his eyes avoiding Springer's.

"Come on in. Sit down." Springer had never seen Mal's hair so in need of a trim. His sideburns were bushed out, uneven. He had on a fresh shirt but it was missing the second button down. No tie. His suit was badly creased in all the places a suit creases when it's been worn for several days straight. This was Mal but not the same Mal, Springer thought. Different in the eyes and the set of his mouth. That Marcie had stolen more than gems.

"How was the retreat?" Springer asked to begin.

"It was okay."

"Just okay?"

"The food was bad."

"The no-talking part must have been worse."

"Truth is I didn't get there."

"Oh?"

"I was in Pennsylvania but not there. I was in New Hope."

"Great name for a place. Does it live up to it?"

"For some people, maybe."

"What did you do in New Hope?"

"Nothing. Went for walks, tried to sleep a lot. Nothing." It was evident that Mal was ambivalent about being there, facing Springer. He kept glancing in the direction of the door, even had one leg out favoring that side of his chair, ready to take the first exiting step. "What's happening with Jake?" Mal asked.

"He goes in for his second chemotherapy tomorrow morning."

"Poor kid." Just two words but with a lot of caring in them.

The sorting pad on Springer's desk was bare now. Springer had hurriedly scooped up the goods and put them away, only to eliminate the distraction. He sat back, studied his uncle for a long moment, noticed that he'd cut himself while shaving and there was a trace of styptic powder, paler than his complexion, where he'd stopped the bleeding. "Mal," Springer said evenly and with plenty of voice, "what you did stunk."

"I'm sorry. I'll always be sorry," Mal mumbled, hanging his head.

"Sorry isn't enough."

"What can I say?"

"I don't know." A noisy sigh from Springer conveyed exasperation. "But . . . to just up and leave me here to take care of the business the way you did was no fucking way to treat a partner."

"Huh?"

"Maybe you've forgotten how much there is to do. People have goods out on memo and need a nudge, people owe us, clients are in from out of town, there are sights to go to London for, there's always something." Springer's words were harshly angled.

"I thought—"

"What it looks like is you want a free ride. Well, let me tell you, there isn't going to be any free ride. Not on my back."

It was like pumping up a person. Mal sat taller. His chest filled out, and so did his neck and face, visibly recovering.

Springer kept on. "And now, after weeks of fucking off, you show up, but do you show up ready to carry your share? No, you come in a mess, looking like you've been on a train for five days and nights. Christ."

"What do you want me to do?"

Springer sat forward, got Mal by the eyes, told him calmly, softly, "I want you to go home. I want you to stop kicking the shit out of yourself, have a relaxing long weekend, and come in Monday fresh and all set to deal. Can you manage that?"

Mal nodded. Even his eyes had regained some of their former spark. Possibly some of that was because they were welling.

"Did you find what you were looking for in your desk?" Springer asked.

"Yeah. I . . . uh, I just wanted to get my loupe and a couple of personal things. Nothing important."

Springer got up and went to the safe.

"Maybe you should have the combination changed on the safe," Mal suggested, thinking Springer might have already done that.

"Why? Only you and I know it." Springer returned to his desk with a black alligator-covered book: Mal's most recent address and number book with hundreds of active entries in it, from Adele to Zelda. "I figured this was too valuable to just leave there in your desk drawer," Springer said.

Mal accepted the book self-consciously.

"Here's something else," Springer said.

A briefke, no coding or any designation on it.

Mal unfolded it, saw that it contained a dozen diamonds of assorted grades and cuts from a half carat to two carats. With his old practiced hands, Mal shifted the diamonds about, made them show their all, tilted the briefke one way and then the other so the diamonds ran up and down its inner crease. He looked questioningly to Springer.

"A starter kit for your personal use," Springer explained, keeping a straight face.

After Mal left, Linda came back in and she and Springer got started on the new goods. Each stone had to be weighed to the hundredth of a carat, measured to the millimeter, classified, given an appropriate coded identity, placed into its briefke, and itemized on a confidential master list. It was a painstaking task, even for two experienced professionals. It would take days.

They went hard at it, working systematically, doing the colored stones first, not deciding on any prices for those until Linda had a better, longer look at them and the current market. There was more latitude, more room for personal appreciation and opinion in determining the value of colored goods. On the other hand, the value of diamonds was about as fixed as a monetary system. A well-cut two-carat E-graded diamond of VVS1 quality was worth specifically so much on any given day.

Springer told the receptionist to hold all calls except one. That one came in at five o'clock.

"It's been such a long day," Audrey said.

"What have you been doing?" Springer asked.

"Mainly?"

"Mainly."

"Loving the presence of your absence for one thing."

"What else?"

"How about *yearning* you?"

"Nifty."

"Are you looking out your window?"

"I am now."

"Can you see this?"

On a high corner of Trump Tower nine blocks up Fifth Avenue Springer made out a little on-and-off flash, as if the building itself was scintillating in that one spot.

Amused, he asked, "Is that your smile?"

"It's the light in my eyes for you, lover. Telling you to get your ass home."

Audrey was at one of the downtown facing windows of her apartment catching and reflecting the late-day sun with a silver-framed hand mirror.

"You're a compulsive flasher," Springer told her. "That's what you are."

"You'll be forever discovering such colorful things about me."

Springer liked the forever.

"When will you be finished there?" Audrey asked.

"Another hour, hour and a half."

"That's ages. I'll have cobwebs between my knees by then."

There was in her voice the quality that Springer had come to recognize meant if he were to say he'd be there in a few minutes, upon arrival he'd find her supine, waiting.

"What is it you're doing that's so important?" she asked.

He told her what he was doing.

"If you absolutely had to, you could leave there in ten minutes?"

"If."

"Good. I'll also leave here in ten minutes. I'll walk down the shady side of the avenue, you walk up, and we'll meet halfway. We'll shop some windows and you can buy me a triple-dip Häagen-Dazs to get me to do something ingeniously lewd later."

She clicked off before he had a chance to turn down or agree with her suggestion. He knew if he called her back she'd just let it ring. He gathered up the goods he and Linda had processed and those they had yet to do and locked them in the safe. They would continue with them tomorrow.

On the hook on the back of his office door was his suit jacket. Also, hanging there by the strap of its holster harness was his .451 magnum automatic pistol exactly like the one Audrey had fired at the *Town and Country* faces pinned to the old barn in Sherman. Ever since the Townsend robbery, Audrey wouldn't let Springer go anywhere without it. Each time he was leaving the apartment she frisked him to make sure. He tried to kid her out of it but she was adamant, repeated that club-and-sword reasoning of hers, and reminded him again that the world was more violent than ever, merely cloaked in controls.

Disagreeing with her was always such a disagreeable thing for him that he just went along with her on it. It was only a phase, he told himself, probably some temporary offshoot of that craving she had for danger. Would pass.

To accommodate the wearing of her own .451 automatic, Audrey had bought quite a few new things by Giorgio Armani and Perry Ellis. How she wore the weapon depended on what she happened to be wearing. With an opaque and roomy top she wore it in a shoulder holster. With the new looser-legged slacks she wore it in an ankle holster. When neither was the case she tossed it into her carryall. One night when they were dining at La Grenouille she had on a regular-length dress with a rather fitted top. Springer believed she had to be *sans* her .451. She'd given up on it, he thought, gladly assuming that he would no longer have to go everywhere with death under his wing. When he broached the subject she guided his hand beneath the table to her inner thigh, and there it was.

Now, Springer flexed his shoulders to get the elasticized straps of the harness comfortably situated. Attached flat to the face of the straps were three extra clips, loaded. The holster was compact, especially made for the .451. The snubby silencer was attached. Springer shifted the holster slightly to make sure of its position. It fit close against his upper side. He had gotten somewhat used to the hardness of its being there.

He put on his jacket, adjusted his shirt cuffs. The receptionist had gone but he heard Linda on the phone in her office. She would lock up. He reached in under the receptionist's desk and pressed the button to let himself out. While he was in the corridor awaiting an elevator, his watch showed he had one minute to spare of the ten Audrey had specified.

The instant he stepped out of the 580 Building he saw the brown Daimler limousine at the curb. Audrey was in the rear seat and Groat, the chauffeur, was attending the open rear door. Springer's immediate thought was there had been a change of plans that involved Libby. He was disappointed. The walk and intimacies Audrey had proposed were far more to his liking.

Springer was halfway across the wide sidewalk when he sensed something wasn't right. He paused, took everything in. There was another man, a driver or whatever, in the Daimler's front seat. The man had his back to Springer, was half turned to Audrey. The glass partition between the driver and passenger compartments was down. On the opposite side of the Daimler, double-parked parallel to it, was a black Cadillac limousine, two men in its front seat. All but its front windows were tinted dark. The thing about the Cadillac that struck Springer as a bit strange was how close it was to the Daimler, within a couple of inches. It gave him the impression that the two cars were related. Then came the realization that the Cadillac, positioned as it was, would prevent anyone from getting out of the Daimler on the driver's side, and yet Groat was out, Groat was standing there with his hand on the rear door handle, the corners of his mouth unwillingly pulled up to appear pleasant, as if he were trying to coax a bird into a cage.

Audrey was up on the edge of the rear seat, leaning out to him,

GERALD A. BROWNE

her hand extended to him. She was smiling, but not with her eyes. Distress in her eyes, Springer thought. "Hello, darling!" she greeted loudly.

The giveaway.

They never said hello or goodbye to one another.

Springer continued on across the sidewalk to the car door. He reached in to accept Audrey's welcoming hand, seemed to be getting in, when he stepped back and pulled. Yanked Audrey out past a surprised Groat.

As soon as there was sidewalk beneath Audrey's feet she began to run. Springer still had her by the hand and she was practically towing him. But now that she was out of the Daimler and on the crowded street, shouldn't they stop so he could find out what this was all about?

Springer glanced back. He saw three men and then another getting out of the Cadillac. They stood tall, scanned the moving crowds on the avenue. They were heavyset men, the Libby sort, the type that constantly cordoned her with their physical efficiency and expert lethalness. But why, Springer wondered, were they so aggressively concerned with him and Audrey? He glanced back at them again, saw they were in pursuit, keeping to the curb and the gutter so not to be impeded by the sidewalkers.

The traffic light at 48th Street was in its warning DO NOT WALK phase. Springer and Audrey just made it across before the cars got the green and shot eastward. Not many private cars at this hour, mostly taxis contending possessively for every inch of their right-of-way. Yellow after yellow in fast tandem, they prevented anyone from crossing 48th now. Those four men of Libby's were among the pedestrians who had to wait.

Midblock between 48th and 49th Springer slowed Audrey to a mere hurry. Out of breath, she told him, "They were going to take us for a ride." There was high color in her cheeks, and her expressive eyes were showing more of their whites than usual. "They had me at gunpoint. Just a squeeze and I would have been a goner."

That didn't make sense to Springer. Why should Libby want such a thing done? "Are you sure it was a gun?"

"I know a gun when I see a gun."

"But—"

Audrey's hand was no longer linked with his.

"Audrey!" Springer shouted. "Audrey, hold it!"

His words hit unavailingly upon her back as she bolted ahead, went zigging and zagging around and past person after person. Springer had no choice but to follow after her. She angled toward the curb, stepped off behind a bus into a sooty cloud of exhaust, didn't hesitate, assumed Springer was behind her, and continued out into the swiftly moving traffic. Across the grain of its speed, with Audrey leading the way, they darted, scurried, dodged, and several times stood stock still, sucked in their stomachs, and felt the rush of metal come within an inch of their lives. When they finally reached the opposite curb even Audrey had to come to a stop and mentally pinch herself to ascertain that she was still living. Springer got her elbow, grasped it firmly, just short of hurting, to prevent her from taking off on the run again. He steered her across the sidewalk to in front of one of the display windows of Saks.

There, Springer decided, was where he was going to stop and figure out what the hell was really going on.

He looked to the opposite side of the street warily. If the Libby men were still coming, they would stand out in a crowd, but Springer couldn't see them. Nor were they, that he could make out, among the people crossing at the intersection down the street. Perhaps that idiotic death-defying scamper across merciless Fifth had been unnecessary. He looked to Audrey. She shrugged and did a contrite, synopsizing smile. Kept her eyes on beam with Springer's, as though that was her best defense.

How many times in their lives would he have to put up with such melodramatic nonsense? To what extremes would she carry it? He felt like shaking her. To help keep from doing that he turned to the Saks window and the neutrality of two smartly bored, serious-mouthed mannequins dressed in bright red against a black background.

Audrey coupled his arm with hers, claiming him and at the same time securing herself.

Springer resumed loving her without reservation.

If it hadn't been for the Saks awning, the way the shade it provided took the glare off the window glass . . . if it hadn't been for the black background of the window display . . . Springer probably wouldn't have seen the man's reflection. He appeared so suddenly and so close behind them it was as though he'd materialized there. Certainly, had the window glass been even a bit glary, Springer wouldn't have seen the pistol. At that he got only a glimpse of its blue-black metal as the man was slipping the pistol down to firing level, keeping it close to his body, using his unbuttoned jacket to shield it from sight.

In that instant Springer realized the man's incredible intention—and the practicality of shooting someone point-blank on Fifth Avenue at the height of rush and indifference. Shots fired from a pistol equipped with a silencer would be unnoticed spits in the din. The victim's collapse would appear to be caused by a stroke or heart attack and before anyone could realize that it was actually a matter of blood and death the shooter, whom no one could remember seeing, would have drifted into being just another of the many side-walkers, gone.

It was about to happen.

Springer spun around. In the same motion he brought his knee up. It was not a heroic move but one of desperation. He brought his knee up full force into the inverted V formed by the man's stance, felt the flacid mass of the man's scrotum that his knee smashed. He saw the man's mouth open to an oval in a face gone pale with the awful pain. Despite the distortion of the face, Springer recognized it. It was the one called Fane, the one who'd done the serving that afternoon in Libby's inside orange grove when Springer had delivered the Russian diamonds.

Springer's knee had beaten Fane's finger by the merest split of a second. Now Fane couldn't move that finger enough to pull the trigger. He was like a man turned to stone, incapable of breathing. His legs gave way and the rest of him crumbled. As he went down he lost his grasp of the pistol. It skittered metallically on the sidewalk among stepping feet, and although the pistol appeared real enough no one wanted to get into the trouble of determining whether or not it was. It lay there, something to be momentarily curious about while it was avoided, until a fellow selling twenty-five-dollar rip-offs of three-hundred-dollar Gucci handbags walked over and picked it up. He put it out of sight under the edge of the sheet his wares were displayed on. What pistol?

Fane, meanwhile, was down and retching. His contorted bulk and, to a greater extent, the puddle of his puke was a mess to keep clear of.

Springer and Audrey surely wanted nothing more to do with him. There were three others like him they had to contend with. Springer, a believer now, quickly led the way to the Fifth Avenue entrance of Saks. Anywhere inside seemed, for the moment at least, to be safer than outside on Fifth Avenue. They went in through the Saks brushed bronze doors to three thousand pairs of panty hose on the left and, on a counter opposite, the heads of three neatly decapitated all-white women wearing contented expressions and the annual straw hats. Springer had his hand extended behind him for Audrey to hold onto, for him to be assured that she was there, as they rushed down one of the central aisles, feeling the press of their pursuers in the stir of the air behind them. Those kill-bent men of Libby's would be more determined now that one of their kind had been felled.

Where was safe?

Not at a counter where three lightfooted fellows were critiquing perfumes by sniffing tiny strips of cardboard. Not behind a display of cummerbunds and pleat-fronted evening shirts or at the peninsular end of two aisles where certain previously overpriced summer scarves were slightly reduced and being jostled for.

Nowhere.

Springer and Audrey had reached the rear of the store. The up escalator offered itself. They took it, and during the diagonal, higher ride Springer was able to survey most of the main floor. His eyes were selective, only vaguely regarding counters, the merchandise, the ordinary shoppers, as they sought and . . . saw the three Libby men.

There they were!

Undoubtedly them. They had separated like a combing military unit, each taking an aisle, were headed toward the rear of the store. An instant before the second-floor level cut off Springer's view he believed he saw the Libby man in the center aisle raise his head the slight bit needed to take in the profiled escalator. Springer wasn't certain, couldn't be at that distance, but there was a chance that the man had spotted him.

"We could sneak you into one of the Ladies' dressing rooms," Audrey suggested and added lightly, trying to take the tight edge off, "It'll be close quarters in there, but I could try on a lot of what they call *better* lingerie."

An intolerant grunt from Springer. He was reasoning that if those Libby men now knew he and Audrey were in Saks, the smart move would be to get the hell out of Saks, as quickly as possible and unseen.

They rushed up the escalator to the third floor. Springer's idea was to take the elevator down from there, to backtrack so those Libby men would be pursuing in the wrong direction. There was a bank of eight elevators and no interim way of telling which was in service. Springer and Audrey paced and waited for the pinging sound and the red light that would indicate one that was going down.

Ping! White light.

Ping! White light.

The waiting seemed an age. Audrey called Springer's attention to a red EXIT on the wall to the extreme left of the bank of elevators. They hurried to it, and as soon as they were on their way down . . . *ping!* went another up elevator.

Among those who stepped out of it was one of the Libby men.

Springer and Audrey ran down the stairs, dashed out of Saks, and stopped on 50th Street as though they'd run into an invisible wall. There at the curb was a black Cadillac limousine with dark tinted windows, in all respects like *the* one. Springer couldn't verify the driver, who was looking straight out at them with what seemed to be more than incidental interest.

"Not hers," Audrey said, noting that the limousine did not have an LHH license plate.

However, there at the curb were three other identical black Cadillac limousines with drivers in them, and pulled up bumper-to-bumper as they were, the license plates weren't visible. Any one of them could be the Libby.

Outside wasn't safe again.

Springer and Audrey fled across 50th Street to the south side entrance of St. Patrick's Cathedral. They took the ten granite steps up two at a time and went in through the open sixteen-foot-high double doorway. Springer intended to use the cathedral as a passageway to 51st Street, to walk straight across the width of it to where another doorway led out. He changed his mind, decided that doing the obvious would be more elusive. He and Audrey went about halfway up the center aisle to a vacant pew. They sat as far in from the aisle as they could, next to one of the huge supporting columns, which concealed them to some extent.

Springer didn't really know St. Patrick's. Like most New Yorkers he only felt he did. It was there and would be there. Springer knew and always appreciated the shimmering way the cathedral's thirty-story spires used the black sheer surface of the Olympic Tower as its looking glass. He also knew the cathedral from above. Whenever he'd shown goods to out-of-town clients who were staying high up at the Helmsley Palace, he'd looked down on St. Patrick's and seen the simple Latin cross shape formed by its vast blue-gray slate roof, the way it seemed embedded in the middle of the city, as though it had been dropped huge and hard and precisely on that spot from some incredible height.

But he hadn't been inside St. Patrick's since he was fourteen, when once, on his walk home from 47th, he'd cut through it just to see what it was like. It had fascinated him in an eerie way, a great haunted place full of statues and whispers and flickers. At one of the tiered racks that held rows of votive candles in little red or clear glasses, Springer had lighted nine candles and was going for a tenth when he noticed the metal offering box there with its slit of a mouth asking for money. He didn't have a dime on him, so he blew out the nine he'd lighted. He thought of it as having reneged on a deal, and over the years one of the many venial vows that he never kept was to go back into St. Patrick's, light ten, and make it right.

Now, seated in the pew with Audrey and his fear, he glanced about to make sure of his surroundings. He hadn't expected St. Patrick's would be such a diversely busy place. In its own way it was only a few notches down from Saks or the avenue itself.

A priest, so distant at the high altar that he was nearly faceless, was saying the late day mass. His congregation of hundreds was possibly outnumbered by the tourists who were roaming about everywhere, admiring aloud various features of the cathedral, firing flashbulbs at the likenesses of saints. Constantly coming and going were worshipers on their own, to sibilate along with their strings of rosaries and recite Hail Marys. There were also nappers. It was hard to tell the nappers from those who were intensely praying with eyes closed. And some people were even using the place to meet and decide where to have a bite to eat before going to a movie. Springer just happened to catch a glimpse of a business deal being made in the pew across the way, a sheaf of cash being exchanged for whatever a Bloomingdale's shopping bag contained.

It was not unthinkable that Libby's men would take advantage of all this commotion. Springer and Audrey had to keep alert. At least being in the St. Patrick's pew might buy them a little time, give their minds a chance to catch up with their bodies.

Audrey appeared shaken, Springer thought. Not quite a furrow, but a discernable bunching of tension between her eyes, some of the fullness of her lips lost to tightening. He was about to take her hand for a buoying hold when she reached down to check on her leg holster and her .451. She slipped the pistol partway out of the holster, testing to make sure it would come out easily enough, then snugged it back into place. She straightened the bottom of her full slacks and sat up. "Do you have an extra clip to spare?" she asked. "I was in such a rush to meet you that I left mine in my makeup kit."

Springer reached under his jacket, removed one of the clips from his holster harness. He passed it to her. She brought her foot up, undid the lace of her white Italian sneaker to make room. She tucked the narrow metal clip down into the side of the canvas sneaker, took up the slack from the lace and tied it. Surely it wasn't comfortable, but now as she sat back again she seemed more relaxed.

"Can you think of any reason Libby would want us dead?" Springer asked.

"No."

"Any reason at all, no matter how absurd it might seem?"

"I wish I'd brought my pendulum."

"Think," Springer urged. "Maybe we can somehow set it straight." He gazed at the exactly geometric yet irregular-looking ribs of the vaulted ceiling ten stories above while he reviewed Libby. He went all the way back to his initial impressions of her, as he'd seen her that first afternoon on the terrace with Townsend and Wintersgill. Libby holding court, sprawled on a chaise like an empress in a silk dynastic robe that must have taken ten Chinese lifetimes to embroider. Her uglied hands hidden by the sleeves of the robe but her bitterness visible, her egocentricity displayed as though it were a privileged fashion. Her every word in his direction had been honed with superiority, meant to slice him thin to the point of transparency. No regard for the pain of it. Was that then the true Libby—or merely a mood of hers he'd just happened upon?

A poke from Audrey.

Calling his attention to two men moving up the far side aisle on the right. They stood out from the tourists, were both taller, hefty, looked menacing in their proper dark suits. One had a plain brown paper bag in hand. A gun in it?

Audrey crossed her legs so her right ankle was resting on her left knee. That put her pistol within an instant of her fingers. Springer's right hand went reflexively in under the left side of his jacket. They watched the two men come up the side aisle, peripherally saw them stop at a spot about twenty-five feet away beyond a section of pews that were mostly unoccupied. The men didn't appear to be taking special notice of Springer and Audrey, as, of course, they wouldn't. In fact they seemed rather detached from their surroundings, oblivious to the milling tourists. Next, Springer and Audrey expected, the two men would cross over to the near aisle and sit in the pew just behind them and be within point-blank range of the back of their heads.

However, the two men turned away and gave their attention to the tiered rack of votive candles positioned in front of one of the small railed-off chapels along that side of the cathedral. There was the sound of metal scraping marble floor as they moved the pedestaled rack a couple of feet away from the railing. The glass candleholders rattled in place. One of the men knelt and, with such a big bunch of keys it was like a nosegay, reached in under and unlocked the metal offering box that was a permanent part of the rack. He pulled out the drawer of the offering box. It was so crammed that bills and coins dropped to the floor, causing him, annoyed, to express the need for larger drawers that would require fewer collections. The other man held the mouth of the bag open so the contents of the drawer could be dumped into it. The stray money was retrieved. The drawer was noisily replaced, locked, and tried, and the tiered rack shifted back into position. The two men, church custodians, continued on up the aisle to the votive candle rack of the next side chapel.

The false alarm was such a letdown for Springer and Audrey that it was therapeutic, slackened their tension a bit. Springer fixed his eyes almost straight ahead on the baldachin that served the high altar. Gleaming, golden bronze, intricately detailed with figures, floral finials and tracery, the archlike baldachin created the impression that the altar was standing on the doorstep of some surely holy realm. Springer noticed that on the topmost point of the baldachin, about five stories up, was the figure of an angel. He didn't know that it was the Archangel Michael but he saw that the figure had a sword and it occurred to him how that supported Audrey's theory. If an angel couldn't go anywhere without a sword, who should?

While Springer's eyes remained on the baldachin, his mind resumed with Libby. It seemed to him that her initial vitriol was something she just had to get out of her system. Because since then she'd been consistently congenial toward him. More than that. She'd gone out of her way to be generous, well-intentioned. Only the day before yesterday she'd phoned and inquired about Jake, said she'd taken the initiative of contacting the Head of Medicine at Johns Hopkins for his recommendation of an oncologist to care for Jake, whoever in the world was most advanced and knowledgeable in the

area of osteogenic sarcoma. She'd been referred to a doctor in Edin-
burgh, had spoken with him, explained the circumstances, and persuaded him to make Jake his priority case. One of her personal jets
would fly Jake over. Everything would be arranged. Please, allow her
to help, she'd said. And now, two days later, she'd sent her private
armed guard out to kill him?

A Libby man.

Springer saw him come in by way of 50th Street. No doubt about
him. He was the one who had spotted Springer in Saks. He had gray
hair with some blond left in it, but dark eyebrows. His saunter
conveyed that he was disregarding where he was. At the center aisle
he turned his back to the high altar and searched the pews with his
eyes, took his time, systematically scanned the pews on the right and
the left.

Springer and Audrey were to the left of him only about fifty feet
away. They felt obvious, were tempted to duck down out of sight,
but any quick move would draw attention.

"Pray," Springer whispered to Audrey.

Slowly they knelt on the red plastic-covered knee rest, placed their
hands on the back of the pew in front of them, hunched forward, and
lowered their foreheads to their hands. Over their knuckles they
could still see the Libby man. He stood there for a while longer,
concentrating his survey on the pews to his right. Then, apparently
satisfied, dropping his shoulders a bit as he gave up, he turned and
walked out the 51st Street doors.

Springer and Audrey continued to pray.

"Did he see us?" Audrey asked.

"I don't think so," Springer replied.

When, after five minutes, the Libby man didn't reappear, Springer
and Audrey sat up. They were quite confident that they'd given their
pursuers the slip. They agreed that for margin they should stay in
St. Patrick's at least another half hour. Audrey began massaging the
back of Springer's neck, a conclusive gesture. While her fingers
kneaded caringly, Springer's thoughts returned to the perplexity of
Libby.

Okay, he reasoned, say there was some one-sided misunderstanding serious enough for Libby to want him done in, just say there was, then what about Audrey? These men were out to also do away with Audrey, and Libby wouldn't want that, probably not under any circumstances, no matter how obsessively envious she might be of Audrey's many fewer years or jealous of what Audrey and he had together. Nothing short of insanity would call for such drastic action. No, it just didn't wash.

He felt like taking his head off and giving it a few hard loosening shakes. The answer, anyway the clue, to this Libby thing had to be stuck in there somewhere. Did it perhaps have to do with the Russian diamond deal? He went back over the times he'd been with Libby, what had been said. Words of hers ran across the front of his mind. Several fragments went zipping by at the speed of thought but insisted on coming back for replay:

I have enough people here . . . quite capable people and very loyal.

That had been Libby's reply when they were down in her vault at the Greenwich house putting the Russian diamonds away and he'd inquired about her security. He remembered wondering at the time how she could be so certain the staff of men that protected her was so capable . . . and loyal . . . and she had told him:

Wintersgill finds my people for me . . . recruits and screens them intensively.

Wintersgill. The getter, the front, the green floodgate.

Wintersgill. The bloodlined lacky with marriage ambitions.

If Wintersgill found these men weren't they his? Didn't they owe their selves to him? If he screened them wouldn't he make sure they knew from whom their bonuses were coming? Hell, yes. Groat and Fane and all the others were, when push came to kill, Wintersgill's own task force. Then, of course, it followed that Wintersgill, not Libby, had sicced these men on them. A purge. More than likely, not they but Libby was the main mark, and wherever she was at that moment, she too was in mortal danger.

Perhaps she was already dead.

That shivering thought brought Springer to remind himself all this was mere surmise. His scenario. It stacked up a lot more neatly than anything else, though.

He put it to Audrey, what did she think?

"Wintersgill." She nodded.

"But why? What would he have to gain?"

She looked up at stained glass windows of the north transept, as though the answer was up there among the colors and the tracery. "Maybe," she said, "gain isn't his motive. Maybe it's a matter of what he has to lose."

"We've got to get to Libby."

Springer looked off to his right and left and then turned and looked behind.

There they were.

Ten pews back.

Two Wintersgill men. The gray-haired blond and another. Their eyes held on Springer's. They were smirking malignantly. Evidently they'd been sitting there for some time, enjoying their edge. The gray-haired blond must have spotted them and not let on, gone around, and come in through the front entrance.

What to do now?

They sure as hell couldn't be outsat.

Mass ended. The hundreds attending got up from the pews and were filing out. Springer and Audrey saw it as a chance. They joined those leaving by way of the center aisle, got as close in among them as possible, using them as a shield. The two Wintersgill men waited for Springer and Audrey to pass before joining the flow. Springer and Audrey would go out to Fifth Avenue, would, as soon as they were a foot out of the cathedral, make a dash down the steps to the sidewalk, the curb. Luck and timing would be with them. An available taxi would be coming along, would be right there and they'd jump in and be swiftly carried away to safety.

Now they'd reached the end of the aisle. The crowd diverged in the main vestibule. The main way out was closed, as it usually was on weekdays. There was the choice of going out by way of the north or south vestibules. Springer and Audrey chose the south, hurried through the doorway to it and were about to step outside when they saw Groat. Unmissable in his double-breasted brown twill livery, shiny beaked cap, leather leggings. Groat and another with him, at the corner of the exterior landing, were waiting for them, watching for them. Saw them.

Impasse.

Wintersgill men ahead and coming on behind.

Springer noticed a door just inside the vestibule, an ordinary single door. No telling what it might lead to. He tried it. It came open. He and Audrey darted in and quickly closed the door after them. They, along with an old tin dustpan and a wornout broom, were at the bottom of a steep spiral stairway, so narrow they would have to go up single file. Clear glass lightbulbs of twenty-five watts at most were suspended from outdated fabric-covered wires. A banister that followed the curve of the white plaster walls offered its assistance.

Because of the sharp continuous turn of the steps, they had to be taken one at a time. Audrey went up ahead of Springer. Her feet were almost level with his eyes and he saw the repetitious blur of her heels as she scurried up and around, up and around. It was dizzying. Desperation made it seem all the more so.

When they'd climbed three complete spirals, they heard what surely had to be the Wintersgill men on the stairs below: the heavy, pursuing steps of perhaps as many as three. Springer and Audrey could only be mentally spurred on, for their feet were already going as fast as possible. At the completion of the fifth spiral they had climbed one hundred fifty-three steps, about the equivalent of ten stories. At that point the stairway ended at a landing. There was a closed door on the right, a solid wood door with a hundred-year-old brass knob that had never been polished.

No time to catch a badly needed deep breath.

Springer turned the knob, pulled. The door seemed to be locked, but he noticed there was only the knob, no keyhole. He pulled harder. The door, swollen in its jamb from humidity, gave slightly. He attacked the door with a sudden yank. It complained stridently and came open a foot. Just enough to squeeze through, Audrey first. While Springer pulled the door closed from inside, Audrey reached down and got her pistol. Springer saw it in her hand and took his out too.

They quickly assessed the space they had entered. It was indeed a space more than an area. The inside of the inside, an attic of sorts situated between the cathedral's vaulted ceiling and its roof. It was long, about a hundred and fifty feet, but only about ten feet wide. Overhead, cutting down on the space, was the diagonal underside of the roof, its beams burned brown with age. There was no floor. Instead, a catwalk made up of unnailed wood planks ran the entire length. The only light came from weak bulbs suspended every twenty-five feet or so.

Springer and Audrey rushed unsurely along the catwalk. The uneven planks rumbled beneath them; their swiftness aroused dust. As they were avoiding the hang of the first lightbulb they heard the door being tried, then the rasp of it being jerked open, followed, almost at once, by three consecutive spatting sounds, the distinctive sounds of shots from a pistol being compressed by a silencer.

Springer anticipated the jolt, the pain, the burn, whatever would be felt from a bullet in the back. Then, as though acting on their own, his legs stopped, refused to run, his feet pivoted.

The Wintersgill man seemed small, vague, too far away.

Springer fired three times.

One bullet missed. Another passed through the fabric of the man's jacket and shirt and the skin and subcutaneous flesh that covered the sixth rib where it curved around his side. It grazed the bone of the rib and went on through. Springer's third bullet struck approximately four inches to the left of the second. At a velocity of one thousand one hundred feet per second, the hollow-nosed slug entered the man between his sixth and seventh ribs, spread to nearly twice its diameter when it met the resistance of the cartilage that connected the two ribs, and tore through the walls of the left ventricular chamber of his heart. It veered as tissue slowed it, so that it partially penetrated and lodged in one of the transverse processes of the man's spine.

He was the gray-haired blond Wintersgill man. The impact of the bullet caused his arms to spring out from his body. He lashed fearfully, surprised, as though he'd stepped on a snake. Driven back, his heaviness slammed against the door, forcing it farther open. He slid down, a dead heap.

GERALD A. BROWNE

Audrey had taken aim but had not had time to get off a shot.

She and Springer continued quickly along the catwalk and found that it went at a ninety-degree angle off to the right. Forty feet along they came to the dead end of it. They went back to the place where it angled and took up position there, where they could see down the long narrow attic space to the door that evidently was the only way in or out, keep a watch for their other pursuers.

It was a relief for them to kneel, to take air in deeply. Springer was stunned by what he'd done. Killed someone. His hand and the pistol in its grasp seemed fused, would forever be. The pistol was extremely heavy, requiring tremendous effort to keep it from weighing him over, lopsiding him. The endogenous old dragon in him had been let out of its lair, had finally flicked its ferocious tongue. He had killed someone, in a church of all places.

"That was some shooting," Audrey complimented.

It mattered, Springer told himself, that it had been a kill-or-be-killed situation. His reflexes, only his reflexes were to blame. That bastard's bullets were him asking for it, deserving it. How about that gleaming angel with the sword? How about bloodbaths and holy wars? Springer decided he wasn't off the hook . . . but he could live with it.

Springer and Audrey peeked warily around the corner, kept watch on the door at the far end of the catwalk. Every couple of minutes around the edge of the jamb a Wintersgill man fired blindly in their direction. Just to keep them put. After a half hour of this the door was closed.

"What do you make of that?" Audrey asked.

"The door?"

"Yeah."

"They're trying to sucker us out."

"What time is it?"

"Almost seven."

"The cathedral closes at nine thirty."

"Closing time is probably what they're waiting for. When the lights are turned off they'll make their move."

"Can't hit what they can't see."

416

"Who knows what they'll come up with?"

"I hate being cornered in here like this," Audrey said.

Springer could hear the fear behind the anger in her voice. He took her hand in his for some mutual transfusion. He stretched out and tried to make himself more comfortable on the hard dusty planks. He thought of where they were, visualized the cathedral as he'd occasionally seen it, objectively, from high above—the huge cross configuration of it shaped by its slate roof. He marked their position with an X on his mental view. They were under the left arm of the cross. It would seem, philosophically, a safe place to be. He went on thinking about it and recalled how symmetrical and immaculate the roof of the cathedral had always appeared to him. No debris on it, every slate in place, well kept. It occurred to him that in order to repair and maintain the roof there would have to be some way to get out onto it. He looked around the corner, ran his eyes along the underside of the slanted roof from beam to beam. He caught upon an interruption in the texture, a square, darker area. It could be a hatch. It was about thirty feet down the catwalk in the direction of the door.

Audrey kept her pistol sighted on the door, would fire upon any movement there. Springer went swiftly down the catwalk and found that it was indeed a hatch, about three feet square. It was easily accessible, at about waist height. Hinged at its top, held by a pair of large hooks and eyes at its bottom. On the nearby horizontal beam lay a length of broom handle.

Springer undid the hooks and heaved the heavy hatch open. Its hinges were begrudging, made a loud, rusted, croaky sound. Springer signaled Audrey to him. She climbed out over the raised collar of the hatchway. He followed her out, removed the propping broom handle, and quietly closed the hatch.

They were at the south edge of the cathedral's vast roof. Fiftieth Street was ten stories below. A narrow walkway ran between the roof and a stone balustrade that served as a decorative railing all around. They decided on a position about ten feet from the hatch. The situation was still a standoff, but anyone who attempted to come out through that hatch would be an easy target.

The sun was going, was already weak enough to be looked directly at without squinting. About a third of it was already behind the seventy-story Rockefeller Plaza Building. Across the way the linear blackness of the Olympic Tower was being raked by late sun yellow, and off to Springer and Audrey's right many of the windows of the fifty-floor Helmsley Palace Hotel were ignited patches. Those buildings surrounded, dominated. Springer had the feeling that there were thousands of spectators looking down on his and Audrey's plight but if he signaled for help they would probably just wave hello back. It would be equally futile, he knew, to try yelling down to anyone on 50th Street. The surface of the city created an impenetrable, constantly rising cloud of noise.

"Going to hell in high places," Springer thought aloud.

Audrey was more optimistic. "Seems to me everything is pointing in the *other* direction." She meant the spires of the cathedral pointed heavenward, as did its many pinnacles and gables.

Springer was reminded of one of his unresolved childhood wonderings: Why was heaven always believed to be up—even after the world took half a turn and what had been up was down and what had been down was up? His father, Edwin, had only claimed to be a Protestant whenever officially required to do so. His mother, Mattie, had thanked the life source (which Springer presumed was God) for beautiful blessings prior to Christmas dinner and other special meals when they'd had turkey. So he'd never been religious. Once, when someone had inquired what his religion was, for candid amusement he'd replied, "D-flawless." Lately, though, since Jake had become ill, Springer had often found himself pleading with some determining power beyond himself to intervene favorably.

He leaned back against the balustrade. Its weather-eaten stone ground roughly into his spine.

Audrey relaxed against the slant of the slate roof. The roof was more steeply pitched than it appeared from street level, had a 60-degree angle to it. From the edge of the roof up to its ridge was at least thirty feet. Along the ridge was an ornamental upright of wrought iron about four feet tall, a fencelike grille in a repetitive pattern of foliate tracery and spiky finials.

As he looked around, Springer realized the carved stonework did not include any gargoyles, not a one. He called Audrey's attention to the fact. "All Gothic cathedrals are supposed to have them. Fork-tongued monsters, griffins, bulgy-eyed lizards, things like that. The uglier the better."

"I don't miss them," Audrey said impassively.

"Know the purpose of gargoyles?"

"To scare the devil out of everyone."

"Nope."

"Okay, then they're for spouting water from the roof, so it doesn't just run down the wall and ruin the masonry."

It never really bothered Springer when she stole his thunder. "You're very well read," he told her.

"Just another of the countless reasons why you should be glad I'm yours," she said with mock immodesty. The levity helped briefly.

They didn't talk much for the next twenty minutes, kept their eyes fixed on the hatch, waiting for the slightest movement. Their impatience built; they felt that as long as an encounter was inevitable it might as well happen and be over with.

"Maybe they've given up on us," Audrey said.

"I doubt that."

So did Audrey. "They still think they've got us trapped in that dead end."

"They'll wait until nine thirty."

"Then what?"

"Find we're not there, find the hatch, and come on out."

"And we'll plunk them," Audrey pledged grimly.

Springer parried that prospect with a grunt. He'd been considering the wrought-iron embellishment on the ridge of the roof, thinking that to get from this side of the roof to the other side would require climbing over that spike-topped obstacle. Four feet tall, it would be more than an inconvenience. What it suggested to him was there might be another hatch on the other side that gave into another attic. In fact, that same wrought iron followed along every inch of ridge of the cross shape of the cathedral, dividing the roof into four sections. There might even be four hatches to four separate attics. That would be the reason why the attic they'd been in hadn't gone all the way around the transept, the arm of the cross shape. The huge, high windows at each extremity of the transept preempted attic space.

If he was right about this, Springer thought, it could be their way out. Go up and over the ridge to the other side of the roof and then down through the hatch there. Leave the bastards prowling around in the dark with no one to shoot at but one another.

Springer explained his notion to Audrey. It sounded reasonable to her; anyway, was certainly worth a look. At once she took a testing step up the roof. Springer stopped her, told her, "You stay here and watch the hatch." The pitch of the roof appeared dangerously steep.

"You don't have on the shoes for it," Audrey said.

She was right. His leather-soled shoes would slip on the slate shingles. But, he thought, barefoot he'd be able to manage it.

While he was removing his shoes and socks, Audrey took it on her own to make the climb, was already partway up. There'd be no stopping her now, Springer knew. Anyway, perhaps it was best that he remain there near the hatch where the greater danger would come from. He saw that the gum soles of her sneakers were providing her with excellent traction. He'd leave his own shoes off in case she had trouble and he had to get up to her. He kept shifting his attention from the hatch to her.

Audrey found the going difficult. It was nearly impossible to compensate for the steepness by leaning forward, and she kept stubbing her toes on the angular juts of the overlapping slate shingles. When she was halfway up she stopped and inserted her pistol into the waistband of her slacks, and that allowed her to resort to a climbing crawl. She reached ahead hand over hand and trusted merely the toes of her sneakers to provide adequate grab. It was much easier. At two thirds of the way up she lowered her head and looked back between her feet—just for the belly-hollowing sensation of it. One good long look was enough.

She continued up.

And soon she reached for and grasped the wrought iron. It was sturdier, thicker around than she'd thought it would be, and pocked rough. She pulled herself up so she could see through one of the spaces in its tracery. If she saw a hatch anywhere on the other side of the roof she'd signal Springer to come on up.

She saw a Wintersgill man.

The one called Fane, the one Springer had kneed in the crotch. Fane now appeared none the worse for it. He was about six feet to Audrey's right and halfway up the other side of the roof. Barefoot, trouser bottoms rolled up to midcalf. Wearing no jacket now, his backup pistol and holster harness showing. Fane was intent on climbing, making sure of the placement of his feet, not looking up at that moment.

Audrey ducked down out of sight, pressed herself against the surface of the roof.

She could, she thought, just pick him off. Let him have it without even a warning. Don't have any compunctions about doing that, she told herself. She was suddenly aware of the force of her outward breaths, felt that the merest tightening of her throat would cause them to become some kind of audible animal sound. Her heart was pounding. Also, she realized, she was still clinging to the wrought-iron tracery. Fane might notice her fingers. She slowly released her grasp, withdrew her hands from the tracery. Her pistol was in her waistband, hard beneath her. She humped up her middle and reached for it. Only for an instant was she careless about her toes, but that was all it took for her sneakers to give up too much of their hold. She slid down the roof a short way, tried to brake herself by turning her feet sideways, putting more of the rubber soles of her sneakers to the slick slate. But the grab of the sneakers was too sudden. Her weight and momentum overwhelmed her ankles and the next thing she knew she was sprawled parallel to the line of the roof. Unable to resist its sharp pitch, she tumbled swiftly down, seeing sky, buildings, roof, sky, buildings, roof. Her full length struck so hard against the stone balustrade at the bottom, the wind was knocked out of her.

Springer thought she'd just slipped. He knew nothing of Fane. He rushed to her.

She rolled over and kicked at him, kicked him away. She didn't have the breath to tell him about Fane, nor was there time. Surely

Fane had heard the clatter of her pistol on the slate. He'd have his bearings.

Audrey had her pistol in hand now. She fixed her eyes upon the ridge of the roof, the spot along the wrought-iron embellishment where she thought Fane would show. Her skeet-shooting experience would help. But damn Springer. He was still trying to minister to her, asking her if she was all right, making it more difficult for her to concentrate.

The first move Fane made was what she expected. She saw only the slight motion of the little black hole that was the muzzle of his silencer as it appeared in one of the curved, smaller spaces of the wrought-iron tracery. Fane was positioning his pistol before bringing his eyes up to aim it. He'd come up to it all at once and then take aim, Audrey figured.

Which was exactly what he did.

Audrey saw through the tracery the incongruity of Fane's features, especially the plane of his forehead.

Springer also saw him now.

Before Fane could get set to fire . . .

Audrey squeezed two shots.

The first hit Fane at the hairline. Because of the upward angle of its course the slug creased through his scalp and glanced off his skull. It hurt but didn't hinder all that much, by no means stopped him.

Audrey's second shot missed Fane completely.

It was very close but, nevertheless, a miss. The slug struck the wrought-iron tracery to the right of Fane's head, ricocheted off, and with its hollow nose already spread, entered Fane's left temple to plow through dura mater and cerebral cortex and nerve cells and glial cells and blood vessels. It didn't stop until it had slashed through Fane's middle cerebral artery and was deep in his brain, a kernel of death. The impact of the slug snapped Fane's head to the right. The rest of him followed, flipped over. He slid deadweight down the roof.

Audrey had regained her breath. She flexed and stretched to make sure everything was in place and functioning. Instead of giving in to thoughts of Fane, she apologized to Springer for having kicked him.

She ignored her bruises and her badly skinned left knee, and retrieved the two spent casings. More souvenirs.

The other Wintersgill men would be coming now, Springer thought. They must have heard when he'd opened this hatch and figured, as he had, that there'd be another on the other side of the roof from which they could make a surprise move. Fane had been the first, probably others were already over there. How many? Two from four left two, but there was Groat as well, and the one who'd held the gun on Audrey in the Daimler. So, possibly four. They were professionals, Springer reminded himself. That gave them plenty of edge. He scanned the ridge of the roof, ran his eyes back and forth along it a couple of times, fearing they might at that instant be somewhere along it, concealed by the wrought-iron tracery, taking aim.

For sure, Springer realized, he and Audrey couldn't stay there. What it had gotten down to was the chance that he was right about there being separate attics, not only on this long section of the roof's cross shape but also farther up, beyond the transept, on the shorter section, the apse. If not? Think positive, Springer almost said aloud.

He didn't know what to do with his shoes. When he stuck them in his jacket pockets toe first, they were heel-heavy and dropped out. Heel first they were bulky, would get in the way and might cause a costly, possibly even fatal awkwardness. Yet being barefoot made him feel vulnerable. Somewhat against his better judgment he flung the shoes as far as he could and didn't hear or see them land below on 50th Street.

He and Audrey moved along the walkway to the transept roof. They went up it side by side in their climbing crawl, all the while sensing the Wintersgill men taking aim on their backs. Up and over the wrought-iron tracery, noticing that the spikes on its top were not really as pointed and menacing as they appeared from a distance. Down the other side of the transept roof, feet first, to where the walkway continued and then, on it, around the corner to the roof of the apse.

It hadn't been mere wishful thinking, Springer saw.

There was another hatch, identical.

It would lead to the south-side attic of the apse and there would be a catwalk and a door to another spiral stairway that would take them down to the wide area around back of the high altar called the ambulatory. They wouldn't even hesitate, would walk across the ambulatory, the entire width of the cathedral, with Springer's bare feet padding along the slightly gritty marble floor, would walk across that atmosphere of sibilant implorations and gratitudes, feel the pious air of the place slip more easily, like an invisible silver fluid, down into them. They would leave the cathedral by way of the small northeast door that led to the pathway alongside the parish house that would take them out onto Madison Avenue. With none of the Wintersgill men aware, none of them following.

Springer tried to lift open the hatch. It was held solidly from inside. He got a better grip on its overlapping lip and pulled up so hard his face was crimson with strain. Audrey had him make room for her, and when they both had good grips they pulled together. Hers was the additional strength needed to make the large hooks and eyes within the hatch surrender the deep holds their threads had bored in the hard, aged wood.

Twenty-five minutes later Audrey's BMW was fifth on line at one of the exact-change toll booths of the Tri-Borough Bridge.

Audrey was driving.

Springer was hastily digging for quarters to make up the dollar-fifty toll. He came up a quarter short and had to rummage around in the glove compartment among a bunch of wrongly folded road maps, two plastic windshield ice scrapers, an owner's handbook, and a very old, overlooked, still unopened Devil Dog.

"They have a lot of preservatives," Audrey said, grabbing the cellophane-wrapped cake from him and placing it on the hump near the hand brake.

Springer vowed to himself that he wouldn't let her eat it no matter what. As soon as they were on the highway he'd throw it away. He found three dimes, closed the compartment, and sat back.

They'd gone to the apartment for Springer to put on a pair of loafers. While there, Audrey had disguised her voice and phoned Libby in Greenwich. Hinch had answered and said Mrs. Hull was not to be disturbed, which, despite Hinch's usual phlegmatic monotone, sounded awfully foreboding, Audrey thought. She was most anxious to get up to the Round Hill house and see if Libby was all right. Springer was also concerned about Libby but he was understandably ambivalent. Here they were bound for danger when they'd just spent hours struggling to escape it.

Three cars to go.

"What are you thinking?" Audrey asked.

"About those two guys we killed. What happens when their bodies are found?"

"More than likely the others will see to it that they're not found. For their own good."

That sounded feasible, Springer thought.

"Even if they leave them up there in St. Patrick's," Audrey said, "I doubt that much will be made of it. The church won't want it known, and the police and the church are close. Hoodlums are always killing hoodlums . . . and these days in the strangest places."

Still, Springer was glad he'd had the presence of mind to throw his shoes away instead of leaving them as clues. By now his shoes were probably on some bag lady's feet or crushed beyond recognition from being repeatedly run over. He glanced past Audrey's profile to the car in the next toll lane over, a blue Plymouth with two men in it. The man on the passenger side was looking Springer's way. Springer had never seen either of the men before so he thought nothing of it. It was just a matter of a stranger momentarily taking in another stranger.

The BMW moved ahead.

Audrey dropped the dollar fifty-five into the toll receptacle. EXACT CHANGE was what all the signs demanded, but evidently overpayment was acceptable.

The BMW took off with a bit of tire squeal. Audrey maneuvered it diagonally across the flow of cars bound for Long Island.

In the blue Plymouth, Fred Pugh and Jack Blayney, the two State Department men, were just then pulling up to the toll booth, getting change back from a ten. They watched the taillights of the BMW disappear down the ramp.

"Want I should keep up with them?" Blayney asked.

"Don't kill us doing it," Pugh told him.

Besides, Pugh knew where they were going.

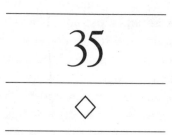

35

Libby.

All of her in the *bergère à la reine,* her legs folded under her, her toes finding the snug chasm down alongside the seat cushion. The Scalamandre silk upholstery fabric felt pleasantly compatible with her cotton pajamas, slick through that cotton which had exploded out of prized plants of the Nile delta and been spun into a cloth so fine and light it came close to floating when tossed in the air. Her pajamas were dark blue, piped in white, exactly cut for ampleness. As a general rule she detested feeling bound by whatever she wore, particularly by anything she lounged or slept in. On the second finger of her left hand a thirty-carat Kashmir sapphire performed a solo, shooting flares of blue that needed no accompaniment from diamonds.

The chair Libby was in was her favorite. In the winter she had it positioned at a nice close angle to the fireplace in her large second-floor bedroom, and although she wasn't one to merely sit and waste time dream-gazing into the flames, the chair would for various hours be her base of operations. A telephone was always within easy reach in the event she wanted to talk to anyone anywhere in the world, and, as well, there was on hand a remote electronic signaling device to summon and have come running whomever of her staff a particular button designated.

But it was summer now.

Her favorite chair was situated before the tall French doors on the south side of her bedroom. Beyond the open doors was her private balcony with its substantial balustrade. It was a dark night, only the merest sliver of a moon, and for some reason the darkness seemed a willing transport for the fragrance of the white alyssum flourishing in the deep loam of the garden bed directly below. Libby had specified on the groundskeeper's plans that, without fail, alyssum be planted there each season—a wide crowded carpet of it—anticipating the contribution that it would make to evenings such as this.

Earlier in the day she had given thought to keeping the Palmer dinner invitation she'd seen noted on her "possible" agenda. At that time she'd felt it a bit more likely than not that she'd feel like showing up. Dell Palmer was the reason, Lois Ward Palmer's third and youngest-ever husband. It was quite courageous of Lois Ward at her age to marry anyone so vigorous and demanding and straight, was Libby's opinion, while so many other older well-offs under similar circumstances buckled under to their estrogenous shortcomings and chose to charade with the sort of men who were long proved to be light of foot. Chic it wasn't, but courageous, yes. Never mind that Lois Ward had bitten off much more than she cared to so frequently chew, her thirty-eight-year-old Dell was a handsome hound with giveaway large hands and feet, and now, even after six months of marriage, he was doing far better than most at sustaining an acceptable semblance of authentic breeding. The last time Libby had dined at the Palmers', Dell had flattered her four times, twice verbally.

As the day passed, so also did most of Libby's inclination toward the Palmer dinner. She called Lois Ward and, not wanting to waste much effort on it, offered the most transparent kind of excuse. It was so readily accepted Libby was put back a bit. The least Lois could have done, Libby thought, was coax a couple of times. It made her wonder how much of a bore people considered her to be.

Fuck introspection.

Came twilight she leisurely bathed the day from her. She was in a pleasant passive mood, confident of life, not chafed by any of the usual looming vulnerabilities. Up to above her head in a sense of well-being, she dabbed her personal Guerlain here and there, chose to put on the dark blue pajamas, and took to her favorite chair.

For ten minutes precisely she allowed two of the dogs in. The black-and-white King Charles spaniels responded with the anticipated enthusiasm, unable to suppress a few zealous yaps as they bounded in and saw Libby's hand patting the signal which offered a share of the bergère and herself to them. They smelled not at all doggish, even their breaths were sweet. Libby wooed them each by nuzzling them in the hollows under their chins with her knuckle. The last she gave to them was a two-handed squeeze, feeling their tiny rib cages squirming as she put them to the floor, dismissed.

She ordered dinner, decided it should be early and light and served to her there. A double Gloucester cheese soufflé, baked to a crisp around the sides, and endive salad, a brochette or two, and a bottle of Swiss white for a change. She had the wine brought in advance, a '52 Dézaley l'Arbalete from the slopes that formed the bowl that held Lake Geneva.

While sipping, Libby went over the preview catalogue of the Fasig Tipton sales soon to be conducted in Saratoga. One yearling in particular piqued her intuition. A Secretariat colt with some Hoist the Flag in him. Using her solid-gold DuPont pen, Libby circled the lot number several times, which, in her mind, despite whatever bidding-up there might be by Texans, Japanese, or Kuwaitis, made the colt already hers.

Faced away from the door, she heard it being opened and closed but she didn't look around to see who it was. Long ago she had developed the attitude of conserving energy by being presumptive about the nearly constant scurry and bustle that went on around her, chambermaids, waiters, and such. It did occur to her now, though, that whoever had entered hadn't bothered to knock and, still without looking in that direction, she made a reproachful comment. She did not realize it was Wintersgill until he'd come deeper into the room, well within the periphery of her vision.

"Thomas!" The single word carried her surprise and vexation.

Wintersgill acknowledged her with a nearly imperceptible nod. He appeared to be mainly concerned with the room. He looked about it slowly as though it were something being presented for his selection. Libby's strict edict that no one was allowed into her private apartment unless invited included Wintersgill. It had been three years since he'd been in this bedroom with her.

"What is it?" Libby demanded.

No reply from him.

She sat up abruptly, placed her wine goblet on the table at the arm of the bergère. It was a feint on her part, an incomplete motion meant to forewarn that strong action would be taken. "I want you out of here this minute," Libby said with an unequivocal clip. "Out!"

"We have matters," Wintersgill said as much to the setting as to her. He drew over a side chair that was intended to be admired more than bear weight. He sat diagonally opposite her with one leg crossed over the knee of the other, the fingers of both his hands loosely laced.

Libby resumed her comfortable position in the bergère, told herself she would put up with this not a second longer than five minutes. She hoped that she would be able to return to the mood she'd been in. What was this all about, anyway? Why didn't Thomas come right out and say? If he was there to again campaign for marriage she would discharge him, banish the son of a bitch despite the inconvenience it would cause, send him packing to his former job of socializing on behalf of various charities such as little ballet companies and obscure repositories for the elderly, maneuvering, for a commission, the expiatary tithes of well-offs. A step back into that kind of whoring would serve him right. Just let him even mention marriage.

She tensed the corners of her mouth into a small measure of smile, casually spun her crystal wine goblet by its stem before taking a sip. Studied him while she waited for him to explain why he'd stepped over the line of being there. Thomas seemed, she thought, more relaxed than usual, even in that dreadful, unreliable chair, settled in as though for a long conversation. His ease was emphasized by what he was wearing. A gray cashmere cardigan sweater, probably from Dunhill, light-gray flannel pleated slacks, a creamy silk shirt, and off-white antelope oxfords. An incongruity was the black strap and snap of the elastic garter holding up the pale gray sock on his right leg. This outmoded, prosthesislike accessory was revealed to Libby by the way his trouser bottom had ridden up. Wintersgill had probably started wearing garters early in life, a childhood event, Libby thought. He would always be the garter sort.

"Well," she said impatiently, "what is it . . . business?"

"Yes."

"Then it can wait."

"Yesterday, the twenty million we spoke about. . . . It didn't go into Townsend's account in Liechtenstein, so you can save yourself the bother of having someone run that down."

Actually, Libby hadn't given a thought to that twenty million. The bank transfer receipt for it was already forgotten in the handbag she'd carried yesterday and might not carry again for months, if ever. Her indifference toward the money was not out of disrespect. Twenty million was a formidable amount, but it was gone and she'd never had it in hand and it was impossible for her to feel deprived of anything so abstract.

Calmly, Wintersgill told her, "The account in Liechtenstein that it went into is mine."

Oh, so that was it, Libby thought. Wintersgill's conscience was chattering and he was there to unload, needing her to forgivingly wipe his most recent misdemeanors from his brow. No doubt this was a result of the way she had laid him bare yesterday. Pity she wasn't in the frame of mind to skin him a bit. He'd caught her at a good time. All she wanted was to be rid of him, not let him spoil her night. Magnanimously, she changed the subject. "Did you by chance look into getting that Whistler portrait from Brooke Edgerton's estate?"

The question passed through Wintersgill. He didn't believe her reaction. It exemplified how devious she was. No matter, he'd get her to cooperate. From his sweater pocket he brought out the red kidskin pouch. He undid its drawstrings and spread its mouth and poured from it into his cupped hand the twelve Russian diamonds. He watched Libby's eyes narrow, heard her breathing catch, knew he had reached her.

During the next few moments Libby realized what, up to now, she'd been too self-involved to see.

The knots behind the composure of Wintersgill's face.

The cinching knots of madness.

She was sure of it. That was his reason for being there. He'd snapped, was deranged, and had chosen her to reveal it to. She would have to be extremely careful with him, not to tighten those psychotic knots more or cause them to become uncontrollably unraveled. She felt fright emptying her stomach, transmitting to her every pore and nerve end. Don't let it show, she warned herself. But what should her attitude be? Could a single wrong word set him off? She believed so. She had to get him out of there somehow. She needed help. The electronic button to summon help was on the side table, but her hand told her it would be unwise to suddenly reach for it.

Wintersgill jiggled and tossed up the diamonds, tauntingly. They clicked together and sent flashes into one another, reciprocally intensifying their brilliance. "As you see," he said in that same calm tone, "your diamonds weren't lost in the Townsend burglary."

"Marvelous!"

He sat forward, held out his hand.

Was he offering her the diamonds? She cupped her hands together to receive them. For a long moment he was ambivalent about what to do, and just when she was sure he was going to drop them into her hands, he curled his fingers around them possessively and stuffed them and the pouch into one of his sweater pockets.

Libby eliminated the awkwardness of her empty hands by having them pour a glass of the wine for him. While doing so she remembered aloud, as though exemplifying her thoughtfulness toward him, that he preferred a high grown white such as this over most reds, and it was he who had introduced her to the Swiss vintages. "Over the years there have been so many things like that," she exaggerated. "I don't think you realize, Thomas, what an influence you've had on me."

When he genteelly accepted the compliment and the glass of wine, smiled softly, and said a credible thank-you, Libby thought perhaps she'd been wrong about his mental state. She'd allowed her imagination to run away with her. This was the same Wintersgill as ever, acting a bit out of pattern, admittedly, but didn't everyone have their spells of that? She raised her glass and with a confident voice from the first syllable recited a toast that he would know from having heard it before as one of the ones she reserved for meaningful intimate occasions. It had to do with the longevity of everything beautiful.

He drank to that.

Over the rim of her glass, careful not to be caught staring, she searched his face and saw the knots still there. If anything, they were tighter, more pronounced, bunched up particularly in the flesh over his cheekbones and along his neck. The sinews of his neck stood out as though he were holding up an extreme weight.

Another wave of fright passed through her. It was all she could do to keep it from transforming into panic.

Wintersgill didn't help with his talk about Townsend. He sat there and, in an almost chatty manner, related why Townsend had been murdered, told how the twenty million in Liechtenstein and the fifteen million in Russian diamonds fit in. He made it sound as if it was an opportunity that only a fool would have let pass. Everything about it, as he saw it, was simply feasible, a good piece of business.

Libby had always felt there was something smelly about Townsend's death. Townsend was too much of a clawer for suicide, and the notion that he'd slipped on the wet marble floor and gone over was, in Libby's opinion, absurd. She hadn't, however, made anything of it except dinner-table talk. After all, Townsend wasn't anyone that she held dear, not a person of quality by any means. He was a merchant, a purveyor, and a procurer as well. Give him a *rest in peace,* if that was what was called for, and let it go at that. It had never once occurred to her that Wintersgill was connected with the Townsend mess, although now it seemed obvious.

Murderer.

Which brought Libby to the terrifying question: Why was he divulging it to her? Surely not because he was in need of a confidante. She would, she knew, have to be more femininely resourceful than she'd ever been in her life, reach down into herself for the precise sort of charm, say every right word, convince him.

She began by getting his eyes with her own, holding them. It was difficult for her to soften her facial expression but she managed, and purposely slow, degree by degree, taking at least a full minute, she increased her smile and the fondness in it. "I was dreadful yesterday, wasn't I?" she said with some contrition.

Wintersgill agreed with a single definite nod.

"When I left the club I kept looking back and feeling sorry. Several times I was on the verge of telling Groat to turn around and take me back . . . to you . . . but I thought by then you would probably be gone. So I had to suffer through the evening trying to distract myself. I was a sulk over dinner and so fidgety at the theater that the man seated behind me complained. Imagine."

It seemed to her that he was hanging on her words. She was encouraged.

"It was all my own doing, of course. I couldn't have a thought without it being crowded by the picture of you somewhere, wounded, and I the disconsolate inflicter. Oh, God, if only we could take back into our throats words that should have been left unsaid, unheard. Impetuous defensive words that just come out, by habit more than anything else." She lowered her eyes, slightly quivered her lashes. "Do you understand what I'm trying to say? Do you?"

"Yes."

She contrived a small, self-conscious laugh. "I'm afraid I'm not very good at apologies . . . or asking for . . . second chances." As though to mask the nervousness brought on by such an admission she took a cigarette from the bronze and crystal box on the table. She tamped it on the back of her hand, tamped it again and again, pretending that an important thought had drifted her off from what she was doing. No doubt read by Wintersgill as a thought of him. After a moment she simultaneously brought the cigarette to her lips and sat up very straight in the chair. She stretched catlike, bowed her spine, and flexed her shoulders back as though they were wings. There was, she knew, a promise of more active passion in such suppleness and, as well, she was quite aware of the way it caused her breasts to thrust and her nipples to punctuate the fine cotton of her pajama top.

She reached for the table lighter.

The heel of her hand pressed several of the buttons of the signaling device. There! It was done and she was certain Wintersgill hadn't noticed. Soon plenty of strong-armed help would arrive and she'd tell them to throw this idiot out—*sans* her diamonds. There was always help on duty just down the hall, Fane or Hinch or someone. On the average it took them only thirty seconds to get to her. She'd timed them on occasion and she was certainly timing them now, calculating that an inhale and exhale of her cigarette took seven seconds.

Well over thirty seconds passed, then more than a minute. Where the hell were they? Was it possible the signaling device was on the blink? Unlikely, inasmuch as it had been working less than a half hour ago when she'd ordered dinner. She was almost certain she'd pressed the buttons firmly enough. The help was fucking off. She'd discharge the lot when she got out of this. Automatons such as they were a dollar a dozen. Damn! Why didn't they come? Until they did she'd have to carry on with this ridiculous love-humbled role. Wintersgill seemed to be growing agitated.

"Thomas," she said as though it were pleasant for her to form the name, "do you remember telling me years ago that you believed I resembled the actress Madeleine Carroll?"

"I do."

Actually, the resemblance had been commented upon by numerous people at various times. "It was, as I look back on it now, one of the sweetest compliments anyone ever paid me. I've never forgotten it. *But lovelier than Madeleine Carroll,* you said, and I was unable to just accept it, had to think it was merely a blandishment. I don't suppose you'll ever say that again or have reason to, just as I suppose you'll never ask me again."

"Ask you what?"

"To marry you."

No response from him.

Libby believed that if she could get him to again ask her to marry him she would accept enthusiastically and be on safe ground. Why should he ask for a future and then harm it? "Serves me right," she told him, making her lips into a pouty moue, a little artifice that had gotten her her way countless times. Someone, a Frenchman whose name was as forgotten as a meal, had told her that expression on her mouth was like a proposal for oral sex. "I know," she went on, "you're going to make me do penance for all the times I've disappointed you. I beg of you, please, Thomas, don't put me through all those punishing traces."

He stood abruptly.

She believed he would come over to her, to eat from her hand, but he just stood there and again studied the various aspects of the bedroom in a selective manner.

She got up and went to him, taking her wine goblet with her. Standing well within the prospect of an embrace, she told him, "We could be married in Saratoga during the summer meeting. It will be terribly warm there but we won't mind. Everyone who is anyone will want to celebrate us. Think of it. Besides, there's a Secretariat colt going up for sale that I want . . . as my wedding gift to you."

She beseeched with her eyes, tried to will him with her eyes, offered the silence into which she expected he would place his compliance. She believed she saw the knots in his face slackening. She heard his breathing and reasoned that the cause of his rapid, shallow breaths was her closeness. She heard him wet the inside of his mouth and swallow. She thought how much she hated him.

She transferred the wine goblet to her other hand. The cabochon sapphire she had on hit the rim of the crystal goblet, causing a resonant little ring.

The sound flung open a gate in him, and immediately his mind was overrun.

The back of his right hand lashed across Libby's face, snapping her head around with such force that the rest of her body had to spin with it. Her balance was lost for a moment, but the hard side of an intricately lacquered armoire standing against the near wall kept her from going down.

She'd never in her life been struck.

The right side of her face felt scorched, but that was not as painful as the abasement of it. Her reflexive impulse was to protract claws and attack.

Instead, she made a dash for the door. Was within inches of reaching the ornate knob when Wintersgill got her from behind by her hair, yanked her back with such suddenness that it felt as though her scalp was torn.

She screamed obscenities.

He flung her across the room.

Her arms, flailing for balance, swept precious possessions from the marble surface of a console. She went sprawling to the floor and at once began a scurrying crawl, like some startled, scuttling sea creature, trying, it seemed, to gain the protection of the crevice beneath the bed. However, what she was really going for was the .32 caliber automatic pistol she kept in one of the *encoignures* that flanked her bed. She got the elaborate marquetry cupboard door of the *encoignure* open, got the pistol in her grasp.

Wintersgill's hand clamped around her wrist. He wrenched her slender wrist as he would a branch he was tearing loose. He must have broken it, for her hand flopped useless, unable to hold the pistol, which dropped to the floor.

He clutched and twisted the front of her pajama top, lifted her upright by it. He was surprised how extraordinarily frail she seemed to him, practically weightless.

She heard her own screams. She cowered her face in the crooks of her elbows.

He tightened his right hand into a hard fist. Drove it full force into the pit of her stomach, doubling her over, cutting off her scream.

She could not breathe. Her windpipe felt bound. It was as if the blacks of her pupils expanded beyond the limits of her eyes as she lost consciousness.

Wintersgill continued to beat her. He held her up and smashed her face with his fist again and again, until the silicone implant that had composed her perfect chin showed whiter than bone through the split flesh. Until her splendidly shaped nose was laid open on her cheek.

Even after she was dead he went on beating her, splattering himself with her blood. Finally he stopped, stepped back, and blamed her for his being out of breath.

He tore the pajamas from her and lifted her dead weight to the bed. Pulled on her and arranged her so that she lay face up straddling the corner of the bed, her limp legs falling left and right of the corner. The soft mass of her pubic hair was offered up, floss on a mound. He knelt between her legs, ran a finger through her pubic hair, combed through it, and parted it in several places with his fingers, his face close down to see what he was doing.

From his second sweater pocket he brought out his straight razor, his ancestral razor. He opened the blade to its best angle. Stretching the skin of her mons with the fingers of his free hand, he applied the cutting edge.

There was a crackling that would have been almost inaudible under ordinary circumstances, but was now like loud electric static, as the razor shaved a three-inch-wide swath down the left section of her mons. The shorn skin was whiter from having been protected.

Wintersgill pinched it in several places, poked at it with the tips of his fingers.

Using the razor again he cut into the flesh of her mons, made an incision about two inches long. The outer skin and the underlying vascular tissue parted like a lipless mouth and pooled with blood. The blood obscured the honed edge of the blade, but Wintersgill knew almost exactly where to cut, and anyway it didn't matter if he made a mess of it.

He felt a change in the resistance under the blade.

He cut deeper.

As though it were something animate, eager for liberation, it emerged, slipped up and out from between the folds of the fatty tissue that had comfortably nestled it.

Stone 588.

That it had come into Libby's possession was a coincidence to begin with. It merely happened to be among the goods stolen from the Springer & Springer safe. The thieves had acted on their own, unaware that this stone was special. As far as they were concerned, what they had stolen were just diamonds, all good, some better. The thieves sold the entire package of swag to Townsend for a million and a half. He wasn't altogether sure that what he'd bought were the goods of Springer & Springer. He'd heard of that robbery, of course, and because of the coinciding timing, rather surmised that firm had been the source, but in keeping with the code of stealer and buyer he hadn't inquired.

While sorting through the package Townsend had come upon the stone. He recognized it immediately, from having examined it that night after dinner in Libby's library.

Townsend, in one respect, knew what he had, and in another he didn't know. He didn't know the veracity of the stone, its power, nor did he take the time to determine that. Maybe he felt so certain it was a hoax that he didn't want to weaken his bargaining muscle by proving he was right. What he did know he had was something Libby believed in and would pay plenty for. He knew her.

With Wintersgill acting as intermediary, Townsend struck a deal with Libby for the stone. She agreed to the first price Townsend asked: two hundred million. To be paid in substantial installments out of Hull Foundation funds over the next two years.

Twenty-five million sealed the deal.

Stone 588 went to Libby.

The very next day Libby flew to Madrid, where, under an assumed name, she had the stone implanted in the adipose tissue of her mons. Wintersgill took care of all the arrangements. The young plastic surgeon who performed the simple operation was already acclimated to eccentrics. He was told the reason Libby wanted the stone implanted, particularly there, had something to do with her Mephistophelian religious beliefs. The plastic surgeon was fascinated to the point of doing a little research for precedent cases and discovered the little-known fact that Burmese warriors used to implant rubies beneath their skin, believing they would protect their blood from the poison of enemy arrows.

The plastic surgeon's incision healed. Libby's pubic hair grew back and concealed the fine, tiny scar.

Libby had stone 588 and its righting power all to herself for as long as she lived. She was virtually guaranteed that she would never suffer a sick day.

Only Wintersgill knew she had it.

Now his fingers dug in and plucked the stone from her opened flesh. For a moment he gazed at it, saw in it the means by which he would regain the wealth and prestige that had once belonged to the Wintersgill line. He wouldn't sell the stone outright, as the fool Townsend had, nor would he keep it to himself like the vain, selfish Libby. He would control the stone, dole out its power. The wealthy sick would plead to pay him vast sums.

Hurrying footsteps out in the hall.

Wintersgill stood up as—

The bedroom door was opened by Audrey. Springer was with her.

Wintersgill's mind said his eyes were mistaken. Springer and Audrey were supposed to be dead and somewhere never to be found. There *couldn't* be anyone left alive who would have reason to come after him, who would cause him to put more locks on all his doors.

Springer and Audrey were stopped, stunned into immobility by the gruesome sight: Libby on the bed, so obviously dead, her face bashed in, raw, her blood everywhere. Wintersgill was splattered with it. Her blood was on his hands.

Wintersgill stood there, caught in the ghastly tableau.

And the next moment he was not there, had disappeared like a phantom. He'd taken advantage of Springer's and Audrey's state of shock, had been no more than a blur to them when he dashed out through the French doors to the balcony and, without hesitating, went over the balustrade into the black of the night.

Springer and Audrey hurried out onto the balcony. With their pistols in hand they peered down, but by then Wintersgill was part of the thick, pervasive darkness. He was not even as much as a shadow or movement.

Wintersgill landed in the bed of alyssum fifteen feet below. The soft loam there cushioned his drop. He kept to the flower bed, ran along the south side of the house for a short way before taking to the lawn. Within five strides on the lawn he had set off one of the external security systems of the house: an undetectable, ten-foot-wide pressure grid beneath the sod, which electronically responded whenever weight in excess of a hundred pounds attempted to move across it. The grid was continuous, circumscribing the house like a reassuring moat.

Activated by the pressure of Wintersgill's weight, the grid automatically switched on numerous powerful floodlights.

Wintersgill was revealed out on the open lawn. He was sixty-some feet away and running.

Springer and Audrey brought their pistols up, simultaneously aimed, simultaneously squeezed the slack from their triggers. It would take an exceptional shot at that distance.

Wintersgill's arms flew up as if he were saying hallelujah. His upper torso twisted, and it appeared that he'd tripped over his own feet. He stumbled, lunged, went down, convulsed a couple of times, and lay motionless.

Was it Springer's or Audrey's shot that had felled him?

Neither.

Neither Springer nor Audrey had fired.

Audrey climbed up over the balustrade, hung from the lower edge of it, and dropped to the alyssum bed. It was something she'd done many times years ago from a similar balcony outside her own second-floor bedroom when she hadn't wanted to take the long way to the outside. She reached Wintersgill before Springer. Wintersgill was lying face up in a contorted position. He looked dead. He was dead. But who had killed him?

Wintersgill's right arm was doubled beneath him. His right hand was a loose fist.

Audrey spotted something.

A shiny hint of something protruded ever so slightly from the cranny formed by Wintersgill's fist. She felt influenced to know what it was. She pried open the dead fist enough to get at it. She straightened up and then Springer was next to her and she was about to tell him that she had stone 588—when a voice from behind them, intimidating in its clipped gruffness, told them, "Right there!"

Springer and Audrey did as told, remained in place and motionless.

Fred Pugh and Jack Blayney came out from between a row of euonymus shrubs. Blayney had a big revolver, a .44 magnum, with a silencer making it look all the bigger.

Springer assumed that was the gun that had so surely killed Wintersgill.

Blayney kept the .44 pointed while Pugh took the pistols from Springer and Audrey and frisked them for any additional weapons. "Just so no one gets hurt who doesn't deserve it," Pugh explained.

A reassurance and a warning, Springer thought.

Blayney put away the revolver. He'd killed Wintersgill because Pugh had officially told him to. Simple as that. He'd also kill these two if Pugh gave him the word.

Pugh knelt and searched Wintersgill's body. First found was the straight razor. It puzzled Pugh momentarily. He confiscated it. Then he found the twelve Russian diamonds. They didn't puzzle him at all. Counting them more than examining them, he dropped them back into the drawstring pouch and put them in his pocket.

Springer surmised that the diamonds had had something to do with the murderous rampage of Wintersgill. And that they were what these men were after, what they'd killed Wintersgill for. These two were probably Wintersgill men turned disloyal, making the best of an opportunity. What else?

Pugh continued to search Wintersgill's body. He was very thorough about it, practically stripped the clothes off. He removed Wintersgill's shoes and felt inside them, peeled Wintersgill's socks off and turned them inside out, even went so far as to stick a finger into Wintersgill's mouth and probe around between the cheeks and gums.

Finally, Pugh stood up. Apparently he was a bit confounded. He considered Springer and Audrey for a moment, then Wintersgill's body, then Springer and Audrey again. "Let's go over there where we can sit down," he suggested.

They went across the lawn and down the slope a way to the terrace inset among the willows, the same terrace where Springer had met

Libby that first afternoon. The furniture had white sheetlike covers to protect it from getting damp. Blayney uncovered a couple of bergères and a settee, arranged them so they were facing and close enough. He and Pugh took the bergères, Springer and Audrey the settee.

Pugh pinched an itch from his nostrils, stretched his nose, sniffed once and began. "I figured this would be the windup." He gestured in the general direction of Wintersgill's body. "I figured he'd end up with the stone. Either him or, somehow . . . you."

"What stone?" Springer asked.

"Don't give me that," Pugh said, squinching up his face. "You're in no position to give me that."

"No position," Blayney echoed.

"Are you talking about stone five eighty-eight?" Springer asked.

"I don't know about any numbers," Pugh said. "Is that the stone that's supposed to heal? If it is, that's the one."

Springer was puzzled. How did these guys know about stone 588? Who were they to be after it? He asked.

"State Department," Pugh told him.

They didn't look like diplomats to Springer. There was nothing tactful about that big .44 revolver.

Pugh read Springer's skepticism. He took out his over-sat-on wallet and flipped to the acetate sleeve that contained his laminated State identification. He insisted that Springer take a good long look at it.

It seemed authentic, but Springer was only three quarters convinced. He recalled Danny having told him about a place in Queens where for as little as fifty bucks one could get anything from a car title to a Harvard Medical School diploma. "How do you know about stone five eighty-eight?" Springer asked.

Pugh told him. Anyway, enough of it for Springer to gather that somehow, through Norman, particulars about the stone had leaked out. It didn't matter to Springer. He told Pugh, "I don't have the stone. I wish to God I did."

"We've all got problems," Pugh said with the appropriate degree of sympathy. "One of yours right now, I must point out, is Blayney here. All I have to do is tell him and he kills you. He's like that."

Springer believed Pugh.

Audrey asked, "Say we do have the stone, just say. And say we handed it over to you. Would that satisfy you? Would you allow us to walk away and that would be the end of it?"

"I'm not soft," Pugh replied, "but the way I see it everybody who deserved to be dead is already dead."

Springer glanced up to the house. Through the lacy droops of willow he saw the lights of Libby's second-story bedroom. The old time-fighter had lost, he thought regretfully. Audrey seemed to be taking it well. Probably the reality of it hadn't yet hit her.

Audrey did a loud, submitting sigh and told Springer, "Give them the stone, darling."

"Huh?"

"Let them have it. To hell with it," she said.

"But . . ."

"I'm not about to suffer another scratch, much less give up living, for any stupid phony stone," she said.

Pugh got the *phony*. All along it had been his own unexpressed opinion that this fuss about a stone that could heal people was just a lot of wishful jerking off. Still, an assignment was an assignment. It was his obligation to bring the stone back to Washington to George Gurney. The Department could test it out. If it didn't work, it wouldn't be his ass. As for the twelve Russian diamonds, they'd be his and Blayney's unmentioned fringe benefit. They were entitled.

"Give the man the stone," Audrey told Springer impatiently.

"I don't have it," Springer said, trying to understand the tack she was on.

"I gave it to you," Audrey said.

"You didn't," Springer said.

"It's right there in your jacket pocket," Audrey claimed. "Don't be so stubborn."

Just going along with it, Springer reached into that pocket. His fingers were surprised to feel some sort of stone. It felt about right. On their way over here to the terrace Audrey must have slipped it into his pocket. But where had she gotten it?

Before Springer could say anything, Audrey ricocheted a little self-inflicted slap off her forehead. "Whatever am I thinking of?" she exclaimed. "I didn't give it to you. I only thought I *ought* to give it to you." She stood in order to dig into the pocket of her slacks. She brought out her pendulum.

"That's not it," Pugh said. He had a general idea of what the stone looked like, its size and all. A third-hand description.

"Of course it isn't," Audrey said and kept digging in the pocket. She brought out a rough diamond of fifty-some carts. It was what she called her "similar" stone, the one she'd taken as a souvenir of the Townsend burglary. Something had told her to carry it around for luck. She handed it over to Pugh.

He examined it, held it up, and turned it every which way. A smile and nod conveyed his acceptance.

Springer hung his head, feigning defeat.

Audrey raised her chin and looked away, acting vindicated.

At that moment someone was coming down the floodlighted slope. It was Hinch. He paused at Wintersgill's body, then stepped over it and proceeded to the terrace. He addressed Audrey. "Please pardon me for interrupting, Miss Hull, but I was wondering if anyone would care for some refreshment."

Springer was astonished by Hinch's thick-skinned composure, even more so by the flexibility of his loyalty. Hinch, evidently, had done a body count and knew Audrey was now on top of the Hull heap. He wasn't just offering refreshments, he was offering to continue on in her service.

"Nothing for me, Hinch," Audrey told him. "But perhaps these gentlemen . . . "

"I'll have a rye and Seven," Blayney said.

Springer declined.

Pugh ordered a frozen banana daiqueri. "What's your name?" he asked Hinch.

Hinch told him, spelled it for him.

"We had a terrible thing occur here tonight, didn't we, Hinch?" Pugh said.

"Yes sir, we did."

"A robbery."

"A robbery," Hinch concurred.

"The three thieves who broke in . . . there were three, weren't there?" Pugh said.

"Three."

"Who broke in and killed Mrs. Hull and Mr. Wintersgill . . . but you weren't able to get a good look at them, were you?" Pugh said, leading.

"No, sir."

"Why not?"

"They had nylon stockings pulled over their heads so their features were compressed beyond recognition." Hinch said. "I couldn't even determine the color of their hair."

"What were they wearing?"

"Black coveralls and leather gloves."

"They held you at gunpoint."

"Yes, indeed. The shorter of the three kept a gun on myself and another servant while the other two went through the house."

"Did they take anything?"

"I'm certain they did. At least a few valuable things that Mrs. Hull had around," Hinch said. "I'll have to see exactly what."

"You do that."

"Yes, sir. Mrs. Hull must have refused to reveal the combination to the vault. And Mr. Wintersgill must have tried to defend her. Such a valiant gentleman, Mr. Wintersgill."

"We all agree on that," Pugh said.

A couple of pros cleaning things up, Springer thought.

Hinch looked to Audrey again. "Miss Hull, may I inquire whether you and Mr. Springer will be spending the night here or going into town?"

"We're going into town," Audrey said.

Hinch, with an absolutely straight matter-of-fact face, told her, "Groat is waiting to drive you if you wish."

36

"You don't have to creep. I hear you."

"I thought you were asleep."

"I was just lying here thinking. What time is it?"

"Going on twelve."

Jake switched on his bedside lamp and squinted at Springer. "I had a feeling you might drop by tonight," he said sitting up, punching his pillows and placing them against the headboard. He had on pajama bottoms. Before his leg got sick he'd worn only the tops, but he didn't want Gayle and everyone always taking looks at his leg hoping to see some sign that it was better. "Did Audrey come with you?" Jake asked.

"She just dropped me off. She had to go home."

Audrey had thought it best that Springer take care of this alone. But her heart and hope would be there with him, she'd said. "She sent you her love," Springer told Jake.

"How much of it?"

"A bunch."

"What in?"

"A hug, for one thing."

"Well, give it to me."

Springer sat on the edge of the bed so he could put his arms around his boy. Hold him close. Jake's desperation was like a radiance that passed into his own body. Springer kept holding, wanting to absorb all of it.

Gayle came in bringing the coffee Springer had requested. Strong and black. Along with two slices of the pecan chocolate pound cake from Greenberg's that she knew he liked as much as Jake did. Gayle looked harried but seemed stronger than ever, not just persevering but prepared to fight the long fight. She placed the small tray on the table next to the chintz-covered armchair she'd moved in from her bedroom. She spent a lot of time in that chair by Jake's bed, the precious time. "If you need anything more I'll be in my room reading," she said pleasantly and went out, closing the door after her.

"Want a hunk of this cake?" Springer asked Jake.

Jake burped, pardoned himself, and said he wasn't hungry. He broke off a corner of one of the slices of cake, just to share. "I'm sure tired of taking soda bicarb," he said. "All I do is burp. In the last month I must have said a couple of million pardon-mes." Jake's intake of soda bicarbonate was essential. His system had to be kept alkaline to offset the toxicity of the chemotherapy.

"Can I use your bathroom?" Springer asked.

"Don't forget to lift the seat." Jake playfully mocked Gayle.

Springer went in, took only one look at himself in the mirror, realized he hadn't seen himself since early that morning. He thought the image that looked back at him was a bit glary-eyed. He removed his jacket, rolled up his shirt sleeves, and splashed double handfuls of cold water on his face. That helped him feel fresher. He got stone 588 from his jacket pocket. He noticed now that it was partially coated with blood dried a reddish brown. Wintersgill's blood, he thought, or possibly Libby's by way of Wintersgill's hands. Springer ran warm water over the stone. The blood adhered stubbornly to it.

He used a fingernail brush to scrub the blood away. He dried the stone with a kleenex tissue. When he held it up to the light, it appeared restored and he felt better about it. He put it into his shirt pocket and, leaving his jacket off, went out to Jake.

"Your coffee's getting cold," Jake said.

"You stuck your finger in it?"

"My toe." Jake grinned.

Springer sat in the armchair, ate the cake, and drank the coffee while he and Jake talked about anything . . . except tomorrow. Springer knew how much Jake dreaded having to go back into Sloan-Kettering for more chemotherapy and all its distressing side-effects. He was waiting for Jake to fall asleep.

Jake yawned. "I'm sleepy," he said, "but I just can't seem to let myself fall into it."

"We all have those kind of nights," Springer said.

"I'm going to die, I think," Jake said, right at Springer. It was the first time he'd expressed the fear in words.

"No you're not."

"They're going to give me chemotherapy for as long as they can, then they're going to have to cut off my leg, and eventually I'll die anyway . . . in ten years or so."

"Who told you that?"

"I read about it in some medical books Mom got. She didn't show them to me. I sneaked a peek at them when she wasn't around. She had the places all marked and everything. I know."

"Well, you're not going to die."

"Why not?"

"Because we're going to do everything within our power to make sure that you don't."

"For instance?" Jake challenged a bit hopefully.

"For one thing we're going to *believe* you're not going to die. We're going to believe that with *all* our inner strength. We're going to all put our believing together so it's stronger than dying."

Jake pictured it. "Sure," he remarked dubiously.

Springer paused to choose his tack. "Did I ever tell you about your great-grandfather's believing stone?" he asked.

"His what?"

"Believing stone."

"Nope."

"I thought I had."

"What was my great-grandfather's name?"

"Willard."

"You probably told somebody else about it."

"I wouldn't. It's strictly a family thing."

"Confidential information."

A conspiratorial nod from Springer. "One day way back when your great-grandfather was about your age, he was looking for arrowheads in a field up in New Milford. It was springtime and the ground had just been plowed up, and he knew that was usually the best time to find arrowheads."

"What kind of Indians used to be up around there?"

"Mohawks," Springer said, which was the first tribe that came to mind. "Anyway, your great-grandfather . . . "

"Why don't you call him Willard?"

" . . . Willard didn't find any arrowheads that day but he did find a pretty stone, and he took it home and everyone agreed it was so different from the sort of stones seen in those parts that it must have come from somewhere else. Willard was proud of it and it got so he always carried it around with him, and before long he discovered that his stone could do things for him."

"What sort of things?"

"Well, whenever he got low on believing all he had to do was hold the stone in his hand and it would give him a refill."

A skeptical side glance from Jake.

Springer didn't let it faze him. "That stone came in handy countless times for Willard. He always caught trout even when the water in the streams was too warm or too low. Once he caught an eighteen-inch brown with his hands by just grabbing in under the grassy overhang of a bank. And in winter when he wanted to go sledding there was always good ice for him on one hill or the other. Simply because he had enough belief that that was how those things would be."

Jake shook his head incredulously. "You expect me to believe all that?"

"Are you sure I never told you about the believing stone, never even mentioned it?"

"Never."

"Want to see it?"

"You got it with you?"

"I carry it with me a lot." Springer took stone 588 from his shirt pocket, handed it to Jake.

Jake looked it over. "What is it, quartz?"

"I don't know."

"Maybe it's even rock crystal." Jake offered the stone back to Springer.

"Why don't you hang on to it for a while," Springer suggested.

"What for?"

"Seems to me you're low on believing. You could use a refill."

"All I have to do is hang on to it, right?"

"Just hang on."

"For how long?"

"For as long as it takes."

Jake's eyes got blinky and he finally fell asleep. With stone 588 in his hand. When his fingers relaxed and released the stone, Springer found an Ace elastic bandage in one of the dresser drawers, the sort of bandage Jake used to use when he turned an ankle or pulled a muscle playing volleyball. Springer, careful not to awaken Jake, placed the stone on the inside of Jake's right wrist and wrapped the elastic bandage around it just snugly enough to keep it in place. He dimmed the lamp by draping a towel over it, so he could still see for sure the stone was there.

He removed his shoes, hunched down in the chintz-covered chair, settled into his vigil.

It was up to stone 588 now, he thought. Either it was doing what it was supposed to be able to do or it wasn't. He'd risked all for it, he'd stolen for it, he'd been almost killed, and he'd killed for it. Now was no time to start doubting it.

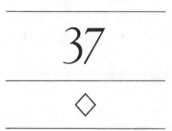

37

The following morning at half past ten Springer was in Dr. Stimson's office at Sloan-Kettering. He was alone and feeling it. Jake was down on the second floor being x-rayed, so his condition could be assessed prior to chemotherapy treatment. It was routine. Dr. Stimson was with Jake. He'd told Springer he'd return in fifteen, twenty minutes at most, but Springer had been waiting close to an hour.

The time that it was taking did not bode well, Springer thought. It probably meant the x-rays showed unexpected complications, a severe worsening of Jake's condition, medical decisions having to be made. But maybe, Springer told himself, trying for ease, they were just having equipment problems, or it could be as simple a thing as they'd run out of film.

Springer got up and walked out of the office, went down the corridor to the drinking fountain, sucked up a mouthful, and went back into the office and sat again. For about the twentieth time. He took a medical journal from the hundreds that were stacked around. Turned to any page. His eyes struck upon such phrases as *limb salvage procedure, resection surgery, distant metastases,* and *fully malignant.* He closed the journal, placed it back on its stack cautiously, as though otherwise he would unleash its contents.

Dr. Stimson finally returned, with a large manila envelope containing x-rays. He appeared solemn, distracted, even a bit rattled. He apologized perfunctorily for having made Springer wait and got right to the point. "We need your consent to do another biopsy on your son's leg," he said.

Those were certainly not the words Springer had hoped to hear.

Dr. Stimson removed a large x-ray from the manila envelope. As it bent and buckled in his hands it sounded like make-believe thunder. "We must obtain some fresh tissue samples in order to evaluate the cells and determine exactly what is going on," he said, clipping the x-ray onto the lighted viewing panel on the wall.

Springer had never seen an x-ray of Jake's leg. It was strange to be able to look into flesh that he'd helped create. There was Jake's thigh and knee with the affected area so obvious, the tumor interrupting and misshaping the femur bone like an ugly growth knot on a limb, crushing in the bone, relentlessly overwhelming the adjacent flesh, blood vessels, nerves. It looked so painful to Springer that he had to close his eyes.

How ridiculous of him, he thought in eyeshut, to have put his faith in anything so illusory as stone 588. He'd been thinking with his hope. But the stone had worked for others. Why hadn't it worked for Jake? Was some sort of moral requirement involved? Could it be that the reason it hadn't worked was he'd stolen for it, killed?

Dr. Stimson meanwhile had clipped another x-ray to the light panel, on the right of the first. "Our initial thought was that the technician had made an error," he said, "that possibly she had developed the wrong film and what we were looking at was someone else's x-ray. Subsequent exposures eliminated that possibility."

Springer's eyes were open now.

Stimson explained. "These are nearly identical views of your son's leg. This one"—he indicated the x-ray on the left—"helped us make our diagnosis. It was taken a month ago. This"—he directed Springer's attention to the x-ray on the right—" is one of the x-rays we took today."

Stimson pointed out the difference between the two, how the most recent x-ray showed both the outer covering of the bone, the periosteum, and the compact bone within it to be perfectly intact, how the surrounding tissues and vessels were not distorted by malignancy. In fact, there was no sign of a tumor there or of one ever having been there.

"We don't know what to make of it," Dr. Stimson admitted. "Our entire Solid Tumor Task Force is down there now theorizing. The Cornell people who came over to take a look say that we must have misdiagnosed. I'm for making sure, doing another biopsy."

Springer was staring at today's x-ray. He knew what he was looking at.

The Righting of Jake.

He had a pang of guilt for having doubted, but that was easily offset by joy. "Where's Jake now?" Springer asked.

"Waiting on two. Do I have your consent, Mr. Springer?"

"Thank you, but no," Springer said and headed for his boy. He had a huge happy lump in his throat, and although he walked down the corridor it certainly felt like dancing.

38

◇

In the most incorruptible, comfortable-looking casket money could buy, Elizabeth "Libby" Hopkins-Hull was placed on a stone shelf in the family crypt in Greenwich. Her shelf was directly above the one occupied by Audrey's mother, Gillian Croft.

Audrey thought of it as the reunion of a couple of high-spirited adventuresses, sensuous cavorters, both better off having each other to gallivant with on the other side. Audrey left all her regrets in the crypt, which was swiftly bolted and sealed. What she took away were only pleasant, easy-to-carry memories.

For the entire week after the funeral, Audrey was kept busy with legalities and other matters having to do with the Hull estate. She was rushed from one meeting to the next, day and night. She faced, down the lengths of conference tables, so many sincere-suited attorneys and their dry, affected competence that they all began to look and sound alike to her.

The attorneys soon discovered that she wasn't the sort to just take their word for everything and sign whatever documents they placed before her. They patiently patronized her when she wanted to know not only *what* she was being asked to sign but *why*. It put a sycophantic strain on their polish when she tried to cut through their legal triple-talk.

The attorneys and executives she met with kept referring to this or that Hull holding, this or that Hull position.

Audrey tired of it. She requested a list of the various businesses and ventures Hull was into, everything it owned outright, controlled, or had any stake in.

It wasn't, she was told, that simple.

"Fuck it," she said, causing the clearing of several old phlegmy throats. "Make it simple."

She didn't realize that she was trampling on their autonomies, that this thing called Hull was so far-reaching and complex, purposely structured in a way that would confound even those who believed they were overseeing it.

Naively trying to get to the bottom line of all the bottom lines, Audrey asked what did the Hull holdings aggregately amount to? (She was beginning to talk like them.)

In other words, how much was she, Audrey Hopkins-Hull, worth?

Did she mean personally worth or worth within the Hull Foundation or what?

How much could she, to put it plainly, count on? That's what she meant.

They looked to one another.

Billions was the closest they could come to answering her. Billions.

Audrey, exasperated, asked one more question: Was there enough money so that she would never want no matter what she wanted?

They blew like correctly attired whales, as though it had been absurd of her to ask. More than enough, they told her, with emphasis on the *more*.

Not really satisfied but thus assured, Audrey graciously withdrew and let them get on with the business of making money. She'd been neglecting Springer, she thought, which was to say she'd been neglecting herself.

Springer did, indeed, feel somewhat deprived of Audrey all that week, but he too was kept busy—with classifying, pricing, and putting into inventory the goods from the Townsend haul and with having to keep convincing Gayle that it was all right for her to allow Jake to go out and play volleyball or whatever. Naturally Gayle found it difficult to accept that Jake was so soon wholly recovered, and nearly every afternoon there would be an SOS from Jake asking Springer to come over and liberate him.

Also, Springer was mentally preoccupied with trying to figure out how stone 588, stolen from his safe, had ended up in Wintersgill's hand. He imagined all sorts of explanations (a few were close to the truth) but not one, he felt, filled the gap acceptably. It bothered him that he'd never know.

Something else that weighed even heavier on his mind was what to do with stone 588.

Now it was Friday night and he was stretched out on the sofa in Audrey's living room. Ample light was being provided by the electric aura of the city. An Usquaebach and water balanced on his bare chest while he talked on the phone with Norman.

"I was sure you'd want it," Springer said.

"I'll admit it's tempting, but—"

"Any doctor would jump at the chance to have it."

"Not this doctor," Norman said.

"Why not?"

"I've given it adequate thought, Phil."

"Just tell me why not."

"Well, I'd probably start off with good intentions, telling myself that I'd only resort to using it whenever a case had me stumped or was hopeless. Before long, though, I'd be doubting my professional self, my decisions, every diagnosis. I'd begin to rely more and more on the stone. Not because of any weakness in my character, mind you. It's only human nature to want to be surely right. I would no longer have to know much, if anything at all, about medicine. Everything I've strived for all my life, all my years of study and training, would be superfluous, time wasted. I'd never even have to lay eyes on another medical journal, keep up with things, attend another symposium. There would be no more challenge for me."

"But you'd become a world-reknowned doctor," Springer put in.

"I intend to become that anyway." Norman laughed to temper his immodesty. "You know, Phil, it's ironic—actually, in a way, perverse. Here we are striving so hard to overcome all the horrible physical puzzles and along comes a panacea, a cure-all, and it brings us to realize it's not the best thing that could happen. For some reason, perhaps having something to do with the ongoing collective spirit of mankind, we're better off with our two-steps-forward, one-step-backward ways, rejoicing in our discoveries, being grateful for them."

Springer couldn't argue with that.

"Besides," Norman added, "if I had stone 588 to work with I wouldn't even be a doctor, I'd be a shaman."

"So?" Resigned.

"So, by the way, I had lunch with Janet yesterday. We had an enjoyable talk. God, she's bright. She came down here for a couple of days with someone whom she referred to as her special friend. Seems to me she's smitten."

"Great for her. And what about *your* love life?"

"Let's just say it's an expendable necessity."

"Find someone," Springer urged. "Take time to look."

Norman too quickly promised he would. "Don't eat too many *éclairs au chocolat,*" he said.

"That's not my department. So long, doctor."

"Take it easy, dealer."

A click again put 250 miles between the two brothers.

Springer lay there thinking that perhaps what he should do was just keep stone 588, sock it safely away, and only bring it out whenever there was an emergency. Wouldn't that be unconscionably selfish? The first time some friend was ill—the first time he even heard of anyone seriously ill—wouldn't he run and get the stone to make them well? And how many times could he do that, no matter how clandestinely, before word of it got out and he was descended upon by all sorts of people who had anything wrong with them? He'd become more of a miraculous attraction than Lourdes. He'd become a messiah. He certainly didn't want that.

Could he, then, hand over stone 588 to some well-established medical institution? No matter how ethical and well-meaning the institution might be, it would have to compromise itself. The stone took several hours to perform a Righting. Say, four hours on the average. That meant six people each day would be able to receive its benefits. Two thousand one hundred and ninety people over a year's time: a mere fraction of a fraction of the seriously ill of the world. Who would determine which two thousand one hundred and ninety out of the many millions most deserved to be healed? What would be the qualifications? Wealth? Probably; no—the way the world ran —surely.

He could, of course, let the government have the stone. Just drop it into the hands of power and let it be used for that. A dose of medical extortion to augment questionable statesmanship. Every ailing adversary who became a healthy ally would want to remain healthy, stay in line. No doubt that was why those two State Department guys, Pugh and Blayney, had been after the stone. They were only a taste of the extent the government would go to if it got wind of the real stone 588. Anyway, Springer decided, he wasn't that much of a flag waver.

What to do with stone 588?

Springer imagined himself throwing it away, imagined standing on a hill that he was familiar with up near the house in Sherman, the stone in his hand. Bringing his arm forward, letting it fly. He knew he wouldn't be able to do it.

He remained there on the sofa a while longer, considering alternatives. Then he picked up his shoes and his drink and went upstairs.

Audrey was among her pillows at the foot of her bed. She had on a pale blue silk charmeuse teddy and matching spiky heels. Her hair was severely slicked back, looked wet, and her eyes were darkly shadowed and penciled in an exaggerated way that gave them a strong oriental hint. She was wise about varying herself for Springer.

"The pendulum says we should stay at the Crillon," she said.

"I promised Jake the Ritz."

"I had Ainsworth arrange for a double suite at the Crillon." Ainsworth was the man who'd been chosen to take Wintersgill's place as head of the foundation.

"I have confirmed reservations at the Ritz," Springer told her, settling it.

"Well," she said, "we'll keep the Crillon suite as a backup. Who knows, perhaps the Ritz will run out of linens or something. What time do you want to leave?"

"Our flight is at ten Sunday morning."

"What flight is that?"

"Concorde."

"Oh. I forgot to tell you. Ainsworth arranged for one of the Hull jets at Westchester. A seven-oh-seven or something. It'll save us from having to go through all that rush and hassle at Kennedy, and we can take off whenever we're ready. I thought we might leave Saturday night and sleep in nice big beds all the way over. Doesn't that sound the better way to go?"

"I already picked up our tickets," Springer said.

"No problem. Ainsworth will see that they're returned or whatever."

Springer wondered why he so resented Ainsworth. He hadn't yet even met the man. Maybe Wintersgill had soured him on Ainsworths, but then, maybe that wasn't it at all. "We're flying Concorde and staying at the Ritz," he told Audrey firmly.

"Yes, sir, boss," she said, tongue in cheek. She brought her knee up and examined the healed-over skin where she'd scraped it on the roof of St. Patrick's. She tilted her head, glanced up at Springer, and when she saw that he wasn't aware that her eyes were on him, she used the chance to steal some from him and thought how much, how marvelously much, she loved him and always would, and that never would she let anything come before him, no matter what it cost her. Life without him would be for her like floating along without feet, like reaching out without hands. He was the love of her life, this life and the next and the next, just as surely as he had been her love before and before and before. She wanted him. She wanted him now. She felt herself go wet with her want of him.

She got up and put a Maureen McGovern on the stereo. Maureen started with "The Very Thought of You."

Springer sat in the chair kitty-corner from the foot of the bed. Instead of taking off his socks he put on his shoes.

"Going somewhere?" Audrey asked calmly.

"I have to meet a guy."

"Who?"

"Just a guy. Business."

"Before pleasure."

"I shouldn't be long."

She suspended time with a couple of long silent beats. Even her stance was candid. "You know, of course, I fully intend to have my way with you as soon as you get back."

Springer didn't get up and go over and kiss her because he knew if he did he wouldn't be able to leave. He smiled his I-too-want-you smile at her with his mouth and eyes and went into the dressing room. He put on his Audemars Piguet watch. Counted out and put to pocket five one-hundred-dollar bills. In the front left corner of the top drawer of his dresser was the precious Czar Nicholas II Fabergé box that Libby had given him. It contained stone 588. He decided against the box, took only the stone. For extra measure he went into the Mark Cross leather box in which Audrey kept her current everyday jewelry. He hastily chose a pair of plain gold ear clips and a casual gold bracelet set with pale various-colored Ceylon sapphires.

When he passed through the bedroom to go downstairs, Audrey, among her pillows again, was reading her Blavatsky and taking the first bite of a Heath Bar. To not see Springer go, she didn't look up.

As soon as Luis spotted the guy he was for doing him.

Not Frankie. Frankie thought the guy looked too easy, the way he was walking along like nothing could happen. No one walks along like that at night in New York. It was almost like the guy was asking for it. Could be a setup, Frankie believed, a cop who'd put the clamp on them when they made the move. Last thing Frankie wanted was to do a cop. Luis was still a juve. All Luis would get was another lecture from a judge. Frankie had turned eighteen. His next time he'd do time.

They were on Lexington Avenue between 81st and 82nd on the west side of the street. About mid-block, so they looked enough like they were waiting for a bus rather than a score. It was a good area for them, only a block over from Park. Rich people were always walking their dogs, were braver with their dogs. Luis and Frankie had made moves and scored okay around there a few times.

Frankie gazed down Lex. It didn't matter either way about the guy any more. The guy was gone. Frankie was sorry now that they hadn't done him. It would have been a good thing, he felt.

Luis made Frankie feel worse about it by bringing up the watch, the flash watch they'd both noticed the guy was wearing.

Frankie said it was probably a fugaze. Lots of people were going for shit watches, rip-offs of Rolexes and Cartiers, all kinds.

Luis said he didn't think it looked like a fugaze. What if it wasn't?

So fucking what, man? Frankie flared.

About the time they got the guy out of their minds here he came again. Around the corner of 82nd and on down Lex. Right past them.

The thing that convinced Frankie to do him was the cane the guy was walking with. Cane with a carved ivory handle. Frankie got a good look at it when the guy went by. Also a better look at the watch. No cop would be out with a cane like that, Frankie told himself.

The guy, walking slow, crossed over at the corner and went east on 81st Street. Eighty-first along there was darker, just brownstones, no storefronts or anything. Cars parked on both sides.

Frankie ran full out down 82nd to Third Avenue and around so he'd be coming at the guy in the opposite direction on 81st Street. Luis went down 81st Street, walked faster than the guy. He timed it so he caught up, came up behind the guy exactly when Frankie blocked the guy's way.

From behind Luis told the guy to give it up. He flicked a knife in front of the guy's face.

Frankie stared mean into the guy.

The guy was like standing up dead. That scared, Frankie thought. He didn't even peep while Frankie unloaded him, every pocket. Then Luis gave the guy a shove and the guy went down in the gutter between the bumpers of parked cars.

Frankie and Luis walked away fast, didn't run. They didn't even look back at the guy. He was done. As far as they were concerned, what guy? It was one of the easiest moves Frankie and Luis had ever made.

At 77th Street they went back over to Lex and caught the subway downtown. Got off at 8th Street. They were sure Benny would be at his place. He was there every night all night. At a tenement on 6th Street between First Avenue and Avenue A. The top floor rear of a seven-story walkup. Benny didn't live there. It was just where he did business.

Parked on the street across from Benny's was a beige 1980 Chrysler Le Baron. Behind the wheel was Ralph Ciccone. Luis and Frankie were what Ralph had been waiting for. Not specifically, but the sort. Ralph worked his right-turn signal light to get their attention. He rolled down the electric window.

Luis and Frankie came over.

Ralph asked them what they had.

Frankie didn't say, just patted the pocket of his jeans. Luis and Frankie knew Ralph as one of the fences who hung around outside Benny's wanting to get to guys and their swag before they went up. Benny didn't like it.

Frankie said they were going up to see Benny.

Ralph persuaded them to let him have a first look. Luis and Frankie got into the rear seat of the Chrysler. Frankie passed the swag to Ralph, who used a flashlight to look at it. The watch, the sapphire bracelet, the ear clips and something else. How much did they want for the package?

Luis said two large.

Ralph said Benny would offer them one large tops.

Frankie said they'd take eighteen hundred.

Ralph said he'd go for twelve.

Fuck, man.

The deal was made at fourteen.

Ralph counted it out and Luis and Frankie split it and felt good about it. They'd already split the five hundred they'd taken from the guy. They took off down the street, headed for spending.

Ralph was left with a choice: Wait around to buy more swag or go out to Staten Island and get laid.

He drove downtown, took the Manhattan Bridge across to Brooklyn, got onto the Brooklyn-Queens Expressway and then the Gowanus Expressway to the Verrazano Narrows Bridge.

Ralph always felt good when he was going across this bridge. Like he was really going somewhere. He lowered all the windows and turned on the radio and tried to dial in some Sinatra or at least something with words he could understand. He settled for Greek music.

He'd done all right tonight, he thought, reaching down into the brown paper bag on the floor below his seat. He felt for and took out the watch. An Audemars Piguet with an 18-karat band. He had a private who would, in a breath, give him twenty-five hundred for it. The same private might also go for the sapphire bracelet. He'd ask four large for the bracelet. Take three. The ear clips were worth at least a couple of hundred in melt.

What the fuck was this other piece?

He held up the stone.

It didn't look like anything valuable that he'd ever seen. Just a rock, maybe even just a piece of glass. Nothing anyone would want, nothing anyone would pay anything for. He was used to thieves trying to fatten their packages with all kinds of worthless shit.

Ralph flung the stone out the window.

It sailed over the rail of the bridge.

It fell through the damp night air and made an insignificant disturbance when it landed on the surface of the water of the Narrows. Slowly, its descent determined by its meager weight, it sank to the bottom. Came to rest on a bed of silt and sand.

The currents would gradually carry it from lower New York Bay. Out past Sandy Hook and even farther out into the Atlantic.

On some distant day on some distant shore it would be found again.

By a boy perhaps.

Or by a sick old man.